Father Andrew Greeley is a priest, journalist and sociologist as well as a bestselling novelist. Considered one of the top people shaping religious thought today, he is programme director at the National Opinion Research Centre in Chicago and a Professor at the University of Arizona.

Also by Andrew M. Greeley

ANDREW M. GREELEY

Angels of September

Futura

A Futura Book

First published in Great Britain in 1986 by
Macdonald & Co (Publishers) Ltd
London & Sydney

This Futura edition published in 1987

Published by arrangement with Warner Books, Inc., New
York.

ISBN 0 7088 3233 4

Reproduced, printed and bound in Great Britain by
Hazell Watson & Viney Limited,
Member of the BPCC Group,
Aylesbury, Bucks

Futura Publications
A Division of
Macdonald & Co (Publishers) Ltd
Greater London House
Hampstead Road
London NW1 7QX
A BPCC plc Company

For Father John Shea

Who taught me to tell stories of God

And warned me of the appeal of theologies of divine retribution

And was gracious enough to give me a head start in writing fiction

I have set before you life and death—therefore choose life, loving the Lord your God, obeying His voice and cleaving to Him.

—Deuteronomy 30:20

St. Michael the Archangel, defend us in battle. Be our protection against the malice and snares of the Devil. Restrain him, O God, we humbly beseech thee. And do thou, prince of the heavenly hosts, by the power of God, thrust into hell Satan and the other evil spirits who roam through the world seeking the ruin of souls.

—Prayer at the end of Low Mass in the pre-Vatican Roman liturgy

Then war broke out in heaven. Michael and his angels waged war upon the dragon. The dragon and his angels fought but they had not the strength to win.

—Revelations 12:7–8

NOTE

Enough time has elapsed since the strange meteorological phenomena at the end of September in 1983 so that it is possible to tell the story of the apparent cause of these bizarre events which did so much damage on the Near North Side of Chicago. Readers familiar with the area in which these strange occurrences took place will recognize the pains I have taken to disguise and protect the actual people involved. The names are fictional, of course, and no amount of searching in either this story or the newspaper accounts of the time will reveal the real-life counterparts of my characters.

The "Mother of Mercy" school fire ought not to be confused with another Chicago school fire which happened many years later.

Nevertheless, the reader is given all the raw material available to "Father Ryan" from which he fashioned his final report to the Archdiocesan Chancery on the possibility of diabolical influences in the case.

The reader must decide whether "Father Ryan's" conclusions are adequate to the data.

A.M.G.

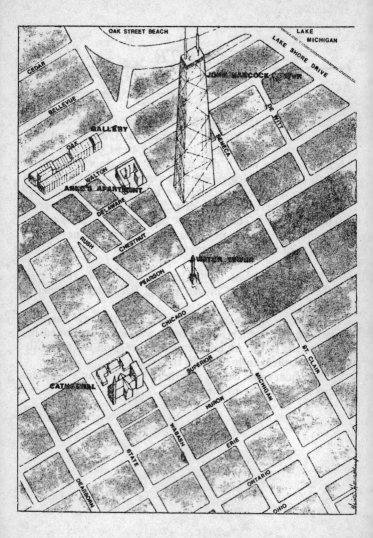

OAK STREET BEACH

LAKE MICHIGAN

LAKE SHORE DRIVE

CEDAR

BELLEVUE

JOHN HANCOCK CENTER

DE WITT

SENECA

GALLERY

OAK

WALTON

ANNE'S APARTMENT

DELAWARE

RUSH

CHESTNUT

WATER TOWER

PEARSON

CHICAGO

SUPERIOR

ST. CLAIR

CATHEDRAL

MICHIGAN

HURON

WABASH

ERIE

STATE

ONTARIO

DEARBORN

OHIO

BOOK
ONE

1

"He makes Hieronymus Bosch's hell look like an idyllic scene in Monet's garden," the Cardinal said.

Unlike many of his confreres in the Catholic hierarchy, Sean Cronin, the Cardinal Archbishop of Chicago, liked women. In the presence of a lovely woman art dealer he was quite capable of showing off his artistic knowledge—even if it meant stealing a line he had heard Father John Blackwood Ryan deliver as they walked from the Cathedral to the gallery for a preview of the exhibition of Father Desmond Kenny's paintings.

If you're a Cardinal, Blackie Ryan mused to himself, you don't have to footnote.

"Look at this poor thing," Anne Reilly said, pointing with a graceful finger at the lower left-hand corner of the canvas. "She has almost escaped, but the swamp has slowed her down. One demon has caught her breast in his claw and the others are closing in on her. I suppose he's saying that you don't make narrow escapes from God's implacable justice."

The victim, naked as were all the damned in Des Kenny's lunatic painting "Divine Justice," was writhing in terror as the devil's pitchforks plunged toward her fresh young flesh. Her eyes pleaded for mercy and despaired of it.

Anne, the Cardinal, and Blackie Ryan, the Rector of the Cathedral, were standing on the landing between the first floor and the basement of the Reilly Gallery, a brownstone on Oak Street just around the corner from Michigan Avenue. The basement showroom was packed with the paintings and sculpture of the late gifted if insane Chicago priest-artist. "Divine Justice," the most famous and, according to local art critics, the best of his paintings, had been placed strategically on the landing to attract potential

1

customers downstairs. Anne could hardly have filled her first-floor showroom with the twisted bodies and contorted faces of Kenny's sexually aroused and diabolically tormented saints and sinners. Window-shoppers would have thought it was a sadomasochistic freak show. As it was, Anne had done the Church a big favor by agreeing somewhat reluctantly to the Cardinal's request that she market Kenny's bequest to the Archdiocese, a gift made in 1949 just before he disappeared into an asylum from which he was to emerge only for his funeral thirty-three years later.

"The resignation on her face says that she knows she's damned," Blackie said, trying as always to be helpful.

"Maybe she received Holy Communion after breaking her Eucharistic fast with a glass of water," Anne said thoughtfully. "It was a mortal sin in those days, Your Eminence. She thought she could get away with a small mortal sin and was killed in an auto accident coming home from church. She gambled against God's justice and lost."

The Cardinal shivered slightly. "Our God doesn't work that way, Anne," he replied fervently. "He never did."

"We were taught that he did." Anne was not so much arguing with a prince of the Church as wondering about the New God and the Old God.

"Those teachers were wrong." The hoods that usually obscured Sean Cronin's brown eyes momentarily parted and his face glowed like the faces of some of the saints in Des Kenny's manic paintings, though in Cronin's case the glow was of passion and not fanaticism. "A proper portrait of God's justice would picture him dragging all of us into heaven by the skin of our teeth."

"Or other available parts of our anatomy," Blackie added, continuing his attempts at helpfulness. "By Her own admission, God is horny."

Products of an earlier era, the Cardinal and Anne continued to ignore him.

"But what if they were right, Your Eminence," she sighed, "and you're wrong? It matters a great deal, doesn't it?"

The question of God's forgiveness was clearly more than just an academic problem for Anne O'Brien Reilly.

Cathy Curran, whose paintings—mostly nudes and sunbursts—had hung in the Reilly Gallery, had insisted frequently to Blackie that Anne was one of the most beautiful women in the world, a proposition her cousin Blackie was not disposed to challenge. Much of her beauty, he thought, depended on a precarious, but somehow durable, balance between youth and age and a parallel tension between fragility and fortitude. You wanted to put your arm around Anne Reilly to protect her from any more tragedies, and in the very act of embracing her, you would find yourself sharing in her courage and strength. She was all the more interesting as a sex object and a sexed person because you perceived that the battle still went on inside her and that she had yet to make the decisive choice, urged by the Deuteronomist, between life and death.

"Coz, she has absolutely the most exquisite back I have ever seen," Cathy Curran argued, an observation based on data collected at the Women's Athletic Club, just down the Magnificent Mile from the Reilly Gallery, where Cathy Curran and Anne Reilly swam and did battle with ingenious medieval torture machines called Nautilus. "I wish she'd let me paint her," Cathy said. "She proves that a woman's erotic desirability can increase with age."

"That, Coz," Blackie had replied, trying to sound like one of the authors of the Books of Wisdom, "is for sure."

It was true. Even with all her clothes on, Blackie noted, Anne Reilly exuded sex appeal—a finely mixed blend of genetic endowments designed to withstand the assaults of time and strongly willed self-respect. Replace the gray slacks, white blouse, and gray sweater (matching her eyes) tossed casually around her shoulders with the elaborate gowns of the eighteenth century and Anne would look like a woman who had stepped out of a canvas by one of the great English portrait painters.

As a girl she must have been a classic, a black Irish beauty, with soft pale buttermilk skin quick to blush and impossible to tan, dark hair, flashing eyes, a firm and supple figure, and a rich musical voice in which one could hear the laughter of the dancing streams and the Little People.

Age—she was in her early fifties—had not so much

faded her beauty as softened it and made it more mellow and more intriguing. The lines on her face and throat, the tastefully adjusted silver and white of her short, swept-back hair, and the raised veins on her hands all revealed that she was no longer young, but the lines hinted at character and wit and enhanced the delicacy of her high-cheekboned face and her hands moved with such subtle charm that, veins or not, you would have liked to have been caressed by them.

She was tall and slender, her body's appeal drawn with quick and elegant strokes hinting at lithe and graceful rather than voluptuous sensuousness. And her eyes were the best part of her—sometimes as placid as Lake Michigan on a windless, cloudy day and other times swirling like a crater of lava, alive with fire and passion.

"Shall we look at the rest of his work?" she asked discreetly.

"Of course," said the Cardinal, as though he were whispering in a library or at a wake.

Anne led the way down the stairs, providing Blackie with a rear view quite as spectacular as Cathy claimed. A man would not stop his careful inspection at her waist, however. And from the way her slacks fit, Anne did not intend the inspection to stop there either. *Hooray for the Nautilus*, Blackie mused.

Her eyes also disturbed you. While there was self-control and strength in them, as well as passion, you also saw, as through gray mists, enormous pain. Whatever her genetic luck and however great her skill with cosmetics and fashion, a woman remained beautiful at Anne's age for psychological more than biological reasons. You did not doubt her resources of self-esteem or faith. But whence the pain? And of what sort the conflict between the pain and the faith? And what would happen to her delicately balanced beauty if pain should win the raging conflict?

Her finely honed beauty would disappear overnight.

"You knew him, didn't you, Mrs. Reilly?" the Cardinal asked as they walked slowly among Des Kenny's compelling yet demented fantasies, some of them so violent and sadistic as to be almost blasphemous.

"He was at Mother of Mercy parish when I was a little

girl," she said quietly. "He was very kind to us after the fire. I lost two sisters in it. He and my father became good friends and he remained close to our family even after he was assigned to the seminary to teach."

When Cornelia Graham owned the gallery, it was simply two large exhibition halls, one on the first floor and one in the basement. The top two floors, entered from the side, of the old home were occupied by a firm of architects in whose offices there was so little activity as to suggest they might be a front for the Outfit. Portable walls were moved about occasionally to separate exhibits. Anne had redone the interior—thick carpet, sound-absorbent ceiling, track lights, arches, nooks, niches, alcoves, and rooms of different sizes and shapes. The changes created a sensation of surprise and expectation as one wandered from chamber to chamber, provided different perspectives, and challenged the ingenuity of the exhibitor. As Anne admitted, she had to fight every day the impulse to confuse the roles of art dealer and museum curator. If she yielded too much to the latter propensity, the gallery would soon become the most interesting bankrupt gallery in Chicago.

The canvases of Desmond Kenny, overpowering in their energy and rage, were almost unbearable when you encountered their furious reds, dismal blacks, and terrifying purples in a small alcove. The trio's progress through the gallery was like a journey in a dank swamp of fetid water, rotting vegetation, and eerie mists with an occasional ghostly light flickering in the distance. You sensed that there was the ever present possibility of quicksand, which would either swallow you down or cough up half-decayed corpses.

"What was he like?" the Cardinal asked. They paused at a picture of a martyred matron losing her lovely classical breasts to a delighted, drooling executioner, a hideous yet compelling oil that seemed to overpower the tiny room in which it was the only exhibit. "He had been institutionalized by the time I was at the seminary," he added, "but his legend lingered."

"It's so hard to remember. I was in second grade when he came to our parish—1935, the year of the fire. He was

very energetic and enthusiastic. Being a parish priest was
more important to him than being an artist. Cardinal Mundelein persuaded him that he could be both when he had his
breakdown after the fire. Then he moved into the Cardinal's house. He was there the night the Cardinal died, you
know."

Sean Cronin nodded. "And he never recovered from the
shock, though his most striking work was done in the years
when his sanity was slipping away." He paused. "Was he a
homosexual, do you think?"

Anne drew her sweater closer around her shoulders although it was the September finale to the hottest summer
in a half-century. "I would not have known what the word
meant in those days, but . . . well, I don't think so, Your
Eminence. He was a strange man. Not very stable, I guess.
Enormous energy and talent and, as my mother used to say,
not much common sense. That's why he collapsed under
the strain of the fire. He tried to heal single-handedly all the
wounds in the parish."

"Instead of putting him in an asylum, today we'd make
him a consultant to our Liturgical Art Commission,"
Blackie offered, "and let him roam freely about. The bound-
aries of acceptable clerical behavior have expanded toward
infinity. I don't think he liked women very much, but then,
that's not untypical for priests."

The other two continued to ignore him.

"This is a remarkable piece of work," the Cardinal
said, picking up a nude statuette in a corner of the next
room, a piece perhaps a foot and a half high, of a young
woman in the first flower of her womanhood, kneeling with
hands clasped. Innocently confident of her newly discovered beauty, she was like one of those chaste delights
sculpted early in the nineteenth century by Lorenzo Barto-
lini—modestly naked and chastely erotic, the kind of slender classical objet d'art one wouldn't want to put down. "So
different from the others, serene and gentle."

Anne nodded in agreement. "The critics say it's the
best thing he ever did. They wanted me to use it on the
cover of the brochure. I'm afraid that would have been de-

ceptive. His eroticism was rarely that tranquil." Her hands clenched.

"Rarely that sane," Blackie muttered. "For my money, Des Kenny was a gifted crazy. The mistake was not in putting him away but in ordaining him in the first place. His career is still cited in the Archdiocese as evidence that you cannot be an artist and be sane."

Reluctantly the Cardinal replaced the statue. "Like the work your cousin does, Blackie. Erotic but not obscene."

"Ah, I am visible after all. Might I use this precious moment of visibility to observe that the alabaster piece you're holding, Eminenza, establishes that Father Kenny was capable on occasion of merely admiring a woman without having to destroy her."

Blackie quickly became invisible again as Anne replied to the Cardinal.

"Or like Peggy Donlon's watercolors," she said, slipping her arms into the gray sweater.

They paused again at "Divine Justice."

"Is there still a hell, Your Eminence?" she asked, buttoning up her sweater.

"I doubt it," the Cardinal replied briskly.

"There has to be the possibility of refusing the offer of God's love," Blackie interrupted. "But it wouldn't be like that canvas. God doesn't torment those who won't love Her back."

"What kind of a place is it, Father Ryan?" Anne asked, with the curiosity of one asking about a foreign country one is planning to visit.

"A place where God puts people until She figures out a way to give them a second chance."

"God cheats?" she asked dubiously.

"All the time."

"I wish I could believe that."

"He's usually right," the Cardinal observed.

They took their leave of one another with many "Your Eminences" and much kissing of rings. Sophisticated art dealer though she might have been, Anne Reilly was nonetheless an old-fashioned Catholic. And sophisticated new-fashioned bishop that he was, Sean Cronin liked neither titles nor ring kissing. But he was sufficiently captivated by Anne Reilly's gray eyes that he graciously accepted her old-fashioned respect.

"For the office, not the man," Blackie mumbled.

As he and Sean emerged on Oak Street he glanced back. "Divine Justice" could be seen at floor level. From a distance it was the kind of scene trapped coal miners might see before a raging inferno enveloped them, a mass of dark and twisted colors, of fire and suffering.

And determined hatred.

2

On the way to her office at the rear of the first-floor showroom, Anne paused to consider "Divine Justice." It was a startling contrast to the quiet light-bathed French provincial street scenes of her first-floor exhibition.

Like the poor child in the swamp on the outer fringes of hell, she had been trying to escape all her life. No matter how fast she ran, she was still trapped in the swamp. When she was younger, she thought that someday she would be free. Now that time was running out, she knew that escape was impossible in this life and probably in the next too. Her guilt was like a heavy piece of luggage that seemed to grow more onerous the longer she carried it.

She sighed. That was the way it should be.

The conversation with Cardinal Cronin and Father Ryan had given Anne a headache, as did every conversation about punishment and forgiveness. Priests taught very different doctrines these days. Intellectually she found the new doctrines appealing. Love was more attractive than punishment. In her heart she did not see how she could be forgiven, not even by a God who, if Father Ryan was to be believed, cheated on His own rules to capture those He loved.

She turned away from Father Kenny's painting and walked slowly toward her office. *Poor Father Kenny*, she thought. She had visited him a couple of times before his death. A feeble, pleasant old man who did not remember her. Hardly the angry, violent painter of four decades earlier.

Anne took off her sweater. Much too warm for a sweater. Why had she worn it? Old women were afraid of the cold.

Sandy, at her desk outside Anne's office, looked up from the letter she was writing to her husband. Such a beautiful man the Cardinal, spoke to her in Polish and kissed her hand, Polish style. So like Jan Pavel.

Anne was not certain the Archbishop of Chicago would relish the comparison.

Her private phone rang. She picked it up automatically. "Reilly Gallery, Anne Reilly speaking."

At first she heard only silence—then the scratching of a very old phonograph record.

> "Irene, good night
> Irene, good night
> Good night, Irene
> Irene, good night
> I'll see you in my dreams."

The world stood still, her fingers froze on the phone, her breathing seemed to stop. When the song ended, there was silence again. Then the needle scratched the record once more. They were playing the song over.

She hung up, quickly and nervously. It could not be a coincidence. Someone must know what that song would mean to her today. Yet how could anyone know?

"Missus is ill? She looks so pale."

Anne glanced up. She had not heard Sandy come in the office.

"No," she said, trying to sound brisk and businesslike. "An unpleasant phone call."

"I did not hear phone," Sandy said with a baffled frown.

"I picked it up right away," Anne replied.

Then it rang again. No 1940s music this time. Renee Hughes of the Cadwallader Gallery, an insufferable busybody and gossip—a person to whom you had to listen if you wanted to know the worst things that were happening in the art world. You wanted to know them all right, because they might be happening to you.

"I want you to know that we think it is terrible," Renee said with exorbitant enthusiasm.

So something was happening to her, Anne thought. Renee was a lesbian, which did not disturb Anne greatly after she had turned down Renee's first pass. The subsequent passes, however, were infuriating, especially as Anne felt that even if she were not mostly straight, she would not find Renee an appealing sexual partner.

"I'm glad you do," she replied guardedly.

"After all the work you put in on La O'Cathasaigh, it's not fair for Peter Ruben to carry her off, so to speak."

Anne's heart sank. *Oh, no. I'm counting on that exhibition to pull us out of our slump.*

"It's a free market," she replied casually. "Shelaigh is not tied to me by any contract."

"She at least might have let you bid," Renee said spitefully. "You know how lavish Peter is with promises."

"Yes, I do. We'll have to see what happens."

"So it's not final, then?" Renee came to her point. She had heard rumors and was fishing for information.

"In the art scene nothing is ever final," Anne replied smoothly.

After she had hung up, fingers trembling slightly, Anne realized that the rumors were probably true. Expected behavior from Shelaigh (born Julie Cassidy and innocent of any knowledge of the Irish language) and Peter Ruben.

Shelaigh was an authentic Irish Gypsy (or Tinker or Itinerant, as the rest of the Irish call them, or Traveler, as they call themselves), but that was about all that was authentic about her, except her ability to create wondrous impressionistic canvases of the Irish countryside.

Anne had learned to believe nothing that Shelaigh said—

she may or may not have been the illegitimate daughter of a P.P. (Parish Priest) and a sixteen-year-old Traveler. She may or may not have attended Trinity College. She may or may not have borne three daughters, each by a different father. She may or may not be thirty-five (Anne guessed closer to forty-five, but it was hard to tell because the woman's red-haired, freckle-faced, full-blown good looks were durable, despite the abuse to which she subjected her body). All that was certain was that she was a near-alcoholic, a chain-smoker of cigars, a habitual liar and thief, and practically a nymphomaniac—with no regard for the sex or the age of her bed partners.

And a painter of modest talents whose oils, Anne knew the first minute she saw them, would have considerable appeal to the affluent Chicago Irish, whom the art trade cheerfully ignored.

Despite the woman's faults, Anne liked her, partly because she was a charming and likable woman and partly because Anne had discovered that in the mid-nineteenth century there was a Laverty (her mother's maiden name) ancestor who was a Tinker woman—explaining, Anne reasoned, both Aunt Aggie and herself.

It would not be hard for me to become a drinker and a whore if I let myself go, she thought. *I may feel a little envy for Shelaigh. And a liar and a thief too.*

She had found Shelaigh dead drunk, sleeping behind a statue at the Chicago International Art Fair at Navy pier. Shelaigh had come to Chicago, quite possibly on a stolen airline ticket, to try to peddle her oils to a dealer, any dealer. Anne had sobered her up, fed her, resisted her at-first feeble and then not-so feeble advances, and bought all her paintings. (The best deal an unknown like Shelaigh could have expected was a consignment deal.)

Anne was not simply giving in to her propensity to try to cure birds with broken wings. In the first place, it was not clear that Shelaigh's wings were all that broken. Secondly, Anne knew she had a find.

Now, just when she needed the money from another O'Cathasaigh show, she was losing her find. Absently she placed a call to what might or might not have been Shelaigh's studio in Limerick. She waited nervously for the Tinker woman's raspy, nicotine-damaged voice. No answer.

Unlike most novices in the art scene, Anne was a competent financial administrator. She avoided cash-flow problems with some skill and had thus far not been taken in by forgers. Yet, she had trouble with a weakness about which Corny Graham had warned her. "You are not in the museum business, dearie. You must not buy pieces merely because they will look nice in your gallery. A work that doesn't turn over is a liability even if your books claim it is an asset."

Anne glanced at the Carlos silk screens that hung in the alcove outside her office, over Sandy's desk. She loved them. She had better love them, because they were going to hang for a long time. Chicagoans were uninterested in abstract representations of Mexican poverty.

Her worst mistake, however, was the group of Dali-like woodcuts of Miroslav Sobanek, an obscure Czech from the 1930s who was very much in fashion these days. He had worked in watercolors mostly, and Anne thought she'd made a superb deal when she purchased his graphics from a Munich art agent at a price that wiped out her working capital but was still a bargain.

After she had announced the special Sobanek exhibition and hung the works, she discovered the reason for the bargain price: The People's Republic of Czechoslovakia had discovered literally thousands of Sobanek prints in sheds on his old farm in Moravia and clumsily dumped them on the art market in hopes of improving their dollar reserves. Moreover, since Miroslav had not destroyed his woodcuts, the Prague Ministry of Art struck as many more prints as it could before the cuts became unusable. Anne's prints were practically worthless.

Anne was counting on O'Cathasaigh to move her back toward solvency. Now that hope was likely to be dashed. She could, of course, call on her son Mark for help. Yet she had made a rule for herself that she would either make a go of the gallery without running to Mark or give up.

And because she was a person who believed in rules

and stuck by them, she might well have to give up the gallery.

That would be almost as bad as giving up life—and probably much worse than giving up Mark's father, Jimbo Reilly.

She poured herself another cup of herbal tea and slumped into the chair behind her desk. She wished she had not given up smoking. Just one. . . . No.

Outside the tiny, barred window behind her desk, in the narrow alley, clogged with trucks, a few sprouts of red and gold cheerfully announced the coming of another autumn. She hummed the melody of "September Song," a tune from her girlhood. . . . "The days dwindle down to a precious few . . . the September of my life." One less year.

Chicago alleys—that would make an interesting exhibition.

Often she envied Sandy. However ambivalent the blond Polish Juno's relationship with her husband—always referred to as "Colonel Kokoshka," as in "Colonel Kokoshka did not write this week"—there was passion in her life, formal and courteous passion, but passion nonetheless.

She had discovered Sandy from a newspaper story. A thirty-five-year-old Polish immigrant, graduate in art history from the University of Kracow, wife of a colonel in the Polish army, mother of two children still in Poland, working as a cleaning woman in north shore homes, she had been mugged, raped, and nearly beaten to death on an L platform and threatened with expulsion by the Immigration and Naturalization Service while still unconscious.

Anne had acted decisively. Her lawyers fought off the INS. Her doctors got Sandy out of the hospital and into Anne's apartment. Her therapist found someone to whom the Polish woman could talk. And Anne rented her a couple of rooms on Wrightwood, just off the Drive, from which Sandy could take a bus every morning to the gallery, changed her name from Alexandra to Sandy, a "truly American name" of which the Pole was inordinately proud, and hired her as an assistant.

Sandy was, as Anne later told her son Mark, a wise

investment. "Colonel's wife," as the Polish woman some-times defined herself, possessed excellent artistic taste, a shrewd business sense, and a capacity for dogged loyalty that soon turned into worship. The two teenagers, solemn, polite children, came from Poland to live with their moth-er, and the Colonel received carefully composed letters every week.

"Missus's assistant," another self-label of Sandy's, was a few years too old to be Anne's daughter, but she treated her employer like a revered grandmother anyway.

"Why did you leave Colonel Kokoshka?" Anne asked her once, slipping into the formal, article-lacking Polish style.

"Colonel drinks too much," Sandy snapped.

"Do you love him, Sandy?"

"Oh, Missus . . . " she sobbed, throwing herself into Anne's arms and making Anne cry too.

So it was vicious to envy Sandy. She had risked her life for her children. She had been humiliated and beaten and raped—left for dead in a strange country whose language she barely understood. Separated from a husband whom she still loved. And, unlike Anne, she had done nothing to de-serve such punishment.

Anne had never been battered or raped. Forced sex with one's husband hardly fit into the same category as what had happened to Sandy. There was no reason to wish she were Sandy.

Except she had nothing to live for and Sandy did.

After wishing she could return to her old habit of mid-day drinks, Anne poured herself another cup of herbal tea.

"Missus's assistant does not wish to disturb. . . . " Sandy stood at the doorway, statuesque autumn loveliness in a brown- and red-striped wraparound dress. With a few dollars in her purse, Sandy showed that she had excellent fashion taste too.

"Of course not." Anne tried to recapture her wandering thoughts.

"Would Missus speak to Financial Commodities Speculator?"

"Missus," according to Father Ryan, was a bad translation of *panie,* but Anne hardly wanted to be called "my lady." And "Financial Commodities Speculator," however precise, was not what Mark might have thought proper either. Nevertheless Anne and her son agreed that Sandy's penchant for formal titles was too appealing to be tampered with.

"Hi, Mark." She tried to sound alert and happy on the phone, owing that at least to her youngest child.

"How did it go with the Cardinal?"

Why did the boy have to be so anxious about her? *Because he loves you more than you ever loved him, that's why,* Anne thought.

"Splendid. I kissed his ring, he kissed Sandy's hand, and Father Ryan went through his weird-old-priest act to perfection. June has already got out a press release."

Something gnawed at the fringes of her consciousness. There had been a bad moment during the Cardinal's tour. What was it?

"I'd have liked to have heard the Cathedral rector on the subject of Des Kenny." Mark's voice seemed to relax. His mother had survived another crisis. "I'm afraid I made only two thousand dollars on your account today."

"I'll disown you." She laughed. "I hope you did better for your wife."

"Lost her twenty-five dollars." He joined in the laughter. "But then, she doesn't know I trade in her name."

Two years ago Mark had opened accounts for both the women in his life, reimbursed himself for their original capital from the profits of trading in such obscure commodities as Ginny Mae notes and T-bills, and had then made them both enough money so that they could face the proverbial rainy day with all the financial protection they would ever need.

"Give her my love."

"I sure will."

"I bet."

They both laughed again.

From the most unorganized teenager one could imagine, Mark had become a creature of precise routines. At the end of trading each day he first phoned his mother, then rode the Lake Street L home to River Forest, finishing his homework on the way. Then he consumed one drink, made love to Teresa, his wife (who had spent the morning in class at Rosary College), took a nap, probably made love to Teresa again, played with the kids, mixed a second drink, helped with supper, and then drove in the family Mercedes back downtown to Loyola for his night-school courses in English literature.

"So that I won't be a rich dummy," he explained, "of whom my kids will be ashamed."

For six months he had taken the L to Loyola until Anne and Tessie had conspired to make him drive.

My one success as a mother, she thought, *and I had nothing to do with it. And God help me, try as I might, I can't love him as much as the others.*

Mark had been a mistake, conceived after too many martinis and born into a family where there were already too many problems. She had had no energy left over to worry about him or to protect him with special concern. And he had not been particularly attractive as a child—big, ungainly, silent.

He had matured into a determined adolescent athlete, good, but not good enough for college sports. He dropped out of college after six months, became involved with drugs, and experienced some trouble with the police. In desperation Anne found him a job as a runner on the Board of Trade, despite Matt Sweeney's prediction that the boy would always be in trouble.

Mark fit perfectly into the warrior world of commodity traders. A couple of old-timers took a liking to the zealous young runner and rented him a seat of his own. Shortly after his twentieth birthday he married Teresa, a high school graduate of three months before, over her parents' noisy objections (her father was an immensely successful Irish Catholic surgeon who was convinced his power of life and death made him God). By the time their first child—Anna—was born a year later, Mark had already purchased the home in which he had been raised in River Forest and earned more annual income than Tessie's father.

When Matt Sweeney walked out on Anne and she thought she would die, indeed hoped she would die, Mark bought the gallery without consulting her, took her to it one day after lunch at the Cape Cod Room across the street, gave her the keys and a book of checks for the first exhibition, and told her it was all hers.

She had made enough money in four years to pay much of the "loan" back—and suspected Mark used it for another trading account in her name. Now she was scared to admit to her son that she was on her way to being the failure that she thought he might be when he was a few years younger.

Anne had watched Mark's spectacular success in business and marriage with stunned disbelief, always expecting, even today, that the bubble would burst. She worried about his casual laughter when he said that trading in stock market index futures would make the CBOT the biggest casino in the world.

And she tried to love him as much as he loved her, so far unsuccessfully, not understanding why Mark—and Tessie too, for that matter—adored her. Yet when she said her prayers at the end of the day, there was more intensity in her pleas for Beth and David and for the repose of Jimmy's soul—if he was really dead—than in her prayers for Mark.

Mark was a success in life without his mother's concern or her prayers. Perhaps he didn't need them as much as the others did.

"Oh nonsense," Dr. Murphy, her psychiatrist, had insisted. "You have to come to terms with the truth that your mother love was more effective when it was distracted. You should face the fact that you gave the others too much attention. That was not love. Mark is really returning the most generous, because least self-seeking, love you gave any of them."

"I don't understand," she had stammered.

"Yes, you do," the therapist had insisted. "It will take some time to admit that you do, however."

She resisted the temptation to make another cup of tea. She had missed her swim yesterday and did not dare to miss it again today. Why she still cared about her body, she did not know—even though Dr. Murphy persistently demanded, "Why don't you let yourself fall apart? Don't you deserve to look ugly?"

"Damn it, Doctor, maybe I do. But I'm not going to."

"Why?"

"You don't," she replied defensively.

"I can answer the 'why' question. You can't."

"Then why?"

"I'm the doctor and I don't have to answer your questions."

Anne signed a stack of checks that the indefatigable Sandy had prepared and reached for her purse. She would walk down Michigan Avenue to make up for not swimming yesterday. Look at all the gorgeous kids and wish she were one of them.

A gnawing memory again. *Something wrong in the Cardinal's visit. Oh my god. The Venus. The Cardinal had not noticed. Most people wouldn't. But Father Ryan's quick little eyes had caught it instantly. A mistake. Too much integrity.*

She ran down the steps. *Must not be too late for the pool or the late afternoon crowd will be there.*

Anne grabbed the fragile little figure and dashed across the showroom. *Dummy to try to run in high heels. Put it in the safe in my office.*

She passed "Divine Justice" and did not even glance at it. She was almost at the top of the steps when the shock wave hit her and she felt herself floating through space. *Must have tripped on my heels. What a crazy way to die.*

She nestled the figurine against her breasts. It did not deserve to be broken.

"I'm sorry."

Was it a scream or a silent prayer?

Then there was nothing.

3

The Cardinal and Blackie walked down Michigan Avenue toward Superior Street, a venture that on a warm day in mid-September compared favorably with a walk along the French Riviera. Sean Cronin, however, was distracted by problems.

They paused at the window of the Wally Findlay Galleries, across from that old wedding cake phony, the Water Tower. They were showing Philip Auge—sensuous alabaster women, cool, remote, and draped in gorgeous gowns, appropriately for a former fashion designer.

"More peaceful than Des Kenny," Cronin said thoughtfully.

"He paints without a model," Blackie said, continuing to be helpful. "Indeed, paints them nude and then drapes the clothes on them. They're not my idea of erotic women, but everyone to his own taste."

"Nor mine. I guess we Irish go for the healthy type like your friend Anne. . . . How many of these will they sell?"

"Probably all of them. They're the Cadillac dealers of art. Been in business over a century. Head office in Paris. Handle only oils, have a stable of fine artists. They're often sold out on the strength of their brochures even before the exhibitions open."

"Anne is not that fortunate, I presume."

"Hardly. Some galleries deal in expensive works, half-million, even million-dollar pieces. They're more like brokerage firms than galleries. Brokerage firms and museums. Some of them are very important in the art life of Chicago. Richard Gray, for example, to whose twentieth anniversary in the business celebration you will certainly go next month, even if I bring you at gunpoint. He's especially generous with new and young artists—like Anne will be if she can ever afford it. Others in this crowd are so strong and so distinguished that everything they do turns to gold. But most galleries operate in the claw-and-scratch marketplace of a free-market economy in which half the upper-middle-class suburban home owners want at least a worthwhile graphic or two in their front room. It isn't easy."

"You know a lot about it," Cronin said, turning away from Auge's pale shoulders and throats.

"My parish," Blackie said simply.

"Do you think Des Kenny was the fourth person in the house the night Mundelein died?" the Cardinal asked, changing the subject and neglecting to note that past rectors of the Cathedral could not have cared less about art galleries, save to dismiss them as hotbeds of homosexuality.

"I don't know. What do you think?" Blackie replied, turning the question back on him, as he had intended him to do.

"I don't know any more than you do, Blackie. There are no records. The clerical folklore says that there were four men in the house that night—my predecessor of famous memory; his secretary, Tommy the Cork Corcoran; a friend of President Roosevelt; and a man of mystery. That Kenny was the mystery guest is not part of the folklore. But Mrs. Reilly takes it for granted that he was there. A different tradition, perhaps."

"And she obviously does not know the rumor that the Cardinal was killed by a homosexual lover."

They paused at Superior, heedless of the riptide of pedestrian traffic.

"No proof of that rumor," he said thoughtfully.

"But something strange seems to have happened that night. And if Kenny was involved, it would explain the rapid decline of his sanity."

The Cardinal reached into the pocket of his tailor-made black jacket—chosen without doubt by his sister-in-law Nora Hurley—and removed the catalog of the Kenny exhibition. "Sleek-looking little fellow, wasn't he?" he said, studying the ordination picture of Des Kenny on the first page of the listing.

Desmond S. Kenny, the son of a clerk at the Pullman Company, was indeed sleek looking, but the haircuts of the early 1930s and the high pontiff Roman collars, always attached to a shirt with French cuffs, would have made anyone look sleek.

"The eyes," Blackie replied.

"Yes, of course, the eyes. Even in 1932 the same kind of wildness as in that horrible painting. Three years in Rome, studying the history of Christian art, then he falls out of favor with Mundelein and is sent to Mother of Mercy. After the fire he has a nervous collapse. My predecessor indulges in one of his rare reconciliations with a fallen protégé. Then Kenny's back in favor and becomes court painter at the seminary. After Mundelein's death he is picked up by Barnie Sheil, Mundelein's auxiliary and the loser in the succession fight, a proper gombeen man, that one."

"Sheil drops him, as he eventually dropped everybody, and Des bounces into the Marian asylum, whence he emerges only for his burial .... What do you want to bet that when you check the records, you'll find that Des was not officially living in the house at the time of Mundelein's murder?"

They walked slowly up Superior Street toward the Cathedral.

"Possible murder. That's all we'll ever be able to say." Cronin paused. "It hardly seems to be the same Church. No wonder the poor guy went mad. An administrative genius my predecessor may have been, a nice man he was not. Bouncing between him and Sheil, from Annas to Caiaphas, would have driven anyone nutty."

Sean Cronin knew what Blackie thought of the way the Church destroyed its most talented members. The Des Kenny case, however, was different. "He had a good eye and a powerful brush, Eminenza, but he was nutty as the proverbial fruitcake—a word I use advisedly—when that ordination picture was taken. He'd never have made it past the psychological profiles today."

"I think we would have taken better care of him," the Cardinal replied. "I visited him at Marian," he continued, "after I was named administrator. He was a dotty old man, gentle, sweet, and harmless. He thought I was Pat Hayes, Mundelein's secretary. The nuns let him say Mass till almost the end."

The Cardinal's passionate sense of fairness for a gifted priest who had been abused was responsible for this last exhibition of Des Kenny's work. The curious would come in droves to gape at the paintings of an allegedly crazy cleric. The critics would write of the raw power of his talent and the tragic loss caused by his "illness." And Sean Cronin would see only the rehabilitation of a talented priest who had been badly treated.

And now he was considering the disturbing possibility that the talented priest might also have been a killer.

"A remarkably appealing woman, isn't she?" he said, changing the subject.

"You noticed."

"According to our official teaching, sexual attraction exists for purposes of reproduction. To divorce it from reproduction is to pervert it. Why then does the Almighty permit there to be an ever-increasing supply of gorgeous women whose reproductive years are long since passed?"

"Maybe She is like us—enjoys looking at them."

"Perhaps," he mused, ignoring Blackie's change of God's sex. "I will have to pose the question to my blue-eyed Polish colleague when next I visit the Vatican. I suspect he enjoys looking at them too. In any case . . . do you know much about her background?"

"One branch of our family remained on the West Side after my mother and father made the fateful pilgrimage to the South Side. I think my cousin Mike Casey the Cop went to grammar school with her."

"A tragic life, poor woman." His hand was on the door of the Cathedral rectory. "Is she going to make it, Blackie?"

"As an art dealer?"

He shrugged. "As a woman and a human being. I have the impression that the question is not settled yet."

"Even money." Blackie gestured as if he were an Outfit odds maker.

"Why did she ever go to bed with an idiot like Sweet Matthew Sweeney?"

"Pity and guilt, I suppose. We merchandised a lot of guilt in the old days."

"Tell me about it," the Cardinal said bitterly. "The

Church is probably responsible for most of the strain in that poor woman's life."

"And much of the strength that keeps her together and lovely."

"I suppose," he conceded, for some reason not ready to leave the bright September sunshine for the mausoleum interior of the rectory.

"You noticed the curious phenomenon at the gallery?" Blackie asked, knowing damn well that he hadn't.

"Which one?" Cronin shoved the rectory door open.

"The ivory figurine."

"Striking little thing," he said with a sigh of relief. "Suggests that he was heterosexual after all and that our speculations are wrong."

"It's the same woman who is trying unsuccessfully to run away from the suburbs of hell."

"Oh?" Cronin pushed Blackie ahead of him through the doorway. No protocol for the Cardinal, no way.

"And the face on both of them is that of Anne Marie O'Brien Reilly."

"God help us!" exclaimed the Cardinal.

"She may have to before this one is over."

As Blackie closed the door its dark stained-glass window rattled. Far away, or so it seemed, there was a faint sound of something like a sonic boom.

4

"I'll be out in a few minutes," Casey said in Spanish to Patrol Officer Deirdre Lopez when she had double-parked their squad car on Oak Street in front of the Reilly Gallery.

"Sí, Jefe," she replied.

Casey had six different drivers, one for each day of the week, as he explained—black, Hispanic, and a white of each sex. No one could say that he discriminated. (There were, he admitted to the other Deputy Superintendents, more than two sexes, but six drivers was enough of a concession to equal-opportunity employment unless the morons who were federal judges wanted to find him gay drivers of both sexes.) While he much preferred a woman driver and for obvious reasons, no one could accuse him of sexual exploitation.

As a firm supporter of a bilingual police force in a city with 600,000 Hispanics, he insisted on speaking Spanish on the days when his drivers were Deirdre Lopez or Hermano Mendoza.

Deirdre—the Irish won at names if nothing else—was a graduate of St. Scholastica High School and daughter of active parishioners at some parish in Logan Park. His Spanish was better than hers. But that was all right, because she was easily the prettiest of his three women drivers.

So it went.

Mike Casey's title varied with politics and racism in Chicago. And with political racism. He was at different times Superintendent, Acting Superintendent, and Deputy Superintendent. The title did not matter. He ran the Department and without him it could not run. The political hack who was the titular head of the Chicago police was always smart enough to know that without Casey's insolent professionalism, the Department would grind to a halt.

Casey spent half his day at a desk at Eleventh and State, the surrealistic police command center, and the other half roaming the streets of the city, sometimes in a blue-and-white squad, sometimes in an unmarked car, listening for radio calls. The cop on the beat could never be quite sure when the "super" would appear, a strong but not determining motive for honesty and fairness.

A risky way to live—eventually some drug addict with a gun would catch up with him. But it was said of Michael Patrick Casey that he lived for his family and the Department and nothing else.

And now only the Department.

He was disgusted with what the last two mayors—incompetent disgraces—had done to a department that had briefly been the most professional in the country. No great achievement, perhaps, but still better than it used to be. In twelve months he would finish his thirty years. Then he would get out and stay out.

Let the Department suck itself.

He issued himself a mental reprimand for thinking the obscene word. *You only stopped speaking them when you stopped thinking them.* No coarse language was tolerated in the Deputy Superintendent's presence when women officers were also present. Women, he argued, would transform police work and humanize it, but only if they were not forced to imitate the macho vices of men. To the argument that the mouths of women were these days as foul as the mouths of men, he would reply laconically, "That proves my point."

A lost cause, of course. All causes were lost. And lost a long time ago.

You don't have a fucking idea of what is left in life when you stop being a cop, he told himself as he nodded to the two male patrol officers standing guard at the entrance of the Reilly Gallery and returned to his past.

The two men stood stiffly at attention. However secret were the "super's" movements, cops knew instinctively these days when he would appear and were ready for him— frightened but ready.

They have me figured. It's time to get out.

The gallery was a shambles—front windows and doors blown out, paintings knocked from the walls, desks overturned, papers and catalogs swept against the walls, police and fire types milling around, testing the air, looking for the cause of the explosion.

"Anyone killed, Sanders?" he asked the black lieutenant who was in charge.

"No, sir," the officer replied crisply. "Dr. Reilly's assistant, a Ms. Kokoshka"—he checked his clipboard to make sure that he had the strange name right—"is in Henrotin Hospital with a probable concussion. Dr. Reilly has cuts and bruises, but refused to go to the hospital."

Dr. Reilly? Ah, the Irish were resilient. They lost in

politics and city employment, so they muscled into the academic and art worlds.

"What caused it?" Casey asked tersely.

"A shock wave seems to have originated in the basement, sir. It hit Dr. Reilly on the staircase. Judging by the destruction of the windows, she was fortunate not to have been seriously injured or even killed."

"Shock wave, Sanders? You mean explosion?"

"Neither our personnel nor the fire department personnel have been able to find any trace of an explosive device, sir. The gallery is a mess, but nothing besides the windows has been seriously damaged."

"You can smell an explosion . . . and a fire too."

"Yes, sir," said Lieutenant Sanders. "I mean, sir, that you can smell something that smells like an explosion, but the firemen don't know what it is."

"Sewer gas? Ruptured gas main?"

"Sewer gas apparently, sir."

"Apparently won't do, Sanders."

What the hell was the matter with them?

Casey wandered toward the stairwell where the blast had hit Annie. A godawful painting. "Divine Justice"? He picked up a tattered catalog. Ah, yes, the insane priest.

He walked into the basement exhibition room. What crap!

Strange that the blast had created less of a mess down there. Most of Desmond Kenny's paintings were still hanging neatly in place.

He climbed back to the main floor. If Annie had been on the landing when the blast occurred, and the blast was powerful enough to shatter the windows, she was very lucky to be alive.

His heart was beating very rapidly. He could hardly wait to see her and at the same time was afraid to face her.

The door to her office was closed. He hesitated, decided that he ought to leave without talking to her, and knocked on the door anyway.

"I heard the call on the radio, Annie. Thought I'd make sure you were all right."

Walking through the door into her office seemed like driving out of a long dark tunnel on a brilliant sunshiny day. His eyes blinked as the light jabbed at them and his whole body tightened in a protective reflex.

"Mickey!" She rose from her chair rather shakily and extended her hand. "Always thoughtful. You remember my son Mark?"

A big handsome kid, with his father's shoulders and his mother's smile. Trader. Millionaire probably. Real owner of the gallery, no doubt. The only serious conversation he'd had with Mark's mother in three decades was when she called about a narcotics charge against him when he was a teenager. Sometimes favors do work out.

"I'm so glad you came, Superintendent," said the young man, delivering a warm handshake. His mother's graceful charm too, probably the result of careful imitation.

Casey was so jolted by the physical impact of seeing Annie again that he hardly noticed the details his brain quickly recorded—as he insisted in his *Principles of Detection* text, the brain of the good detective always records details no matter what the distractions.

An office/workroom in white and black—white walls, white desk and worktables, black leather chairs with aluminum legs, black calendar cube and black leather—probably Mark Cross—desk set, papers in orderly piles, just the right amount of indirect lighting, a small computer console with a neat plastic cover, a white-on-white painting on one wall, and, to break the theme, a Monet lily print on the other. A flawless office from the pages of *Interior Design*.

Arranged, of course, to highlight the vigorous and stylish beauty of its occupant, wearing Stanley Korshak clothes, Chanel scent, Elizabeth Arden makeup, circumspect Cartier silver at her neck and wrist—a figure you wanted to hold in your arms. Badly shaken by the blast but coping effectively. Poor woman, she'd had to cope all her life.

Why had he come? To see if Annie was as beautiful as her pictures? To learn whether she smiled the way she used to smile? To find out what time and age had done to her? To probe that mysterious spot in his character in which there once had been a terrifying and ecstatic response to Anne Marie O'Brien.

The spot was still there, as vulnerable to a touch of her hand as it was in 1950, the quick and overwhelming sensation that, body and soul, they would always belong to each other.

"Relax, Sergeant," he said to the black woman officer who was also in the room. "Mrs. . . . I mean Dr. Reilly and I were in school together before you were born."

"He was in school then; I wasn't," Anne said with her contagious laugh. "He has me confused with my mother. Do sit down, Mickey, so the sergeant can relax."

You can trust me, Annie. I've come to help as I should have long ago. I'll take care of you if you need me.

Casey was assaulted by as powerful a sexual hunger as he had ever known. Shaken by the strength of his reaction to her, he settled into one of the chairs, something that Mies might have designed. His hands were wet with perspiration and his head seemed to be spinning.

"Are you sure you're all right?" he asked stiffly.

"Dr. Reilly declined first aid treatment," the sergeant said anxiously.

Maybe you have to be my age, to realize how beautiful she is. No, that's not true. She'd take any man's breath away.

"Shame on her."

Anne's blouse was torn and her face was smudged. There was a trace of blood on her fingers. *And she's laughing at me.*

"That's a lot of crap you're exhibiting downstairs, Annie," he said, realizing instantly that he was making a fool of himself.

And his eyes were stripping her, enjoying what they saw. *Damn it, I don't do that to women.* She seemed amused rather than offended, confident that she was worth stripping. And in that clever way women have, she was secretly evaluating him, liking what she saw too. He found his lips smiling, and not the contemptuous smile that terrified his subordinates more than any words of condemnation.

She smiled back. "Don't play the anti-intellectual cop with me, Michael. I read the Art Institute contributors' list."

Now she's making me blush. She's a little flushed herself. My God, doesn't it ever go away?

"I thought it was an Art Institute contributor's judgment."

"He had enormous raw talent," she pleaded, now wanting his approval. Her head was bowed, her eyes averted from him, her face tinged with a lovely flush, a novice talking to a bishop. He remembered the same pose from long ago. It still turned him on.

"Which never developed," he said crisply. "Did he do that?" He picked up the lovely figurine from her desk. "If he did, I withdraw my previous opinion."

Anne was suddenly nervous. "Yes, it's rather different from the others, isn't it? I was carrying it upstairs when the explosion happened. It's a miracle it didn't break."

She swayed, appeared momentarily about to topple over. His hand reached out to steady her. He eased her back into her chair.

Oh, no. It never stops.

"Mark," he said to her son, "take your mother to a doctor and then take her home. She lives right around the corner, doesn't she? Maybe you or your wife can make her supper. The Chicago Police Department will protect her gallery till tomorrow morning."

"Don't give me orders, Superintendent," she said, pretending to be angry but still laughing at him. Long ago it would have been real anger. Everyone had mellowed a bit.

"There being no snowbanks handy, I wouldn't dream of giving you an order, Dr. Reilly. It's Mark I'm telling what to do."

"Sandy . . . my assistant . . . can you find out how she is? . . . Please."

And at her most beautiful when she worried about others. The new Annie had developed compassion.

"She's okay, but I'll confirm it for you soon. Now, Mark . . . "

"Yes, sir, Superintendent, sir," the young man responded with a grin. Likable kid.

Casey slumped into Annie's chair as Mark helped her to the door. She turned as she was leaving. "How do you know where I live?" It was half-question, half-taunt. Same old Annie.

"A good cop knows everything."

He should never see her again. The delight and the fear were as strong as ever. It was too late anyway. It had always been too late.

Before he left the gallery—with an expression of somber dissatisfaction that left Lieutenant Sanders trembling—he looked more closely at "Divine Justice."

Absolute crap. And mean crap too.

The odd smell—cordite maybe, but not quite—remained in the building.

"I want this one cleaned up in a hurry, Sanders. The press will be over us, with his exhibition of crap opening here next week."

"Yes, sir."

In the squad he ordered Patrol Officer Lopez to confirm by radio call that Alexandra Kokoshka was in good condition at Henrotin Hospital.

"She is a very beautiful woman," the driver said in Spanish.

"Señora Kokoshka?"

"No, Jefe, Dr. Reilly. Doña Anna Maria."

"I went to grammar school with her for a few years," he said by way of explanation.

"Oh."

Not enough explanation. What would happen if he should proposition Deirdre? Would stern Catholic principles or hero worship triumph? He would spare her the dilemma. He should not even think about it. A few minutes with Annie and he was a dirty adolescent boy again.

"We fought most of the time."

"That is a shame," she said quickly. *Cop or not, young woman, you are still a Latin romantic.*

"Sometimes it was kind of fun," he replied, hoping that he had rebuilt the aura of mystery proper to a deputy superintendent of police.

"Jefe?"

"*Sí.*"

"You observed the broken glass?"

"Of course I observed the broken glass."

"Is it not strange?"

He thought rapidly. There had been something strange about the glass. "Any theories?" he snapped, covering his failure.

"Why would anyone put shatterproof glass in the window of an art gallery, glass that powders like an automobile window?"

Why indeed?

"Find out why, Deirdre. When it was installed and by whom. I want to know by noon tomorrow."

He thought there was something strange going on in that gallery. *Annie couldn't be mixed up in criminal behavior, could she?*

Nonsense.

That night, sipping the Jameson's neat that served as his usual nightcap on the balcony of his Outer Drive East apartment and watching the boats in Burnham Harbor—gems on black velvet—Casey tried to tell himself that it was absurd to think that he and this woman he had hardly spoken to since 1950 were some sort of weird soulmates, capable of helping and hurting each other almost without limit. He remembered the big fight with Annie, so long, long ago. He had almost forgotten it, consigned it to the trash can of irrelevant memories. The same trash can to which she herself had been consigned—even to the extent of avoiding newspaper articles about her.

Annie had changed for the better in forty years. He hoped he had too, but was not altogether confident that he had. Just become better at covering up.

He resolved that he would not make this afternoon's mistake ever again.

5

"Obsolescent," said Sister Alphonse Mary, a young nun with the serene loveliness of an ivory statue. The year was 1942.

"Obsolescent, O–B–S–O–L–E–S–C–E–N–T, obsolescent," volunteered the boy. "It means out of date, as in the P-thirty-eight fighter plane is obsolescent."

The class groaned as if someone on the other team had made a free throw. They were weary of Mike Casey's preoccupation with the war.

But none of them had a father in the jungles of Guadalcanal.

"Or," he added brightly, "as in spelling bees are obsolescent."

The class laughed. Mike Casey could always get a quick laugh from them, even if they did not like him.

"That will do," S'ter said sternly. Much of S'ter's energy was devoted to restraining her impulses to laugh at the seventh grade several times every hour.

"We'll let you try 'enervate,' Anne Marie." She turned to the other side of the crowded classroom, where Mike's last opponent was standing.

Loud cheers for the other side. First and goal.

"That is if your noisy supporters will give you a chance to spell it."

It was an old battle. For the last two years Anne Marie O'Brien and Michael Casey had been the finalists in every contest in the class—and education in St. Ursula's was mostly contest.

Mike always won.

And Anne Marie despised him.

"It means 'wear out' or 'tire,' " said the little girl with the long black hair and blazing gray eyes and the first hints of a woman's body, "as in contests with Michael Casey enervate me."

The class howled, as they did at every joke at Mike's expense. He was too smart, he worked too hard, and his family was reputed to be rich.

Anne Marie they worshiped. They had little choice. The alternative, doing battle with her strong will and wild anger, was terrifying. "That little O'Brien girl is going to grow up to be a black Irish beauty," his aunt Katie had said, "and she'll have the temper to go with it."

"No personalities, Anne Marie." S'ter did not even try to hide her own laughter. "Stop stalling."

Sister Alphonse Marie was the only one who dared to challenge Anne Marie and hope to get away with it.

"Yes, S'ter, stop stalling, S–T–O–P, one word, S–T . . . "

More merriment from the seventh grade. But not this time from S'ter.

"I'll disqualify you, young woman," she warned stiffly, a referee giving a last warning before throwing a player out of the game.

"Sorry, S'ter." Anne Marie was contrite. Only S'ter received apologies from the reigning monarch of the seventh grade. "Enervate," she said smiling appealingly. "E–N–N–E–R–V–A–T–E, enervate?"

She was uncertain. Mike knew he'd won. When Anne Marie lost her confidence she was finished, like the Japs would be once they began to lose the war.

"One more chance." Sister Alphonse Mary was as solemn as King Solomon preparing to cut the baby in two. She liked Anne Marie and found Mike a trial. But unlike many of the other nuns at St. Ursula, she played no favorites.

"E–N–N–A–R–V–A–T–E?"

S'ter pounded the hand bell, a nun's badge of office and the gong of defeat for Anne Marie. "If you spell it right, Michael, you win."

His heart beat rapidly with the thrill of victory, as though he were fighting Japs at the edge of Henderson Field.

He loved victory over Anne Marie, who was the Monstress of Mongo from the Flash Gordon comic strip.

"I believe that Anne had it right the first time except for two *n*'s," he said.

"I'm the teacher, Michael," S'ter said impatiently, "just spell it for us."

"E–N–E–R–V–A–T–E." He trailed out the letters, savoring his triumph and the frustrated rage on his opponent's pretty, elfin face.

"Michael Casey wins again." S'ter pounded her bell three times.

The class booed.

"That will be quite enough, class, unless you want to spend your Christmas vacation doing homework."

The class settled down promptly, like soldiers when a top sergeant came into the barracks. S'ter Alphonse Mary was pure poison when you made her mad.

They had many reasons for not liking Mike. Because his uncle, Monsignor Quinlan, was the Cardinal's secretary, the priests made a fuss over him. His mother and father were separated—"divorced," many parents said in hushed whispers. His father was rumored to be a "Communist and an alcoholic." His mother was running her family's manufacturing business, making parts for B-17s; most people in St. Ursula's did not think it was right for a woman to preside over a factory, despite the fact that she did so for "the war effort." She rode in a chauffeur-driven LaSalle with a "C" gasoline ration sticker. Even if Mike had not earned himself the reputation of being a "walking encyclopedia" in his first week in school after he and his mother had moved into St. Ursula's, the other things would have caught up anyway.

He pretended it did not matter, that he did not need friends, that he did not mind the envy of his classmates, that their taunts did not hurt him.

But they did hurt. His mother often said, as though discussing a physical handicap, "Michael is so sensitive, just like his father."

He retreated into a dreamworld of books, radio programs, and war reports and looked forward eagerly to escaping from St. Ursula's to the seminary, where he could begin his studies for the priesthood.

Anne Marie walked back to her seat, her mouth a razor-thin line.

She whispered a very vulgar word as she walked by his desk.

The girls around her giggled.

"What's going on back there?" S'ter thundered.

"He called me a name, S'ter." Anne Marie was outraged innocence.

The daughter of Judge Larry O'Brien, Anne Marie came from a family whose Catholicism and political clout—which were virtually the same thing—were unquestioned on the West Side of Chicago. She was pretty, she was fun, she was popular.

And she received special sympathy from the nuns because her two sisters had died in a school fire.

"Did you, Michael?"

Sister Alphonse Mary was familiar with Anne Marie's tricks. Yet she would show no preference either for the daughter of a politically powerful judge or the son of a rich divorcée with her own war plant.

"No, S'ter, I'm going to be a priest. I don't use vulgar language."

The class groaned.

"We are well aware of *that*," said the nun. "It's not necessary to remind us. We will talk about this after school. Both of you will remain when class is dismissed. I do not want to hear another word out of either of you. Do you understand?"

"Yes, S'ter," they responded in a meek duet.

The nun was not eager to begin the conversation after school. She busied herself with record keeping while the two of them sat anxiously at their desks, Mike in the second seat of the third row, near the chart with the stars after the names of those who went to Mass every day, and Anne Marie at the back of the second row, under the pictures of the Holy Land that S'ter used for her Advent lessons.

Mike opened his geography book and began to read about copper mining in Chile. Copper was essential to the war effort. He had heard his mother say on the phone one Saturday that she didn't care how much it cost or where they bought it, she had to have more copper.

No one in St. Ursula's ever mentioned his father's dispatches, which appeared almost every night on the front page of the Chicago *Daily News* with the dateline "Henderson Field, Guadalcanal." The Japs were closing in. Some experts felt that Henderson Field would fall soon. The marines were virtually cut off.

Yet his father's stories were lighthearted and cheerful, much like the handsome reporter himself, though Mike could hardly remember what "Patrick M. Casey" looked like. His mother never mentioned him, not even when he won the Pulitzer prize for his stories about the war in New Guinea.

She did read his dispatches every night, however. Even when his uncle, a dapper little man in clerical vest and French cuffs, would visit them and assure her that the "annulment" was "coming along."

Michael tried to explain at first to his classmates the difference between an "annulment" and a "divorce." They were not interested.

He looked nervously at his watch. If S'ter kept them too long, his mother would be home before he was and would worry about him. Whenever he seemed to do something wrong, she worried that "Casey blood" might turn him into an alcoholic.

He would also miss *Don Winslow of the Navy; Jack Armstrong, the All-American Boy;* and maybe *Little Orphan Annie.* And if his mother was angry at him, she might forbid him to listen to *The Lone Ranger* after supper. She often said that he read too much and that, instead of being glued to the radio, he should become friends "with the other boys your age."

From the corner of his eye he watched Anne Marie; she was fidgeting like a tiger in a circus cage. With loud sighs and noisy pen scratching, she pretended to be busy at work on an arithmetic problem.

An hour passed. S'ter worked implacably at her records. The seat of his desk was as uncomfortable as a concrete slab. The minute hand dragged itself slowly around the clock.

Anne Marie caught him looking at her. She made an ugly face and turned away in disgust.

"Daydreaming again, miss?" S'ter demanded. "Making up those silly romantic stories of yours?"

"No, S'ter," she said.

"Yes, S'ter, is what you mean. Leave your dreamworld and return to your arithmetic, if you please."

"Yes, S'ter."

Anne made up stories too. Wasn't that strange? He thought he was the only one in class who lived in a dreamworld.

The Monstress of Mongo. Mike hated her with single-minded fury. She was everything he wanted to be, popular, brave, athletic, a leader.

Even though he was tall, he was clumsy and useless at sports. And his mother wouldn't let him play football for fear he would hurt himself. His health was "delicate," just as his disposition was "sensitive." He broke his finger playing softball and missed a week of school.

Anne Marie had fractured a collarbone during a game against the eighth-grade volleyball team from Tower of Ivory parish and had not shed a tear. Two days later she was back on the team, playing with a cast.

"Just sitting there?" S'ter looked up at them in mock surprise. "Make yourselves useful. Erase the blackboard and clean the erasers. Get on with it."

Under other circumstances it would be a sign of favor to help Sister Alphonse Mary after class. Now it compounded their disgrace. It was also a sign that they were in very serious trouble. A long wait and then the erasers were invariably a prelude to a severe tongue-lashing.

It might be easier, Mike thought, to be fighting Japs at Henderson Field.

Quietly they erased the boards and gathered armfuls of erasers to take outside.

Anne Marie stuck out her tongue at him.

Monstress.

"Going out without your wraps? Too busy with your

sinful fighting to notice that it's December? We had the spelling bee because it's the last day of school before Christmas, don't you remember that?"

"Yes, S'ter, no, S'ter," they said in unison again. Mike was afraid that they had the words in the wrong order and that would infuriate Sister Alphonse Mary even more.

"Do you want both your mothers to complain about my ruining your health? Put on your coats this minute."

"No, S'ter, yes, S'ter." This time they had said it right.

Suddenly Mike felt very angry. He had done nothing wrong. His only offense was to win a spelling bee. It would be unmanly, a Casey-like weakness, to lose to placate Anne Marie. She had caused all the trouble and he was being punished for it.

Worse than Ming's daughter.

Outside the wind was bitter. Mike shivered as he pounded the erasers against one another, sending clouds of chalk dust floating like frozen mist over the snow piles at the edge of the school yard.

"If you tell her it was me, sissy, I'll make you pay. . . . "

Mike wanted to smash her nasty little head between the erasers.

Of course he wouldn't tell. To do anything to hurt a woman was unmanly.

The threat of a winter storm was still on S'ter's face when they returned to the classroom.

"Take off your coats and come up here to the front of the room. Now, then," she began when the two of them were standing side by side in front of her desk, heads bowed before the solemn bar of justice. "I think everyone knows that Michael does not use vulgar language. He is invariably courteous to women."

"I–N–V–A–R–I–A–B–L–Y, " said Anne Marie, a hint of her most winning smile flashing across her piquant face.

"That will do, miss. You lost the spelling bee, as I remember?"

"Yes, S'ter," she said contritely, but her tiny hands were clutched in fury.

"Do you like Michael?"

The girl was thrown off-balance. And Michael wished the floor would disappear beneath him.

"What . . . what do you mean, S'ter?"

"You know very well what I mean, miss."

"Well"—she hesitated—"Mickey would be kind of cute if he wasn't such an overgrown sissy and a stuck-up mama's boy."

"Indeed," Sister Alphonse Mary sniffed indignantly.

The Casey in him took charge. "Annie would be the prettiest girl in the class, S'ter, if she didn't have a mouth like a marine."

The nun didn't even bother to try to hide her laughter. But Anne Marie flushed in embarrassed anger.

"That will do," said S'ter, more to herself than to them. She sighed and then tried again. "Eventually this terrible war is going to be over and our country and our Church are going to change. We will need bright and attractive young people like you. But you will have to give up your apparently incorrigible Irish propensity to fight with your own. Do you understand?"

"Yes, S'ter," they said politely, though they did not.

The young nun sighed again. "Can't you understand, Anne, that Michael's father is in a place where his life is in danger every moment? Can't you have some sympathy for that?"

"He ran away because he was a drunk." Anne Marie's voice raced like the Burlington Zephyr rushing by a crossing gate. "And his grandmother killed his grandfather and his aunt Kate is a Communist."

Sister Alphonse Mary tapped her pencil on the spotlessly clean blotter of her desk. She stared at Anne Marie as though she were watching a spider crawl across a wall.

Mike noticed the look S'ter gave her and thought, *You know she's a Monstress too.*

In the silence, Mike heard the ticking clock, the voices of some boys in the school yard (a world far away), and his own breathing.

"You may be the most vicious human being I have ever known," S'ter said quietly. "Apologize to Michael."

"I apologize, Michael," she said crisply, "for being the most vicious human being S'ter has ever known."

"She doesn't mean it," he flared back.

"So you are capable of anger?" The nun considered him curiously. "Accept her apology anyway."

"Yes, S'ter. I accept your apology, Anne Marie . . . "

"Fine," said Sister Alphonse Mary.

" . . . the same way you made it," he finished.

"You are both impossible." The nun pushed her pencil away impatiently. "You will suffer greatly for your stubbornness. Very well, I give up on you. You may go home now. And I hope you will find time to reflect on Christmas Day about what the Christ Child must think of both of you."

"Yes, S'ter," they said.

They left the school by separate doors. Mike glanced at his watch. His mother would be home by now.

But at least he would not miss *Jack Armstrong, the All-American Boy.*

He hummed the program's theme song, "Wave the flag for Hudson High boy," as he sloshed through the snow in the fading light on the long and lonely walk to his family's house on the Oak Park side of the parish, one more thing about which he was teased.

Mike took it for granted that he would always be lonely. He was the kind of person no one seemed to like—too smart, too clumsy, too sensitive.

Since he was a little boy adults had warned him that he would not amount to much unless he changed. And as long as he could remember, children his own age had reacted to him the way the seventh-graders at St. Ursula's had. He would have been astonished if his classmates had welcomed him when his mother moved into the parish, to be near the plant and to flee from the bitter memories of the old house in Lake Forest. A few laughs at his quips and then the same old dislike.

It would stop when he was dead.

As he crossed Mayfield Avenue the first snowball banged into the back of his head.

Surprised and unprepared, he turned around and was

hit in the face. His attackers had been hiding behind bushes and trees. They came at him from all directions, pelting him with snowballs, some of them rock hard. Instinctively he threw up his hands to protect his face. Someone tackled him. He crashed into a bank of freshly shoveled snow.

They formed a tight ring around him and continued to throw snowballs, like Indians attacking covered wagons. Then two of them held him in the snowbank while another, Joe Kelly, repeatedly shoved globs of snow against his face, into his mouth, up his nose. He did not fight back. His mother told him that fighting was unmanly.

"Wash his face clean," shouted Anne Marie, who was lurking behind the boys in the darkness. "Priests ought to have nice clean faces."

The snow burned his skin. Tears of humiliation and rage poured down his face.

"Cry, baby, cry," Anne Marie taunted him. "Go home to momma and cry for her."

They circled around him for a final barrage of snowballs and then slipped away into the winter night.

Mike lay in the snowbank, panting. Then, slowly, he struggled to a sitting position, wiping the melting snow from his face and coughing to clear his throat.

He would miss *Jack Armstrong* now, a world in which good people won instead of lost.

Someday he would show them all. He might even be a monsignor like his uncle. Then they would respect him.

But for now there would be loneliness, misery, pain.

Why couldn't he be on Guadalcanal with his father?

"Enervated?" Anne Marie was standing under the streetlight at the corner of Mayfield and Potomac, savoring her triumph.

"One *n*," he muttered.

"And your father's a drunk," she spit at him.

Deep inside Mike Casey something churned and then tore loose. He sprung from his sitting position and tackled her, dragging her into the snowbank with him.

They rolled over in the snow. She slipped away like a squirming goldfish and tried to run. He grabbed her again. She fought back, kicking, clawing, biting. They tumbled into the bank, struggling like two wounded animals in the pale glow of the streetlight. She clawed his face with her fingernails.

"Explain that to your bitch of a mother," she said, trying to shove her knee into his groin.

All the anger of Mike's life fused inside him and became a white fire like that of an acetylene torch.

He hit her in the stomach, once and then again. She folded up like a summer deck chair in a windstorm and collapsed into the snow. He pinned her against the ground with one hand and raised a massive handful of snow above her head.

Then in the faint light of the street lamp, he looked into her flaming gray eyes and saw himself.

His pain and loneliness and misery in her eyes. How could that be? What was she doing with his feelings? Why would she feel that no one liked her either?

Such terrible pain, much worse than his. Why?

She was not afraid of the wet snow, she didn't care about that. Yet, she was afraid.

Just as he had always been afraid.

She must see herself in his eyes just as he saw himself in hers. They shared even the surprise of discovering their own reflections.

Their pains merged, one loneliness, one fear, one despair over worthlessness.

Mike lowered the hand that held the lump of snow.

And time ground to a halt, like a streetcar lurching to a stop for a red light. The rest of the world drifted lazily away. There was only Anne Marie and Michael. And the snowbank and the pale illumination of the streetlight.

They were no longer two persons but one, united by their agony and then by something that went far beyond agony. Michael/Anne Marie or Anne Marie/Michael . . . wrapped up together like two infants in a thick winter blanket, a warm protective envelope of peace and then joy.

He wanted to kiss her and knew that she wanted to be kissed. He was afraid to touch her lips, as he would be afraid to profane the chalice a priest used at Mass. She was wonderful, beautiful, and terrifying. So he touched her face with a wet glove. She smiled gratefully.

When, later in life, he tried to analyze what happened on that shortest day of the year in 1942, he often asked whether it was merely blossoming sexuality. His intellect, trained to probe and suspect all human emotion, could never explain the merging of the two persons at the foot of the old-fashioned streetlight. But, whatever it was, it was not just sex, not as sex is normally understood.

Something much less.

Or much more.

Slowly the warmth disappeared, like a spectacular summer sunset at the end of a day when vanilla-ice-cream clouds had chased one another across the sky above a lake, leaving only two seventh-graders in a snowbank, two seventh-graders who would never be quite the same.

Mike helped Anne up and brushed the snow off her coat.

"I really deserved to have my face washed," she said.

There seemed to be nothing for him to say.

"It isn't a very deep scratch." She touched his face and caused a lingering trace of the joy to flicker briefly inside him. "Wash it off as soon as you get home so it doesn't get infected. Your mother won't even notice."

And no need to say anything.

He picked up her bookcase, dusted off the snow, and gave it to her.

"If you hurry, you won't be late for supper. . . . " Her need to talk was as strong as his need not to talk.

Anne sounded like a mother, not his mother, not her mother, but someone's mother.

She turned to walk down Mayfield toward the O'Brien house, halfway along the block to Division Street.

Then she faced him again, buried her chin on her chest, and murmured, "Sorry . . . "

She ran away rapidly, as though someone were chasing her.

Mike found his voice. "Don't fall, it will enervate you. . . . "

He strode home briskly with cheerful music playing in his head, Christmas music. It did not matter that he had missed *Jack Armstrong, the All-American Boy*.

As long as there was one other person in the world who hurt as badly as he hurt, he was not alone. Life was filled with promise and possibility.

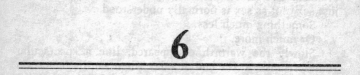

She wanted a drink. But her rules said that she didn't drink alone, not even on a day when the Cardinal visited her gallery, when an explosion sent Sandy to the hospital, and when Mickey Casey walked into her office. Instead, she turned on her radio to WMET, to The Fixx doing "One Thing Leads to Another." Her addiction to rock, picked up from her children, was a carefully concealed vice.

She had drunk too much at her lunch with Joan Powers, an early lunch so she could be back in time to greet the Cardinal—three glasses of white wine for her and at least four martinis for Joan.

Instead of examining her notes for the next session with Dr. Murphy she thought about Joan—strange that she had seen her and Mickey the same day. Mickey had certainly worn better than Joan.

Joan was obese, there was no other word for it—one massive oblong, her face, fit tightly on another massive oblong, the rest of her. She was a drawing from a geometry textbook, dressed in a hideous blue gauze dress with frills and ruffles, decorated with more and more expensive jewelry than Anne owned, and blurred by several coatings of useless cosmetics. She had, she assured Anne, just returned from a "fat farm" where she'd lost twenty pounds and been given a new lease on life. She would be able to have nothing more than a salad, despite the fact that she "adored" the Arts Club's menu.

When Anne arrived she had found Joan already halfway through a martini. The only question was whether it was the first or the second.

Joanie, the inseparable companion of her girlhood, the beautiful and shapely matron of honor at her wedding, had become the kind of woman that Joan would have ridiculed when she was in her teens.

"Well, I hope you don't expect me to visit that new exhibition," she began her assault of Anne as soon as Anne had sat down—their lunches were always assaults, carried on in the name of "shaping you up at last."

"Up to you," Anne had replied, biting her tongue because she suspected that she was the only one who ever took Joan out to lunch these days—always at "that divine Arts Club," where Anne would pay because Joan, despite her husband's wealth, was constitutionally incapable of reaching for a check.

"I said to Tony, I said, 'I can't believe she's doing it. He was a little prick,' I said, 'nothing more. She doesn't owe him a thing,' I said."

"The Cardinal asked me. . . . "

"Does he know about what happened that summer after Dickie boy didn't come home from the wars?"

Always the nasty crack about Dick Murray. Joan had to stick the knife in. In Joan's vision of the past, Anne had taken him away from her. She refused to remember that Anne had dutifully asked whether Joan objected before she responded to Dick's interest.

"Of course not," Anne had replied. "No one does."

"Well, I said to Tony, I said, 'I wouldn't let that prick's stuff into my gallery for all the cardinals in the world,' I said, 'and he didn't have a very useful prick either as far as that goes,' I said."

Vulgarity, obesity, alcoholism—no one could have anticipated such fates for the genial young Joan O'Malley.

I know she hates me now, Anne had thought, *but I'm all she has left. Tony plays around, her kids can't stand her. What would happen to her if I let her make me angry and fight back.*

"I get a third of the take," she said lightly, mentally

gritting her teeth. "Can't beat the profit motive, whatever happened long ago."

"That's the trouble with you." Joan had jabbed a salad fork in the general direction of Anne's cream of watercress soup. "You don't understand that you're a grandmother and should act like one. I said to your daughter-in-law the other day, I said, 'What does it feel like to have a mother-in-law who is mixed up in a business with a bunch of faggots,' I said, 'especially when with all your husband's money,' I said, ' . . . she can settle down in River Forest and have lunch at the country club every day with the rest of us old women?' Of course Teresa agreed. She's a very intelligent young woman."

Poor Tessie, cornered by such a harridan, probably at a supermarket.

"We're doing Peggy Donlon's watercolors next," Anne had murmured softly. "She's almost twenty years older than we are."

That comment had launched Joan on an attack on the Donlons, especially on Hugh, "an apostate priest, that's all he is," and Maria, "cheap little dago." It was not aimed at the Donlons as much as it was aimed at her. Joan knew that Anne and Maria had become friends and jealously could share Anne with no one else.

Poor old woman. Dear God, don't let me ever become like that.

And then she had felt guilty about the arrogance of her prayer and apologized to God for it.

"Well, I hope nothing happens during this exhibition," Joan had continued, draining her third drink (at least). "That little prick had some weird powers. I hope he doesn't come back to haunt you."

By which she meant that she devoutly hoped and prayed that something terrible would happen during the Kenny exhibition.

Anne had paid little attention to the curse as she guided her weaving friend to the taxi. After what had happened later in the afternoon, she wondered if perhaps . . .

Nonsense, she told herself crisply, *you're too intelli-*

gent to be superstitious. Forget about Joan and get back to the more serious matter of Mickey Casey.

She looked over her notes—"felt like melting butter." She could not use such a cliché in reporting to Dr. Murphy. Indeed, there was no reason to tell Dr. Murphy about Mickey Casey at all. Why tell her about his thin silver hair, his thin pink face, his thin hard body, and his pale, pale blue eyes?

Yet by the pact she had made with herself, she was bound to tell her therapist everything except the most terrible sins in her life. If ever the wall between those sins and the rest of life should collapse, she would die.

She thought about Father Kenny's painting of "Divine Justice" and the poor girl with the devil's claw in her breast.

With a shudder she drove the picture out of her mind and tried to concentrate on her notes. How many women were silly enough to make notes for an hour with a shrink?

It would be humiliating to talk about her schoolgirl crush on Mickey Casey, but it might make up for what she was hiding from Dr. Murphy. And maybe the doctor could explain the strange electricity between her and Mickey, a schoolgirl crush, of course, yet more than sex. Much more. But what?

She poured herself a second cup of herbal tea, removed the dinner dishes from the washer, and trudged back upstairs to the room that served as her at-home office and occasional guest bedroom. Mark had chosen the old 900 North Michigan apartment building between Delaware and Walton because it was the only rental building near the gallery that at not unreasonable cost provided two upstairs rooms, each with its own bath.

As he had tried to explain to Teresa, it was perfect for her—snug and comfortable inside with the noise and the bustle of Michigan Avenue outside when she wanted to feel the pulse of the city all around her.

The downstairs room—parlor and dining room combined—was blue and cream, with mirrors and a hint of Second Empire, leather couches and chairs, richly textured cream fabric on the wall, blue drapes, a couple of strategically placed candelabra that glittered in the mirrors. Snug and at the same time opulent despite the fact that the space was so limited. Coolly reassuring when she came home exhausted at the end of a day's work.

When she wanted total peace, she shut the windows and turned on the air conditioners. Only the fire engines and the ambulances broke through the soothing din of the old window units, which had been badly overworked this long hot summer.

"But we love you," Tessie had protested, tears in her big green eyes. "Mark, the kids . . . we want to be near you."

Tessie had made her a delicious omelet and opened a bottle of white wine while she showered. Bumps and bruises, the doctor said. And Sandy would be out in a day or two. Only a headache and the smell of the explosion remained.

And then over the omelet, her daughter-in-law had extolled the virtues of a "cute little house" only a block away from theirs in River Forest. With Korshak's moving to One Magnificent Mile and rumors that the 900 building would be demolished to make room for another high-rise, wasn't this the time to think about River Forest?

"I mean, Mrs. Reilly, you could have all the privacy you wanted and you'd still be close to us. And it's a safe neighborhood."

"I don't need any privacy, unfortunately. And this is as safe a building as anyone could want. Filled with old widows."

"You're not an old widow," Tessie had said stubbornly. "And I want my children to grow up knowing a great lady."

The little redhead's passionate affection embarrassed Anne, especially as she was unable to return it. If her own daughter, Beth, who disliked and patronized her, should even hint at living in Winnetka, she would move tomorrow. Teresa worshiped her and Anne kept her distance.

At first Anne had dismissed Mark's young wife as an empty-headed flake. But she was an honor student now at Rosary and she clearly wasn't a slut. Anna had been born more than thirteen months after the marriage, so pregnancy had not been the reason for their hasty wedding.

Anne could not explain to the intense young matron that River Forest had too many memories of a failed marriage and that her own son recalled memories of her being beaten until she was semiconscious as a prelude to forced sex with her drunken husband, who found her more useful than a punching bag because punching bags did not cower, plead, and then cry out in pain.

"I have to be near the gallery for a few more years. Maybe when I retire . . . "

Tessie had laughed nervously. "You won't ever retire, Mrs. Reilly."

And you won't ever work up enough courage to call me Anne. Maybe I should follow Beth's advice and look more like a grandmother.

"Oak Street Beach is more fun than the pool at Butterfield."

"We don't want you to be lonely," the younger woman insisted.

Taking pity on her, Anne said, "If I ever feel lonely, you and Mark will be the first to hear about it. Whatever hour of the day or night."

Dismissing the memories of that conversation, she pushed aside her notes for Dr. Murphy. No, she would not talk to her about Mickey Casey.

There were two kinds of loneliness. The first, a loneliness of boredom and emptiness, did not bother her. Her life was busy and challenging, too much to do rather than not enough. Perhaps River Forest and grandchildren would make sense if she did feel bored and empty.

The other kind of loneliness could be filled only by a man who loved her. Or a God who loved her.

Having a man of her own had always been more painful than not having one.

And she had lost a God of her own long ago. Nevertheless, He lingered on the fringes of her life, as though He were waiting for her to do something that might let Him back in, a guest dismissed from a birthday party, but perhaps not permanently.

She finished her herbal tea and placed the cup and saucer on a table in the upstairs corridor so that she would remember to bring it down to the kitchen in the morning. Fussy old woman.

She removed her bifocal contact lenses and placed them in the container in her bathroom. Virtuously she rubbed facial cream into her face. *Bifocal contacts*, she thought, *periodontal work and reconstruction for my rotten Irish teeth, the Nautilus and diet for my figure, cosmetics of every imaginable variety*, Vogue and Bazaar *every month for the most recent discoveries, Inderal for what the doctor calls a benign heart arythmia; all the protections against time that human ingenuity had devised and I'm still growing old.*

Carefully covering her makeup jars, so as not to waste any cream, she swallowed two more of the pills that the doctor at Henrotin had given her. Maybe they would help her sleep. And banish the raw acrid smell from the explosion that still lingered in her nostrils.

Then she hung her robe on the hook behind the door in her bedroom, a cozy cocoon in pink and white prints with contrasting white lamps, chaise, and armoire curtains. *I'd never have the nerve to design a room like this in River Forest*, she thought.

It was almost ten o'clock, but she was not interested in the ten o'clock news. Whatever they said about the explosion at the gallery would be said whether she was watching or not. She needed a good night's sleep.

Dear God, she prayed, *tonight I want to ask for one good night's sleep. No dreams please.*

Then she prayed for the repose of the souls of her mother and father, her sisters and her brothers, and of her son Jimmy, in case he was really dead. Next she asked God's blessing and protection for her children and their families and for Jimmy if he was still alive. She begged the Lord to restore Sandy to health and to cure the pain that separated her from "Colonel Kokoshka."

Finally she prayed for the three men in her life, all of whom she had failed so badly.

"And forgive me for everything I've done wrong," she said, ending her nightly prayers as she always did.

She fantasized that the cool flow of air on her shoulders from the air conditioners was a benign response from the Lord. Father Ryan would probably say that it was.

Within the comfort of her sheets, she wondered how long ago she had stopped praying for Mickey Casey. Probably when he returned safely from Korea. Ought she to add him again to the list? She had not failed him, had she? Well, maybe him too.

And maybe she would do so again, a thought both stimulating and appalling.

Well, she would pray for him anyway.

She fell asleep quickly, benign images of the mystery of Mickey in the snowdrift slowly yielding to much more terrible memories.

7

A thick cloud of oily black smoke hovered motionless against the dull gray winter sky, a twisted dirty handkerchief hung from a clothesline on a windless day. Occasionally red fingers of fire stabbed up from colorless brick buildings to disturb the immobility of the cloud. And everywhere in the neighborhood the smell, thick, black, and dirty like the cloud, a smell like a hundred overheated coal furnaces, a smell of foundry and mill.

A dull, respectable neighborhood of two- and three-flat apartment buildings, and an occasional older wooden home. Working men and their families struggling out of the chasm of the Great Depression without complaint over the blighted dreams and the spoiled lives. Unemployment increasing again, but still contempt for "relief" and for the "WPA idlers" and fear of the Communists in some of the new unions.

At the center of the neighborhood the gray Gothic church finished just after the Crash, a church where on Friday afternoons and evenings more than a thousand women prayed to the "Sorrowful Mother of Jesus" that their husbands or sons would find steady work and lighted candles with a plea that someday their "ship would come in."

And across the concrete courtyard from the church the old school building, built at the turn of the century, to protect the faith of the children of the immigrants, a school building in which now a generation was dying.

Screams and silence, horror stifling all other sounds. Screams of anguish from parents searching for their children, screams of joy when a child was found, screams of despair when a priest or nun shook his or her head sadly, screams of frustration from firemen whose equipment was not adequate to their task—ladders too short to reach to the window ledges on which scores of children clung, forced to choose between the concrete of the courtyard and the flames at their backs.

Screams of parents pleading with their children not to jump when a child had fallen to the ground and lay motionless on the concrete, and screams pleading with them to jump when another windowful of little ones was incinerated by the racing flames.

And, worst of all, shrill and pathetic screams of children: terror and confusion among those who had escaped, their faces covered with grease and dirt; unbearable pain from those who were dying in their classrooms; and more pain from those who lay on the ground, suffering from broken bones, savaged lungs, and scorched skin.

A black-haired girl in the school uniform hanging from a window ledge, fire consuming a child behind her. The black-haired girl—her sister Kathleen—lost hold with one hand, clung desperately with the other, then with agonizing slowness regained her grip. A burst of smoke in her face. A cry of horror as she fell. A fireman desperately lunging to catch her. And missing.

Judge O'Brien's daughter, the crowd murmured, as someone put a blanket over Kathy's body.

More fire equipment. Water from the hoses freezing

against her skin. The Monsignor shouting incoherently at the firemen. Father Kenny trying to quiet him.

A sweet smell, like candy cooking. "Varnish," said a man, "those shining floors are like gasoline. I hope the goddamn nuns are happy."

Then fire nets, finally, and with enough firemen to hold them. A knot of older girls at a window on the third floor. In the midst of their frightened faces her sister Connie. *Oh, dear God, save my Connie for me.*

A great whoosh of red flame and a terrible breaking noise.

"The roof! The roof is going!"

An avalanche of fire consuming Connie and her classmates. And more screams, her mother yelling at her, angry that she was still alive and Connie dead. Her father clasping her in his arms and murmuring, "She doesn't mean it, she doesn't mean it."

And then, much later it seemed, canvas bags in front of the church. Limp children being placed inside the bags.

"What are those bags for, Daddy?"

"Hush, child, everything will be all right." Daddy was sobbing, but he held her as if he would never let her go.

She knew what was inside the bags, however.

In two of them were Connie and Kathleen.

8

Mary Kate pushed the record button on her cassette player.

Patient was nervous today and appeared under considerable strain. Continues to dress like a fashion model, mulberry Ultrasuede suit today, with coordinated blouse and hose. Devastating. Doubtless to impress me. I'm impressed.

Small wonder that she was nervous. There was an ex-

*plosion in her gallery yesterday afternoon. Unnerved me
because she revealed relationship with relative of mine.
Unnerved me more with story of peculiar psychic experience with him.*

*I put aside my ballpoint pen. Mike Casey the Cop a
psychic?*

I added the word ongoing *before psychic.*

*I was uneasy about the patient. My brother the Punk
was her priest. She knew of the relationship, of course, but
never mentioned it. A compliment to my integrity or a
challenge?*

*And now a long-term attachment to my cousin. She
must realize that he is mixed up with the Ryan/Collins
clan. His mother, Margaret Ryan Casey, was my father's
older sister.*

*I hardly know the man, since he remained on the West
Side when we migrated to the South Side after the Second
World War. Yet I don't like the coincidence. Should I con-
front her about it? Maybe it's not important. And there are
other matters that came up today that are probably more
important.*

*I have a reasonably good relationship with her be-
cause, like her, I am an Irish Catholic wife and mother and
professional woman, with more than my share of guilt and
hang-ups. I'm ten years or so younger and less concerned
about propriety. I'm happily married, indeed, disarmingly
so. And I can't really claim that men have been cruel to me
or that the Church has repeatedly screwed me.*

*If I had suffered all the things she's suffered, I'd be
permanently institutionalized.*

*She's a strong woman and gorgeous and I like her more
than I like most of my patients. She's made considerable
progress against the depression that brought her to my
couch.*

And she's lying to me. I'm not sure why.

*So I'm going to replay part of today's tape and call the
Pirate (my husband, Joe, who is a Jungian) and see if he has
any references on this joint ecstasy stuff.*

"You feel yourself still attracted to this Mickey Casey?"

"Yes. Is that wrong?"

"Do you think it is?"

"Why am I attracted to him after all these years?"

"You think that the years eliminate sexual attraction?"

"It's more than sex."

"Why does it have to be more than sex?"

"I don't know why. It just is."

"Does he need you like the other men in your life seemed to? Does he appeal to your propensity to sacrifice yourself for a man instead of relating to him as an adult?"

"Do I do that. . . . Oh, you mean that I try to protect them because I was unable to protect my father from the Great Depression."

"You admitted during our last session that taking care of a man, assuming responsibility for him, treating him like a spoiled little boy has been typical of your relationships. Is this police person a spoiled little boy? You find that amusing?"

"Only because I called him that long ago. Actually, he wasn't a spoiled baby then and he isn't now."

"So he doesn't need you?"

"No. Well, he needs someone. He's lonely. I can see the pain in his eyes. . . . "

"Like the pain in Father Sweeney's eyes?"

"Not at all. Mickey needs a woman, not a mother."

"And you can't permit yourself to become intimate with a man who doesn't need a mother. Even your senator needed someone to take care of him."

"I'll have to think about that. Mickey certainly can survive nicely without me. He had a wonderful mother once. So he doesn't need another one."

"Therefore, you are afraid to be intimate with him."

"Yes, I am. But, I know this sounds contradictory, I want nothing more."

Mary Kate pushed the pause button on her cassette

player. The last comment was typical of the patient's rigorous and intelligent honesty about herself. She did not avoid the kinks in her personality. She knew that she wanted a little boy and simultaneously wanted an adult man. So far the little boys hadn't satisfied her. Perhaps now she would try a man. She released the pause button and spoke before she went on replaying the session.

And despite her claims, I thought the Senator was a little boy—though not an infant like her two husbands.

"Do you want to go to bed with him?"

"No . . . Maybe . . . I don't know."

"Would you if he asked?"

"He won't ask."

"Why not?"

"You're not listening to what I've said. We're afraid of one another. We knew that we could hurt each other terribly. It's too intense. Even now."

"Your romp in the snowdrift when you were children, was it not a sexual interlude? Didn't you say it was like being naked?"

"I said it was worse and better than being naked. There wasn't anything about me that he didn't know totally—my fears, my pains, my guilts, my loves. And I knew everything about him too. There wasn't anything physical that day. We just became one person."

"There was something physical when he held your arm yesterday."

"Of course. We're no longer innocent children."

"Children are not innocent, but let it go. And you saw into his soul yesterday too?"

"He's still suffering because of his wife's death, feels guilty that he didn't love her enough. Wishes he'd spent more time with his children. Resents the tricks politicians have played on the Department. Misses his parents, especially his father. Disillusioned with his work. Looks forward to retirement next year and is afraid of the emptiness it will bring. Fears loneliness and despair."

"And finds you attractive."

"Yes."

"Very?"

"Extremely."

"Couldn't all of this be merely quick insight?"

"You don't believe me! Damn it, I'm telling the truth!"

"You're angry at me?"

"I'm sorry."

"You don't have a right to be angry?"

"I like you."

"Can't you be angry at someone you like?"

"I suppose."

"You do want to have sex with him?"

"Yes . . . except . . . "

"Except what?"

"Except when our personalities blend like that, sex seems almost unnecessary."

"Under those circumstances sex would not be good?"

"Oh, no. It would be much better."

"There was a promise of sex in the snowdrift?"

"I suppose so. We were both too inexperienced to . . . . well, to recognize it. I wanted him to kiss me, that was all. He didn't, by the way."

"You both recognized it yesterday?"

"Yes. It was like a powerful invitation to complete with our bodies what, well . . . , what our souls had already done."

"I see."

Mary Kate turned off the tape for a minute. She had lied there. She didn't see at all. She fast-forwarded the tape to Anne's account of their brief college-age romance.

"There was just one other interlude between the two of you?"

"Yes. We were polite and kind to each other after that night at Mayfield and Potomac. Then he went to the seminary and I went to Trinity. His family moved out of the parish when his father and mother came back from Berlin. I was a senior in college, living with my aunt near Lincoln Park, finishing up at Loyola, feeling very free and reckless and sophisticated."

"He'd left the seminary by then?"

"Yes, only I didn't know that. I was in a bar on Wabash in the Loop. The college crowd gathered in bars in the Loop in those days. Rush Street and Old Town had not yet developed."

"Of course."

"I was wearing one of those grotesque 'new look' suits, blue with fur trim, skirt halfway to my ankles."

"You remember what you were wearing?"

"As though it were yesterday. I saw him across the bar. Then he saw me. He came over to talk. He was gorgeous, tall and lean, with a thin face and jet-black hair, kind of like Tyrone Power. He really hasn't changed much—silver hair now, like me. Anyway, when he reached me, all the other noises faded away. He took my hand, told me that he was sorry about my parents' death, said I was very lovely—more of a compliment than I had ever heard from him."

"I see."

"Then he said that he had left the seminary and the Church and was going to the University of Chicago. He claimed that he didn't believe in God anymore, but I knew that he did."

"Another casualty at the University of Chicago?"

"Of course not. I went there later and didn't lose my faith. Anyway, he returned to the Church that year, before he left for the war in Korea."

"Because of you?"

"I don't think so. Well, partly, I guess. Mostly it was a group of Catholics at the university. I was on the fringes of the same group later on when he was in Korea."

"What did you talk about?"

"We didn't say much, just held hands and looked into each other's eyes . . . he has the most incredible blue eyes."

"You said nothing?"

"I told him I might go to graduate school at the university and study art history. He wanted to know why—unlike most boys he didn't say that it was ridiculous for a girl to waste her time in graduate school."

"And your explanation?"

"I don't know. I was an unlikely intellectual. Still am, I suppose. Maybe because when I was in high school the art nun brought us to the Art Institute one day. I fell in love with it. I used to ride the L downtown. I told my mother I wanted to shop at Marshall Field's and went to the Art Institute instead. I'd sit for hours in front of El Greco's 'Assumption' and Monet's 'River' and Renoir's 'Little Girls.' "

"How did he react?"

"He just kind of smiled. I felt that maybe he didn't understand, but still deep down he understood, perhaps better than I did."

"You dated?"

"A few times. We were both fascinated and frightened. We went to movies and held hands, listened to Mozart and cool jazz at my aunt's apartment, hummed 'Good Night, Irene' and 'Mona Lisa' on the Clark Street trolley—you didn't need a car for dates in those days—kissed each other good night."

"There was obvious sexual attraction then?"

"Oh, yes."

"And you did nothing about it?"

"No . . ."

"Sounds idyllic."

"It was wonderful and scary. . . . There was one night . . . "

"Yes?"

"We'd seen Rashomon, the Japanese film about rape. It was, well, very arousing. In the vestibule of my aunt's apartment . . . "

"Yes?"

"We became very passionate. Me especially. I was his for the taking that night, Dr. Murphy. My aunt wasn't home."

"And he didn't take you?"

"No."

"Sorry about it?"

"I don't know. My life would have been very different. . . . "

"This was the only relationship you two had between your grammar-school days and the present?"

"Yes. He called once or twice after that night. Then he went off to Korea. We never really crossed paths after that. I suppose we both did our best to avoid it."

"And it was his fault that the relationship was not pushed?"

"No, not completely. I probably wasn't too enthusiastic on the phone the times he called. I could have written him."

"Why didn't you?"

"I was afraid."

"Of what?"

"Of being known the way he would know me."

"I see."

Mary Kate pushed the pause button again, then began dictating.

I still didn't see at all. But the patient is intelligent and sophisticated—as long as religion isn't the subject. I must take her account seriously. There is unquestionably some special chemistry between her and Mike Casey the Cop, and one of remarkable durability.

The citation provided by my Pirate to an obscure and characteristically convoluted Jungian journal made me feel even more uneasy. It was entitled "Soul Marriages" and was by (of course) a Swiss analyst who summarized three cases, a big sample for a Jungian. When you had plowed through the permutations and combinations of animus's and anima's (or should I say animi and animae?) you came to this summary paragraph:

"In such a blending of personalities, caused as we have seen by complementary and symmetrical sensitivities, originating in acute childhood loneliness, there need not be a sexual result at all. Indeed so powerful is the mutual sensitivity that sexual relations seem unnecessary or even terrifying. The bond in these relationships appears to be lifelong, even if the partners do not see each other for many years. Often, for reasons which will require more clinical

*investigation, there is a struggle between one partner and a
third person for the possession of the anima of the other
partner.*

*"Sometimes this struggle may take the shape of a war
between light and darkness."*

Oh shit! That's all I need—a war, a goddamn Jungian
war, between light and darkness!

9

"I have a report on the plate glass, Jefe."

Patrol Officer Lopez was dressed in a skirt today instead of slacks and looking prettier than ever, a brown-eyed,
olive-skinned beauty whose trim little rear seemed ready to
twitch and sway in flamenco rhythms. Casey considered
whether the image was racist and concluded that it was.
Patrol Officer Lopez was much more likely to be devoted to
rock 'n' roll. All right, he could imagine her undulating to
soft rock.

Such reprehensible but enjoyable images forced him to
abandon his nostalgic contemplation of the south end of
Grant Park and the space where the Illinois Central Terminal used to be. Who would have thought in the 1940s that
Chicago could do nicely without the IC terminal?

Now it was merely a memory under the soft blue of the
first autumnlike day of September. Maybe the big heat
wave was over.

"Okay, Deirdre, shoot. And sit down, for the love of
heaven. I'm not a general."

Casey treated with undisguised contempt the propensity of some of his colleagues to walk around in tailored uni-
forms with three or four stars on their shoulders—like
Douglas MacArthur, for Pete's sake.

"It was not shatterproof glass. Ordinary, no-glare plate
glass." She sat at the edge of a hard chair, discreetly tugging

the hem of her skirt into place, so that he could only guess that she had knees. A lot of things had changed in the Church, but Catholic high schools still strove to produce young ladies, though now young ladies who were feminists.

"It can't have been. . . . "

"I know, Jefe, but it was. The main window was damaged last winter when the high winds blew debris from the construction at One Magnificent Mile."

"I remember. We had to close off North Michigan. . . . "

"*You* closed it off," she said, implying a reprimand for a deputy commissioner who directed traffic in a crisis. Women patrol officers could skate a lot closer to insubordination than men, especially if they were pretty. "Anyway, Doña Anna Maria replaced all the windows with nonglare glass."

"All the better to see the paintings."

"Some of them are very lovely," she said, defending Doña Anna Maria against any implication of bad taste. "Here is the copy of the purchase order. The same company has already replaced the windows damaged in the explosion the day before yesterday."

"It's official, then, that it was a sewer gas backup?"

"That's what District Commander Mullens says in his report." She shrugged again. All women cops hated Jeremiah Mullens. "The fire department and the sanitation department think so too."

Sewer gas in Chicago in 1983? Was Jeremiah playing games again? Casey felt a faint hint of suspicion brush against the back of his neck.

"I don't like it, Deirdre."

"*Sí*, Jefe."

"Stay on it."

"*Sí*, Jefe." Just a hint of affectionate ridicule.

The patrol officer departed. *Lovely ass on her. My God, what's the matter with me?*

I suppose I know.

Casey's office was in the new addition of Police Headquarters, a horizontal slab with marble corridors on the first floor, which made an old building look new and modern—

something like the force itself, which now had the appearance of integrity and professionalism that had become essential for big-city police. Jargon, college degrees, smooth-talking public relations. He was part of it. He believed in it. Yet he was not sure that there was a police force in the world, even the squeaky clean western European departments, in which there was not a residue of corruption. The critical question, he thought, was whether you could eliminate most if not all the corruption and still maintain effectiveness. Once he was sure you could. Now he wondered if there was not a negative correlation between the appearance of professionalism and actual effectiveness. Maybe the formation of the metropolitan police departments in the United States and Europe in the middle of the last century was a mistake.

Mike Casey didn't know any of the answers anymore. He sighed. *One time I thought I knew them all. Maybe I've grown wiser and maybe only older. Anyway, in a year or so, it won't be my problem.*

Right now, whether I like it or not—and I half like it— Annie O'Brien, damn her, is my problem.

She's in trouble. There is something weird happening in that gallery. She needs my help. And her ass is spectacular.

Wonderful. Take my mind off other women. So pathetically, beautifully fragile.

How do I help her? What's the mystery this time? Something involving that nut Des Kenny. He was mixed up in it the last time too. He's dead now. He can't be involved.

He poured himself another cup of black coffee from his Mr. Coffee machine and walked back to the window. The IC terminal was going strong in those days. The place where it had been was now park and parking lot, partially obscured by a white brick luxury apartment building into which Mike had been tempted to move. Too close to work, he finally decided, and remained in the Outer Drive East apartment with all its memories of Janet, looking down on the Art Institute with its Vatican exhibit this year.

I never thought in those days at St. Ursula's that I'd be

*living near the Art Institute. To tell the truth, I don't think
I knew there was one. Or an Orchestra Hall, either. Not till
Dad came home.*

It was the summer after that he'd realized he was in
love with Annie.

The war had been over for a year. She was going to
college in the east. He was facing his fifth year at Quigley,
filled with resentment toward his mother and distaste for
his father, distaste mixed with admiration for Pat Casey's
relaxed self-confidence.

He couldn't have been all that confident. He was an
alcoholic, wasn't he?

He had just won his wife back, taken her away from her
son. He had reason to be confident.

*I was so buried in my own worries and problems I
hardly noticed her that summer. God, how dumb!*

They lusted after Jeanne Crain, hummed "It Might as
Well Be Spring," marveled at the new Studebaker, debated
about whether it was a sin to read *All the King's Men*,
prayed for the success of the U.N.O., as it was called then—
Roosevelt's replacement for the League of Nations—worried about a depression.

At least the others did. Mike worried about himself.

He spent the week after Labor Day at the lake, by himself. Stupidly, he refused to stay in the cottage when his
mother and father were there. He knew they were making
love and he hated them for it. He had heard the sounds one
night.

Annie was at her aunt's big house on the other side of
the lake. Her parents stayed away because of all the memories. She was the only one left out of five children. Mike
supposed they resented her like he resented his father. Her
aunt was too involved with her charitable projects to pay
much attention to Annie.

Des Kenny was there too, in Aunt Aggie's guest house.
The little creep. Was he screwing her?

I never thought of that before.

Des was gay. Mike Casey didn't know the word or the
condition then, but he knew Des didn't go for women. And
he knew he was crazy.

Maybe Des was giving her booze. There was a rumor in the neighborhood that she'd taken up heavy drinking after Dick Murray was killed in the Hürtgen Forest. Pour Scotch into an adolescent female and see what happens—that was Des Kenny's style in those days.

Des had been a good parish priest, they said, till the fire.

Mike turned away from the window of his office. He saw himself sitting on the worn pontoon raft on the lake, wrapped up in his own silly little ego. A head, covered with tousled black hair, appeared at the side of the raft. And then those magic gray eyes.

"Hello," she said. "Can I join you . . . ? Oh, Mickey. I heard you were here. Will you be in trouble with the seminary if I sit on the raft with you?"

"Of course not." His heart was pounding. "Anyway, there's no one around to see us."

Since the last time he'd seen her, the night they graduated from grammar school, she had grown into a breathtakingly beautiful young woman, her fresh body bursting at the seams of her blue swimsuit with red and white trim. Long black hair, pale white skin, hesitant gray eyes—she was a woman in an Irish myth, a faerie queen perhaps.

And her pallor, the hint that she had been marked by and for special suffering, made her even more appealing. For Mike, who had seen *La Traviata* the previous winter in violation of the seminary rules and was captivated by its sentimental romanticism, her pale fragility turned her into Violetta, a captive who had to be saved from death.

She talked about religion during each of the three mornings they met on the raft, taking his seminary status as evidence he was expert on such matters.

"Something wrong?" he had asked lightly the first morning when she trailed off into silence after a brief exchange about schools.

"I think I committed a mortal sin last night."

"Oh?" he said, both horrified and fascinated.

"I may have had a drink of water after midnight and I went to Holy Communion at Mass this morning anyway, because I was afraid to upset my aunt."

"We're still on daylight savings time, so you get an extra hour. The fast binds on standard time, not daylight time."

"Really? Oh, how wonderful! . . . but I thought it was a sin. . . . "

"It was still okay to receive Communion to protect your aunt from worry."

She seemed reassured but not completely.

The next morning he helped her climb on the raft, not thinking that the touch of hand on wrist and arm would reestablish the link between them.

They stood motionless on the gently swaying pontoon, his hand on her arm, their eyes locked together. There was terrible fear in her, which the touch of his fingers banished temporarily.

Finally he released her and they sat side by side, feet dangling in the warm water of the lake, shoulders almost touching, oblivious of the cream-puff clouds that were racing across the sky above them.

"I worry about limbo," she said.

So they discussed that place between heaven and hell to which the Church, in those days less confident about God's love and mercy, consigned the souls of unbaptized infants.

And they talked about how God distributed prayers assigned to the benefit of the most neglected souls in purgatory and whether it was better to pray for the soul closest to heaven or the one farthest away.

Also about whether there was really a sin that could not be forgiven. What indeed was the sin against the Holy Spirit? How could you touch the heart of a person so proud of his own sin that he had despaired of God's mercy?

Did you need to say a perfect act of contrition before gaining a plenary indulgence for the souls in purgatory? Did your state of grace affect the payoff for the "poor soul"?

Was Padre Pio's prediction of the end of the world (delicate shiver of wonderful shoulders) by 1950 accurate? And had he heard about the latest miracle at Lourdes?

And so it went.

Crap of course. The Church loaded us with crap in

those days. Sometimes when I yearn nostalgically for the Old Church I think about those arguments and sigh with relief.

What kind of creep is it who can sit on a raft under a soothing blue sky with the most beautiful young woman he has ever known and talk about crap? Maybe he was worse than Des Kenny.

He hadn't touched her after the first morning. But he knew that beneath the minor horrors of mortal sin and the end of the world, she was tormented by something much worse, something so terrible that he wanted to turn away from it and from her.

The last day on the float she was wearing a different swimsuit, white and strapless, as always the fashion leader. She was so dejected—bare shoulders slumped, gray eyes forlorn, finely pointed chin sagging toward her gently swelling breasts—that he wanted to take her in his arms and promise that he would never let her go, that he would protect her for all their lives, and chase away all the demons that tormented her.

He was filled with infinite tenderness, the most powerful emotion of love that he would ever feel in his life.

But he turned away from her and swam to the shore, scared of her beauty and power and terror.

I wanted to help her. Oh, dear God, how much I wanted to help her. I didn't know how.

And I was afraid to ask.

The coffee cup was empty and the IC terminal was still not there.

She needs help now too. The confident, self-possessed businesswoman persona is a good one, but it doesn't fool me. She needs help and she half wants it from me.

I can't help her now either. And the best thing for both of us is to leave it all alone. We're both too old to be hurt again.

10

Anne's tight, queasy stomach felt as if it were in the preliminary stages of motion sickness or intoxication. It desperately wanted to vomit but was not yet quite able to do it.

Exhibition openings were always difficult. There were thousands of serious art buyers in the Chicago area and tens of thousands of men and women affluent enough to buy something more than prints for their homes. But the world of art dealers was still small and often nasty. Buyers could be scared away by rumors percolating through that world and by the swipes of bitchy critics.

Moreover, as a newcomer who was Irish and Catholic and a physically attractive woman, she was an especially appealing target for the vultures who sat on the fences, and watched and sneered.

This was by no means an ordinary exhibition. She was taking a risk, though one that was carefully calculated. Father Kenny would have a certain stylistic appeal—a mad monk. And some of the pieces would appreciate with time. In his saner moments he would have been pleased that the money would be used to finance schools in the poor neighborhoods of Chicago.

Yet the exhibition was a gamble. She had started the day with a headache. It had grown worse by noon and was unbearable by four o'clock. The caterer was late, the wine merchant was later, Sandy was still dazed and not as much help as usual—"I am hokay, missus, really"—and then the crowd was slow in coming.

Earlier in the afternoon there had been another phone call—this time the music was "Old Buttermilk Sky," the other song. The record was even more worn than "Good Night, Irene."

And again Sandy had not heard the phone.

My darn crazy imagination, playing tricks and making up stories.

When the guests at last began to straggle into the gallery, they seemed less interested in it than in the changes in the neighborhood caused by the opening of One Magnificent Mile—for all the world looking like a marble enlargement of a desktop tubular pencil holder. She did not dislike the building; it was a nice wall for the colorful canyon that ran from the river to the lake. But the conventional wisdom was that the new shops which had opened on the ground floor made Oak and Cedar streets look like Paris or New York. And that was not so.

Anne could not forgive the shops that had left the 900 North Michigan building for the new structure. She thought their style was not elegant but chichi. And she strongly believed that Chicago looked like itself, which was certainly better than New York and comparable in its own way to Paris.

She wanted to scream that they were fools. And then she wanted to vomit.

Moreover, the first comments on Father Kenny's works were hardly flattering. Maybe it had been a mistake to hang "Divine Justice" on the landing. She found herself defensively praising the "power and clarity" of his vision.

Whatever the hell that meant.

And it seemed to her in one sick-making glance that "Divine Justice" had changed. The demons were closer to the girl in the swamp.

That could not be. She was too busy rushing about to look carefully.

Then the crowds arrived and the comments became more favorable. Anne should have relaxed and enjoyed the rest of the party, maybe had a glass of wine.

But her stomach protested against the wine, and, now wound up, she could not unwind.

She was talking to Catherine Curran and her two cute little kids, Nicole and Jack.

"Isn't Mrs. Reilly pretty, kids? She's going to let Mommy paint her someday."

The kids nodded in wide-eyed agreement.

"Is your husband coming?" Anne asked, ducking the flattering and frightening invitation.

"Late as always," Cathy said with a laugh. "And we had a monumental fight this morning too."

"Oh, my."

"No sweat. I'll apologize. Nothing like an apology for restoring romance. I should have learned it a long time ago."

If you were married to Nick Curran that was probably true, Anne thought. It would have had no effect on either of her husbands. She envied Cathy and then thought of the price she had had to pay to win Nick—torture in a prison camp in Latin America—and reproved herself for the envy.

"You were in the wrong?"

Cathy looked so healthy and happy that Anne withdrew some of the reproof.

"Who knows?" Cathy shrugged negligently. "Probably. It gives you an enormous advantage to take the initiative. I don't know why most women forget that . . . Hey, our family is here in force. There's my clerical cousin with Mike Casey the Cop. Do you know him?"

The gallery whirled around her.

"Oh, yes."

"He has wonderful eyes, don't you think? And I bet one of his daughters bought that blue sport coat to match his eyes, poor man."

"I had better say hello to Father Ryan."

"We're having supper after at Le Perroquet. If we can recruit Mike Casey the Cop, would you like to join us?"

"I better not. A lot of loose ends."

Father Ryan was lecturing Mickey.

"The issue, Mike, is finally whether there is love in the universe. If there is of course we can't perish. If there isn't then it's all a waste of time. Any position in between is a cop-out . . . ah, Dr. Reilly, the Cardinal sends his best . . . Perhaps you remember my cousin Mike Casey the Cop?"

"I think so," she said, blushing at Mickey's frank approval of her thin-strapped cocktail dress. "Was it in a snowdrift?"

"As I remember, it was." His frosty blue eyes twinkled and his flinty cop's grin turned warm and gentle. "You were not wearing a russet dress then, were you?"

"Wine," said Father Ryan, rolling his owlish, near-sighted eyes in a fair approximation of Father Brown.

"Have to run, I'll be back," she said, trying not to breathe too hard. It was wonderful to see him in the gallery again, but in contrast to the glass of wine, she had no choice about drinking in Mickey.

And he was like rich food. Her stomach protested sharply.

The next time she drifted near them, Father Ryan was still lecturing, now to Nick and Cathy Curran, their two children and Mickey.

"We should never have given up purgatory. It is a wonderfully consoling Catholic story—a place were we are given a chance to straighten out all our fouled-up relationships. And don't tell me you were not told that in school. Those who failed to explain what purgatory was were *wrong*. Then, when we had discarded the story, along comes *The White Hotel* with a powerful vision of our doctrine and turns into a best-seller. Dumb."

He was preaching a sermon to Mickey, who was still grieving over his wife. Why did he feel so guilty about her? *Dr. Murphy would say that he believes he should have died instead of her*, Anne thought.

I am really involved with that family.

And then she realized why she was sick and angry.

She had finally finished the autobiographical sketches that Dr. Murphy had asked her to do. There was no obligation to give them to the doctor, but of course she would.

They revealed too much, and yet not nearly enough.

For a moment she thought she really would vomit. Then the red-faced, sweating caterer asked for another wastebasket.

Damn. Why couldn't he have thought of that before? she thought. There was a metal basket painted with Monet lilies in the closet underneath the staircase. She would rush down and pull it out.

She bounded down the stairs, glancing over the shoulders of two couples who were staring at "Divine Justice."

The demons *were* closer to their victim.

The crowds in the Kenny exhibition were now so thick

that it was hard to move. *We'll sell almost all the pieces. Next exhibition, I'll definitely hang a "no smoking" sign. There are probably a lot of people here who feel as sick as I do.*

Anne rested momentarily against the storeroom door, her hand on the knob, her head against the door panel. *Odd. Both feel hot. Maybe I should turn on the air conditioner.*

She opened the door on a curtain of foul-smelling flame, a thick dark fire, leaping out to engulf her.

The heat scorched her face, singed her hair, drew her unto itself. Responding to its invitation, she prepared to jump into it, as she would dive into a swimming pool.

At the last second, almost as though she had dived and then changed her mind, she slammed the door.

Near her two men were talking about the White Sox. Both were sure that they would not win the World Series.

Am I the only one who saw the fire? Why are they not suffocating from the smell? I've got to find Mickey, call the fire department, I can't permit all these people to burn to death. Please, God, not again.

She could not move, could not speak, could not even think.

I'm losing my mind. I hear the chatter of voices, I see their smooth, polished faces, I can smell the wine as well as the fire, but I'm not in their world.

The door handle, pressed against her palm, was cool and reassuring. What had happened to the fire? The panel isn't hot either.

Gingerly she opened the door. Only Monet lilies on a metal drum.

"Thank you, Dr. Reilly," said the caterer, taking the drum out of her hands.

I am losing my mind.

Slowly, smiling confidently, she walked up the stairs to her office, wondering if she looked as pale as she felt. Only when she closed the door did she dash for the private bathroom at the rear of her office.

And was briefly and violently ill, fortunately into the toilet.

As quickly as she could, she returned to the now-packed exhibition rooms, looking for Mickey's flinty smile.

"Missus is ill?" Sandy, in a closely fitting white dress, looked like a Polish countess.

"Too much cigarette smoke." She brushed her assistant's concern aside.

Father Ryan was now preaching at a TV camera, his round, pudgy face glowing with delight.

"Father Kenny's message was that it is terrible to lose God's love. And indeed it is. Of course, we know that it is pretty hard to do that, almost impossible, as a matter of fact. God is an implacable lover who will not be put off. He even cheats on us sometimes and breaks his own rules, the way lovers do."

"Hell is a state of mind?" said the black reporter, honestly confused.

"Hell is not responding to God's love," Father Ryan said solemnly.

Mickey was leaving. The Currans had not enticed him into supper. She should have accepted their invitation. Then he would have joined them.

For someone who is going mad, woman, you are certainly arrogant about your desirability.

Dear God, take this terrible smell out of my nose and mouth.

"Are you all right, Annie?" he asked solicitously. "You look terribly pale."

"Cigarette smoke. I'm all right. It was wonderful of you to come." She reached out to shake his hand.

He held her right hand and with his left adjusted a strap of her dress which had fallen down her arm.

"This reminds me of a raft on a lake a few Septembers ago."

"White strapless. A little too fashionable," she breathed, totally paralyzed. *His finger is so strong against my skin. Keep it there forever.*

"May I pay you a compliment?" His finger was still on the strap.

"God, yes."

"The view is even more elegantly appealing now than it was then."

Warmth flooded her face and throat and shoulders, her heart did several rapid turns, and her eyes began to tear.

I'm sinking. God in heaven, help me. I want him so much.

"Russet dress," she murmured.

"Wine," he said.

"Wonderful compliment, Mick. Slightly exaggerated maybe, but I don't care."

"Be careful," he said and then he was gone.

Her pink cloud was peaceful and pleasant, but the smell of fire quickly brought her back to earth.

How can I explain it to Dr. Murphy?

And as the crowd thinned out there was yet another smell, distinct from the dirty, acrid smell of a flaming building.

It was the sweet, sickly smell of burning varnish.

BOOK TWO

BOOK

TWO

11

"It was a nasty divorce," Blackie's father, Ned Ryan, said, carefully refilling Blackie's glass of Baileys Irish Cream. "Harriet Reilly was one of those women, of which we Irish have almost a monopoly, who cannot accept the possibility that reality might be different from the way they want it to be. She ticked off a list of problems that reality proposed to her, devised responses which would change reality so that it was more to her liking, and then used her cash to buy those responses.

"Was there medical testimony that her son battered his wife and children repeatedly? She would find doctors to testify that there were other explanations for the injuries treated in the emergency room of Oak Park Hospital. Was it common knowledge that her son spent much of his time in high-class disorderly houses? She would find witnesses to perjure themselves to the effect that it was not so. If you could buy control of reality, Harriet would have done it long ago."

"You won the case, of course?" Helen, his second wife, who knew all the cues, asked.

"You understand, my dear"—he put his arm around her affectionately—"that when I say 'disorderly house' I am casting no aspersions on the owner's ability as a housekeeper. Oh, yes, we won all right. Going away. It was hard on the poor little girl. But she had to fight or lose her children. I must say"—his silver-blue eyes twinkled cheerfully—"she was a good fighter when she set her mind to it, a tough and smart alley brawler who never lost her Catholicgirl's-college dignity no matter how angry she was. Poor Harriet never had a chance."

"Women's college," Helen said automatically.

77

"Not in those days, my dear."

Ned Ryan was about Blackie's height, a gentle white-haired man in his early seventies with a kindly smile, a dry wit, and an incorrigible propensity to tell stories. The family had always felt that the zaniness of the Ryans came from his first wife, Blackie's mother, with whom he fell in love on the Sky Ride at the 1933 World's Fair. After she, the sister of Mike Casey the Cop's mother, died, he married Helen and produced a second family, at least as off the wall as the first. Which kind of shot their theory.

Ned Ryan was an authentic war hero, however hard it may have been to believe of one so kind and even tempered. He was blown off the *Arizona* during the attack on Pearl Harbor and saved the lives of several seamen whom the Japanese were trying to machine-gun in the water. He fought through most of the Pacific war after that, avenging his friends from the *Arizona*, until he won the Medal of Honor in the greatest naval battle in all history at Leyte Gulf. A couple of destroyers and some escort carriers saved the troops on the beach and those waiting to go ashore by charging most of the imperial Japanese Navy, which had faked Bill Halsey into leaving the transports unprotected.

In one of the most amazing incidents of the war, Ned would sip his Jameson's and lean back reflectively as he told the story, the Japanese admiral lost his nerve when he saw this puny force attacking him and turned tail and ran. Halsey got back in time to polish most of the enemies' ships off on the other side of Leyte.

"I'll never be able to figure it out. He could have sent all of us to the bottom of the Philippine Sea and destroyed three American divisions and Douglas MacArthur in the bargain. Instead, as they said during the Korean Police Action, he bugged out. The Little Big Horn in reverse. I sometimes think he imagined my four-stacker was a battleship."

They gave him the Congressional Medal of Honor, to match the Navy Cross from Pearl Harbor. He never wore either, save at black-tie dinners and then only because both of his wives insisted that he looked "distinguished" in the stripes of a retired rear admiral. "Political appointment," he would grumble, but as Helen had noted, he still wore both the epaulets and the medals.

They sent him home to receive the medal from a failing FDR. His wife insisted that Blackie was conceived the first night they were together after the battle, which was possibly but not necessarily true.

His hands tremored slightly, but his mind was in fine shape, and, if one were to judge from the emotions that bounced back and forth between him and Helen, so was the rest of him.

"She was a fine client." He considered his own cordial glass critically and then the remnants of the Baileys and filled the glass. "The only one who could tell me beforehand what the lawyers on the other side were going to do the next day."

"Really?" Helen said, patting his hand.

"Damnedest thing that ever happened in a half-century or so of messing with the law." He settled back to spin another yarn. "Old Elias Burns, who was appearing for the Reillys, swore to his dying day that we had a spy in his office."

"Psychic?" Blackie asked.

"Fine young woman, a real knockout. Her father was a pleasant enough chap, several years ahead of me in law school. Kind of empty, if you ask me. Mr. Eliot's hollow man. Still, able in his own way. Had a habit I never liked— always tried to make others feel responsible for his failings."

"Psychic?"

"I heard you the first time, Blackie." He winked at Helen. "I didn't know the word then. I thought she was fey. Some Irish women are, you know. Your sister Nancy, for example. Not as much as Annie O'Brien was during the trial. She was really on a roll, as we'd say today. I asked her about it and she said it came and went, never been as strong as it was during the trial. Emotional strain, I suppose. Funny thing, sometimes I think she might even have made pens fall off the opposition counsel's table. And tangle up their documents too."

"How spooky!" Helen exclaimed.

Ned Ryan sipped the Baileys thoughtfully. "Fine young woman, still. Perfectly normal, as far as I can see. Probably only a passing thing during the craziness of the divorce. Do candles move around on the Cathedral altar, Blackie?"

"Not that I've noticed," Blackie said, refusing to rise to his bait. (For, of course, he wanted to know why Blackie was asking questions about Anne.) "Psychologists tell me that in most cases these phenomena are episodic. They come and go."

And, Blackie thought to himself, *sometimes they come again.*

12

Again she heard the footsteps. They came slowly up the stairs from the first floor of her apartment, seemed to hesitate at her door, and then walked across the hallway to the guest bedroom, sometimes sounding like the slovenly gait of a weary night watchman and sometimes like the cautious tread of a veteran hunter. The door of the other room closed softly, but not so softly that she couldn't hear it.

Anne gripped the mattress. This time she would not stir out of her bed. It was a trick of her imagination. It was not really happening.

In a few minutes she heard the door open and the steps move across the hallway and stop outside her door. The last time she had flung the door open and found nothing—except a blast of cold air, which she attributed to her thin gown.

This time she would not move.

The footsteps began again, reluctantly it seemed, almost as though they were disappointed. They paced back and forth outside her door, while Anne, her heart throbbing with fright, clung with grim determination to her bed.

Then they went down the stairs and faded away.

Eventually she went to sleep.

The next morning when she awoke from a deep sleep and a horrible dream, in which she and Mickey were cutting each other to pieces with knives, the sheets and her gown were soaking wet with sweat and she was shivering as though she had been sleeping outside on a winter night.

I must be getting the flu, she tried to tell herself.

I am so afraid. Dear God, please help me.

And please forgive me all my terrible sins.

13

Now she was hearing footsteps in her office at the gallery.

She had stayed after closing time to work on a scholarly article that her rules said must be finished by November first. At last the ideas were flowing and she was pounding away at her Model IV while The Motels shouted on WMET about "suddenly last summer."

Above the sound of the music, she heard the steps, slowing and hesitantly prowling through the first-floor rooms and then coming to a halt at the closed door.

Her fingers poised above the word processor, she waited. The steps should soon reverse themselves and fade away.

There was no sound.

Someone, or more likely something, was waiting for her.

Furious at the torment, Anne sprung from her chair, threw open the door, and shouted, "What do you want, you miserable son of a bitch?"

A frightened Mickey Casey looked like he was getting ready to run a 100-meter dash. Away from her.

"I wanted to give you this malted milk—Thirty-One

Flavors—and this pot of mums," he said sheepishly, holding very hesitantly in her direction the chocolate temptations and the bronze flowers. "The outside door didn't chime and I was wondering whether I should knock."

"If there was a snowdrift handy," she said, feeling her face turn furnace hot, "you could throw me into it. Do come in. You want to make me fat and lose my figure, but I'll drink it just the same."

Not bad for a save, she thought, wishing she'd worn something more impressive than a white skirt and an aqua angora sweater with a deep back.

"You should lock the front door when you're here alone," he said mildly.

"Yes, sir, Superintendent, sir," she said, turning off WMET. *I can't let him know I'm into teenage music.*

"I hope I'm not interrupting anything," he said shyly.

"Only a crucial article on Jan Vermeer," she said, gesturing at her notes and the Abrams edition of Vermeer's work. "Sit down, please forgive my rudeness, put the flowers over there, and let's rid ourselves of temptation while we can."

If only my face would stop burning. He looks so handsome. He's into brown and blue sports jackets. This one is wine herringbone. I bet his daughters made him dress up right and now he likes it. Heart, stop pounding.

"Tell me about the article," he said, opening both their malts.

"Well . . . " She drew a deep breath and, feeling as if she were lecturing a hostile crowd of full professors, jumped into her subject as into an ice-cold pool.

"It's about sex in Vermeer's paintings. There are only thirty-four of his works that have survived. Six of them are about love letters and nine more have men and women in close physical proximity to one another. Good academic that I am, I'm going to squeeze two articles out of it, do the love letters next year. He was a pious and devout man. No naked bodies. Wife a Catholic, kids too. Went to a Jesuit Church. Yet there's more sexual tension in his paintings, it seems to me, than even in Bosch. Look at this one, 'The

Procuress.' Beautiful yellow on the dress, isn't it? Compare it with this one of Van Buren, oops, Van Buburen. Lots of tit, huh? But in my friend Jan, it's all indirect. See the complacency in her face? She likes being pawed by the Prodigal Son. Right? They think he's supposed to be the Prodigal Son. Now look at this one. He did it later on when he'd got the color and light thing right. See the girl's skirt? Isn't it wonderful? Anyway, it's called 'The Concert,' two women and a man, one woman singing, the other two playing instruments. They're not even looking at one another. And on the wall behind them Van Buburen's 'Procuress,' with the whore who has the big breasts. His audience knew that music scenes were usually love scenes. But Jan plays it cool. Not a hint of what's going on among them, except for the painting on the wall. You know there's sexual energy in the intensity of their concentration on the music, but you have to figure out what it is. And then look at this one, the girl at the virginal with Buburen behind her again. What is she looking at with that tender expression? Her lover, of course, but you don't even see him. You have to imagine the story. I can't even use this one because the man isn't in the picture. But my theme is that, half Jesuit or not, Jan Vermeer of Delft said a lot about sex. And I'm making a raving idiot of myself, for which I am sorry."

And to herself, Anne said, *I must be gazing at him even more stupidly than the little idiot at the virginals.*

He took one of her hands from the book she'd slammed closed and held against her chest, and put the malt in it. Then he removed the book from her other hand, which he held gently.

His hand is like a tough nylon rope, she thought. *I can't break its grip on me. Is it a lifeline or is it a leash? Or maybe both?*

"Drink the malt. I hope I get credit for remembering the color of the flowers. I think the article is brilliant, but I'd expect nothing less from you." He touched her hair gently. "Why don't you dye your hair black? It would make you look at least fifteen years younger."

She was now thoroughly flustered. "I do use some stuff

to even out the gray and the silver." She gulped at the malt. "And I don't want to look younger."

Oh, my God, what a dumb thing to say.

"Fair enough. Now tell me about yourself."

There was so much strength in the hard, fine lines of his face—and in his broad shoulders, solid chest and flat belly—that it was unthinkable not to obey him. Anyway, she wanted to tell him everything. Well, almost.

So she went through it all, feeling deliciously naked as she talked, thoroughly under the control of his piercing and loving eyes.

Her notes for Dr. Murphy made it easy—Jimbo, Beth, Jimmy, Dave, John Duncan, Matt Sweeney, Joan Powers, Teresa, and Mark, all the people she'd let down.

When she was finished, he still held her hand. She felt unbearably foolish.

"I was at Dick's funeral, you know. In the corner of the church, where you couldn't see me."

"Oh?" What a strange response that was, she thought. What was he driving at?

"After the snowdrift, I was always courteous but did my best to stay out of your way."

"Me too, I guess." She had no strength of will to disengage her hand, even if she'd wanted to.

"I'll tell you a secret. You should have won the spelling matches. You were and are smarter than I am—and you just proved it again with that talk on Vermeer. It's difficult even now for a woman to have confidence in herself when she's competing with a man. By rights, you should have won."

He's more confused than I am. He thinks he still loves me.

"I'm glad you finally admit it." She giggled.

He touched her face as he had in the snowdrift. "What baffles the hell out of me is how someone as bright as you are can blame yourself for the mess other people have made of their lives by their own free choice."

"Zowie," she said weakly. "Mike the Cop drives home his point on the unsuspecting suspect."

He grinned at her, like a father at a funny little girl child. "Time to give it all up, Annie."

He knows, she thought. *Not everything, but almost.*

They held hands while time hung in suspended animation.

If he wants to make love with me he can have me, she thought. *Right here on my glass desk. Like Portnoy.* And then she banished the demon responsible for that obscene temptation.

But he only kissed her on the forehead and said, "I have to run. See you soon."

She mumbled something incoherent as he left. Nice incoherent.

Her body was sunk in contented lassitude. It slowly responded to her stern command:

You have enough problems as it is without acting like a moonstruck adolescent.

14

Mike Casey twisted uncomfortably in his bed. After an hour's sleep he was awake, hovering between an ascent into full consciousness and a descent back into restless unconsciousness, an inky pool teeming with nameless demons. He should not have left the window of his apartment open. It was too hot and sticky without the air conditioner and there was too much noise from the Drive thirty stories beneath him. He had missed his thrice-weekly racquetball game and had not substituted an hour in the geodesic glass-domed pool at the base of his building, mostly because young women in bikinis were a torment to him. Nor had he found time in the last week for his relaxing and quite secret new hobby, the results of which were hidden in the "study" next to his bedroom, a hobby that would have utterly bemused poor Janet.

Moreover, pollen, floating on the still night air, had jammed his nostrils shut. If he got out of bed to close the window, turn on the air conditioner, and take a decongestant pill, sleep would probably elude him for the rest of the night.

He should have drunk a second Jameson's before going to bed. He had held the bottle in his hand and restrained himself just before he tilted it to refill the glass. He would not become one of those lonely cops who drank themselves into oblivion.

He admitted to himself that neither the noise on the Drive nor the humid air, nor his stale muscles nor blocked sinuses, nor the low alcohol content of his blood, was keeping him awake.

It was Annie. She had slipped back into his veins like a virus for which long ago he had lost his immunity. He had seen her twice, touched her once, and already he wanted her wonderful body. He wanted her naked on her back underneath him—simple, direct male lust, primal need, elemental hunger.

She was so incredibly lovely, more so than ever, a woman of experience, mystery, sophistication, charm.

Then there was that other link between them, whatever that was, less simple, less direct, but ultimately more insidious and more compelling. It made him want even more to hold her in his arms.

I love her, I suppose. Maybe I always have.

She's in some kind of weird trouble again. Why is it always mysterious, sinister trouble, Annie, my love!

I must save you from trouble and then you'll be mine at last.

Or maybe it must be the other way. He frowned. That was an especially terrifying thought.

And why was that little fraud Des Kenny always involved?

Jeremiah Mullens had been on the phone today, Jeremiah with an "h", never Jerry. He was the district commander at Chicago Avenue, able as always to adjust to whatever political group was in power, even if the present group of bums were reformers and Jeremiah—red face, big paunch, bald head, cheap cigars—was perhaps the kinkiest police captain in the city.

That was no mean achievement. Some cops were kinky because the life of a cop gave them the opportunity or maybe drove them to it. Others had grown up kinky and become cops because police work matched their personalities.

Jeremiah was born kinky. There was not an untwisted cell in his body. Nothing, absolutely nothing, was ever straightforward with him.

"There's something fucking funny going on at that gallery, Mike," he had begun without preliminaries and with his usual flexible and nuanced vocabulary.

"Oh?"

"Did you read the fucking reports?"

"Yes." He had begun to sketch Jeremiah's face on his inevitable doodle pad. Captain Mullens as a malignant and slightly alcoholic leprechaun.

"Isn't it fucking funny?"

"Sewer gas, Jeremiah? I didn't laugh much."

"A blast that shatters a fucking plate-glass window and yet no one is hurt. Fucking strange."

"Interesting."

"The broad a friend of yours?"

Ah, now we get to the point. He wants me to ask him to forget about the blast because Annie is a friend. That way I owe him a favor, Mike had thought.

"Not particularly."

"You were fucking there after the blast, weren't you?" Jeremiah's gravel voice made it sound like a crime.

"I was in the neighborhood. We went to school together. I don't think I've seen her more than once or twice since we graduated from grammar school, which, Jeremiah, was a long time ago."

"I hear she's a fucking sexy broad."

"I suppose that depends on your taste. She's worn well."

"She's been married twice, you know. Once to a fucking priest."

"Oh?"

"And her kids are weird. One of them is some sort of hippy out in Oregon. Another had a drug arrest. The girl lives up in Winnetka now, but she was mixed up in the fucking days of rage."

"Really," Mike had said. *And one is an MIA in Vietnam. There are no convictions against any of them. Thousands of families have piled up such histories in the last fifteen years.*

"You want me to forget the explosion, Mike?" Jeremiah had said, hinting that he would overlook what might be a major crime as a personal favor to Mike. The man grew kinkier with every passing day.

"What was the size of the insurance claim?"

"Fucking peanuts. New window, some hospital bills, that sort of shit."

"Suit yourself, Jeremiah. It doesn't make any difference to me."

"Yeah, well, all right. There's something fucking funny going on there."

"Could be."

"Yeah, well, good to talk to you, Mike. The daughters all right?"

"Fine . . . Oh, Jeremiah . . . one more odd thing about that explosion. The window was ordinary glare-proof plate glass. But it didn't shatter. It turned to powder, like safety glass in a car. Kind of funny."

Mike had established once again, courtesy of Patrol Officer Deirdre Lopez, the Super's knack for catching the small detail. One that Mullens and his investigators had missed.

"No fucking fooling?"

"You might want to look into it. Nice to talk to you, Jeremiah."

So Mullens would mess around the Reilly Gallery, keeping an eye on it, looking for dirt. He would have done that anyway, regardless of whether Mike had asked him as a favor to drop the case. To add to Annie's troubles, Jeremiah Mullens's mean little pigeon eyes would be watching her every move, not to arrest her, but to create a bond of obligation to use against him.

So it went.

In Korea he had decided that he loved her and wanted to marry her. On the cold nights in the snow and the mud near Heartbreak Hill, with the waves of Chinese attacking in the mists as whistles screeched and bugles blew, he expected never to see Chicago again. The mysterious tension between him and Anne seemed a fantasy of his adolescent imagination.

She was an intelligent, interesting, and lovely young woman. She would make a fine wife and mother. In the unlikely event that he survived, he would claim her when he returned.

He didn't write, because he didn't know what to say. He would have prayed, but he didn't believe in prayer anymore. So he hoped and he dreamed. The image of black hair and pale skin and shapely body kept him alive and brought him home.

Where he discovered that she had married Jim Reilly.

He was furious, hated her bitterly, cursed her in his mind for years. Until he finally forced himself to admit that he had given her no reason to wait for him.

Why did she have to marry that drunken pug! he thought.

Because you blew it, that's why.

Shortly he was married too. Happily, he supposed, though not spectacularly. Janet was a good wife, loyal, faithful, dedicated, corresponding in every detail of her life to the image of the dutiful "heart of the family" of old-fashioned Sunday sermons who found her happiness in sacrificing herself for her husband and children. She could never understand why he wanted to be a cop. After he finished law school and passed the bar exam, she confidently expected he would leave the Department, despite his expressed doubts about practicing law.

"Why do all that work if you're not going to act like a lawyer?" she asked repeatedly.

He had no answer to the question, just as he had no answer to the question of why he wanted to be a cop. Oddly enough, his mother and father were tolerant of his career choice, maybe even a little proud of it. Pat Casey listened quietly to his Korea stories, and nodded in silent understanding, one combat veteran sympathizing with the memories of another combat veteran. He nodded the same way when Mike said he wanted to be a cop, as though he understood. Mike himself did not understand then or now. Probably something to do with the romantic idealism that had drawn him toward the priesthood and a reluctance to risk the vulnerability of that idealism to ridicule. The mud and death of Korea had not wiped out his dreams, only forced them beneath the surface, where they still lingered as a torment and a challenge.

The slow reconciliation with his mother and father had begun.

There could not be a reconciliation with Janet because they never seriously quarreled about his commitment to the Department. "It's like they're the Church and you're a priest," was as far as she would go.

She worried about him compulsively and by her worry made him feel guilty for causing her and their daughters concern. Yet he did no more than promise that he would retire from the force when his thirty years were completed.

Janet was dead two and a half years before that magic day. She died as she had lived, without fuss or complaint—but slowly and painfully as the cancer ate away at her insides.

Toward the end her fear was not for herself or her daughters but for him. Who would take care of him? The girls were all married and she would be gone.

At the very end she worried that he had never really loved her. She accepted his protestations, but in the last moment of her life two little tears trickled down her face, tears not of pain or of reluctance to die but of sorrow over loss.

Twenty-eight years—where had it all gone?

Then he found among her few papers tender and lyrical love poems, written about him but never given to him, composed a long time ago from the feel of the pages. Behind the Sunday-sermon "wife and mother" persona there had hidden another woman, a woman he had never discovered and perhaps as inaccessible as the farthest reaches of a deep and intricate cave.

I might not have found the bottom of that cave, but I never tried to enter it or even bothered to learn that it existed, he told himself at her funeral Mass as he listened to the blathering police chaplain yammer on "a woman without price."

He had thought they had more time. What would have changed if there had been more time? Their marriage was better than most. There were few bitter fights, much quiet companionship, sympathy, understanding, friendship. There was little romance, no heights and depths of passion. Janet, pretty as a bride and never unattractive as a wife, was a sensible, reliable, down-to-earth woman. If he had wanted a romantic, he should have married one.

Why had she not given the poems to him? Afraid that he would ridicule them? He had never ridiculed anything she did. Afraid of the passion they might have ignited? Perhaps.

Why had he married her? He could not remember. It was time to marry. She was available and the best choice among the other availables. The war was over. It was time to settle down. . . .

They had twenty-eight good years together. If they might have been better years, the fault was his, not Janet's. Without realizing what was happening, he spun his own romantic dreams behind the mask of the good, gray, honest cop.

Now he wept silently to himself when he considered the terrible waste and pleaded with Janet to forgive him. He was not sure that he agreed with Blackie Ryan's strange theological arguments about survival, certainly not sure that Janet could hear his pleas, but he prayed to her anyhow.

Annie had not been a specter of a lost love who had hovered over their marriage. He had forgotten about her, experiencing only a slight twinge of regret when he read about her in the papers. Or, to be more honest about it, when he saw her picture or her name and quickly turned the page. She had brought him back from Korea and then passed out of his life.

Not, as it turned out, forever.

Deirdre Lopez had been quite blunt about Annie in the squad this afternoon.

"You should marry her, Jefe."

"Don't you think that's not your affair, Patrol Office Lopez?" he'd replied hotly, digging his fingers into the palms of his hands to contain his rage.

She'd giggled at his unintentional pun. "No, I don't think it's an affair yet, Jefe. You're always saying that women will humanize police work. One of the ways we do that is worrying about the relationships of our colleagues a lot more than men do."

Hoisted on his own petard.

"You would permit the use of the word *busybodies*?"

She had considered carefully. "Interested and sympathetic observers."

He had taken a deep breath and called on his Blarney genes. "I'm flattered and touched by both the interest and the sympathy, Patrol Officer Lopez."

"You look so lonely and so hungry and she is so beautiful."

"She's older than I am," he had said tentatively.

"She is not, Jefe." Deirdre had flared dangerously. "How dare you say that? She's at least ten years younger."

That reaction also probably went with permitting women to be cops. *I could tell her that Annie is a month older than I am and I would be in even deeper trouble. Give a woman an inch and they'll take a . . .* He had repressed Jeremiah Mullens's favorite participle . . . *mile.*

"Do I have permission to play it my way, Patrol Officer?"

"Sure, Jefe. But you still ought to marry her."

"And does she have a chance to make a choice in the matter?"

"Oh, Jefe," Deirdre had said in her most astonished voice, "no woman would turn you down."

He rolled over in his bed and sighed again. Annie was

calling to him above the rooftops of the city. No ESP or anything like that. Merely the knowledge that she was alone and lonely in bed just as he was.

And frightened.

Damnation, were they running trucks down the Drive at night? He'd have the ass of the chief of traffic, if they were.

Mike groped through the dark to the drapes on his balcony windows. Absently he flipped on the stereo just inside the balcony. WFMT through the night. They were playing d'Indy's *Istar* variations. He turned the receiver off quickly. The last thing in the world he needed just now was music about a woman taking off her clothes.

Beneath him on one side was the old straggling S curve and on the other the new and unfinished correction of the S. Despite what the traffic engineers said, he did not think it would eliminate congestion.

What do them experts know? as the late mayor, *the only real mayor, would have said.*

There were no trucks on the Drive, no vehicles, to use a favorite police word, of any kind. The noise was in his head.

He let the drapes fall back into place, turned the FM back on, and reached for his Jameson's bottle.

15

"Bless me, Father, for I have sinned. It's been a week since my last confession. I permitted a man to touch me immorally on one occasion. And I was distracted twice during my prayers. For this and all the sins of my past life I am sorry and ask penance and absolution of you, Father."

The old form of confession and the old sins. The young priest on the other side of the screen was doubtless surprised. It was the sacrament of Christian reconciliation now, not confession or penance. As a young girl she would have accused herself of necking and petting, but the young priest would not understand the terms. How many people confess such sins now? Probably not very many. Those who were old enough to think that a hand on the breast was a grave sin had little opportunity to commit the sin. And those who were young enough to engage in such amusements did not think they were sinful.

Anne was uncertain. Despite Dr. Murphy's accusation that she would not give up the superstitious multiplication of sins that had characterized the Catholicism of her young womanhood, Anne was tolerant of what other people did. But she would not run the risk of tolerance with herself. What if God still thought that a few moments of delicious petting were gravely wrong? She was in enough trouble as it was.

God probably was not deeply offended. She had read somewhere that women's breasts had evolved in their present form so that in addition to feeding babies they would be admired by men. They were designed to be looked at and caressed.

But only by one's husband, so the priests and nuns had said.

"Are you married?" asked the young priest, grasping for a lead in his response.

"No, father. The man is not married either," she added helpfully.

"Do you intend to marry him?"

"No, Father." And then, troubled by the need to be honest to her confessor she added, "At least, I don't think so."

"I see. . . . Do you love each other?"

"Yes, Father."

The day before had been a slow day at the gallery. She had had time to think about the explosion and the fire she had imagined in the storage closet. The explosion was real enough, even if the explanation was a little dubious. The fire had been a trick of her imagination, and certainly connected with her guilt because of Father Kenny. She should never have agreed to the exhibition in her gallery.

She nodded toward the priest.

Now she was having trouble with hot water. That morning she had turned the shower to maximum hot and shivered, despite the steaming water. Imagination again, of course.

She had tried again in the tiny shower in the bathroom of her office in the gallery. She shivered as though she were standing naked in a snowstorm and continued to shiver while she dressed in the small room in which she occasionally spent the night on a couch when she worked late.

Still chilled, though it was another 90-degree day, she had studied the proofs for the brochure of her next exhibition, nervously and pointlessly slashing at the copy and compulsively rearranging the layout of the pictures of Peggy Donlon's flaming watercolors.

The Kenny show would last only two more weeks. She could hold out till then without losing her mind.

Perhaps she should talk to Dr. Murphy about it. Crazy imaginings. Linked to the past. She couldn't tell her about that.

That morning she'd finally awakened a blurry and confused Shelaigh O'Cathasaigh, who doubtless was sleeping off a week-long binge.

"Ah, sure 'tis good to hear from you again, Annie love. How's the art business in Yankee land?"

As delicately as possible she'd asked about the rumors of a deal with the Ruben Gallery.

Shelaigh pretended to be hurt. "Now, you know me better than that, don't you, love? Sure, would I walk out on my only friend in America, and myself not giving you a word of warning either? Wouldn't you be knowing me better than that, now?"

I know you pretty damn well, you shanty Irish bitch, and you'd do it at the drop of an Irish punt.

"Of course I didn't believe it," she'd said aloud. "I said to my friends that I'm sure a famous artist like Shelaigh has lots of offers and I wouldn't blame her for taking one that was better than any deal I could arrange. But she wouldn't do it without giving me the right of first refusal."

"I would not at all, at all," Shelaigh agreed fuzzily. "What's the right of first refusal?"

"The right to match any offer that someone else would make."

There was a second's hesitation on the international line. "You're absolutely right," she said vigorously after the pause. " 'Tis more than business between us. 'Tis friendship, isn't it, love? I wouldn't even talk to anyone else without telling you about it. And I'm not talking to anyone, I swear it."

She might be telling the truth, Anne told herself as she hung up, *and then again she might not.*

In any case there's little I can do about it, except pray every night.

Her accountant had shook his head earlier in the day. "Your inventory is too big," he'd said. "Those Czech and Mexican things simply have to move or you will be in deep trouble before the year's end."

"There's the O'Cathasaigh exhibition," she had said cautiously.

"The Irish woman? She'll have to sell out in December. What if the Chicago Irish aren't buying this Christmas?"

"They'll be buying. The stock market is up."

"For now," he had said grimly. "Do you have any of her paintings yet?"

"It doesn't come till November."

He shook his head again. "Are you doing well with this crazy priest's stuff?"

"It's moving quite nicely," she said. "I'm only taking my expenses, however. It's a charity exhibition."

"I bet you have yourself locked in so you can't write off a tax deduction."

He won the bet. *Why hadn't I thought of that,* she had wondered. *I'm so preoccupied it never occurred to me. Maybe I don't belong in the business world after all.*

"Pardon, Missus," Sandy, always sensitive to her boss's moods, interrupted. "Police Commissar to see Missus."

Mickey, flinty blue eyes, craggy smile—a marine general before a battle.

"Thank you, Alexandra. Would you like to come in, Commissar? Come to buy some crap?"

The Commissar kissed Sandy's hand, and muttered

some words in Polish. Sandy left, pleased and flustered.

"I know enough Polish for wakes," he murmured.

"And enough Spanish to talk to your lovely Mexican driver."

"How did you know . . . ?"

"I read the papers. Now, about buying crap?"

"Is that statue still available?"

"It's not for sale."

They were both standing, on either side of her desk, two fencers feinting for advantage, two elderly boxers sparring with thickly padded gloves.

"What about a picture of you in that dress?"

She was wearing a V-neck sleeveless apricot dress.

She felt her face grow warm. *Damn, I'm blushing.*

And then she wondered if he knew who had been the model for the statue.

"Your cousin Cathy wants to paint me, without the dress, I'm afraid."

"I'd be scared to own something like that." He grinned tentatively.

So he didn't know.

"She's not likely to do the picture."

"A shame. May I sit down?"

She felt frightened. Something was wrong.

"Can I offer you some almond herbal tea?" she said, remembering her manners and feinting so she could recover her poise.

"Please."

Oh, Lord, those beautiful eyes, knife-keen silver blue, shearing away my clothes like neat slices of cheese and drawing me, shivering and exhilarated, into the cold waters of a lake about to freeze.

Avoiding his eyes but very much aware of them, with unsteady hand she poured the tea into a Reilly Gallery cup—also with the Monet lilies on it, as they were on her stationery and the cocktail napkins. The purists thought it vulgar, but the people who bought paintings loved it.

He sipped the tea slowly. "Hmmn . . . good."

"What's up, Mick?" she asked, trying to sound crisp.

He placed the cup on her white desk and rubbed his

chin, a characteristic gesture she suddenly remembered from long ago.

"Is there anything you want to tell me about the explosion, Annie?"

"Do you think I'm hiding something from the police?" she demanded hotly. "An insurance scam?"

"For a new plate-glass window?" he asked ruefully.

"Then for what?"

He shrugged helplessly. "I don't think there's a scam. I think there's a mystery. And I want to help if I can."

"I know as much about it as you do."

Now I'm lying. How could I possibly explain? . . .

"Okay . . . do you know the commander over at Chicago Avenue? Captain Mullens?"

"Unfortunately. He was in here yesterday, leering. I assumed you sent him."

"You assumed wrong." Now it was his turn to be hot.

We are scoring points on each other because we care so much. I must stop it.

"I'm sorry, Mickey. I've been nervous all day."

"Jeremiah is corrupt. He is likely to continue to hang around, looking for something. Don't worry about him. Let me know whenever he shows up."

"Why would he harass me? Because I'm a friend of yours?"

Mickey nodded glumly. "He wants to back me into a corner where I have to ask him as a favor to lay off."

"Would you do that?" she asked uneasily.

"Jeremiah's big fault is overreaching. I don't have to ask him for favors to cool him off if he becomes too pushy."

"You can be very ruthless, can't you, Superintendent?"

He laughed happily, as though she had paid him a compliment. "In protecting the innocent? Hell, yes!"

"And if I weren't innocent?"

"I'd protect you anyway. Now let me take you out and buy you a milk shake. Thirty-One Flavors or Häagen-Dazs?"

"Häagen-Dazs. We can sit at the sidewalk tables and pretend we're teenagers again."

His light-hearted invitation and her equally light-hearted response transformed the tone of their conversation. They were no longer old lovers jousting for position. They were now adolescents having a good time on a date. They chattered happily about their friends and schoolmates from the 1940s as they watched the lightly clad young people of a new decade drift by their table in the failing twilight.

"Are you and Joan O'Malley still close friends?" he asked, draining his milk shake.

"Joan Powers now. I talk to her every week. We have lunch once every month or two. I'm afraid my life is a bit of a scandal to her."

"She has a poor memory."

"Don't we all?"

"Another milk shake, Annie?"

"I'd love one, but I'd better not. Too many calories."

"With your figure you can afford to pig out once in a while."

"Daughter talk?"

"Granddaughter . . . Wait here, I'll get two more."

I was a virgin on my wedding night, Anne reflected. *Joan, who certainly wasn't, thinks I'm a terrible sinner. I am, but not for her reasons. She would be shocked if she saw us here. A divorcée and a widower, acting like two teenagers. So would my liberated Bethie.*

Mick was standing by their table, a milk shake in either hand.

"Something wrong?"

"Merely admiring how lovely you are."

"Oh, Mickey." She felt tears come. "How nice of you. . . ."

She began to sip her second shake, vowing to fast the next day. "You never bought me a milk shake when we were young."

"I was afraid to," he said, taking his lips off the straw.

"And you're not afraid anymore."

"Yeah. I'm still afraid. But I like milk shakes more now than I used to."

"Silly." She pushed his arm playfully, forgetting about the electric current in their touch. Time stopped briefly. Then they returned to their milk shakes and she told him about Joan's family and how strict she had been with her children.

"Really bad memory," he observed.

"I sometimes wonder whether we learn anything from generation to generation."

"Not much," he said laconically. "A little maybe."

"Do you remember the World's Fair?" she asked, thinking of past generations.

"A little, not much."

"We met there for the first time, you and I."

"No," he said in disbelief. "I can't remember that at all."

"Our mothers bumped into each other. We spent the whole day together. I fell in love with you. You were such a kind little boy. Nothing like the—"

"Nerd, as one of my granddaughters would say."

They both laughed, easy, relaxed laughter. Cheap nostalgia.

"I'm a World's Fair freak," she continued. "Even if you have forgotten me, I want an exhibit at the next one."

"I'll see what I can do. . . . "

His eyes darted to the next table. Two young lovers were staring into each other's eyes, oblivious of a napkin that had caught fire in the ashtray between them.

The girl cried out as the fire leaped toward her arm. In another second it would have ignited her frilly blouse.

Mick's hand moved like that of a riverboat gambler, deftly inverting a banana split dish over the fire. The flame disappeared. So quick was his movement and so calm his manner that no one else in the sidewalk café noticed what had happened.

"Fire needs oxygen," he said to the grateful couple.

"Did you learn that at the Police Academy?" Anne asked him, impressed by his speed and skill.

"Korea," he said. "Put out a fire that way once and you never forget it. Another shake?"

Sadly she declined. "Too many calories already."

When they had regretfully finished their second ones, he said, "I'll walk you home."

"You mustn't keep Patrol Officer Lopez waiting."

"She's off duty. I came in a cab."

He looked as if he were going to take her arm and then quickly thought better of it.

They chattered aimlessly as they strolled to the door of her building as the night sky rolled in off the lake. It seemed so natural that he should accompany her to her apartment that she did not feel tense until the elevator door opened.

My God, no. We can't. . . ,

"Good night, Annie." He extended his hand as she extracted a key from her purse with trembling fingers.

"Good night, Mick. It was great fun."

Then his arms were around her and his lips pressed against her lips. She dropped the key.

There was no time, no space, no universe, only the two of them blending together. She was filled with security and peace. There was nothing more to worry about. She need merely trust him. Time to surrender to a man, as Dr. Murphy said.

His hand found its way to her breast, not feeling, not groping, but rather touching, caressing. His fingers slipped underneath the neckline of her dress, gently searching for a nipple, already firm and waiting for him. His lips smelled of ice cream, there was a thin coat of moisture on his face. She snuggled closer to him. His lips and fingers became more demanding. His pale blue eyes, more appealing than ever, drank her in like a milk shake.

She tried to look down, so that she would not fall completely captive to those eyes. He released her from the grip of his arm, eased her against the door, and tilted her chin up so she could not escape the intensity of the demand in his eyes. Fire radiated from her imprisoned breast to the rest of her body.

Mike slid the dress off her shoulder and down her arm. His teeth touched the skin at the top of her breast.

What if one of my elderly neighbors should see us?

The danger of discovery aroused her even more. She was about to lose all control of herself.

She wanted to float on the gently flowing river of his

love forever. *Do with me whatever you want, lover. Do it before it is too late.*

They were almost at the top of the mountain. A few more seconds and she would pick up the key, open the door, and he would come in with her. Where he belonged.

Then they separated, as if by some secret treaty. He picked up the key and gave it to her as she nervously rearranged her dress. "Good night, Annie."

Adolescent fondling. *The exciting sexual games we played when we were young and filled with dreams of an endless pleasure-filled future. What a shame we had to grow up.*

"Would it be inappropriate for me to ask why you don't intend to marry if you love each other?" said the young priest.

They were so courteous and respectful these days.

"I think we're both afraid, Father. We've had . . . ah, unfortunate histories."

He wants me with simple and determined male urgency. He has since the moment those lovely sad blue eyes of his peeled off my clothes when he walked into my gallery the day of the explosion. He will be back. His desire for me and my response to his hunger exist in another world from this dialogue with a nice young priest. My religion tells me I should not let Mick Casey fondle me. It does not tell me what I should do about him.

Please just give me absolution, so I can receive Communion.

"Sexual attraction is designed to overcome those fears. It's God's way of helping us to cancel out unfortunate histories."

Thank God my grandchildren will have a chance to be reconciled to the Church by priests like you. "I understand, Father."

The priest hesitated, sensing that she didn't want to discuss her spiritual problems with him, yet, priestlike, wanting to help.

"The moral issue that is critical in your relationship," he said carefully, "is not whether your emotions on occasion lead you to affection that might not be completely appropriate, but whether you are treating his emotions and yours with sufficient honesty and respect."

"Yes, Father."

Of course, Father, honesty and respect. The new core virtues of Catholicism, replacing purity and loyalty. Not that you're wrong. I shouldn't be treating you like an absolution machine, but I don't know what else to say.

"Very well. Perhaps you should talk to someone about your problem. A priest or a counselor. Anyway, say the Lord's Prayer once for your penance."

Lord's Prayer, not the Our Father. The Prots won another.

"Thank you, Father," and then giving in to the young man's sincerity. "I do have a counselor, Father, and I have been discussing the relationship."

I have a priest too. Your boss, Father John Blackwood Ryan, who, if he knew I had engaged in foreplay with his cousin Mike Casey the Cop, would proclaim a celebration and announce the banns.

She had received Holy Communion, as she did every day of the week at Holy Name Cathedral, with a touch of guilt. She was not sure that she felt much regret about her embrace with Mickey. The violently sensuous woman who lurked within her, dominated but not destroyed, felt strong regret that she had not pulled him into her apartment.

I did enjoy it, she had told herself piously as Father Ryan placed the wafer on her lips and declaimed, "The Body of Christ, Anne." *But I am sorry I offended God, and that's what counts.*

Was it another sacrilegious confession and Communion? she wondered as she left the church and walked briskly down Wabash Avenue toward the gallery. There had been so many of them. Several times in her life she had tried to make a "general confession," covering all the sins she had committed, even the most terrible ones. Usually the priests didn't believe her. She found none of the release from guilt which "general confessions" were supposed to bring.

No one preached about "bad" confessions anymore.

She was afraid to ask Father Ryan what he thought of them. He might laugh at her for dredging up mistakes about which God had forgotten.

Someday, someday, she might be so desperate as to go to him for confession, in one of the reconciliation rooms they had. She would tell him the whole story.

New model priest that he was, he would believe her.

Then there might be peace.

She stopped at the Café Croissant to buy two croissants for breakfast, one for her and one for Sandy. There was grapefruit juice in the icebox—a holdover word from her childhood—at the gallery and she would brew some apple cinnamon tea. Breakfast with Sandy was the most important event in her assistant's day and she could not dodge it because a guilty conscience left her with little appetite.

She opened the door to the brownstone at five minutes to nine. Still a few minutes before Sandy would arrive. The strange smell, like burning varnish, persisted.

My neurotic imagination again. It will all be finished in two weeks.

She put on the teapot and arranged the cups and dishes for their breakfast.

Mickey does love me. With the slightest encouragement he would marry me.

I can't do that to him. He's had enough suffering as it is.

She dismissed the temptation. *Before Sandy comes I had better look at the Kenny exhibition. We may want to rearrange some of the works. We know now which ones are likely to tempt buyers.*

With the first cup of tea in her hand, she walked down the stairs briskly. It had cooled off overnight. More buyers would be in today. A good day's work should make her feel better. Take her mind off her own silly problems.

She had carefully avoided looking at "Divine Justice" since the opening. Curiously she glanced at the lower left corner as she strode by the painting.

The cup slipped through her fingers, shattering on the floor. The demon's claws were on the girl's breasts, and he was pushing her into the swamp as the other pursuers circled around her.

Anne blinked her eyes, trying to clear them. It was her imagination, it had to be.

She shook her head and looked again. There was no doubt: the demon's claws were in both breasts and blood was streaming from them. The despair on the girl's face was now mingled with excruciating pain.

She screamed. And then screamed again.

She heard the door of the gallery open. Sandy.

She choked off a third scream, and on unsteady legs climbed up the stairs. She had to get to the security of her chair behind the desk before Sandy saw her.

I will not survive two more weeks.

16

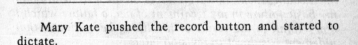

Mary Kate pushed the record button and started to dictate.

I wept while I was reading through—quickly and for the first time—the patient's autobiographical sketches.

The Grand Moguls at the Institute would be fiercely critical. A therapist should not become emotionally involved with a patient's suffering.

Horse manure, you should excuse my favorite expletive.

They're either men or thoroughly masculinized women who would be a lot better off if they could cry once in a while. You don't cry in the patient's presence—though I wouldn't even in principle exclude that kind of display of feeling. But if you're forbidden emotional release in the patience's absence, you've been banished from the human race.

Which is what the Moguls would like to see happen. Transference and countertransference are the name of our game, but the Supershrinks and the Training Analysts are as ashamed of such things as we Irish Catholics are about sex.

Or used to be.

Anyway, the patient is a sensitive and intelligent woman as well as an awesomely—to use my brats' favorite word this summer—lovely one. She's had a hell of a rough life, but she's able to be reasonably objective and witty about herself. With some work and the help of an editor I bet she could publish her little self-revealing essays. Her self-portrait is as deft in its lights and shadows as a late Rembrandt painting and as tart in its clear-eyed, bittersweet nostalgia as a cordial glass of Grand Marnier (on the rocks, please).

The exercise of writing them has been helpful for her. She has acquired a little more distance from herself, and possibly a little more respect for her ability to pull life together when it falls apart on her.

Reading them, however, forces on me a recognition of my basic failure in my treatment of her, a failure which I don't think is the result of my liking her—though that judgment is subject to revision later.

How come this elegant, pretty, intelligent woman of the world is so fouled up?

She's made it so far through life, God knows, and with more style than most women. Still, she's tied up in emotional knots. She's brave enough to want to untie some of the knots, otherwise she would not be draped attractively on my couch. (A position which would drive most male therapists up the wall.) So I have an obligation to help her. The years that remain to her could be extremely creative.

But . . . and it's a big but . . . I haven't made it halfway down the first baseline.

Her problem focuses on the goddamn Catholic Church, you should again excuse the expression. Her monumental guilt attaches itself to the actual or imagined violation of various and sundry Church regulations, laws, norms, canons, and other obligations—past and present.

And heaven knows the Church has gone out of its way to screw her as well as screw her up.

Nevertheless, I have a hunch that the origins of the guilt are deeper, back in her family life when she was growing up. She hints at this in her autobiographical notes.

Anyone with an Irish family structure and belief system will assume responsibility for the death of siblings and parents, particularly the horrible death of her sisters. You feel guilty that you're alive and they're dead. Such guilt can be worked out in therapy, particularly if the patient is as intelligent and cooperative a person as Anne Reilly.

So there's something else going on, something she's not telling me. I suspect she knows she's hiding the key to the puzzle.

Why enter treatment if you intend to hide the core issue?

Why be human?

You expect the therapist to find out what the problem is and deal with it. First of all, however, the therapist has to obtain if not quite your total trust at least more trust than you've ever experienced before in your life.

Anne Reilly has never really trusted anyone. Or if she has, that trust has been brutally betrayed. She can't give herself in surrender to a man because she has never really trusted anyone, not for a long, long time.

I must help her to trust me. I have the unpleasant feeling that she does not have much time left to do that.

17

"Suppose the plane to Washington crashes."

That's what poor Janet had always said when Michael was obliged to represent the Department at a meeting with the FBI or a Justice Department task force. Mike had learned the lingo and the work-avoidance strategies of the federal bureaucracy quickly and was skillful at frustrating the lunacies of J. Edgar. So it was he who usually went to Washington when someone had to make the trip.

"If I crash in the airplane, Patrol Officer Lopez, that's the way things go. But I'd hate to die in a squad car driving to O'Hare."

"Sorry, Jefe. I don't want you to miss the plane. Should I use the blue light?"

"You know better than to ask that."

"*Sí*, Jefe. But if we're late . . ."

"There's always another plane to National. When the world comes to an end, the last plane to fly will land at National."

Janet had been terrified of flying, and indeed distrustful of traveling anywhere. He figured that Korea was far enough for one lifetime and repressed his fantasies of world travel. Now that he was free to wander, he had lost the energy. Or maybe he was afraid of the loneliness of solo travel.

If the United plane should crash, perhaps on the approach to National Airport, he would die cursing himself as a cowardly fool.

He could have made love to Annie last night, something, if he was honest with himself, he would admit he had wanted to do most of his life, even before he knew what making love was.

In that snowdrift, I wanted to make love to her, even if I had only the haziest idea of how to do it. Our souls were bonded, whatever that means. Our bodies wanted the same thing. So too on the raft, particularly the day she was wearing the white strapless suit. And when I touched her hand in the bar. And the night in the vestibule of her aunt's apartment.

How many women lost their virtue in vestibules in those times?

I love her. I've loved her since the first spelling bee. It's not merely lust, even if there's a lot of that. How do you separate the two?

I didn't know what was happening. I didn't have screwing on my mind. Well, not that much anyway. It seemed courteous to walk with her to the door to her apartment. Then before I knew it, we were . . . Oh, God . . . we were preparing to screw. A long way to go, but not very far at all. She was ahead of me, a fire on which I threw gasoline without realizing what I was doing. A few more minutes and there would have been no turning back.

He remembered the softness of her lips, the firmness of her breasts, the hard knot of her nipple, the timidity and the longing in her body.

Oh God, she wanted me so much.

It was a flattering and a troubling thought. Men wanted women and women agreed. In theory, of course, women wanted men too, but Mike Casey had never been the object of such obvious and appealing want before.

I ran as I did the other times. I ran as if I were a terrified eleven-year-old mugger escaping from a blue-and-white squad car even though he's not sure the cop has seen him or knows he's a mugger.

Why did I run?

There's something scary about her. Deep inside of her, there's enormous pain of which I'm afraid. It probably is connected to that crazy explosion that wasn't an explosion.

And to crazy Des Kenny. I ran from her last night, the same way I ran from her on the raft. I let her down again. I have to come home alive from Washington and help her.

I want to be inside her wonderful body. I want to have and hold and protect and love and cherish her—and make the pain go away if I can. No matter how afraid of it I am.

Mike Casey's last big romance.

"Here we are, Don Miguel."

"Good, Deirdre," he said, startled out of his pleasantly terrifying reverie. "Who picks me up? Hermano?"

"No, Jefe, Stash."

"Fine, I'll phone if there's any delay."

"Have you seen Doña Anna Maria?"

"You are being impudent, young woman."

"*Sí*, Don Miguel."

"I bought her a milk shake last night," he admitted grudgingly. "Two of them, in fact."

"I bet you didn't dare kiss her good night," she sniffed.

"You'd lose your bet, Patrol Officer Lopez."

"Oh, Jefe." She exploded in laughter. "You're wonderful."

"I don't think she thinks so," he lied.

18

ANNE'S STORY

I have a picture in front of me of our family at the lake in summertime. I think it was taken the year our lives changed, long before the fire. Momma must have snapped it. Daddy is carrying his golf clubs down the path to his old Packard and we are trailing behind him. He is walking fast, as he always did, his long legs eating up space in great strides. We are following in Indian file, Marty, Joe, Kathleen, Connie, and a very funny me bringing up the rear.

I laugh even today when I see the same scene on the streets of Grand Beach, where Mark, like many of the River Forest Irish, has bought a summer home—doubtless to dispossess the South Side Irish of their birthright. I always identify with the little tyke at the end of the line because I can remember, quite distinctly, to tell the truth, how hard it is to keep up with the rest when you're the youngest and your poor legs are just not long enough to permit you to stay in the pack unless you're half running all the time.

I look at the girl in the picture as though she were a total stranger. I can remember how she felt, always breathless from catching up, but I can't quite believe that she's me.

I'm summer people. I've always loved hot weather. I luxuriate in sand and water and wet swimsuits—and skinny-dipping, which I used to confess until a priest finally worked up enough nerve to tell me that it was not necessarily sinful. (Which, oddly, doesn't make it less fun.) I relish lying out in the sun all day every day and doing nothing but bask—with the proper sunscreen for my pale Irish skin, let me hasten to add.

I suppose this love of the summer goes back to the days at the lake. My children, to say nothing of grandchildren, can hardly believe how primitive summer places were when I was a kid. I point out in the pictures the shadow of the outhouses and they are horrified. I show them pictures of my brothers lugging big chunks of ice—from a horse-drawn ice truck, no less—to our house for the icebox and they shake their heads, like it was the nineteenth century.

Then I tell them that even in the city garbage trucks and milk trucks were drawn by horses till the war and that we didn't get our first refrigerator till 1936, and they are absolutely horrified.

Summer living was more primitive than city living, much more so after we left our apartment in Mother of Mercy two years after the fire and moved to a big new bungalow in St. Ursula's. Yet I didn't mind the stench of the outhouse or the heat of the screened-in porch where I slept with Kathleen and Connie or the buzz of the flies and the complaints of the crickets or the uncomfortable furniture or the tall grass around our cottage that cut your legs.

I was as happy at the lake as I have ever been in my life. I still hear the song about the music going round and round and still see scenes from the movie *Girl of the Limberlost*, which was shown (many times, I think) on a screen in a vacant lot next to the town dance hall. I don't know what the film was about, but I do remember that the girl was very pretty and that she suffered a lot. I cried for her.

Even now I am tempted to cry for her—which shows what a silly romantic sentimentalist I am.

Our house is still there, of course, all modernized and air-conditioned and incredibly tiny. Perhaps I should have kept it, but I sold it after Mom and Dad were killed. Too many memories I wanted to leave behind.

Now that I have a little money to spend I often think I ought to buy it back and paint it pink, like Monet's cottage.

And sit in front of it in the summertime, watch little kids walk down to the lake, and identify with the smallest—although five is no longer the typical number of such groups, not even at Grand Beach.

The summer the picture was taken, as I remember, was the turning point. Before that everything was pure bliss. After that my happiness was always under a shadow to which I could not give a name. Something terrible happened that summer, not as bad as the fire surely, but something that maybe weakened us so that we were less able to cope with the fire.

I know the name of that mysterious something now. It was called the Great Depression. Putting a name on it, however, does not ease the sorrow I felt for something that made my mother and father so unhappy.

Nor, if I am candid, does naming the cause of their unhappiness ease my own sense of responsibility for making them unhappy. Somehow I was always the difficult child—spoiled, hot-tempered, selfish little girl. That's what my brothers and sisters and often my mother used to think. Looking back now, I suspect my mother did not want me, that I was an unwelcome and unpleasant surprise. How did they deal with the birth control issue? I wonder.

If I was the bad little girl who upset my mother so often, perhaps I was also, somehow, to blame for her big sorrows.

It doesn't help now to know that I misread the signs.

Although my father was a lawyer, like his father, he had no political ambitions. I don't think he objected to the corruption of machine politics in those days—no one thought it was wrong, well, almost no one. Rather he wanted for himself and his family a more cultivated life, art, music, the theater, rich friends who did not use vulgar words. As much as I loved him, I guess I have to admit that Daddy was a snob. Until suffering crushed all the ambition to join the north shore elite out of him.

He didn't practice law in those days. Rather he was involved, in ways that are not clear to me now, in "real estate." I suspect that he put most of the money he inherited from his father into land speculation in the then mostly vacant Chicago suburban regions and that the bubble burst for him, as it did for so many others. His "ship" never quite came in.

After the war my mother used to lament about all the money we might have made if we had been able to hold on to that land. Dad was so broken by then that money no longer mattered.

Not that we were poor. After that summer when his "real estate" failed, he was able to cash in on grandfather's political influence to get elected ward committeeman and then to become a Cook County judge. In that era, both jobs were lucrative and no one worried about being indicted.

We couldn't move out of his district until he had complete control of the ward. So we lived in an apartment on the first floor of a three-flat and had much more comfortable furniture and nicer clothes than anyone in the neighborhood. We even had a chauffeur to drive our car, a sign of wealth that was disastrous for me when I went to school. I don't think Daddy was very corrupt by the standards of the time. We didn't have as much money as many other politicians.

I can remember his saying that after the Crash was over, he would go back to "real estate" and we'd be able to move out of Chicago and into a beautiful house of our own. He also said that the Crash would be over when Roosevelt finally managed to get us into a war—although he was a Democrat, Daddy didn't like Roosevelt very much. He delivered his ward for him, however.

We did have the war all right. And there was prosperity. It was too late for Daddy. The price of prosperity had been too high.

There's a picture here in my little pile of Dad and Mom and Aunt Agnes at the lake sometime in the 1920s. Three handsome people. My father tall and bushy haired, a bit like Cary Grant, people used to say, my mother and aunt also tall, both willowy blondes. The old-fashioned swimsuits— Daddy in one that covers his chest and shoulders—don't conceal the magnificent physiques of all three. Middle-class Irish beautiful people of the flapper age, dreaming of wealth and respectability without limit while even then the sands beneath their feet were beginning to shift.

It's hard for me to believe that I'm older than Mom was when she died. Aunt Agnes, God bless her, is still alive and still stunning. I wish I were that beautiful.

Mom and Aunt Agnes didn't have much else besides beauty. The Laverty sisters were both knockouts, but they did not go to college because, as their father, a penurious little clerk who worked at the Pullman Company, said, women don't need an education, especially if they are pretty.

He was right by his own standards. Agnes Laverty snared a wealthy Protestant from Lake Forest and has never had to worry about money since. Mary Laverty married Lawrence O'Brien, a promising lawyer from a powerful Chicago political family. She never knew physical want even at the bottom of the Depression. The tragedies of which she could not have dreamed as a young woman at the lake were certainly not his fault.

As I remember her at the lake when I was a little girl, she was alternately gay and sulky. She delighted in the old piano we had bought for twenty dollars in a sale at Walworth. When she was sitting at the piano, singing for guests in her light, clear voice, she seemed to me to be breathtakingly lovely and perfectly happy, a contented bird chirping on a tree outside our window.

The mess of the house and the noise of the children made her snap nastily at Daddy, songbird become sharp-clawed cat. I'm sure the family financial disaster annoyed her and was beyond her comprehension. She was quite incapable of coping with the later disasters.

Mom, Dad, Aggie—all three of them attractive, shallow people, quite unprepared for the serious pains of life. I weep for them when I look at their pictures. They were as lacking in malice as they were lacking in depth. Fragile plants of the early Irish upper-middle class, yearning for acceptance and modest wealth and tranquil domesticity.

Mom and Dad's garden dried up under the blazing sun of the Depression and was swept clean by the war.

They didn't want all that much. The present generation takes my parents' dreams for granted—and much more besides. So I weep for them again, good people born at the wrong time.

And I weep a little for myself too. I wanted so much more. And I spoiled it all for myself.

19

Father Ryan wandered into his littered and disorderly office in the Cathedral rectory like an itinerant cleric who had been permitted to spend the night and was looking around the premises for the first time.

"Good morning, Dr. Reilly," he said with his hurt leprechaun smile and removed a stack of baptismal record books from a chair so that he might sit down. "I'm afraid I don't have any paintings to exhibit."

"Your cousin is the painter in the family," Anne replied, feeling her serious purpose melt, as it usually did, in Father Ryan's presence.

"I'll not say a thing about the immoralities of that one," he said in a phony Irish brogue. "And herself painting all those people without any clothes on, at all, at all."

"Do you think it would be sinful for me to pose for her?" she blurted, though that was not what had brought her to his office.

"No," he said flatly. "Mind you, we wouldn't hang the portrait in the Cardinal's suite. It might offend some of the visiting Romans—those who have the hormones to notice it."

She felt her face grow warm. "I'll be so glad to get Father Kenny's work out of my basement," she said, changing to the real subject of her visit.

"I can imagine. There is a smell of evil about them if you ask me."

"Smell?" she asked nervously.

"Not a real smell, kind of an atmosphere. I suspect that

when he went mad the genius inside of him turned demon."

"The fire was a terrible event, Father." She seemed to feel an obligation to defend Father Kenny. "It marked us all. He was on his day off. As soon as he heard about it, he rushed home on the streetcar. The Monsignor had collapsed. Father Kenny administered the last rites to scores of us. He consoled all the parents, made all the funeral arrangements, even preached at the Masses the Cardinal didn't attend."

"Trust old George William to squeeze publicity for himself. . . . But, seriously, Anne, I know it was a terrible experience. Most priests would think it was Mundelein's death—"

"I was there, Father," she said firmly. "He had a nervous collapse after the last funeral and was never the same. I'm afraid the smell is that of the fire."

"It was so long ago," he said gently.

"It was only yesterday, Father. . . . Anyway, would you come over this morning? I want to ask you a question about the 'Divine Justice' painting."

"Sure." He seem surprised. "Any buyers for it yet?"

"No, I think it scares people."

"Small wonder . . . Incidentally, Anne, I suppose you should know that Matt Sweeney is back in town, working miracles."

"Oh, my God," she said.

"Don't blame God for Matt."

"Blame me for him," she said bitterly. "I suppose he will have to come and pray over me. I don't need him this week."

"We don't need him any week. In an earlier age we would have burned him at the stake as a witch. I'm not sure it would be a bad idea. Poor Des Kenny wasn't any more demented."

"Yes, he was, Father. Toward the end. See you later?"

"Ten-thirty."

What will happen, she asked herself as she left the rectory, *if he sees the change in the painting too? It will all break into the open, like water smashing through a dam. In a way, I won't mind. It will all be over.*

Each day the demons came closer to the young woman in the swamp. Now they had her pinned in the muck and seemed to be preparing to rape her. Anne resolved every morning that she would not look at "Divine Justice," but she was drawn to it as an iron filing to the magnet, a moth to the candle, an alcoholic to the bottle.

At the corner of Michigan and Delaware, in the shadow of the soaring obelisk of the John Hancock Center, she stopped, frozen in her place by shame, her eyes jammed shut in humiliation.

She restrained her impulse to cover herself with her hands and arms. Cautiously she opened her eyes. Her light blue cotton knit dress was still in place.

Dear God, help me, she prayed.

Hot water had returned to her shower. Her new terror was a sudden sensation of being totally naked in public, a dream fear breaking into ordinary consciousness. She knew in her head the feeling was absurd, but it was so real when it swept over her that she was totally convinced all of her clothes had been suddenly torn away.

Was Father Kenny haunting her from the other side of the grave?

That was a ridiculous thought. It was all her crazy imagination.

She continued on to the gallery as the cabs and buses rushed down Michigan Avenue, a river running to the ocean of the Loop. No one on Michigan Avenue smiled in the morning. At midday the smiles began and by late afternoon almost everyone returned your smile.

She always tried to smile at people, feeling that they turned to glance at her because they remembered that terrible picture on the front of the *Tribune* magazine.

No breakfast with Sandy this morning. Her daughter was being inaugurated as class president at St. Scholastica and Anne insisted that the proud mother be present.

She opened the door of the gallery. The smell again. *What else is new? Will Father Ryan notice it? No one else seems to.*

She opened the door to her office and jumped back in horror. Every flat surface was covered with soot. She leaned against the doorjamb and swayed. Real soot, not imagination-created soot. Just as if there had been a real explosion.

Can I be doing this, like the children who create poltergeist phenomena?

Wearily, as though it were the end of the day, she went into the little room at the back, took off her dress and slip, and put on the jeans and T-shirt—Monet lilies, of course—she kept there. She filled a bucket with water, hunted for a spray cleaner, and set to work.

Only then did she realize that the soot was on the desk and cabinets and coffee table and chairs, but not on the charcoal gray carpeting.

Maybe I didn't want to ruin the carpet.

As she was scrubbing the desk the phone rang.

"Annie, Mike." A clipped voice, accustomed to giving terse orders. "I had to fly to Washington. I didn't have your number at home. I'm sorry I didn't call yesterday. I was in meetings. . . . "

"There was no reason to call," she said stiffly.

"Everything all right?" She imagined that he was rubbing his chin.

"Of course everything is all right. No explosions, no scams, no kinky district commanders."

"I was worried. . . . " Now he was hesitant, wondering why he had called.

"I've taken care of myself for a long time, Mickey."

"I know that," he said irritably, "I was concerned."

"I appreciate your concern." -

A little bit of petting doesn't give you proprietorship— or family obligations.

"I'll see you when I get back."

"That will hardly be necessary."

She replaced the phone. *I'm sorry, darling, that I had to be so cruel. You heard my message, which is what matters. Neither of us can afford to become involved.*

She wanted to cry, decided that she had cried too much that week and that there would be more tears that afternoon with Dr. Murphy, and repressed her urge to weep.

Instead, she directed her emotions to the battle against the soot.

"Missus work hard," said Father Ryan from the door.

"Damn it, don't surprise me that way," she yelled at him, dropping her spray cleaner.

He beamed happily. "So there really is a temper lurking behind the pious exterior of the pious matron?"

"Who told you about my temper?" she demanded, still angry.

He picked up the cleaner. "Mike Casey the Cop, who else?"

"He has no right. . . . I'm sorry, Father. I'm . . . I'm very nervous these days." She wiped her hands. "May I offer you some tea? Gentle orange?"

"Sure, if it's free. Priests don't pay for anything, you know. . . . It's pretty strong between you and Mike Casey the Cop, isn't it?"

"Of course not," she snapped, prepared to be angry again.

"When you two were talking at the opening, it was as though the rest of the world vanished. Like stumbling into someone's bedroom."

"Nonsense," she exploded as her face flamed.

Father Ryan shrugged indifferently. "Nothing wrong with it. Well-matched pair, as far as I can see."

"It really is that obvious?" she said, calming down.

"Uh-huh."

"Drink your tea, Father, and don't play matchmaker."

"Heaven forbid." He blew on the surface of the tea. "Where's Alexandra?"

"I gave her the day off. Her daughter is being inaugurated as class president at her school. I thought I'd do a little cleaning up." She gestured with the black rag. "Lot of soot in this neighborhood."

"I guess." He seemed to be sniffing the air as though not sure whether he smelled something unusual or not. "A cookie?"

"When have I ever turned down a cookie?"

She opened the credenza behind her desk and took out the cookie jar that she kept for visiting children and priests.

As she stood up to offer it to him, the shame assaulted her again, more piercing than before. She knew that her clothes had been torn away.

"Are you all right, Anne?" Father Ryan asked, stumbling to his feet. "Are you going to faint?"

With a desperate effort she recovered her poise and opened her eyes. She was still discreetly protected by the Monet lilies.

"I wouldn't do something so Victorian. I'm okay. Just the strain of this darn show."

"Of course," he said, obviously not persuaded. "You looked like you were Lot's wife."

She almost told him everything.

"Do you want to look at 'Divine Justice' now?"

"Sure, if I can have my cookies first."

"I'm sorry, Father," she said, flustered. "Have two, even three."

He carefully chose three chocolate chip cookies and followed her to the landing.

"Do you notice anything unusual about it?" She stood to one side, not looking at the picture herself.

Father Ryan squinted through his thick glasses. "Nothing more than the lunacy that's always been in it."

"Are you sure?" she said hesitantly.

"Pretty sure." He was watching her now, not the picture.

She looked at it herself. "Oh, my God, it hasn't changed after all!"

"Huh?"

She started to cry, despite her stern resolutions. "I've been imagining that the demons have been closing in on that poor child. Each day they were closer. They were going to rape her before they dragged her back to hell. . . . It was all my imagination."

Father Ryan examined the picture again, this time intently. "Let's go back to your office, Anne."

"You think I'm a nut case," she said, accepting another cup of tea and, without protest, two chocolate chip cookies.

"I think you're under grave strain," he said.

"And half in love too. . . . "

"I didn't say that."

"You're thinking it, a lovesick old woman." She munched on a cookie, thinking she should make them for herself as well as for kids and priests.

"I think maybe you ought to close the show. Today."

"Because I'm losing my mind?"

"Because there is evil associated with Des Kenny, evil that has a special power to hurt you."

"He wasn't an evil man, Father, just deeply troubled."

"God can judge his conscience. I can only look at the life and the art and judge you ought not to be associated with it."

"I sure know how to pick them, don't I, Father?" She half-laughed through her tears.

"Lately you've been showing much better taste."

They laughed together.

"Let me try it for a couple of more days," she said, pulling herself together. "If things don't improve, I promise I'll terminate the exhibition. We've already sold enough to make money for everyone."

He nodded solemnly, then rose to leave. "All right, but stay in touch with me."

There are so many subjects to talk about with Doctor Murphy this afternoon. I won't know which one to choose.

Yes, I will. I'll talk about Mickey. He's part of the real world.

She changed back into her dress, charmed several purchasers, made some sales she had hardly expected, and felt much better about herself.

There was one more interruption before she closed early to escape to the swimming pool and then Dr. Murphy.

"You look pretty as a picture, Anne, a spring flower in early autumn."

Sweet Matthew Sweeney.

Dressed in a black suit and a black tie, his thick wavy silver hair flawlessly shaped, he looked like a fundamentalist TV preacher, which he had pretty much become, though he was still technically a Catholic priest. He was standing at the door of the gallery, waiting for her to come out of the office in response to the chime that rang when the door was open. People came to meet Matt Sweeney. He waited for you, exuding piety and virtue and Brut cologne.

"Good afternoon, Matt," she said coolly. "Please close the door, the chime will ring as long as it's open."

"It's wonderful to see you again, honey." He embraced her and kissed her forehead, a gesture that was as chaste as the handshake of peace between two old nuns.

You slept with me for two years and that's all you can feel for me?

"Are you interested in purchasing some art, Matt? We have some excellent work by a man who was a priest. Perhaps some of your friends in the Movement would be interested? The profits go to Catholic schools in the inner city."

"I have better things to give to my friends and to the poor than money," he intoned in a rich baritone voice. "I have been blessed by the Lord with a great gift. It has nothing to do with me. As you know, Anne, I am the worst of sinners. Through God's power I have this gift of curing the sick and the infirm of spiritual and physical ills and I am bound by the gift to wander about the world healing even as the Lord Jesus did."

"So I've heard," she said dryly.

Matt was once the crisp, efficient president of a Catholic university, dedicated totally to the intellectual life— and the raising of funds for the intellectual life. Now he was a faith healer, appealing to the fringe of the Catholic Charismatic Movement and to those poor souls for whom medicine could do nothing.

He sold healing the same way he sold chairs for his university. Perhaps not much had changed.

"I can feel the power surging in me," he rhapsodized. "Even when I can't heal their bodies, I heal their souls."

"How wonderful."

"I thought we might have supper together. I could tell you about the wonderful work the Lord has done in me. And you're part of it, Anne, a very important part of it."

Does he want to go to bed with me? No, of course not. He wants some of my money. He's heard about Mark.

"I have some appointments this evening, Matt. Now, if

you'll excuse me . . . " She felt her fists clench and her arm grow tense.

"At least let me pray over you. Kneel down, child, and let God's saving grace flood over you. Heavenly Father, look down upon this handmaid of yours. She doubts your tender and loving mercy still, but goodness is in her heart. Reach out your hand and touch that heart, melt the ice around it, open it up to your love, flood it with your mercy, overcome with your gracious healing all the pain and suffering and hatred that lurks inside her. Renew her life and permit the power that you have given me to flow out and soothe her with sweetness and light. Please kneel down, Anne. God expects us to throw ourselves on our knees in his presence."

I'm going to live up to my reputation for being hot tempered again today.

"Get out of here, you phony little hypocrite, or I'll call the police," she shouted at him. "And don't ever come back."

"Are you still angry at me, honey?" he asked softly. "Is there no forgiveness in your heart? Forgive others as you yourself expect to be forgiven. I thought we had talked it all out and understood each other."

Momentarily he had retreated to his earlier self-fulfillment spirituality.

"*You* talked it out," she yelled, "like you always did, you selfish pig. Now get out of here before I throw something at you."

"Anne," he said softly, his arms limp at his sides, a picture of dejected innocence, "can't we at least be friends?"

"No, we can't, you miserable little liar. I don't want to ever see you again. Go cure your sick old women. I don't want to be reminded of what a lousy fuck you were."

A spasm of rage crossed his face. *Sweet Matthew angry! Some things do change.*

"You are sinning against the Holy Spirit!" he shouted at her.

I'll be darned, she thought. *The passive aggressive turns active aggressive.*

"I'll take my chances," she shot back at him, delighted that she had at last made him angry.

"May God's judgment descend upon you and humiliate you for your sinfulness. As Saint Paul gave sinners in his community over to the devil to be chastised for their own good, so I give you over to the devil. You have brought chastisement upon yourself!"

He left, presumably imitating Saint Paul in the righteous anger of his walk.

Dear God, forgive me for saying such a terrible thing. I didn't want to hurt him. But I do want to keep him away.

He really wasn't much of a fuck. Neither was I, I guess.

And who am I to reject healing wherever it comes from? Maybe his prayer would have helped.

Not very likely.

And now I have a curse to bear. Not the first one, either.

20

"So you're afraid that God will send you to hell if you have an affair with this police person?"

"No . . . not for that."

"You're going to hell anyway?"

"Sometimes I think so."

"Then you might as well have the affair. It doesn't matter."

"I don't want to hurt him."

"Ah, God will send him to hell?"

"I . . . I don't know. Probably not."

"In any case foreplay is already serious sin. Why not finish the action?"

"That adds more malice."

"And hurts God more?"

"We can't hurt God . . . you're making fun of me."

"My dear woman, I am not. I am trying to understand so that you may understand. In my judgment you are in love with the man and desperately want to go to bed with him. Probably to marry him too. . . . "

"I couldn't marry him."

"Why not?"

"I. . . I'm not very good at marriage."

"You mean that he is a man you would not be able to control by taking care of him as if he were a child. He would demand surrender and you are afraid to risk that."

"We shouldn't give ourselves that completely to anyone. We become slaves. . . . "

"You're much too intelligent to play that kind of word game, Anne. Life demands intelligently selected gifts of the self to others. Your gift of yourself to your father was not successful. You've never risked a similar gift to another man."

"That's not fair to Daddy."

"You're still playing games with me. Your father didn't really expect you to exorcise the Great Depression."

"I let both my husbands down, and John Duncan too."

"You let down that Matt Sweeney creep?"

"I must have."

"You're afraid of marriage?"

"Yes."

"And afraid of meaningful sex?"

"No . . . I don't know."

"You said you were virtually frigid. You produced four children with few if any orgasms."

"It was different with John. I failed him the worst of all."

"He could have waited."

"It would have been sinful."

"God will send you to hell for the orgasms with John!"

"You think I'm crazy."

"No, I don't, Anne."

Mary Kate stopped the tape to admire the way she'd

said that sentence, just the right amount of support. Having messed up the session that far, she felt overdue for an intelligent response. She stirred uneasily on the couch.

"Sometimes I think I must be a very sensual woman. I mean, deep inside me there is a person who is extremely erotic. I keep her in control most of the time."

"But you wish you could let her out?"

"I like being fondled and caressed. I like . . . intercourse. I love it. I miss it terribly. I want to have intercourse with Mick—make love all night long. I fell apart when I heard him on the phone today. . . . "

"You're ashamed of your intense sexuality?"

"Scared by it. It . . . it makes me out of control."

"Is it bad to be out of control?"

"I might do something terrible."

"I see."

"Why does everything have to be mixed up with sex? Why can't we love one another without our bodies getting in the way?"

"God made an artistic mistake in arranging the dynamics of procreation?"

"Maybe only an aesthetic mistake."

"I see."

"I want him so badly. I never admitted that even to myself."

"A whirlwind romance."

"I don't mean now. I mean always."

"Will he marry you if you refuse to go to bed with him unless he does?"

"Probably. It would be cruel to do it that way."

"He wants to marry you, do you think?"

"I'm not sure . . . . Yes, I am. He does. He may not realize it yet. He's so lonely, poor man."

"So your understanding of the Church's sexual teaching is not a barrier to your consummating this rather mysterious, mystical love affair you've had for so many years?"

"No . . . I guess not."

"Anne, you are an experienced and sophisticated woman. If you love the man and he loves you, if you want *to marry him and he wants to marry you, if you want to have sex and he does too, then are you not capable of arranging these matters the way women have since the species came down out of the trees?"*

"I'm no good, Doctor, no good. He'll find out . . . ."

And then the patient broke down completely.

Mary Kate stopped the tape again, then began to record her own thoughts.

It was an extremely useful session, I think. The essential problem is not Catholic moral teaching—though the version of it she received as a young woman has doubtless aggravated her condition. The basic issue is her own pervasive feeling of worthlessness, a feeling surely reinforced by the unfortunate events of her life.

Indeed, I don't believe I have ever encountered a patient with such low self-esteem. The condition is pathological and perhaps incurable. Doubtless it is responsible for the unwise choices she has made in lovers.

Until Mike Casey the Cop, who is certainly a very wise choice.

She chose him long ago, didn't she. Fought with him until he had to notice her. Considerable ego strength locked in conflict with violent self-rejection.

Interesting.

The question that I would have asked her if she had not broken down is obviously the key to everything. Which is why she broke down, of course.

"What will this police person find out about you?"

21

"Caitlin, I'm calling you in your role as family archivist."

"Sure, Uncle Punk," said Blackie's niece, the Notre

Dame student, a flaxen-haired, long-limbed Viking maiden
with a sunrise smile, in whom the family's recessive ninth-
century Danish genes had emerged in lithe and luxurious
splendor. "Anything to help your curiosity."

There was a time a number of years ago when Blackie
feared that his oldest niece would violate the family tradition for women and become quite sane. Since then she has
reassured him. She may even have exceeded her mother
when it came to zaniness.

"The letters from Marge Casey to her husband, Pat,
when he was wandering around the world in the 1930s."

"They're in the microfilm file at Grand Beach. Any
special reason?"

"I have a hunch there might be something in them I
could be needing."

"An Uncle Punk hunch, huh? I'll make a printout on
the way home this weekend."

"Fine . . ."

There was something locked in the past, Anne's past,
but perhaps Mike the Cop's too. Blackie wasn't sure what
he might find in old love letters between a man and woman
who were separated and then divorced and remarried after a
spectacular adventure. But there might be something useful, something that would eventually provide a little light.

Poor Anne was going to need all the light she could get.

22

Anne stirred.

The fire was out, black rubble steaming in the coat of
new snow. A fireman and a policeman stood guard. The
smell seemed still to hang over the neighborhood. Old men
and women, shuffling into daily Mass, refused to look at
the ruined school, pretending it wasn't there.

Anger replaced fire, anger that would never be extinguished.

The anger of the children who were still suffering in the hospitals; the anger of the parents whose children had died; the anger of the priests and nuns toward the fire department, which seemed to have failed them so badly; the anger of the city over the carelessness with which the school had been maintained; the anger of the people in the neighborhood who felt disgraced and humiliated.

The drunken anger of the distraught pastor. Father Kenny's towering rage. Why, he kept demanding, wasn't the school safer?

The diocesan lawyers and insurance officials poking around, trying to persuade people to sign documents. Her father's anguished screams as he pushed one of them from the house.

All the while the dead were being waked and buried, new names added to the list every day.

The closed caskets and the long lines at the funeral home. Her daddy, red faced and angry, attacking the Church leaders for their incompetence until two other politicians took him aside and calmed him down. Her momma, weary and restrained, now hugging her tightly.

"We might have lost you too. God was so good to us when he spared you. And I didn't believe you were ill."

Joe and Marty, confused and stricken. Many of their friends were dead too. They had fought with their sisters, as brothers and sisters do. Now they would never fight with them again.

The two white caskets, side by side, in the church. An old man in red preaching at great length. No one could understand what he was saying, but they all agreed that it was "beautiful."

The blizzard that sliced into their faces as they stood by the graveside at Mount Carmel cemetery, the snow covering the caskets as Father Kenny screamed the final prayers above the howling wind.

Christmas music on the Victrola while Anne's momma decorated the tree, the carol voices turning to a mumble as her momma, crying over a handful of tinsel, neglected to rewind it.

Her daddy raging at Christmas dinner while they listened in terrified silence. The police had not captured the arsonist. What was the matter with them? It had to be arson. Spontaneous combustion was not a sufficient explanation.

Someone had to be guilty. Such a terrible tragedy could not just have happened.

Her momma's hand on his, gently soothing him.

Father Kenny coming to visit them on Christmas night, no coat or hat and with a wild gleam in his eye.

"The poor boy is another victim of the fire," her daddy said sadly.

"We're all victims," her momma agreed.

Her own voice: "Will it ever be over?"

"No, child, it will never be over."

Then, waking up in her bed decades later, on a hot September night, covered with sweat.

No, it would never be over.

23

ANNE'S STORY

Dear Anne Marie,

First of all, hon, you must forgive me for not writing sooner. I was sick for most of the ride over on the Queen Mary *and they've kept us so busy here at the RD (Replacement Depot) that I haven't had a second to write.*

I've been assigned to the 39th Division, one of the best in Europe, and I should be in the thick of things in a few days, as soon as they can find transport to move us up. Everyone here says the war will be over in six weeks. Then we'll have to finish the Japs off, but that shouldn't take more than another year. By Christmas of 1945 I'll be home with you. I can hardly wait.

I know what your temper is like and I know you're probably steaming at me because I didn't write. The QM is a wonderful boat. Sometime after the war when it has been restored to its old glory you and I will take it across the ocean and I can show you all the places where I was sick— and we can dance in the ballroom and walk the decks arm in arm and be happy together. This trip, however, was no fun. There were seven thousand of us crammed on the ship—I guess I should call it a ship and not a boat—and we had a terrible summer storm, which the crew says is very rare. You know how much I love you, so please don't be mad at me because I was too sick to write.

We'll visit Paris too. It was night when we drove through it, so I couldn't see too much, but even in the dark and the blackout, it was clearly a lovely city. I want to share it with you someday, and I want to share this whole country. The people have suffered terribly through the occupation. But they're bouncing back bravely. You can see it in the way they walk and hold their heads up high and wave to us as we speed by in our transport.

Incidentally, you needn't worry about my virtue with the French women; I have yet to see one who can hold a candle to women from the West Side of Chicago. Still, it's nice to see them smile and wave. The weather has been warm and sunny until now. Today it started to rain, which might slow down our armor and delay victory for another week or so.

I'm a little scared about going into combat, but not too much. I'm proud to be serving my country against that madman Hitler and I know that your prayers will bring me home safe.

There's one thing I have to say. I'm sure I'll come back, alive and well and loving you more than ever. Still, honey, if I don't come back, I want you to know that I will always be with you, loving you the way I have loved you for the last year, the happiest year of my life. I want you to go on with your life, knowing that I will be happy in your happiness, sorry in your sorrows, and victorious in your victories. I want you to continue with your studies as far as you can go and to fill the life of all around you with as much happiness as you've filled mine with since that first date last August.

I'm sure you've been writing every day. Unlike me, you'd write even when you were sick—please, please, don't be mad at me. The APO number is the same. Mail will catch up with me even at the old address. As soon as I find out what my unit will be in the 39th, I'll write to you with the exact address. That will speed mail up by a day or so. I want to hear from you so badly.

Finally, Annie dear, I love you and I will always love you. Pray for me till I'm back in your arms.

God bless you.

Dick

It was the only letter he ever sent me after he left the United States. I received it a week after his parents got the wire from the War Department. I still carry it in my purse. All the other mementos were lost somehow, when I moved out of our house in River Forest at the time of my divorce.

I don't have any pictures of Dick Murray. We were too busy being in love the summer we dated to take pictures. I suppose I could find one in a Fenwick yearbook, if I really wanted to. I don't need a picture to remember him. Every time I hear one of the Big Bands on a radio interlude of "Golden Oldies" (I must confess that I feel neither Golden nor Old) I see Dick's neatly chiseled face with the dimple in his chin, the twinkling blue eyes, the sandy crew cut, the broad basketball player's shoulders. He was my first love, not counting Mickey, who I didn't count in those days, and like all first loves he is magic in my memory.

Bob Crosby and the Bobcats, Jimmy Dorsey, Tommy Dorsey. Above all, poor Glenn Miller. I cry even now when I hear his music. And the music we heard as Dick and Joan O'Malley and Randy Martin and I walked in the dance hall area of the lake—Sin Lake it was called then and not without reason—that last summer when we were together. "Love Letters," "The Last Time I Saw Paris," "The White

Cliffs of Dover," "Old Black Magic," "I'll be Seeing You in All the Old Familiar Places." The last was "our song," and, though we didn't have a wishing well or a café, we did have a tree, under which we necked, although I don't know if it was a chestnut or not. I stay away from the tree on my rare trips to the lake because there are too many sweet memories I don't want to ruin.

I am frankly being a sentimentalist about my romance with Dick. It was a teenage sentimental crush, which might have ended when he came home from the war. Memories of songs and summer and young love under the stars by the softly lapping waters of a lake are much less likely to fade away into the reality of adulthood if your love does not come home to you.

We were so very young that summer. I was going into my junior year at Trinity High School and he into his senior year at Fenwick. Summer love at the lake was urgent during the war, perhaps because many of my friends were dating boys who were in the service and the lake was crowded with sailors from Great Lakes on weekends. I suppose boys used the possibility of sudden death to intensify the pace of the sexual game and perhaps we used it to squeeze more romance into our dull teenage lives. Those dark Friday and Saturday nights at the lake with the Big Band music blaring from the loudspeakers and young people clinging to one another to fend off the thought of death were as steeped in sexual intensity as the air was steeped in humidity; adolescent sexual fantasy released from the imagination by the terror of war.

Beth has always insisted that the same thing happened to her generation during the Vietnam years. But few of Beth's friends went to war and none of them were killed. She does not seem to understand what it was like when all your friends were scheduled to go to war, many of them the summer they graduated from high school, and some of them would surely be killed.

She also scoffs at my memories of the Big Bands. The Beatles, she says, are a much more realistic musical memory than Glenn Miller. We were innocents, she says contemptuously, to be taken in by that kind of shit.

Maybe we were. We were much more reluctant to sleep with one another, although my friend Joan had her love affairs with servicemen in her junior and senior years of high school. We did not know the possibility of drugs. Yet I'm not sure that Beth's generation understands life any better than we did. They talk a lot about poverty and dress like they are poor, but they have never known poverty. We did not talk about it much, but many of us knew it all too well.

Not me, however, God knows.

I'm not sure that the music of the Beatles—and I've come to appreciate them—will ever keep alive the memory of a boy who did not come home.

If Joan didn't go all the way with Randy Martin that summer, or almost all the way, then she was fibbing to me, behavior of which she was entirely capable. Cute, full-fig-ured little innocent-eyed blond with a Shirley Temple laugh, Joan teased boys with deliberate hints of what she was willing to do. I was much more virtuous and restrained about where I drew the line. You could fondle me but only in certain places. You could kiss me but only for a limited amount of time. You could hold me in your arms, but not too tightly. You could open the top buttons of my blouse but nothing else. You could touch my knee but not any higher. If I suspected that you or I had gone too far, not only would I hurry to a priest to confess it, but, bossy little Irish bitch that I was, I would insist that you did so too, often waiting in the back of the church before mass on Sunday morning to make sure you went to confession.

I was not about to have some boy killed in action con-demned to hell because of me.

All the time, of course, I was planning to be a nun.

That I didn't have intercourse with Dick was not, how-ever, the result of my virtue. Partly it was that neither of us really had any idea of how to do it and partly that he had better control of his emotions than I did of mine. I was so mad, crazy in love with him that summer—and through the school year too—that he could have done anything he wanted to me. He was strong, poised, fun to be with, witty, considerate, the captain of the basketball team and class president—every junior girl's romantic dream. He did not need to go off immediately to war either. He could have enrolled in an officers' training program and gone to college for a year or two. I desperately pleaded with him, but he laughed his carefree laugh and insisted, "I want to get there while there's still some fighting left to do."

He didn't have much time to fight, poor boy.

I offered to sleep with him after the Christmas dance if he would enlist in the V-12 navy program, which would have sent him to Loyola or Notre Dame for two years. I think I shocked and embarrassed him.

"That can wait till I come home," he said with a nervous laugh.

He was the first man to touch my naked breasts, on the night of his senior prom. He was very gentle, scared, and respectful and very curious. It was his virtue and not mine that we went no further.

Momma and I made the Sorrowful Mother novena every Friday during the war, praying for Joe, who was a Thunderbird pilot in Europe, and Marty, who was a gunnery officer on the *Indianapolis* in the Pacific. The summer after his graduation I added Dick's name to our list. He moved very quickly from the cap and gown to the battlefield —I would learn later when I was able to read books about the war that the United States was terribly short of replacements for rifle companies that summer. His basic training was finished in late July, and as you can tell from his letter, he was being sent into combat at the beginning of September.

Our novena prayers seemed to be working. The American armies swept across Europe all summer long. Radio commentators were saying that the war would be over by the end of September. I redoubled my prayers, making two and three novenas at the same time.

On the third Friday in September his little sister, two years younger than me, found me in church after the novena, begging God to send him home safe. With tears streaming down her face, she told me that he'd been killed in action.

Later we learned that he had died on the very first day that he was with his new unit in the Hürtgen Forest. Still later I would read in books about the war that many young replacements died that way because the veterans, often men only a few months older, were too cruel or too weary to take care of the replacements. Sometimes they even let the young men die because they were angry at the death of their buddies and had to punish someone. The books also say that the Hürtgen Forest battle was a serious and unnecessary blunder in which many green replacements were cannon fodder, wasted in the pursuit of an irrelevant victory.

Bethie is a peace activist. She marches in demonstrations against nuclear weapons and in favor of disarmament. Which is her privilege. Maybe she's right, I don't know. She lectures me on the evils of war as though I don't understand them, as though you don't know that war is ugly and horrible when a wonderful boy—and he was wonderful, that's not just sentimental nostalgia—with everything to live for is uselessly destroyed as replacement cannon fodder a few weeks after his high school senior prom.

I loved him. I'll always love him. My life would have been so much different if he'd come home.

I can't escape the conviction that I was responsible for his death. I should have tried harder to persuade him to go into the V-12. Perhaps his death was meant as a warning and even a punishment for me.

I survived my senior year in a daze. Joan was a big help—somehow she becomes a mature woman with compassion and strength when a friend is in need. I struggled successfully to maintain my A average, because Dick had insisted that my studies were important—unlike the man I married, he valued intelligence in a woman. Of course, I continued with the Sorrowful Mother novena, for the repose of his soul—to get him out of purgatory and home with God as quickly as possible. I prayed to God not to punish Joe and Marty for my sinfulness.

I guess God did not hear my prayers. Or my mother's or father's. My brother Joe was killed in a plane crash in June after V-E Day in Europe. Marty went down on the *Indianapolis* or was eaten by sharks when the ship was torpedoed—after it delivered the first atomic bomb to Guam.

I don't mean that about God. I know better, I really do. But that's how I felt then. I am resigned to his will, as best I can be.

Momma never quite recovered. She was convinced that she was somehow to blame. There was no shortage of responsibility in our clan. She slipped deeper and deeper into a moody, silent depression. I gave up my plans to go away to school at Manhattanville in New York—I wanted to learn what life in New York was like—and enrolled at Mundelein so I could be with her. I'm afraid I wasn't much of a help to her or to Daddy. I had my own sorrows and my own recriminations.

Momma became worse and Daddy was totally preoccupied with her health. Doctors and psychiatrists did their best, but I don't think Momma wanted to recover. Perhaps I am being harsh. Often since then I have wished that I could escape into a world of painless silence too.

By then Father Kenny had disappeared from our lives, save for an occasional visit from the seminary. He too was deeply troubled, but his problems made him manic, so manic that we could hardly bear to have him in the house. Monsignor Mugsy Brannigan, the pastor of St. Ursula and one of the nicest priests I have ever known—kind of a Father Ryan of his generation—suggested that a trip to Lourdes might help Momma.

"I don't know what goes on there, to tell you the truth," he explained to me, "but the experience of being in a holy place might be a big help to your mother."

It seemed reasonable. It still does. They left on one of the first postwar pilgrimages to Lourdes, and I think the first by airplane. I stormed heaven that the plane would not crash. Dad sent postcards from Gander in Newfoundland, Shannon in Ireland (where he hoped to stop on the return trip), London, and Paris. The Lockheed *Constellation* had made it safely across the Atlantic despite my fears. Then my prayers turned to a plea that Mom recover, that she become happy again as she was at the lake when we were all young. She was still very pretty and had a long life ahead of her.

I was ecstatic when Aunt Aggie—with whom I was

living while they were away—showed me Daddy's cablegram:

"Mary Anne completely cured. Love to Annie. Lawrence."

A truck crashed into their bus on the trip from Lourdes to Paris. Mom and Dad were the only ones killed.

My parents, my brothers, my sisters—all dead. We had been seven and now I was one, the only one. Alone and isolated in a hospital ward. Maybe even a mental hospital ward.

Even now I am not sure that God was not sending me a message.

24

Michael walked through the underpass from Michigan Avenue to Oak Street Beach. The lake was complacently calm, as if it too were taking credit for the Sox pennant triumph. He shuddered at the thought of the traffic and security problems of a playoff and perhaps even a World Series. He was a Cub fan, but unlike Mike Royko, he was quite capable of being a Sox fan too—until he thought of the nightmare of police work a World Series would require. The well-meaning ninny who was acting superintendent would expect him to arrange it, of course, and then would take all the credit.

Unless there were goof-ups. Then the deputy (whatever number he was next month) would catch the blame.

The heat wave had returned. Oak Street was filled with swimsuited people of every age and sex and shape, some still swimming in the warm waters, despite the fact that the beach was officially closed and the lifeguards had departed. At the far end a blue-and-white squad was parked, a silent warning that no one should break too many laws.

He made a mental note to call Jeremiah Mullens and observe that he was certain the district commander had assigned cops who had lifeguard experience to Oak Street on hot Saturday afternoons in September. And October if the water was still warm.

"Who is going to be blamed, Jeremiah, if someone drowns while the cops in the squad watch? You are."

He smiled to himself. *Fix you good, Jeremiah.*

He saw the silver head for which he'd been looking. At the far end of the beach.

He bought two hot dogs with everything and two large Tabs from the sidewalk vendor and, paying no attention to what the sand might do to his Italian loafers, drifted down the beach toward her. Two well-endowed young women joggers almost knocked him over.

I noticed them and they didn't notice me. Sure sign of age.

Anne was wearing a two-piece white-and-black-striped swimsuit, straps off the shoulders, not quite a bikini but not much more, huge white-shelled sunglasses, a wide-brimmed white straw hat, and a thick layer of protective sun cream. She was reading *Paris Match* and listening to music—he was sure it was classical—on a Walkman cassette player.

She had found a place on the beach where there was a little privacy and created more for herself by the sheer power of her physical presence. You knew she had to be visiting royalty.

And she was so lovely that he wanted to crush her in his arms and cover her with kisses.

"I brought you lunch," he said, pushing a hot dog between her and the magazine.

She removed her sunglasses, looked at him with a quizzical eye, took off the earphones, and accepted the hot dog.

"Thank you." She examined the innards of the dog carefully. "How did you know I liked them with everything?"

"It's a cop's job to know. Here's your Tab. Can I join you?"

"It's a public beach," she said, not unkindly, "but you

are hardly dressed for it. I told Sandy not to tell anyone where I was."

"That doesn't include the Commissar of Police." He began to eat his own hot dog.

"We take turns working on Saturday," she explained, eager to establish that she was not exploiting the immigrant woman whose life she may have saved. "And you're staring, sir."

"Can't help it, Annie. You're something to stare at."

A flush spread over her face. "I'm glad I'm not here with you alone," she said easily, ducking her head in the familiar modest novice movement.

"I'm not."

"I now debate whether I should pull up my straps in careful modesty or leave them where they are in feminist defiance."

"Don't touch them, woman. . . . What did you do this morning?"

"Went downtown to the Daley Center and LaSalle Street to celebrate the city's one hundred fiftieth birthday. Great fun. Big Band music. Remember the Big Bands? Happy Birthday, Chicago. You work for the city, so happy birthday to you."

They were still bobbing and weaving, like halfbacks running in open field, but now they were also laughing at each other. *God, how I want her.*

"Only for another year . . . You read French?" he said, gesturing at her magazine.

"Sure. Never been to France or anywhere else, but I read French. You've never been to Spain or Mexico, but, according to the papers, you speak Spanish."

"*Sí, Señora.*"

"How did you learn?" She bit off another large hunk of hot dog.

"Assigned a Mexican-American cop to work with me and gave orders we were to speak nothing but Spanish."

"The lovely Patrol Officer Lopez?" She smiled archly.

"A man cop. It was hard enough as it was. Deirdre came later. My Spanish is better than hers."

"How nice. . . . " She extracted a tissue from her purse and gave it to him to wipe his fingers.

"She thinks you're wonderful. Calls you Doña Anna Maria. Big compliment from a Mexican-American girl cop."

"Put this on your face." She presented him with a tube of sunshade. "You look like you weren't out in the sun much this summer. She sounds like a nice young woman. I'd like to meet her sometime."

"She'd probably freeze up, presence of royalty, you know. . . . Annie, is everything all right?"

"Of course everything is all right." She sniffed indignantly. But her gray eyes lost their sparkle and clouded over. "There haven't been any more explosions. Even your charming Captain Mullens hasn't been around. We've sold half the Kenny pieces. I'll have an empty gallery in a few days."

"I want to help, Anne." *I want to go to bed with you too, which you surely know. And I want to lick every inch of you as if you were an orange sherbet bar. You probably can guess something like that too.*

She stirred uneasily on her black-and-white blanket, which, he noticed for the first time, matched her suit. "I don't need help," she said, rearranging her long lovely legs.

"There's no point in pretending," he persisted, "that ours is a normal relationship. I don't understand what the hell goes on between us. We *know* about each other. I *know* you need help, and badly."

"I do not," she snapped. "You have no right to intrude into my personal life."

"I've seen the warning signs in those gray eyes before—thunderstorm coming."

As if to confirm his reading, a line of rapidly moving gray clouds was sweeping down the lake like a horde of invading Mongol cavalry, turning the water green.

She relented. "Maybe we should call S'ter Alphonse Mary. She's still alive, you know."

"I know. And don't evade my point."

"No, Mickey. I don't need or want your help. There's nothing wrong with me or the gallery."

"Point two and more important. I love you."

Tears formed in her eyes. "I know."

"I want you."

"You can't have me, Mickey," she said sadly, her head bowing back into its novice pose again. "It's too late."

"It's never too late, Annie. Never."

"We are not given second chances," she whispered.

"Hell, woman," he said loudly. "We're given second chances every day of our life. We don't usually take them, but they're there for the taking."

She wiped her nose with another tissue, quickly and deftly obtained. "I'm as fond of you, Mickey, as I ever was. It still wouldn't work."

"Let me tell you a story." He began to drink the remainder of his Tab. "You remember how my mother and father were reconciled after the war? They met in Berlin and came home together. You must remember what a damn fool I made of myself. I resented Dad, mostly because of what my uncle the Monsignor, God be good to him, told me. I was the one to take care of Mom, not him."

"You were not your best in those days, Mickey," she agreed softly. "I knew you'd get over it."

"It took a long time. After I came home from Korea and was married. I mean, I was civil to them, we were friendly, but I never apologized. Then one summer evening at the lake—Janet was home with the baby—I told them I was sorry for being such a dummy and asked if they could tell me the story of what happened in Berlin. They did. It was quite a story of love and adventure, almost like a novel. I loved them both that night. And we had twenty more years of affection and respect because I had had the guts to admit my stupidity and start again."

She was crying steadily now.

He took her bare shoulders in his hands and held them tight. "I want to admit my stupidity with you and start again."

She tried to break away and then leaned her head against his chest. He stroked her hair and kissed her shoulder. Again their two personalities merged. A Michael/Anne Marie person on the warm beach, oblivious of anyone who might be watching their embrace. He held her as though she were a delicate packet of finespun Irish lace.

"I'll take care of you, Annie."

She was silent for a moment, struggling with her emotions as her chest heaved up and down. "Please, Mickey, don't break my heart any more than it's breaking already. The answer still has to be no."

He released her. It was a pretty clear response.

"Okay," he said heavily. "I'm still available if you want help."

"Thank you."

He struggled to his feet and collected the remains of their hot dogs and Tabs. "Don't get caught in the rain."

"The clouds are passing over. It's not going to rain."

He tossed the cardboard containers into a trash can and walked to the squad car. Both the cops were snoozing. Neither of them had lifeguard training.

Chicago Avenue district cops loafing on the job. At least I score some points against Jeremiah.

I still want her. She sounds pretty definite about it. Don't call me. I'll call you. What the hell is wrong! Well, I can't help her if she won't tell me.

So it goes.

Raindrops had already started to fall when he emerged from the underpass on the other side of Michigan Avenue.

25
ANNE'S STORY

I'm afraid to add this postscript to my story about Dick Murray, Dr. Murphy, because it sounds so odd. I've never told anyone about it before. You know that I'm a little psychic at times. Not always, not even usually, but once in a while. Usually unimportant things, like whether to show someone a painting. Occasionally big things—like my parents' death. I saw a plane fall from the sky the exact time their bus was hit.

It's not a big thing in my life, thank God, or it would probably drive me crazy.

Yet there is this one thing that keeps happening. I don't know whether it's important. Still, maybe I'd better tell you.

Three paragraphs to get to the point: Dick visits me.

I don't mean a ghost. He doesn't look like a ghost and he's not at all scary. It's always a pleasant experience and never when I'm frightened or in trouble, though usually before I have to make a big decision, maybe even one I don't know about.

It's happened five, no six times since 1945.

The most recent event was this summer. I was sitting on Oak Street Beach, soaking up sun (through sunscreen, of course) and reading *The Name of the Rose*. I looked up and saw him walking down the beach from the North Avenue end, as casually as he used to walk toward me at the lake when we were kids.

He was wearing his uniform, Ike jacket, and the old-fashioned overseas cap. He wasn't hazy or spooky or anything like that. Rather he was as real as anyone on the beach. He watched the sailboats out on the lake, glanced at the tall apartment buildings, stepped aside for pretty girls.

I wonder if anyone else saw him. I'm always afraid to ask.

He sat down beside me, hiking up the cuffs of his trousers so that they wouldn't pick up any sand. Then he turned toward me and smiled, the same happy-go-lucky smile that broke my heart when we were kids.

Of course, he was still a kid, younger than my Mark. And I was an old woman.

He seemed to laugh at that thought.

He never says anything. Nor do I. It isn't necessary.

He touched my face with his hand, a warm and gentle hand, and winked.

In a little while he wasn't there anymore. He didn't

disappear and he didn't walk away on the beach. He simply was no longer sitting beside me.

After it's over I am relaxed and very happy. I can never describe what happened even to myself. I guess nothing much takes place. I brush briefly against another world and it makes me happy.

A trick of my imagination, Dr. Murphy? As I reread this P.S., I tell myself that of course it is just that. Yet in the hours after such an event happens, I am convinced that ... I don't know what.

I won't even say I welcome these interludes. I know that they're a sign that there's trouble ahead for me. There's a promise of help, of course, but I can do without the trouble, especially as I don't understand what the help will be.

Now I wonder what crisis the visit this summer portends.

P.S. The attached letter arrived this morning.

Dear Mother,

I am writing this to you instead of trying to talk about it on the phone, because you would interrupt, as you always do, trying to defend yourself. You wouldn't listen to me. You never really listen to me, do you, Mother? Always defending the indefensible. So I have to put my thoughts down on paper. You can think about them and then perhaps talk to me. I will not listen to any defenses or endure any more arguments. I am telling you these things for your own good. You should take them very seriously.

It is my own kiddies about whom I'm most concerned. They are entitled to a grandmother who is like the grandmothers of their friends. They are so embarrassed by you that my heart bleeds for them. Little Lise asked me just the other day with tears in her eyes, "Why doesn't Gramma Reilly look like other grammas?"

See what you're doing, Mother, to my children.

To sum up my advice to you in three words: Act your age! You have an obligation to me and to Ted, to Mark and Teresa, and to all your grandchildren, to accept your age and not make our lives awkward by your notoriety.

I was so humiliated by that article in the Tribune Magazine *about "Chicago's Beautiful Older Women"—cheap, tawdry, exploitive male chauvinism.*

At least you didn't wear your bikini in the picture with the article. Yet that terrible strapless dress you wore to the opening night of the opera last year was almost as bad. It was like you were a Playboy bunny.

Ted, my own husband, said to me, "Next thing you know, your mother is going to be a centerfold."

Don't you have any self-respect at all, Mother? It was so awkward for us up in Door County this summer with you parading around in that swimsuit and all the men on the beach ogling you. I wanted to say something to you then, but Ted wouldn't let me.

And again poor little Lise asking me tearfully, "Why do all the men talk to Grams?"

How could I tell her that the reason men look at Grams and talk to her is that Grams has objectified herself, made herself into a superannuated sex object?

You flirt with men too, constantly, like you were a silly little teenager with false consciousness.

You even flirted with my father when I invited him and his wife to dinner. I think our family ought to be civilized, if only for the sake of my children. You deliberately embarrassed me and my father and his wife at that dinner.

As Ted said afterward, "I bet old Jim went home tonight with second thoughts."

What do you prove, Mother, by doing such things? I think it's disgraceful.

Why do you insist on keeping that contemptible gallery? As I've tried to explain to you many times, art should belong to all the people and not merely to the affluent. You cooperate in capitalist exploitation of the artists by peddling their work to oppressors.

And you don't need the money either. I think you do it merely because you enjoy exploiting people.

Face it, Mother, you're an old woman and it's time you should behave like one. Settle down, retire, move into a project for elderly people and play shuffleboard with them.

*Then you won't embarrass your children and your grand-
children and you'll enjoy the last years of your life a lot
more than you do running around the near North Side like
a young society matron and getting your picture in the
paper every couple of weeks.*

*I'm sick and tired of it, Mother, I really am. I have to
defend you almost every time Teddy and I go out to a
dinner party. I cried all the way home after a party at his
partner's the week the article appeared in the* Tribune. *I
was so crushed that my mother would expose herself to
such reactions.*

*Maybe you should see someone, Mother. A therapist, I
mean. I often have felt that you have some deep-seated
need to humiliate us. You owe it to your children and
grandchildren. I realize that you have the shanty Irish prej-
udice against psychiatry. Yet, Mother, Freud was something more than a nasty old Jew who had dirty thoughts
about children.*

*You must really do something about yourself. The
strain you impose on me is quite intolerable. Isn't it about
time you grew up?*

Beth

I have two pictures in front of me, along with Beth's
letter. One of them is an eleven-by-fourteen print from the
picture of me in the *Tribune*. I admit that I look a little like
the Empress Eugenie, but a *Playboy* bunny I am not. It's a
formal portrait of a woman in evening dress of the sort you
see in photographers' windows every day. Not a very pretty
woman. Nice dress, lots of makeup, good camera angle. But
hardly obscene.

As a girl, people thought I was pretty. That changed
long ago. I was never really attractive, much less a centerfold type. People look at me when I walk into the Arts Club
for lunch or at the Women's Athletic Club because the picture in the *Tribune* makes them think they've seen me
before somewhere.

When I say that to you, Dr. Murphy, you laugh. "No

woman ever thinks she's beautiful. Heaven help the men in her life if they don't insist to the point of exhaustion that she is."

I wonder how Beth would react if I did pose for Cathy Curran? I'm almost tempted to do it after that letter.

Her children like me, I know they do. They hang on me all the time when I'm with them, starving for the affection their mother doesn't have time to give them because she's so busy with her causes (most recently campaigning against zoos).

Is she angry at me because she has become fat and dumpy at thirty and because men look at me on the beach and not at her? She doesn't have to be fat and dumpy. She could be an extremely attractive young woman, but she seems to have contempt for that possibility, as though you can be ideologically pure only if men do not find you beautiful.

I must not permit myself to be nasty about her, no matter how much I am hurt by her letter. I love her and want her to love me back.

I'm enough of a realist to know that Beth is firmly set in her ways and not likely to ever change. The mother/daughter conflict out of which many women finally grow will make me sad till I die. We will never be the good friends that I prayed we would be for so many years. Even if I let myself become fat and ugly, she would still find fault. She has always been ashamed of me for one reason or another. She would write me other nasty letters about other failings. There is nothing I can do that could win her approval.

Now I look at the other picture, a much smaller one, to tell the truth. Bethie at two, in a white dress with a pink bow. Another pink bow holds back her short curly black hair. She is as sweet and lovely a little girl as you could possibly imagine. That's the way she looked and the way she acted back in the 1950s when we were all watching Milton Berle on TV, Bethie laughing with Jim and me, although she didn't understand the jokes.

She is my first. It was a difficult pregnancy—I was sick every morning for four months—and a terribly hard delivery. The minute I saw her sweet little girl face I knew she was worth all the sickness and the pain. So did Jim, who had wanted a boy and was disappointed when the doctor told him that he had a daughter.

I adored her. She was so cute, so lovely, so perfect. There was nothing I would not have done for her. I could not have loved her more than I did.

Where, I wonder, did I go wrong? Was I too indulgent when she was very tiny and smiled up at me in adoration when I held her in my arms? Did I make a mistake by dressing her in cute clothes and taking pride in the admiration she always won when she toddled down the street? Did I spoil her by giving her everything she wanted? She seemed so sweet and happy as a little girl. I didn't think I was spoiling her. It's so hard to know.

The divorce, I suppose. She was fifteen when we broke up, and at that age a girl will side with her father. Yet Jim was harder on her when he was drunk than he was even on poor Davie. She had developed into a very cute little teenager, forever listening to the Beatles and the Rolling Stones, whom Jim despised. In his rages he would break her records, smash her stereo equipment, and slap her brutally.

A couple of times I saw him, well, pawing her as if she were a teenage prostitute. One of the reasons I finally left him was that I was afraid of incest, not even daring then to use the word to myself.

She has never forgiven me for the divorce. Somehow it was all my fault. Maybe it was. Now that I've seen how Rita has shaped Jim up, I know what I might have done if I'd had the courage to dominate him completely. I'm afraid I don't have the character to reduce a man to timid silence.

I truly felt sorry for him that night at Beth and Ted's cottage. And for Rita too. They had no more idea that I would be there than I had that they would be coming for dinner. I tried to be friendly, to make light and carefree talk. Rita was stone silent, as she always is when I'm around. Jim tried to respond to me the same way I talked, until one expression from her froze him. So I babbled on, to fill the vacuum.

Jim was such a sad person that night. Thinner than he was when we broke up and absolutely sober, but without any of the combative energy and enthusiasm that made him attractive as a young man; a thoroughly subdued, balding late-middle-aged accountant.

If you have to browbeat a man into complete submission to keep him sober, I wonder if it's worth it.

That's a cop-out. I didn't keep him sober and Rita did. I should give her credit for helping him when I failed him.

I have to say that their three kids, two little boys and a girl, seem pretty quiet too.

Dr. Murphy said that some men want to be nagged and hassled into submission by their wives in the same way they were emasculated by their mothers. She said that even before I told her anything about Harriet Reilly. "Because they want a fat little woman to nag them all day long, it does not follow that their wives should feel constrained to accept that role."

I had not told her, either, that Jim's second wife—his only real wife if I am to believe the Catholic Church—is short and on the heavy side.

Beth blamed me for Jim's remarriage too. "You're making us illegitimate," she wailed at me. I was astonished because she was then also an advocate of complete sexual freedom and had stopped going to church when she made us take her out of Trinity after her freshman year. (She and Ted, who is Jewish, were not married in a church and she is not raising the children to be either Catholic or Jewish.) I did not understand why she would be so upset at a Catholic decision that her parents were not sacramentally married, especially as at that time she dismissed us both as war criminals.

The Church explicitly says that the children of annulled marriages are legitimate. This did not satisfy her either. "Irrelevant and oppressive male chauvinist exploitation," she snarled.

How did my sweet little tyke become such an angry, angry woman? I was her mother. It must be my fault. But where did I go wrong?

I'm sure the roots of the problem are to be found before the divorce and Jim's remarriage, probably in all the things that went wrong in our married relationship. It does not seem fair that such a poor little girl who has never done anything wrong should pay for the sins of her parents.

When did she stop liking me? She was not happy when I brought Jimmy home from the hospital and took an instant dislike to Dave. Poor Mark was not even worth noticing. She did not play the role of little mother to her younger brothers that other children seem to enjoy. Somehow I must have failed in my generosity to her if I was unable to teach her to be generous to others.

"A spoiled little brat that always must be the center of attention." Dr. Murphy said, "She resents you because she's always had to share the stage with you."

"If she's spoiled," I said, "then it's my fault for spoiling her or letting Jim do it."

"Children are in charge of their own lives," she says in reply. "At a very young age, they begin making their own choices. We influence them, but we cannot assume their responsibility."

She sounds like Sister Alphonse Mary when she talks that way and not like a Freudian analyst. Yet I was Bethie's mother, I brought her into the world, I loved her so much when she was the wonderful little tyke in that picture, and I still love the sweet little girl that's tied up inside all her anger and hatred. I want Beth to love me back.

And she never will.

26

"If your daughter's approval is so important, why not sacrifice everything for her?"

Anne hesitated before replying. "Wouldn't that be wrong too?"

"Would it?" Mary Kate waited for her answer.

"I mean, that's what I am. Wouldn't God be angry with me if I denied what I am?"

"That sounds like the self-fulfillment Catholicism you find so objectionable in your second husband."

"Non-husband."

"All right."

"Matt wasn't wrong all the time."

"Let me put it concretely, Anne. You are wearing a charcoal-gray denim shirt dress with lace insert at the cuffs and neck and matching charcoal-gray, not black, pantyhose. I think I saw the outfit in *Vogue* last month. The dress, incidentally, is becomingly low cut and has a rather close-fitting belt that makes no pretense of hiding the contours of your body. Would you expect to walk down Michigan Avenue to my office in such a dress and not attract masculine attention?"

"No."

"Just a whispered no?"

"*No!*"

"Do you want to be admired?"

"I must. Why else care about how I look?"

"Are you not willing to give up being admired by men to be approved by your daughter?"

"Women too."

"I beg pardon?"

"I want women to admire me. I couldn't come into your office looking like a pig."

"I see."

"Do you understand?"

"Of course I understand why a woman wants to look attractive. What I don't understand is why you are not willing to give up some of that vanity to win your daughter's approval."

"I'll be damned if I'll make myself look ugly so that fat little bitch can laugh at me," she exploded.

Mary Kate felt like yelling bravo.

More tears, more guilt about failing her daughter, more recriminations about her own selfishness.

27

Anne closed *The Encyclopedia of Extrasensory Perception* with trembling fingers, one of which remained inside the book.

She looked around the silent Gothic main reading room of the Chicago Public Library to see if anyone was watching her. Everyone, from very old women in gym shoes to teenagers in black jackets and leotards, was bent over a book. Not a sound or a whiff of movement disturbed the dust-filled air.

She opened the encyclopedia again, to the long and mostly unintelligible article on telekinesis. From the descriptions in the article, she seemed to have the kind of background and personality that might generate such powers. Was she like Carrie in the film that had scared her out of her wits?

Her finger was still at the paragraph that frightened her.

There is research evidence (Carlisle, Notingham, 1978) that men and especially women may experience the activation of this power at some critical turning point in their lives, even rather late in their lives, with very destructive consequences. While there is some similarity obviously with the poltergeist phenomenon (Higgins, 1958), this manifestation of telekinetic energies is dissimilar in many important ways to the poltergeist activity, which always relates to a child or early adolescent. The most notable difference is that the child or adolescent always knows what she or in some cases he is doing. The mature source of telekinetic energy, according to Carlisle, seems genuinely surprised and horrified at the results of her unintended and indeed unconscious destructiveness.

One of Carlisle's three subjects spent several years in a mental institution before being released, happily no longer burdened with the extraordinary and unwanted ability to start fires. This particular woman, it might be remarked, was in a situation where recollection of childhood offenses—real or imagined—had been suddenly and violently constrained.

Oh, my God. I lie on the couch in Dr. Murphy's office talking about charcoal-gray pantyhose when I'm starting fires and setting off explosions.

Last night she had rented a VHS tape of *Carrie* on the way home from the gallery. Inside the reassuring familiarity of her apartment she was disgusted with herself for being morbid. She permitted herself a leisurely bath, after which she put on a terry-cloth robe and watched a ballet version of the *Merry Widow* on Channel 11 in a simulcast with WFMT. The lovely music and the attractive young bodies chased away the frightening images which had invaded her head.

She turned off the TV, strolled toward the stairs, and then returned to the VHS player and, with horrified fascination, inserted the rented tape.

The film chilled her to the marrow. She wanted to turn it off, but could not move from her chair. She was not like Carrie, not a shy and neurotic daughter of a religious fanatic. Yet, as she watched the holocaust, in which Carrie wiped out most of her friends and finally herself too, she was not so sure. Carrie had wanted to get even with her classmates too.

She had stared blankly at the screen long after the film had ended. When she finally went to bed, well after midnight, she could not sleep. *Tomorrow I will visit the library and find out more about telekinesis,* she resolved. *Maybe that will help.*

Then she'd heard footsteps in the corridor, louder and more insistent than before.

Maybe it was Mickey this time too. *Oh dear God, I want to see him. If it's him, I'll tell him everything,* she had thought.

Without any thought of caution, she had thrown open the door.

There was no one in the corridor.

Now the encyclopedia article frightened her, instead of helping. It did not say that she could not kill herself or others.

She returned the book to the indifferent young woman at the call desk and slipped out of the library. Numbly she walked up Michigan Avenue. At Chicago, she paused to view the "mountain range," as she called it—five buildings which from that position seemed to be the Himalayas looming ahead of her—111 East Chestnut at one end and Water Tower Place at the other, with One Magnificent Mile, the Playboy Building, and the Hancock Center (the Everest of the range) squeezed in between. The Water Tower itself, a white stone foothill looking very tall from her perspective just beneath it, was the central peak in the panorama.

Usually this range of skyscrapers was warm and friendly, as the center peaks looked on the cover of *Travel and Leisure* magazine in the issue celebrating Chicago's birthday.

Now they seemed cold and hostile.

I wonder if I could make you shake.

The mountains did not move.

Silly, of course they won't.

Anne walked on toward her apartment.

What am I to do? Who can I turn to for help? Dear God, don't let me hurt anyone.

The last of the Kenny works would be gone in a few days, another week at the most. Maybe it would stop then.

Maybe it won't.

She paused at the corner of Walton. I'd better go on to the gallery and make sure nothing terrible has happened. She glanced at her watch and hesitated. Sandy left a half hour ago.

She was entitled to a drink tonight, a large vodka and tonic. Or maybe a pitcher of martinis. Perhaps when she was drunk she couldn't use this telekinetic power she didn't know she had.

Virtuously she plowed by the welcoming entrance of her apartment building, up another block against a stiffening early fall wind which was coming in off the lake, and turned the corner at Oak Street.

The gallery was dark, a dim light in the back, a display spot in the window on a large advance poster for Peggy Donlon. The architects seemed to have left their offices on the second and third floors.

Across the street a large crowd of people was pushing by

Häagen-Dazs on their way to the Esquire for the first film of the evening.

Do you guys know you have a superannuated Carrie on your hands?

The gallery looked fine. *Go home for your drink. No, better be sure.* She walked up the short flight of steps to the first-floor entrance—the door stoop when people actually lived in the house—and put her key in the lock.

It would not turn. She twisted it back and forth and then, with difficulty, pulled it out. *Dummy, you must have used the key to your apartment.*

But it was indeed the key to the gallery. Baffled, she tried a second time. Again it would not turn. She tried to pull it out. Now it would not budge. Stuck in the lock.

Maybe I should call Sandy.

I'll try the basement door first.

She stepped carefully down the steep cement stairs to the little-used basement entrance. In the dim light she hunted for the key that opened that door, solid oak rather than glass-paneled. She missed her key the first time through the key case and tried again. And again.

At last she found the proper key and tried to insert it carefully. It didn't fit at first try. The second time, however, the lock clicked into place and she turned the key. There was resistance in this lock too but it opened.

Hesitantly she felt the thick oak. No heat. Crazy imagination of an old woman. What would she of all people be doing with telekinetic powers?

At first she saw and heard nothing. Then she heard the sound of running footsteps, many invisible creatures this time. Cautiously she reached for the light switch inside the door.

Her hand was blown away by a blast of icy wind.

Oh, no! Not another explosion! I'll be crushed against the concrete.

Then wild screams, like the howling of the damned. She was screaming herself.

A huge cloud of smoke erupted in front of her face, engulfed her, and then swept by her up the stairs and onto Oak Street.

There were more screams, the people in front of the Esquire.

Dear God, no!

More black smoke. And more. And still more. Continuous gusts of black smoke, driven by a bitter cold winter wind.

She fought for consciousness, felt it slipping away, and then blindly staggered up the concrete steps toward the shouting chaos of Oak Street.

In the distance she heard the angry cries of fire engines.

BOOK
THREE

28

Another dream—a dull, quiet afternoon in the second grade. More empty seats than usual because many of the children were home sick with the flu. Sister teaching arithmetic on the blackboard to the bluebirds, while the redbirds, the brightest of the students, were permitted to read from supplementary readers.

Anne was tired of the supplementary reader that she had already read twice, and tired of the second grade. Some of the other children made fun of her, Sister embarrassed her by making her a pet, and the schoolwork was so easy that it did not hold her interest. She was often angry at the other children and fought with them.

Today she felt sick. She wished she'd told her mother in the morning and stayed home from school. Being sick was better than the dull monotony of the classroom.

In the dream the arithmetic class for the bluebirds was repeated over and over. The slow children were very slow that day.

She squirmed restlessly in her seat. The classroom was very warm. Why didn't Sister have one of the boys use a long pole to open the tops of the windows?

What was that funny smell?

Wearily she stared at the front of the reader again. The silly princess in the story was unbearable. She would grow up to be a smart princess.

The heat was worse. So was the smell. Now everyone in the class noticed that something was wrong. They were buzzing back and forth.

Sister's voice drifted into momentary silence. Her disciplinary control declined. The children were talking out loud.

"What is it? What's wrong? What's happening?"

Then the terrible words.

"Fire! The school is on fire!"

A tiny wisp of smoke curled through the bottom of the door.

"Let us say the Rosary," Sister exclaimed. "Pray the fire department will come and save us."

"Why didn't the fire bell ring?" someone asked.

Then the screams began.

A few of the children prayed with Sister, but she was no longer in charge of the class. Some boys pushed a table against the door to keep the fire out. Other children rushed to the cloakroom to get their coats. One big boy smashed a window with the pole. And then another window. The cold air rushed in, for a few moments cooling the room.

Then the heat became worse. The wall of the classroom facing the corridor glowed like a Christmas candle. Smoke seeped in from the other walls. It was hard to see and hard to breathe.

Finally the fire bell sounded. The children cheered; soon the fire department would come. The wall of the classroom collapsed and was replaced by a wall of thick smoke and ugly, dirty fire.

The children rushed to the windows, now screaming hysterically. She was swept along with the others toward the window. It was a long way down and she was afraid to jump. In the distance she heard the sirens. The fire trucks would be too late.

We are going to die, she thought calmly. *I deserve to die anyway for all my terrible sins. I'll say a good act of contrition and wait patiently for my death, like the early Christian martyrs.*

Some of the children jumped out of the windows. Others were caught up in the waves of flame that now invaded the classroom. Still others choked to death in the thick smoke.

Huddled at the cloakroom door, hunched down close to the floor, Anne escaped the thickest smoke and was somehow untouched by the fire.

She saw an opening in the wall where the fire had already passed and, beyond the opening, the stairwell, filled with smoke. She might be able to escape that way. The smoke was thinner the first few inches above the stairs, as it was in the classroom. If she stayed hunched over, she might be able to escape.

She shouldn't run. It was God's will that she die like Saint Joan of Arc in the flames. Everyone else was dead or had escaped by jumping to the courtyard. She was the only one left.

God was inviting her to stay, to come to heaven and be a princess with him forever.

Oh, yes, I would like to be a princess in heaven. I'll stay here and wait for You.

The smoke and fire quickly filled up her escape hole. She sighed with relief. She didn't have to make a decision. *Hurry up, God, it is very hot in here and my uniform dress is ruined. I'll have to get a new dress before I enter heaven. I must look my best when I meet You.*

Maybe they sell new dresses in purgatory. I won't have to spend much time in purgatory, will I? This fire counts for some of it, please.

Then the escape hole appeared again.

Momma and Daddy need me. My sisters are dead. I'm the only girl they have left. Momma will love me now. I'd better stay with them. Good-bye, God. You shouldn't have given me this second chance if You really wanted me this time.

I'll see You later.

Doubled over, so she could hardly see in front of her, she rushed through the hole and into the thick smoke. She held her breath, as if she were swimming, so that the ugly smoke wouldn't get into her mouth and lungs.

She ran and ran and ran, through a long dark night that she thought would never end.

Maybe I'm in purgatory already.

She felt terribly guilty for deserting her friends who were dead. Maybe she should go back to them. Maybe she was already running back to them.

God wanted her in heaven. That's why he sent the fire. No, God didn't send the fire. Someone else did.

Why am I running away from heaven? If I go there, I will be happy with God for all eternity. I'll be a real princess forever.

I can't do that. My parents need me. Connie and Kathleen are already dead. Joe and Marty will die too in the war. What am I thinking? There isn't a war yet.

Momma doesn't love me. She won't care whether I live or die. If I die, maybe she'll miss me. Yes, I want to die. I will die. I will run back to the classroom.

She plunged into the deepest, darkest part of the night through which she had been running.

And emerged into the cold gray daylight.

29

Joe Murphy held Mary Kate's typescript at near arm's length and frowned impenetrably as he read it to himself.

NOTES FOR AN ARTICLE BASED ON CLINICAL EXPERIENCE WITH A WOMAN NAMED A.
(In which I will argue that the patient A represents a normal process of sexual development for some women)

One of the major contributions feminism will make to the field of psychiatry will be to challenge the male-imposed model of sexual maturation that has for so long dominated the field. Freud assumed that physical and psychological sexual maturation occur at and immediately after puberty. The gonads begin to function, hormones are pumped through the blood system, sexual reproduction becomes a possibility, secondary sexual characteristics emerge, and a hungry and vigorous libido is unleashed as the latency period comes to a crashing end.

To a man, male psychiatrists have taken this model for granted; and, while women analysts like Karen Horney have been more flexible in applying the model to their clinical materials, they have rarely questioned whether powerful sexual longings must necessarily emerge at puberty for all healthy members of the human race. Despite substantial clinical evidence that the sexual needs of women develop more slowly than those of men and often become most powerful in early middle age, it has only been in recent years that women analysts have been willing to question in public whether "delayed" sexual development in a woman is in fact the result of an excessive repression of penis envy.

Nevertheless, as women analysts have come to enjoy greater freedom in exploring their own clinical insights, it is increasingly apparent that there are many different models of the libido development process for both men and women and that there is no need that the usual explosion of male libido at puberty be taken as normative.

The patient A is an extremely attractive woman in her early fifties with a heavy burden of responsibility for family tragedy in her childhood and the death of a sweetheart in the Second World War. Her first marriage was to a brutal man who made no efforts to arouse or satisfy her sexually, despite the fact that she provided him with four children. After her divorce from him, she had a long and intense love affair with a prominent public figure with whom she was able to experience sexual fulfillment more or less regularly, but in response to his episodic needs and not as a result of any sustained libidinous emotions of her own. After ending this relationship for religious reasons, she married a former cleric who made only weak sexual demands on her.

When this relationship was terminated, she embarked on a career in a field in which her academic training and commercial instincts were both challenged for the first time. Then she encountered a man of her own age with whom she had had a transient but intense relationship during her school days (with some possible psychic overtones). Almost immediately this woman, of whom one might have said she had minimal sexual needs, experienced a powerful flow of deep libidinous energies—despite strong religious scruples.

Can one really say that her libido previously had been undeveloped? If that were the case, how could it suddenly become so strong and healthy? Was her maturational process abnormal? How, then, can it be that in the late years of middle age her sexuality became suddenly normal?

Is it not much more useful to say rather that her sexual maturation has followed an alternative process, one more suited to her own emotional and physical needs? Do we not have a much more accurate picture of what has actually occurred in the case of A if we observe that the emergence of an active libido in her case has simply proceeded at a different rate from that of most men and many women?

While she has many rather severe emotional problems, she is hardly an incapacitated neurotic. Yet if we speak of her as undeveloped or underdeveloped sexually until her experience with her childhood friend we are certainly putting her in such a category. We would be much better advised in providing her with clinical support if we would content ourselves with asking what the circumstances were that facilitated the most recent phase of her sexual development instead of negatively labeling the earlier phases.

My clinical judgment is that a number of factors are at work: greater physical self-awareness resulting from a consistent program of exercise to maintain her physical attractiveness (of which she is not unreasonably proud), success in an exciting career in which she is her own boss, freedom from the demands of child rearing, reflection on her life in clinical treatment, appreciation and support from a sensitive clergyman of her denomination, and the passionate reaction to her of the childhood friend with whom there was long ago a rather unusual psychic bond.

If one conceptualizes A in such a fashion, one asks how treatment can reinforce a normal and healthy development in her libido and does not escape from clinical *responsibility by dismissing A as a neurotically repressed prude.*

A skilled clinician takes as a sign of growth the glow and the vitality that have marked her since the beginning of her sexual attraction for the childhood friend and does not dismiss it as a regression to adolescent "falling in love behavior." As an adult she may never have "fallen in love" before but it does not follow that either her past sexual indifference or her present sexual intensity is neurotic. The libido blows whither it wills, particularly in women.

"What do you think?" Mary Kate asked her husband, nervously twisting her fingers as she usually did when he read the preliminary drafts of her papers.

"I want the movie rights," he said with his crafty and kindly pirate grin. "It'll sell."

"Bastard," she said affectionately.

"You might add that she discovered in the anima of her lover her own anima, which was waiting to be freed."

"I am not writing for an unprofessional Jungian journal. . . . *Besides*, he discovered his anima in hers too."

Joe became thoughtful. "One thing wrong about the movie rights."

"And that is?"

"You haven't guaranteed a happy ending."

"That's the whole problem," she said wearily. "I'm not sure it's going to be happy."

30

The Reilly Gallery was closed. A small explosion had hardly been worth the newspapers' notice, but a thick cloud of smoke pouring into Oak Street at twilight was front-page headlines. Anne had announced that the gallery would be closed until further notice and that the Kenny exhibition would be available for private showing to interested collectors.

She was making a virtue of necessity. No one would browse in a gallery in which explosions occurred and clouds of smoke appeared without warning.

The future of her fiercely defended business was in grave jeopardy.

The press and TV had yet to link the phenomena with Des Kenny. No one had enough imagination to suggest that the Reilly Gallery might be haunted or possessed.

Would that help business or hurt it? she wondered. It would draw crowds of curiosity seekers by the thousands.

Would it sell art?

Is the Pope Catholic?

As Father Ryan observed, however, to His Lord Cronin, the Roman Catholic Archdiocese of Chicago had enough troubles without being called on to perform an exorcism in an art gallery on Oak Street just off the Magnificent Mile.

"And that asshole Matt Sweeney would be there with his ritual and holy water at the first hint of diabolism," the Cardinal lamented.

"What kind of a demon would be exorcised by Sweetie Mattie Sweeney?" Blackie asked, performing his usual function of reassuring the Eminence.

"True enough." Cronin finished his second cup of post-breakfast coffee and rose from the Cathedral dining room table, a board at which in various times some of the most corrupt luminaries in the Church had sat. "Do you believe in diabolic possession, Blackie?"

"The case on which *The Exorcist* was based was, according to the serious psychiatric literature, a clear example of mental illness made worse by the exorcism ceremony."

"Ms. Reilly does not seem mentally ill."

"You'd better believe it."

"Some enterprising media idiot will think of diabolic possession if this stuff keeps up," he mused, buttoning his clerical collar, quite indistinguishable from any other clerical collar—not even a hint of the sacred crimson. "And we'll be involved."

"Up to the top of your miter."

"Put a stop to it, Blackie," he ordered.

"Your Eminence's wishes are my commands."

Cronin grinned wickedly. "Especially when you've already made up your mind to do the same thing."

"But of course."

So Blackie donned his invisibility mantle and drifted into the Reilly Gallery. A clean-up crew was scrubbing the floors and walls. Ms. Kokoshka was supervising them with a Polish homemaker's zeal—presumably she scrubbed the sidewalks every morning too. Jeremiah Mullens was making himself obnoxious to Anne.

"I can't figure it out, Miz Reilly." He scratched his bald head. "Something funny sure is going on here."

"Obviously, Captain," she replied coolly.

Blackie was not so ungallant as to say that she looked unattractive. Anne Reilly in tight-fitting slacks and a Monet T-shirt always would be enough to slow down traffic. But she looked worn and beaten, an archduchess under siege.

"Not much damage either?" Mullens persisted in his subtle interrogation while police and fire types blundered around, now under serious threat from La Belle Koko when they dirtied an already cleansed area.

"As you can see, we have to clean up everything. Some of the art in the Kenny exhibition will need minor restoration. Nothing worse."

"Hmmn . . . " said the Captain significantly. "And you have no explanation for it?"

"I thought that explanations for crimes were the responsibility of the police."

"Hmmn . . . , well, yes. We have to consider the motivations for crimes too."

"Would you care to suggest an explanation"—Anne held up a dirty rag and a dirty hand—"for my motivations in creating this filthy mess? And almost choking myself to death in the stairwell last night?"

"Now, Miz Reilly." He held up his hand soothingly. "I wasn't suggesting anything like that at all."

"I'm glad," she said.

"It sure is funny that you can have a big fire in here and lots of smoke and yet nothing gets burned. . . . Oh, hello, Father Ryan. I didn't see you. What are you doing here?"

"Snooping, Captain," Blackie said blandly. "Like everyone else."

Jeremiah took his leave hastily. The priest's presence seemed to make him nervous. *Perhaps he thinks I'll suggest he go to confession,* Blackie mused, *not that I have a couple of days to spend on that bootless exercise.*

"Mike Casey the Cop been here?" he asked.

She shook her head and leaned against the edge of La Koko's desk in front of her own office.

"No, he hasn't."

By which she meant that he had not been there mostly because she had brushed him off and that he was a son of a bitch for not coming.

"Ah."

"He sent one of his aides, however, to scrape up some of the soot."

"From the little fire which wasn't there. Which aide?"

"The Mexican woman."

"Ah, Señorita Lopez."

"Deirdre." She made a funny face and then softened. "Actually she is very lovely and very sweet. And very much in awe of me. Calls me Doña Anna Maria, if you can imagine."

"I can imagine. Adores Mike, I suppose."

"I suppose. He is a very attractive man."

Long pause. Time to sail on another tack.

"What's happening, Anne?"

Her shoulders sagged. "I don't know, Father. I really don't."

"Terminate the Kenny exhibition."

"Not yet."

So he began his investigation. Looking back on it, he felt he should have insisted she get Des Kenny the hell out of her gallery. A lot of suffering and terror could have been prevented.

I am not proud of my part in the story, he reproved himself later. *I had all the clues in my hands early. Indeed, the answer was in the Marge Casey/Pat Casey correspondence, which I'd already read. I missed them all. And mostly because I permitted my prejudices against diabolic possession to interfere with my seeing the obvious solution.*

31

"I have a tough one for you, Lenny," Mike Casey told Len Mulhern, his white male driver.

"No point in wasting my talents on anything else," the short freckle-faced, red-haired young sergeant said with a wink and a grin.

Lenny was a street mick, a short, cocky loudmouth with a quick mind and a quicker tongue. With seasoning, he could easily become a captain. Sometimes Mike wondered whether he saw in Mulhern the son he had always wanted, the kind of disrespectful punk with dazzling flair that he could not help but like more than his respectful, serious sons-in-law, who treated him as if they were junior executives in the presence of a senior vice president of another corporation—not permitting themselves a hint of the blasphemous thought that the old man might be a senile fool.

"I think our kinky friend Jeremiah Mullens is up to something strange over at the Reilly Gallery."

"Yeah?" said Len, obviously interested.

"He seems too happy about that explosion, even though he can't explain how it happened."

"The last one, you mean?"

"Right ... I sniff that Jeremiah knows more about

what happened than his reports indicate. They're a little too neat for his ordinary style."

"He wouldn't do it himself," Len said thoughtfully. "He'd have some of his friends talk to some of their friends."

"Right. Find out who those friends are."

"No problem," Len said, waving his hand casually.

Most cops would ask for directions and wonder if their ass would be covered if they were caught filling such an unorthodox instruction.

"Don't get caught."

"No problem," Lenny said again. "Jeremiah out to put heat on you through this chick?"

"You speculate too much, Sergeant Mulhern," he said gruffly. "Jeremiah does kinky things not necessarily because it is to his advantage, but because it is in his nature. . . . And Len . . ."

"Yeah, I mean, yessir?"

"Not a word to Patrol Officer Lopez about this assignment."

Len winked. "Who she?"

32

ANNE'S STORY

In our wedding picture we look extremely happy. I'm demure but smiling. Jim is beaming merrily, an athlete who has won another prize. He is looking forward eagerly to deflowering his prize, which he will do, without much skill or delicacy, in a few more hours. Another big victory for Jimbo. A comeback.

We were married the week after Douglas MacArthur had come home from Korea, to local acclaim. "The country is going to toss out that goddamn hat salesman," my Jimbo said after he had cheered himself hoarse at the MacArthur parade. "He stole the election from Tom Dewey anyway. Send the fucker back to Missouri, where he belongs."

Jimbo had lost a couple of thousand dollars on a hundred-to-one bet against Truman three years earlier. Fortunately, he was too busy with his fantasies about what he would do to me—most of which he proved quite incapable of doing—to bet on a coup against Harry Truman.

I must be careful in telling the story of my marriage not to permit my anger and bitterness to obscure two important facts: I failed him at least as much as he failed me. And, because no one, anytime in my life, prepared me for marriage, neither my family nor my church nor my friends, I was utterly unready for it.

Not just sexually. While I had been told in my pre cana conference that men were the head of the family and women the heart of it and believed this quarter-truth, I had no knowledge of how men and women must adjust to live together. My only strategy was to give in on everything, which was precisely what my husband didn't need and deep down didn't want. Those things that I couldn't change by surrender I ignored. And the few things I couldn't ignore I suffered. I didn't believe that a man's authority over his wife—and I had no doubt about that authority, it was based on the Bible, wasn't it?—gave him the right to beat her. (I supposed that it did give him the right to force her physically to have sex with him whenever he wanted.) Yet I assumed that if a man did beat his wife, she had no choice but to suffer the pain and offer it up to God as a prayer that he would drink less.

Long before Dr. Murphy, I learned that if you repress your hurts and your hostilities, your resentments and your aggressions, all the time, they will erupt later like a dormant volcano. Matt Sweeney, my second "husband," was wrong in his "let it all hang out" approach to intimacy. But I didn't let anything hang out with Jim Reilly. So when I finally blew up, the accumulated anger of fifteen years tore the poor man apart.

Jim is, or was, till Rita took him over, a point-scorer. Like my Mark, he was a great high school athlete at Fenwick—four sports: football, basketball, track, and boxing—

who wasn't quite good enough to make it in college. Unlike Mark, he never found a satisfactory alternative.

Jim peaked in his senior year in high school, like Rabbit in Updike's novel. His whole life was an attempt to recapture the simple, competitive innocence of the senior football field, when his intensity and enthusiasm made up for his size and his limited intelligence.

That's pretty devastating, isn't it? I don't mean to be devastating. As a suitor he was considerate and generous and filled with fun ideas—like renting a forty-five-foot boat on Lake Michigan for a summer party in which all of us dressed as pirates. He was a superb entertainer—singer, dancer, storyteller. Some people said that if his parents (by which they meant his mother) had permitted it, he could have replaced Bob Newhart at the Holy Name Breakfasts on the West Side, from which Newhart stepped to national recognition (how many times we heard that Gettysburg address routine before it went on the hit record!). I doubt it. He was certainly funny before an audience, but he lacked the strength of character and the ambition to succeed in show business.

Even during courtship he was obsessed with scoring points. If I was late for one date, he would keep me waiting for the next one. If I wanted to see a film he didn't enjoy (like *The African Queen*), then I was forced to sit through some horrid war film he was sure I wouldn't like the next time.

"It's the only way you're going to learn, hon," he'd say by way of explanation.

What it was that I was supposed to learn was not clear to me.

He even kept me waiting in our hotel room on our wedding night for fifteen minutes while he went down to the bar for a drink, because I was fifteen minutes late at church that morning.

What happened when he did finally come to the room was hardly worth waiting for.

He lived in a world where if people did things to you, you did them back at once. Getting even was essential to life, a matter of self-defense and self-preservation. It was as natural as breathing. So too was the assumption—which Jim was incapable of questioning—that everyone was out to score points against him. The human race was composed entirely of point-scorers. No other kind of human relationship was possible. If I snapped at him at breakfast, which I did rarely, save when I had morning sickness, he would not talk to me at supper. I had tried to "get" him at breakfast. He "got" me at supper.

That's all retrospective analysis, of course. I was hardly aware of it then, though I knew what he was doing to hurt me. Every time. For I loved him, you see. Or thought I loved him. I was happy during the courtship. I knew that he needed me. He had not done well in college and had lost his first job. When he started to date me, he settled down, did well at his second job (which his parents had found for him), and cut down on his drinking.

He was still overweight and drank too much—you can see his beery stomach protruding in the wedding picture—but his mother insisted that I had done wonderfully in helping her "Jaymo" to grow up. That was what I wanted to hear.

It was much later that I learned that she had carefully selected me as the young woman most likely to restrain her errant son and had promised him a fifty-thousand-dollar present on his wedding day if he married me.

She was wrong, as it turned out. I wasn't just what her Jaymo needed.

So the beautiful young bride in the wedding picture looks happy. She had found a place in life and a mission. She had to give up her graduate work at the University of Chicago in art history because Jim didn't approve. "I'll take care of you, hon," he insisted. "It wouldn't be right for me to feel that you were obliged to have a job. What would the guys say, if you were the only wife who had to work?"

His mother feared the dangers of Communist paganism in the University of Chicago.

I finished my courses for the M.A. and the comps and then quit the program with little sense of loss. After all, I had learned at Trinity and Mundelein that a wife's career was to be found in the complete devotion of herself to her husband and children. I wanted to make that dedication of myself as totally as I could. Perhaps, I thought, it would make up for the failures of my past.

Almost everyone in my class was married already. Joan Powers was pregnant with her first child and joshed me about turning into an old-maid schoolteacher. Jimbo wanted to marry me and no one else seemed to. Why not marry him?

So we danced to the tunes of "Come On to My House" and "Getting to Know You" and "Kisses Sweeter Than Wine" at our wedding banquet (at the Drake—it was a massive event, twenty-six people in the wedding party, all but Joan and Aunt Aggie's son Tim and the bride from the Reilly side of the family). It was a little too loud and noisy for my taste, what I imagined a high school locker room would be like after a football victory—too many toasts to Jimbo, "a real winner." Yet I was sure that after we were married we would be blissfully happy.

We were intermittently happy for the first years of the marriage. Jim certainly did not tire of me as a sexual partner. He loved the children in his own roughly playful fashion. He did well in his work and went easy on the drinking. Well, easy for him. I kept my disappointments and resentments to myself.

Of course they showed up. I got even too in my own way, with silences and condescension and headaches and lack of enthusiasm and by devoting all my attention and affection to the children. I didn't think of it as getting even. Rather, I thought I was showing him that I was disappointed. It was quite beyond Jim's limited powers of empathy to hear such subtle messages.

Nor did he understand what I meant when I put on the lampstand on his side of the bed a book about women and sex. "I don't need this stuff," he said brusquely. "We're great in bed."

Great for him. Not for me. He thought he was. I knew he wasn't.

There was nothing in my Catholic background that enabled me to be blunt about sex. Perhaps just as well. It might have destroyed his image completely if I had told him he was a lousy lover.

I wonder now how much of it was caused by his size. You'll notice in the wedding picture that he's straining a bit, strong jaw jutting upward so as to give him more height. Actually, I'm a half-inch taller than Jim and no matter how low my heels, he could never quite tower over me, which was necessary for his self-image as the powerful dominant male. My veil probably added another inch in the picture. So, no matter how hard he hunched his massive shoulders or strained with his thick thighs or tilted his solid, square Irish face, he was still shorter than I in the wedding picture.

And for all of our marriage.

He could have worn elevator shoes, of course, but that would have been a violation of his male ego at least as painful as being shorter than his wife.

As a young bride, I couldn't imagine that making any difference. Now, when I see how short Rita is, I'm not so sure.

Despite all of these problems, I think we might have made it, particularly if I had insisted on family counseling and if I'd taken a stronger line with him. We were making some progress after Jimmy was born. Jim had begun to learn with some very subtle teaching how to be a better lover—not first rate, but not hopelessly unskilled. I was learning how to stand up to him and very subtly draw the line. Perhaps, most important, I was not pregnant as I had been for almost every week of our marriage (I had morning sickness on our honeymoon at Acapulco, the only time I've been out of the country save for an art dealers' convention in Montreal last year), and I was not quite so exhausted from taking care of the kiddies as I had been.

Unfortunately, none of that lasted.

I should say I enjoyed the university very much. There were occasional cracks from my fellow students and a younger professor about my being a "repressed Irish Catholic Virgin" (which were doubtless true), but they respected my work and I loved the challenge of the intellectual life.

There were only a few Catholics at the university then, more than there had been, however, in the years before the war, when Cardinal Mundelein would not even assign a priest to be chaplain for the Catholics who were students and faculty and forbade priests to attend. My teachers and fellow students viewed Catholics with the same mixture of curiosity and affection that they would have displayed for an animist from central New Guinea.

I was too innocent or perhaps too naive to find any incompatibility between studying the history of art and remaining a Catholic. Much of what we studied had, after all, been created by people who shared my faith.

I was never quite part of the University of Chicago community, not even of the small and very self-conscious group of Catholic graduate students, filled with the vision and jargon of Catholic Action, who were extremely active in university life at the time. I didn't live in the Hyde Park neighborhood, I wasn't planning an academic career (I wanted to learn more and thought that meant more school), and I was a little too chic (gloves and even hats, would you believe). I dated a couple of boys once or twice, went to a few parties, and felt dreadfully inarticulate and naive in the presence of such high-powered intellects.

"You're really quite intelligent," a doctoral candidate in English told me at a party in an apartment on Greenwood Avenue, a tone of disapproving surprise in his voice. "If only you weren't such a proper young Catholic lady."

"I see no reason to stop being either of those things," I said, which was the truth, though hardly an appropriate response.

"How dreadful," he sighed.

In those days I was too sweet to tell him that I thought he was even more dreadful in his reverse snobbishness.

If I hadn't married Jim, I might have finished my doctorate at the University of Chicago in another year or two and might have become equally dreadful. The environment could easily have swallowed me up. Maybe I was there just long enough.

I even worked up enough nerve several times to wander across the adorable little quadrangle between Goodspeed

Hall and the Divinity School and peek into Bond Chapel, a marvelous pseudo-Gothic gem. It was Protestant, of course, and I was afraid I might be excommunicated if I prayed inside. Now they have Mass there every Sunday.

The department was a colorful place in those days. We joked that the official language was Viennese, because most of the senior faculty were refugees from Germany and Austria, virtually all of them colorful wildmen. One was later fired for "moral turpitude," an offense that is utterly impossible for an academic today.

They all treated me, however, with elaborate and very Mittel-European courtesy, as though I were a great lady. One of them bowed very ceremoniously after he'd read my paper on the Virgin's dresses in Fra Angelico. "Ya, young woman, you have an absolutely first-rate mind inside of that pretty head of yours. Don't let anyone tell you differently."

I'll never forget that compliment, even if I blushed for a week after it. No one had ever suggested to me that I had a mind at all. I got good marks, but I didn't think that made me intelligent. Even today, I'm not certain.

I found the university a curiously gray sort of institution, its atmosphere—I'd say "ambience" today—well matched to the somber Gothic walls and dark corridors. When Abbot Suger of Saint-Denis designed his church, it was, I think, in a burst of exorbitant and energetic playfulness. Ralph Adams Cram's "Gray City" on the Midway was architecturally neither exorbitant nor energetic nor playful. And the work inside the Gray City was serious and determined and responsible, a little too smooth-edged and graytinged for my West Side Irish youthful spirits. My fellow students and teachers were more profoundly committed to the academic life than I was to anything besides my religion. I had no idea then that I would become an academic or at least a quasi-academic. Even now, with objective scholarly credentials that are impeccable, I am still an Irish Tinker like my great grandfather, much more at ease in the Gypsy bazaar of art peddlers than I am on my occasional visits to the ponderous respectability of my alma mater—at which, oddly enough, I am something of a folk heroine, a

boasted-about alumna who one of these years will be elected to its board of trustees, even if she is too chic and too
attractive to be taken seriously as a scholar.

However, when I bid a cheerful farewell to Goodspeed
Hall and my beloved little quadrangle, just bursting into
spring glory, I was convinced that raising children was a
more important and more fulfilling challenge than scholarship, even Gypsy scholarship. Perhaps it is. It is certainly
more difficult. But judging from the outcome, I was much
better at academic work than at raising children.

33

"It's a fucking freak show," moaned Jeremiah Mullens
disconsolately over the phone.

"Really," Casey said with a touch of resignation in his
voice. Outside, summer had disappeared, to be replaced by a
gray, rainy, unhappy autumn day. *Only a couple of days
ago I was with her on the beach,* he thought. *It was almost
ninety.*

One more summer gone. Not all that many left.

"A fucking fire with smoke and soot all over the place
and a terrible smell. Yet we can't find anything that's
burned."

"Sounds weird." Jeremiah's tune had changed since his
preliminary report. What was going on?

Pearl Crawford, his civilian secretary, appeared at
the door and shook her fists as though she were playing
castanets. Pearl had a silent signal for all the regulars who
came to the office. The castanets meant "muchacha"—Patrol Officer Lopez. He nodded that the young woman might
come in.

"Fucking freaky," repeated Jeremiah. "It kind of scares
me, Mike."

"You scared, Jeremiah? Come on."

He waved a solemn Deirdre Lopez into the office and gestured toward a chair. She sat primly on the edge. *I am going to be lectured on my obligation to go up there.*

"Maybe you guys can put it in the manual."

"Maybe the broad ought to have a psychiatric or something."

"You might recommend that, Jeremiah. I doubt that she'll take kindly to the suggestion, but it's up to you. You could, of course, ask for a court order, which would require an arrest. Do you have enough grounds for an arrest?"

"Hell, no, Mike," Jeremiah said nervously. "I mean, we thought it looked like arson at first. Now we don't know."

"Do what you have to do." He wanted to get rid of Mullens but the old pig was hanging on for dear life. And why hadn't Lenny Mulhern reported in?

"Yeah, okay, Mike. We'll kind of wait to see what happens."

Patrol Officer Lopez had not batted a pretty eyelash during the conversation. She knew who he was talking to and could probably guess what was being said on the other end of the line.

"You should go up there, Jefe," she said softly. "That lovely woman needs you."

I can reprimand her for interfering in my personal life, and that will do absolutely no good at all. Or I can try to explain. Maybe when I retire they can give me a job being a wise man for young women patrol officers.

"I think she does too, Deirdre, but she has made it quite clear that she thinks she doesn't. I figure I'd better stay away until she changes her mind."

Her lovely soft brown eyes widened. "Really? You asked her and she said no?"

"I followed your advice, young woman, and made my move. She said thanks but no thanks."

"You really made the move, Jefe?"

"Everything short of rape."

"Gosh. She's such a lovely woman too.   Why, Jefe?"

"At the risk of probing into your personal life—and I realize that, with a woman, turnabout is never fair play— you do have boyfriends, don't you?"

"Oh, sure, Jefe." She dismissed them with a casual wave of her hand. "I don't sleep with any of them, if that's what you mean."

"Your virtue is not the issue, Deirdre. When you become really serious about a man, I mean serious enough to spend your life with him, don't play the courtship ritual games of thrust and counterthrust. Tell him you're his if he wants you and leave it at that. It's the only way two people can begin with clear air and a clean table."

"I'd really have to trust a man a lot to say that, Jefe. I never thought about it. You're right, I suppose; that's the way the game should be played. . . . And she still said no?"

He nodded.

"Gosh . . . I guess I'm too young to understand."

"Do me a big favor and don't ask her why."

"Oh, no, Jefe, it's too heavy for me to mess around. She's making a mistake, though. I guess maybe she knows it. She certainly needs your help. I don't like it up there at all, Jefe. There's something strange happening. Very strange."

"I know, Dee-dee, I know. What did you find out about those charred fragments?"

"That's what I mean by something strange. The boys in forensic are scared by them. They're pieces of flooring."

"What's so scary about that?"

"They've been thickly coated with varnish recently."

"So?"

"The kind of varnish used has not been manufactured since 1940."

34

Blackie began his investigation by reading about the fire in a basement reading room at Tribune Tower—on a microchip reader, of course. Despite the machines, the room seemed like a musty cave from which the faintly corrupt odor of decaying newsprint had not yet been exorcised. The first headline said, "Fear Twenty Die in School Fire." A later edition said, "Fifty Die in Catholic School Fire." Then the last edition: "More Than Ninety Dead in Catholic School Blaze."

In those days, with no TV and little radio news, the various editions of the papers contained hour-by-hour reports of breaking news events.

Blackie tried to imagine the horror of people who saw those headlines, but it was quite impossible. Even on the pale green screen, the stories seemed to have come from another planet.

The O'Briens were prominently mentioned. The Judge was the best-known man in the parish. The tragic loss of two children was news. There were pictures of the Judge and his wife from 1933, at the Inauguration Ball in Washington, handsome, handsome people. Then the next day a picture of them coming out of their apartment building with their two grim-faced sons, both students at St. Mel's high school. A few days later there was a picture of their daughters' wake at a funeral home. A determined little girl was holding her mother's hand with fierce protectiveness.

What was going on inside your head then, little girl? What could you tell us if we called you back and asked you?

The inquest and investigation were severely critical of the fire department for not responding quickly enough and not having the right equipment, and of the staff of the parish and the school because the fire bell did not sound soon enough. Yet there were no indictments or even a suggestion of indictments. Some parents charged "whitewash," but there was little the blue-ribbon jury could recommend. The school was a firetrap perhaps—so too were most schools in those days. There was evidence of rags and varnish stowed under the stairwell, in which the fire may well have started. However, the floors of the classrooms had been varnished the week before and the painters were coming the next day to remove their equipment, which for a week had been in the stairwell next to the newspapers collected in the annual

Thanksgiving collection for the poor. The principal had refused to permit them to take away the varnish until she personally inspected every classroom.

The principal had died in the fire. Everyone knew that the nuns kept Catholic schools spotlessly clean. How could you blame a dead woman for a stairwell that had been messy for a day or two?

The pastor made a fool out of himself on the witness stand. There had been two great blessings from God. Many children had been home from school because of a minor influenza epidemic. God had saved them from death. And the fire had leaped up the stairwell to the second floor, leaving the first unscathed for a few minutes. Most of the primary grade children had been able to scamper to safety.

How odd that God would discriminate against the older children and in favor of those who were home sick.

It was easy, however, to criticize the poor man with the wisdom of hindsight, Blackie thought. What would he himself do if there were a fire in the Cathedral school? He resolved to check all the alarm systems that evening.

And as for God, someday He would have to explain many things. Nor would He be able to escape with the ploy He used on Job: "This is my world; how dare you question me?"

We Christians dare.

The papers reported that the rumors of arson continued. The pastor insisted that there was an arsonist and that the police knew who he was, a boy who had been expelled from school and had a record of arson attempts. But the jury said, "While we cannot positively exclude the possibility of arson, we could find no evidence of it."

In those days, of course, they did not have the sophisticated investigative technology that even small fire departments have today.

Father Desmond G. Kenny was hailed by the papers as the "Hero of the Mercy fire." He had anointed most of the dead and dying, consoled parents, even saved the lives of some of those who were thought to be dead and in fact still breathed. He visited all the homes of the dead that night, stayed close to the injured in the hospital, wore himself out with wakes and funerals. Judge Lawrence O'Brien issued a statement praising him as the one person "who is totally without taint in this tragedy." *Our tainted parish's solitary boast.*

In the pictures in the old papers Des looked even more frail and tiny than in his ordination photo. And his eyes gleamed more brightly. On the witness stand, when asked how he explained the fire, he replied, "God's Divine Justice punished us for our sins of the flesh."

Blackie shivered a bit and wondered how he could confirm that Kenny was with his classmates on the Thursday day off (traditional for the clergy in those days), the afternoon of the fire.

There was much more for the rest of the year, ending with some incredibly tasteless stories about Christmas in the homes of the fire victims. "God will unite us and our daughters just as He was present in the stable at Bethlehem," Judge O'Brien was quoted as saying. He had a genius for clichés all right. Yet what was the poor man to say? He was a politician and he could not refuse to talk to the press.

There were still some references to the fire the next year, a bland editorial on the anniversary, a picture of an honors student in high school who had recovered from burns—and then it faded from the press. And from the active memories of those who had not been touched by it. Most of the parents whose children had died, perhaps all of them, were now dead themselves, Blackie realized. As were many of the surviving children.

Anne Marie O'Brien was, however, very much alive. In her mind, the fire was still alive too, mentioned casually in her conversation on occasion, as on the day Sean Cronin and Blackie had visited the gallery. It was not, he was sure, merely a casual memory. Obviously, it had shaped much of her life. Not knowing what else to do, he figured he would try to learn more about what the fire meant to her.

He called the Cathedral rectory and asked the youngest of the curates when the rectory had had the most recent inspection of its fire equipment.

"The first day of school, boss. Always on the first day of school. It's a tradition in all the schools of the city."

The Catholic Church may be slow to learn, but when it learns, it learns for keeps.

He then called the school board office and received a surprisingly quick answer to his question. The nun he wanted to locate was the principal of a high school in the northwest suburbs.

He struggled through the rain and the inevitable repair work on the Kennedy and found Sister Alphonse Mary in her office at the end of the school day.

She was a vigorous and cheerful woman in her sixties, dressed in a gray suit that fit better than most nunnish gray suits. Her office was so orderly that it would frustrate the most fastidious of marine drill instructors.

"Oh, yes, I remember her very well, Father. It was my first year teaching. I was all of eighteen then, not much older than my students. We did our college work in the summertime. A lot has changed since then. I'm not sure that custom should have been abandoned. I had a lot of fun and learned a lot more about children than I would have in college."

"How did you know what to do, S'ter, I mean, Sister?" he asked, not unimpressed by the woman.

"I tried to act like the toughest nun I had when I was in junior high, which we didn't call it then. I think she was about my age. Even now Annie admits that, while they liked me, they were scared stiff of my anger. She still doesn't believe that I went back to the convent and laughed at her—all of them, of course, but especially her."

"Ah, you see Mrs. Reilly?"

"Yes, indeed, especially in the last few years. She donates money for our art scholarships, takes some of the best students on tours of the galleries downtown. Even gives us an occasional lecture. Remarkable woman."

"Surely. The memory of the fire seem to haunt her much in those days?"

"She never mentioned it, Father, never once. Some of the other nuns said that her temper explosions were because of the anguish from the fire." Sister did not seem in the least interested in Blackie's reasons for inquiring about

Anne Marie's past. Presumably the rector of the Cathedral had the need to know and that was enough.

"You disagreed?"

"I certainly did. I felt she would respond well to challenge and that neither the fire nor her father's prominence entitled her to special treatment."

"Obviously, it worked, or she wouldn't be your friend today. Tell me, Sister, was there any sign of special, uh, sensitivities on her part?"

"Now, it's strange you should ask that, Father. On the one hand, she was a loudmouthed little fighter, pretty as a picture and as tough as a tiger. On the other hand, she had a nose for people who were hurting and was extremely kind and compassionate to them, almost unnaturally so."

"Unnaturally?"

"She seemed almost too good, if you know what I mean. Her compassion was authentic, to use a word I've learned since then, but way beyond her years. I'll never forget the relationship between her and young Mike Casey, who went to the seminary. He's the Deputy Superintendent of Police now, you know."

"Yes."

"The first day he walked into the classroom there was this thing between them. I've never seen anything like it since."

"Thing?"

"Chemistry, magic, whatever. They avoided looking at each other or talking to each other. Fought whenever they could. He had the same kind of compassion too, but not enough self-confidence to show it. That's the way boys are at that age. I always hoped they'd get together later on, but they never did."

"A shame."

"Well, they might yet. They're both free now, you know. 'Course, I mind my own business."

"Come on, S'ter, you and I both know you've never minded your own business."

They both laughed. After a decent interval and a cup of tea, Blackie took his leave and fought his way back downtown in the rush-hour mess. The rain was worse than before.

So. Two psychics with a life-long link. He liked it. But he didn't like it at all.

His cousin Mike Casey the Cop had better be very careful.

There was not a chance in a billion that he would be.

35

Mary Kate pushed the record button and began to speak.

The patient's message was on my answering machine. There had been a fire at her gallery last night. She would not be able to make either of our sessions this week. She would be in touch with me next week about scheduling future sessions.

She might call and then again she might not.

I read the account on the fourth page of the Trib about her fire. Quite spectacular, smoke pouring out on Oak Street. Lèse-majesté to dirty up that stylish thoroughfare.

Minor damage, the paper said.

How the hell can you have minor damage when you produce enough smoke to scare people on Oak Street? And there had been some weird sort of explosion there last week too. The one that had caused Mike Casey the Cop (AKA "your police person") to materialize.

Weird. Truly weird.

I will read through her autobiographic sketches again and see what I missed.

I will also do a quite unconventional thing for an analyst, though typical enough for an Irish Catholic mother. I'm going to pray for her. I think she really needs it.

36

Anne trudged from the elevator to her apartment door as though she were fighting her way through a winter blizzard. She was as tired as she had ever been in her life, even when the kids were little and Davie or Mark would wake up crying in the middle of the night.

Her fingers, still trembling, fiddled with her key case. It seemed a strenuous effort to unlock the door. She opened it cautiously. No smoke inside. She stumbled into her parlor, closed the door quickly, opened it to make sure there was no one following her in the corridor, and then slammed it shut hard to make sure it was closed.

Almost furtively she locked the two extra inside locks.

Sandy had begged her to leave a half hour ago, four o'clock.

"Missus is exhausted. I will see that these incompetents finish the cleaning. Missus should go home and get good sleep. Drink martinis maybe."

Wonderful idea, Alexandra, especially about the martinis.

She kicked off her shoes, peeled off her dress, tossed it carelessly on the floor, and sank into the deep comfort of her leather couch, luxuriating in the sensuality of peach-melba underwear on cream-colored leather.

What a wonderful couch this would be on which to make love, she thought.

Her imagination was flooded with erotic fantasies, at first pleasant and comforting, then suddenly violent, demanding, monstrous.

She struggled off the couch. My God, what's happened to me? I don't have those kinds of thoughts.

Her lust receded but lingered in the back of her brain, as primitive and heedless as a winter storm on Lake Michigan. She shook her head to dispel the images. *That darn painting. I should get rid of it tomorrow. Throw out all of Father Kenny's paintings. End the exhibition.*

She had known as much that morning, but her will seemed paralyzed, unable to take any action. If she did not do something soon, she would become a prisoner of the Kenny exhibition.

She picked up her dress from the floor. She never threw her clothes on the floor either. She had always pleaded with Beth to treat dresses with respect. Beth just laughed at her.

Renee had called again today with more rumors about O'Cathasaigh. "Aren't you going to fight back?" she demanded.

"We'll see what happens," Anne replied dully.

"You taught that asshole Pete Ruben there was a market for Irish crap and now he's exploiting it."

"Maybe he'll serve Baileys Irish Cream at his openings," Anne replied curtly and hung up.

Again there was no answer in Limerick. She should fly to Ireland, like she had always wanted to do, and drag a signed contract out of the O'Cathasaigh. Since her parents' death she had been ambivalent about traveling to Europe—superstitiously afraid of flying across the Atlantic and eager to break away from the superstition. She even called a travel agent to inquire about the cost. It seemed terribly high. Yet it would be worth it if she could keep Shelaigh in the stable.

She fantasized momentarily about traveling to Ireland with Mickey, found the image quite tasty, and then quickly dismissed it.

She didn't make the reservation. She lacked the physical and moral energy to fight for Shelaigh O'Cathasaigh.

She turned up the thermostat. It would be a cool, nasty night with fog and mists swirling in off the lake. She should go upstairs and put on a robe. *Why bother?* she thought.

The phone rang. Indifferently she reached for it.

"Hello, Mom. You weren't home earlier." A tone of mild reproach. Davie seemed to expect her to be waiting at the phone for his very rare call.

"Hello, Davie, how are you? It's good to hear your voice again."

"I'm like fine, you know. But I mean, the generator isn't working and winter comes early up here, you know."

Reproof in his voice, as though she were responsible for the broken generator. The commune produced all its own electricity, mostly from sun and wind power. Anne had visited it on the same trip when she had met Jennifer's new husband. The "natural" life on the commune seemed brutally harsh, especially for the women, who, while theoretically equal, were little better than slaves, responsible for the housework, the children (of whom there were many), and the gardens. Women and children were all held in common, so Davie had no idea which of the children might be his. "We're not, you know, possessive about anything here," Davie explained. "Like no one owns, I mean, anything."

Fine, except any man could have any woman he wanted anytime he wanted and the women were too busy with the work to want any more sex than they were obliged to accept. The guru of the commune, a fat bearded man named Harold with a vast stomach rolling over the belt of his jeans, had drunk Anne in with gluttonous eyes. She suspected that if she had accepted Davie's invitation to stay overnight, Harold would have wanted to exercise his rights over her. She had quickly declined, even though it meant a bumpy ride down an uncertain road in darkness.

"I'm sorry to hear that, Davie," she now said, playing her assigned part. "How much will it cost to repair the generator?"

"Harold says like it will cost a couple of thousand dollars and, I mean, with the cost of lumber for the winter you know . . . " His voice trailed off in a plaintive whine.

"I see."

"We need it right away," he added impatiently.

Anne imagined Harold's argument: *"Rip off your mother again, she's a rich establishment parasite."*

Davie, I hardly knew you. I didn't want you. Yet you were such a nice little baby when I held you for the first time. You were never a bother, so quiet and peaceful. And so sad. What does Harold do for you that I didn't?

"I'll put a check in the mail first thing in the morning."

"We really need it in a hurry."

"I'm sure you do. Dress warmly in the cold, Davie."

"Sure, Mom. Like we need three thousand, you know."

"All right, Davie. I love you."

"Yeah, sure, Mom. Don't forget. Harold says we need it real bad."

He didn't even say thank you. He never had.

Anne shuffled into the kitchen and mixed her martinis. She was too tired to make supper. There was a bag of potato chips there somewhere. She would pig out on martinis and potato chips.

If only Bethie and I were friends. I could call her and pour out my heart.

"Divine Justice" had changed again today. The demons had the girl spread-eagled in the swamp and were plunging flaming pitchforks into her. She was writhing in pain, her face torn by agony and fear.

No one else can see the changes, so they have to be in my imagination. But they seem as real to me as does that Vermeer print on my wall. My dissertation topic—kitchenware in Vermeer's painting. She giggled. A silly exercise in academic ritualism, but kind of fun to do.

I'm becoming hysterical.

I must be doing all these things to myself. The way some of those poor people imprint traces of our Lord's wounds on their bodies. Some of them anyway.

Did the article say that mature telekinetics can do harm to themselves? No, it didn't, but then, who knows?

She slipped back into the luxurious comfort of the couch and began to eat and drink her way into oblivion.

Tomorrow I will have to do something. Close the gallery for a week or two. Have someone else get rid of the paintings and sculpture. Spend a few days with Mark and Tessie in River Forest. Maybe take a real vacation.

Lust returned, sweet and gentle. Mickey loving her on the couch. She had never experienced fantasies about lovemaking with him before. Then terrible, hateful images.

She was too tired to fight them off, would drink herself away from temptation. *Lead us not into temptation. I haven't said my night prayers. Dear God, consider them all said tonight. Please.*

She poured herself another drink.

Sometime later she staggered to her closet to find a shawl, wrapped herself in it, and collapsed back into the couch. "Pig," she muttered to herself. The potato chips were finished, there was still some liquor in the pitcher. She emptied the pitcher directly into her mouth.

"Keep this up and you'll be as fat as Beth," she said, giggling, as she went back to sleep.

Then much later she heard the phone ringing from a great distance.

She tried to ignore it. *I don't know where I am or what time it is, but something is wrong and I will not face it.*

The phone kept ringing. Reluctantly she climbed out of the deep black pool in which she had been swimming and fought her way to consciousness.

Where am I? What's going on?

Her head hurt, she was dizzy, her stomach was protesting vigorously. *I'm drunk or very sick. Maybe I'm having a heart attack. Oh, my God, I am heartily sorry. . . .*

The phone was still ringing.

I'm on the leather couch in my apartment. Half dressed. I must have drunk all the martinis in the pitcher. What's the matter with me?

The phone, yes, the phone. Coming, coming.

"Good evening, Missus, Andrej Kokoshka is speaking."

"Yes, of course, Andy." The kid sounded scared. "Something wrong?"

"Mother has not returned. Jadwiga and I experience some worry."

"What time is it?" She looked around the room, still befuddled.

"It's eleven-thirty. Mother is never this late."

"She worked terribly hard today." Anne struggled for an explanation that would reassure the young man. "Maybe she fell asleep just as I did. I'll run over to the gallery. Not to worry. I'll call you from there in a few minutes."

Dear God, did I save that poor woman only to destroy her?

I've got to pull myself together. Sober up. Figure out what to do.

Call a priest first. Just in case. Maybe she's not in the

gallery. Maybe she is. Start there. A priest, yes. Call a priest.

She didn't remember Father Ryan's number in his suite at the Cathedral. Fortunately, she had left her contact lenses in place. She found the number in her little Mark Cross phone book and punched it out on the phone.

"Cronin."

"Anne Reilly, Your Eminence." She blushed to be talking on the phone to a cardinal, half-dressed. "I was calling for Father Ryan. I think we may have more trouble at the gallery."

I hope I sounded poised and sophisticated.

"He's right here."

"Good evening. This is Father Ryan."

"Anne, Father. I'm worried sick about Sandy. Her kids just called. She hasn't come home. Never stayed this late before. Could you meet me at the gallery in a few minutes?"

"Of course." A brisk and efficient Father Ryan, no longer the dazed leprechaun.

Her next request flowed out without any reflection. Later she would tell herself that it was the martini speaking.

"Would you call your cousin and ask him to come too, if he can?"

"Mike Casey the Cop?"

"Yes, please."

"Of course. See you in a few minutes."

They'll both know I'm drunk, she thought as she struggled back into her dress.

It doesn't matter. Please, oh, please, God, don't let me have hurt Sandy.

37
ANNE'S STORY

I remember when I realized that I no longer loved Jim Reilly, if I ever had. For the first time in our marriage I stood up to him. Looking back on it, I suppose he was in the right and I was in the wrong.

It was 1954 and our marriage was improving. Beth was still resentful of Jimmy, who was a much more even-tempered and steady child than his sister and already, even as a toddler, loyal and protective of me. I was now able to sleep through the night. Jim was drinking very little and doing well on the job. I wasn't exhausted every morning. My health was good again. I had regained my figure, which I thought I might have lost forever. Our sex had some rewards for me too. We went to the movies occasionally—we saw *Roman Holiday* the week before the fight and I think we were in the process of becoming friends. Although I was under no illusions about his character anymore, I now thought that he would respond to my love and that we could make it.

The fly in the ointment was that we were practicing birth control. Or rather he was and I was going along with it because a priest told me it was all right to do that, so long as I didn't actively approve of the birth control.

It bothered my conscience because, while I did not approve of what he was doing, I certainly approved of the results: I wasn't pregnant. The house was usually quiet through the night. We had a little breathing space between babies and our marriage was improving.

Then I went to the parish mission. We had already moved into River Forest (in the house Mark owns) despite my feelings that we were not ready for the expense of the monthly payments of a big suburban house. Jim's mother had insisted that she make the down payment.

In those days, men and women made the mission separately, the women the first week. So I left Jim to watch the kids and the Army-McCarthy hearing on our tiny TV screen (at least it seems tiny now) and dutifully walked over to the church every night.

The two men, the one older with long white hair, and the other very young, almost as young as me, with a thin face and rimless glasses, were not very good preachers. Their talks were standard mission material—God's justice, damnation, bad confessions, Communism, and devotion to Our Lady of Fatima. That particular year there was also strong praise for that great Catholic hero, Senator Joseph R. McCarthy. The talks could have been given in the least-educated parish in the Archdiocese as well as ours, where everyone had gone to college.

I remember deciding that I was a snob for thinking that.

I was not receiving Holy Communion on Sundays because, while the priest had told me that I was not sinning, I did not want to take any chances that I might be.

During the mission I became more and more uneasy, especially about all the sins of my past, which I had confessed but perhaps without the kind of remorse I ought to have had.

On Thursday night, the night I planned to go to confession, the older priest gave a long, long talk on "race suicide," which was a code name in Catholic circles for birth control (that anyone could have seen the swarms of children we were producing in the fifties and think we were engaging in race suicide would now seem amusing if it were not so sad). He told us that if we were practicing birth control, we were nothing more than mutual masturbators, a phrase that caused a titter of shock among us devout women.

I made up my mind before I went to confession to the young priest (who seemed to be rather sympathetic) that I would not confess that Jim and I were practicing mutual masturbation. The priest who had given me advice—I knew him from graduate school—had sternly instructed me not to worry about it or mention it in confession.

So, with an uneasy conscience, I bravely sailed into a list of my impatiences with my husband and children, harsh words, unkind thoughts, distractions at prayer, and takings of the name of God in vain.

"How many children do you have?" Father Placid asked, for that was his singularly inappropriate name.

"Two, Father."

"And how old are they?" he demanded sternly.

"Two and a half and one and a half," I replied, knowing what was coming.

"You're not pregnant?"

"No, Father."

"You and your husband are having intercourse on a regular basis?"

"Yes, Father."

"So you're practicing birth control?"

"My husband is."

"You continue to have intercourse with him nevertheless?"

"A priest told me that it was all right."

"Madam, that priest lied to you. It takes two to commit a sin of birth control. You should refuse to permit your husband into your bedroom until he agrees not to practice birth control. Is he using artificial devices?"

"No, Father." My face was now flaming with embarrassment, and perhaps anger too.

"Aha, then he is performing an unnatural act?"

"I suppose—"

"Suppose nothing, yes or no?"

"Yes, Father."

"And you are taking pleasure in that act too?"

"Not intentionally, Father."

"Yes or no?"

"Sometimes." I did not have the courage to say that it wasn't very great pleasure.

"You know what God would be perfectly justified in doing to you?"

"Sending me to hell, Father?"

"Surely that. He would also be perfectly justified in taking your two children away from you. If He should do so, you would have no legitimate cause for complaint."

I dissolved into tears.

"God wouldn't do that."

"He might and He might not. My point is that if He chooses in His justice to do that, you would be responsible. Could you live with that responsibility?"

"No, no, no!"

Dear God, didn't I live with enough responsibility?

"Now you cry. You should have been weeping every night you luxuriated in your sinful pleasure because of the grave danger in which you were putting your children. Damn your own soul if you want, woman, do not run risks with the lives of your children!"

Shattered and broken, I promised him that I would give up our unnatural sex.

I was absolved and sent home to tell my husband that I could not sleep with him unless he agreed to complete the sex act in the natural way.

He'd been drinking, only a beer or two, but enough to make him surly when I interrupted his TV program.

"That priest is full of shit. He's probably a faggot. I'll make love any way I want."

"Not to me you won't."

He was startled, as well he might have been. It was the first time I'd ever stood up to him.

"The hell I won't."

"I will not permit you to endanger the lives of our children merely for your lustful pleasure."

"Don't tell me about lust, you frigid bitch," he shouted and slapped my face.

I ran to our bedroom, sobbing—he had never actually hit me before, not counting some of the things he did while we were making love—and locked the door from the inside. He kicked at it for a while and then gave up.

The next morning I apologized for my hysteria and proposed that we practice rhythm.

He agreed grudgingly. "All right, if you want. It won't work, but it's no skin off my ass. You're the one who will get pregnant. Not me."

Sure enough. In six weeks I was pregnant with poor innocent Davie, whom Jim despised and whom I didn't want—just as my mother had never wanted me. I was sick again and Jim was angry. The fragile structure of our marital contentment fell apart.

It was my fault for being taken in by that dreadful priest (who, I learned later, married the nun who was the superior of his parish school). I was so worried about our children and so hysterical about the others God had taken from me that I was irrational. I could have called my friend from graduate school and asked for his opinion.

I did not do that because I was angry at Jim for not trying to understand and be sympathetic. Instead of calming me down and reassuring me, he paid no attention to my feelings. He was an insensitive boor and always would be.

I got even with him. I slipped into the point-scoring game and caused terrible things to happen to our marriage and our family.

38

Rain was still falling, now a chilling mist that cut through clothes and flesh like a powerful solvent, when he slammed his car to a stop in front of the Reilly Gallery. Anne arrived at the same moment, soaked to the skin because in her panic she had forgotten raincoat and umbrella.

Blackie was already standing on the top step, in the shelter of the building, apparently dry without any help from a raincoat.

"Give me the keys," Mike barked at Anne.

She fumbled in her purse, like a drug addict compulsively searching for a hypodermic needle. "I can't find them," she cried. "I'm afraid I had too many martinis before the phone call."

He took the purse from her and searched for the keys.

"I've locked myself out of the apartment," she wailed.

"No, here they are, caught in the wallet. Steady, Anne, we'll be inside in a minute."

He held one of her arms as he opened the door. Why was she drinking alone? Something had to be done to protect her, even if she didn't want protection.

The way she leaned against him suggested that she wanted it now.

"No smoke, no fire, no explosion," observed Blackie calmly as the door swung open. "And I believe there is a light switch here."

The bare white walls and the empty stands on the first floor of the gallery made the exhibition room look like a mausoleum in a cemetery—clean, antiseptic, and dead.

Anne broke free of his supporting hand and tottered to the back of the room, paused at Sandy's desk as if she were trying to conjure up the immigrant woman's earlier presence, and then flung open the door of her own office.

"She's not here," she sobbed. "Not here. Oh, my God! What have I done to her!"

He rushed after her, put his arm around her waist as she swayed in the doorway, and eased her to the big judge's chair behind her desk. "You're drenched, Annie," he said quietly.

"Don't worry about me," she pleaded. "Find Sandy!"

"We'll find her. You stay here," Blackie said soothingly. "Come on, Mike. Let's do the basement."

"The bathroom and the dressing room first," Anne mumbled, her head collapsing to the smooth surface of the desk. "She uses it too."

The private suite in back of Anne's office was so tiny that only a woman would think of it as more than closet space, a narrow shower, a minute bathroom, and beyond them, a small dressing room with a mirror, a vanity table, a couch, and a portable screen. A light in the alley outside cast a dim, almost ghostly glow on the white couch.

Blackie, who seemed to know where all the switches were, turned on the lights. "Not much room to hide here."

"No one here, Annie," he said as they returned to her office and raced toward the basement.

Blackie paused on the landing to remove "Divine Justice." He carried it to the basement and hung it on a small stretch of wall space at the foot of the stairs. "I don't like this thing," he complained.

They searched everywhere, in the exhibition rooms, the workshops, the closets, even in the lily-decorated trash containers.

"She's not here, Mike," Blackie said tersely.

"I didn't think she would be. Someone took her on the way home. We've lost her, I'm afraid."

"She made it the last time."

"People are not that lucky twice."

"And now?"

"Call her apartment again to make sure that she's not returned since her kids phoned Anne. Then we'll put out an APB and get Anne back to her apartment. I'll drive up there and comb the neighborhood."

He nodded. "It's weird, Mike."

"Happens every day."

"On Michigan Avenue and Lake Shore Drive?"

They returned to Anne's office. She looked up hopefully from the desk, saw the expression on their faces, and began to sob again. "Dear God, I've killed her."

"This is no time for hysterics, woman," Mike ordered harshly. "Pull yourself together and call her home. Maybe she's there, safe and sound."

Anne mastered her emotions quickly and punched the numbers into her desk phone.

"Jadwiga? Mrs. Reilly. Is your mother home yet?" A cool, collected businesswoman's voice. "Now, don't cry, honey. We'll find her in a few minutes. I'll call you back."

"Anne, you have to go home and get into some dry clothes and drink a cup of coffee." Mike barked his orders before her hysteria could return. "None of your damn herbal tea. I'll put out a bulletin about her, call the local district and have them start a search. Have to drive up there myself. I'll come back and pick you up in a half-hour or forty-five minutes."

"Of course," she said briskly, in possession of herself again. "I'm sorry I'm such a mess. I don't get myself drunk this way often."

"An attractive mess," he said gruffly, wishing he could take her home himself. Much better that such a delightful task should be entrusted to a priest, who, if not immune to her appeal, could be counted on to keep his passions under tighter rein.

"What could have happened?" she asked, now seemingly quite somber and self-contained. "There was no reason to stay here after five-thirty. She was afraid to go home after the rush hour, especially when it was dark. She was almost killed the last time. . . . "

"We'll find out, Anne. Don't worry. We'll find out."

"They never caught the men who brutalized her on the L platform," she said, her voice fading.

"This isn't the last time," he replied, reaching for the phone.

"I don't think she left here," Blackie said, like a man waking from a long reverie. "She has to be in the building. . . . "

"We searched everywhere."

"I know." He shook his head. "But she's still here. . . . "

He walked to the door of the office. "Anne, is that her purse on the chair behind her desk?"

Anne ran out of the room. "Yes, it is. We missed it when we came in, because the chair is pushed in under the desk. Oh, look, Mickey, her keys. She couldn't have left the gallery without taking them along to lock the door. She has to be here."

"Or vanished from the face of the earth," Blackie said. "Come on, Mike, let's go over the rooms again."

"I'm coming with you this time," Anne insisted.

They searched under every workbench, behind every painting in the storerooms, inside every carton in the closets.

Anne sagged against the wall of the workroom. "Where can she be . . . ? My God, who moved 'Divine Justice'? "

"I did," Blackie said. "I don't like it. . . . Anne, do you keep clothes upstairs in that little suite?"

"A few things," she said, mystified. "Grubbies, a robe, a change of underwear."

"Where? There's no dresser."

"In the closet."

"We didn't see any closet, Mike, did we?"

"Oh, it's probably behind the screen. The room's so small there's no place else to put the screen except on the closet door. Do you think . . . ?"

The little priest, whose movements were always slow and seemingly indifferent, raced up the stairs as if he had been launched from a rocket.

He had thrown aside the screen and pulled the door open when Anne and Mike caught up with him. "Insanity," he shouted, "insanity!"

Mike looked over Blackie's shoulder. Inside the closet Sandy was collapsed in a heap, face and arms deathly white, her eyes staring like those of the dead.

A blast of frigid wind, as though someone had opened the door of a cold-storage locker, assaulted Mike as he lifted her out of the closet and laid her on the small couch.

"My God, Mickey, she's freezing," Anne screamed. "Is she dead?"

Blackie was already making a sign of the cross on the woman's ivory forehead. Mike searched desperately for a pulse. Sandy's wrist was so cold that he could feel nothing. He rested his head against her chest, listening for a heartbeat.

He heard a beat, low but steady, and felt a slight but regular movement in her breasts.

"Heart's still working and she's still breathing," he said.

"She's so cold," Anne said, grasping Sandy's hand.

"There's no cold in here anymore," Blackie said, darting back to the closet.

"It escaped," Mike agreed as he prepared to carry her out. "Come on, we have to get her over to Henrotin—no, Northwestern this time of night."

He took off his raincoat, wrapped Sandy in it, and lifted

her in his arms. A big, solid woman, but pleasant in his arms. *Her husband must be a fool*, he thought.

"Blackie, take your parishioner home, make her drink coffee and dress herself presentably, and then bring her over to the hospital. It might be a long night."

"Will she make it, Mickey? Will she be all right?"

"I don't know for sure." He looked at Sandy's face, in repose so like that of a peaceful child. "She has a chance."

"What could have happened to her? Where did the cold come from?"

"Perhaps," Blackie said grimly, "from the basement of Dante's hell."

39

"Looking back on it," Jimbo Reilly said, his eyes carefully examining his folded hands, "I often think she was too smart for marriage. These days maybe it's different, I don't know. But then, most women were content with home and family. Good marriage until she went to graduate school. Thought she was something special. Too smart and too much imagination to be a good wife."

Jimbo was a stoop-shouldered, bald little man with only a hint of the former athlete in his arms and chest. His office in the 111 West Washington Building was long and narrow and pin-neat, the shabby desk clear of everything but his hands and a Monroe calculator that was as obsolescent as its owner.

Jimbo was a minor accountant in a mildly successful private practice, doing uncomplicated tasks with the reformed alcoholic's compulsive reliability.

"Imagination?" Mike asked casually.

He had come to talk to Reilly on the hunch that Anne's trouble might be some sort of long-delayed revenge from her former husband. A few minutes' conversation had convinced him that he was barking up a wild goose chase, as Lenny Mulhern would have said in one of his more manic moments. There was not enough fire left in Reilly for revenge. Not even for suspicion that he might be a suspect in the explosion at the gallery.

"Dreams. Nightmares. Woke up screaming." The knuckles on his folded hands were white from pressure. Jimbo did not like talking about such incidents. "Scared me too. Fire."

"Really."

Mike was asking questions because of Lenny Mulhern's report.

They have no idea over at Chicago Avenue what caused the explosion. Jeremiah made up the sewer gas explanation to cover for you. Then when you weren't grateful, he had some friends of friends of his scatter soot all over the gallery.

Then it seems the same friends made arrangements with other friends to torch the place, make it look like an insurance arson. Apparently the Reilly Gallery has some financial problems. Figured it would really put you in his debt to cover up.

But why and how varnish from the 1930s and how explain Sandy's imprisonment? Were the friends of Jeremiah's friends that creative? Not likely.

Don't ask me why Jeremiah didn't find any evidence of arson. The friends of his friends are pros. They say they didn't do it. Everyone is scared stiff—Jeremiah, his friends, the friends of his friends, and my friends who know the friends. Anyway, I'll keep trying to break it open.

Mike's "informal chat" with Jimbo was a hunch he had followed because he felt he had to do something, a poor hunch, as it turned out.

"Mother of Mercy fire. When she was a kid. Two sisters died. Dreamed about that mostly. Should have forgotten it. Went to graduate school to run away from memories."

"There could hardly be a connection between a fire almost a half-century ago and an explosion last week, could there?" Mike asked, rising from his hard-backed chair.

"Don't see how. Lots of enemies. Temper. Second husband maybe. Religious nut. Strange woman."

They shook hands—a weak, diffident handshake from Jimbo—and Mike left the office. Watching the sunlight on the great rusty Picasso face in the Daley Civic Center, he pondered. Strange woman indeed. And intelligent. Her brief little lecture on Vermeer—flashing eyes, spinning pages, miming hands, flushed cheeks—was a masterpiece. Jimbo had it wrong. It was her mind that had kept her sane and vital despite the tragedies of her life.

Her mind and her wonderful body, he thought with a quickly banished spasm of desire.

But she had always been mysterious. Even as a girl, the first day he saw her at St. Ursula's, she'd seemed to be a bit uncanny. Why? Her temper? Her flashing eyes? The tenseness of her body?

The eyes still flashed, but the temper seemed well under control, and the body relaxed. Yet there was still a hint of mystery. Could there be a connection between the Mother of Mercy fire and what was happening today?

Stash pulled up in the squad. As Mike climbed in, he told himself that he was acting like a superstitious Irishman who had never read, much less written *Principles of Detection*.

The woman he loved always seemed a little mysterious.

Nonetheless, he would find out if there were any cops around who knew the inside story of the Mother of Mercy fire.

40

It was a long night. By 5:00 A.M., however, Alexandra Kokoshka was pronounced in serious but stable condition.

Anne Reilly, sober, chastened, and grateful to both God and Mike Casey the Cop, had been delivered to her apartment, after promising that she would stay away from the gallery and close down completely the Des Kenny show.

The aforementioned Mike Casey was by then on his way to O'Hare to take the day's first plane to National Airport for some absurd Justice Department paper shuffling, after making the unsolicited promise that he would call Annie virtually every hour.

The rector of Holy Name Cathedral was preparing to say the first Mass of the day, a responsibility the other members of the Cathedral staff felt went with his job.

The aforementioned rector wondered why, given the fact that he had discovered Alexandra, his cousin was receiving all the credit and affection.

He was not, however, all that puzzled.

He had his usual modest breakfast of melon, cornflakes and bananas and cream, bacon and eggs, English muffin with raspberry jam, and black tea.

Thereupon he retired to his modest and solitary bedroom to engage in an ancient clerical practice known as "reading the fathers." After two hours of patrology, he awakened, refreshed and invigorated and resolved to resume his investigations.

First, he called the Chancery office and informed His Lord Cronin of the previous night's events.

Silence. Then: "I'll check with the press office on how we might best conduct an exorcism."

"They'll want you to do it, with minicams from all channels present. Satan on the five o'clock news. Your friend in the Fourth Floor of the Vatican will like that."

"I bet. I thought I told you to take care of it."

"One tries, my Lord, one tries."

That was the first stop. Next he approached Anne's Aunt Aggie, who lived in a Gold Coast high-rise apartment, approximately as modest as the Taj Mahal, on the north end of the Cathedral parish.

Seated in her living room, which overlooks the lake, and sipping late-morning tea (brought by two servants as though she were the Dowager Empress), he heard Aunt Aggie on what was clearly her favorite subject—her niece Anne Marie.

"She's got more spunk than a cageful of tigers, let me tell you." Aunt Aggie was a presentably blond-haired woman, pushing eighty. "Would you believe all the terrible things that have happened to her? And she keeps bouncing right back. Gumption, I call it, gumption."

"Losing all one's family as a girl is statistically improbable," Blackie said. "But it does happen."

"I know, I know, Father. Sometimes I wonder what's wrong with us. 'Course, I haven't had any tragedies. My husband made it to eighty-two and I'll at least match him. I wonder if God had something against the O'Briens."

"Anne thinks that?"

"Sure she does, but she keeps right on plugging away."

"Did she have any premonitions about the deaths?" Blackie said, throwing the ball toward the end zone and hoping there were some receivers in the vicinity.

"Now, that's strange. How did you know that? I remember when we watched that funny plane with the three tails take off at Midway, Annie standing next to me holding on for dear life and crying her heart out. 'I'll never see them again, Aunt Aggie. I'll never see them again.' "

"Indeed."

"My sister Mary, her mother, told me that she knew before she went to the novena that her boyfriend—what was his name now? I can't remember; it doesn't matter—had been killed."

"How terrible."

"She was surprised about her brothers' deaths, come to think of it, so it doesn't work all the time."

"Father Kenny was a big help to the family, wasn't he?"

"A big pain in the you-know-what, if you ask me. Hanging around like a beaten spaniel. I think that poor Annie took care of him instead of the other way around."

"They were very close, I understand, after her parents' death, when she was going to college."

"There was that summer when he stayed in the guest house at my old place up at the lake. I didn't much like it.

Annie was forever taking in stray dogs and cats and mothering them. I didn't mind that, but I told her we should draw the line at stray priests."

"So she didn't seek him out."

"Seek him out? Ha! She was too devout to say what she thought: he was a creepy little pansy. She took care of him because he was there."

"I see. You were not worried, then, that he might, uh, be romantically interested in her?"

"She made that mistake with a priest much later. I don't know though, Father. He was a strange one. There was something in his eyes when he looked at her that was odd. Maybe he was a switch-hitter."

"Possibly. He's dead now, poor man."

"I don't think that priest she married was completely straight either," Aunt Aggie plunged on. "He needed help and Annie was a sucker for someone who needed help."

"Aha. That was probably a result of the fire trauma."

Aunt Aggie squinted her eyes, trying to remember. "Maybe, maybe not. Even as a little tyke, she was taking care of birds with broken wings and little dolls with broken arms. If I believed in any of this modern psychology stuff, I'd say that was because her Mother didn't want her. Poor Mary was terribly upset when she found she was pregnant again. Kathleen was supposed to be the last, if you know what I mean."

"Of course. Anne knew this?"

"How could she? Kids don't catch on to that kind of stuff. Mary loved her after she was born, of course, and especially after the fire."

Blackie left Aunt Aggie's private elevator feeling some distinctly unpleasant thoughts. He could not consult with his sister, Mary Kate the Shrink, because he suspected that she was the therapist about whose sex Anne was so obscure. On the basis of the facts, however, there was sufficient reason for him to think that they had on their hands a troubled woman with considerable guilt and anger and perhaps powerful psychic abilities.

He preferred that explanation to any appeal to diabolic possession. When he considered the Anne Reilly who was an active member of his parish, a successful art dealer, and, if the *Chicago Tribune* magazine is to be believed, the most beautiful "mature" woman in Chicago, he could not picture her, even subconsciously, trying to freeze poor Alexandra to death.

Or even tormenting the poor woman until they found her and saved her.

But there was not much to choose from. He began to wonder how the Archdiocesan media office would want to stage the exorcism.

Joan Powers was not much help, either. If Aunt Aggie was a charming old woman, Joan Powers was a flighty late-middle-aged bitch. It was hard to picture her as a contemporary of Anne. Moreover, as she guzzled her mid-afternoon old-fashioned in her vast and untidy home in Western Springs and he his soda water with lime, it was also clear that she had never really liked Anne. Close friends from girlhood they might be, but this fat, faded woman with the wispy hair and expensive rings resented Anne. Her house was steeped in the scent of powerful perfume, the stultifying and oppressive smell of wilting blossoms in a flower car on the way to the cemetery.

"I always thought she was her own worst enemy, Father. I told her she shouldn't marry Jim Reilly. Then I told her she should stick by the poor man. He gave her a good life—money, furs, cars, everything a man could do. He drank a little and maybe was rough at times, but, I said, our religion used to stand for cleaving to your husband, no matter what. It's been no bed of roses with Tony, let me tell you"—loud and significant sigh—"but where would we be if women ran out on their men every time the damn fools are obnoxious. Don't you agree?"

"Where indeed?"

"Like I say, I said to her, I said, 'Annie, Dick Murray is dead. He isn't ever going to come back. Maybe if he did,' I said, 'he wouldn't be the dreamboat you thought. Jimbo's your husband, not Dick,' I said, 'and he's the only husband you have.' "

"The Church didn't seem to think so."

"That annulment stuff. They were *married*, father. And she walked out on him. Rita Finnegan showed what a woman with gumption could do for poor Jimbo. Annie didn't do any better with that priest, did she? Now she's a two-time loser at her age. Who'd want her, even if she has kept some of her looks?"

"Who indeed?"

I could provide a list of a half-hundred men, headed by my cousin Mike Casey the Cop, a good catch if there ever was one, Blackie thought.

" 'Annie,' I said to her, 'you're going to have a lonely old age. One of your kids is dead, one's a permanent hippy, you've never liked your daughter,' I said, 'and they're going to catch up with that kid on the Board of Trade.' "

He did not ask who was going to catch up with Mark. Sean Cronin's friend Hugh Donlon, who was a trader, among other things, said that Mark was the best of his generation.

"It's all because of Dick Murray, Father. I fixed her up with him so that I could keep an eye on him in case I needed someone to ask me to the Fenwick senior prom. She took him away from me."

"I'm sure you went to the prom anyway."

"Certainly I did. I can't remember with whom, but that's not the point. The point is that she not only took him away from me, she went gaga over him. He was all right, Father, nothing spectacular, if you know what I mean."

Blackie agreed that he did.

"I was sorry when he died, of course. 'Life goes on,' I said to her; 'you can't carry the torch for him till the day you die.' I think she still does."

"How can an ordinary husband compete with a dead legend?"

"Huh? Well, she prays to him. Would you believe that? I said to her, I said, 'That's the most morbid thing I've ever heard of.' Don't you agree, Father?"

"We pray to some strange people."

"See, what did I tell you? She's always been hung up on religion too. I suppose you know that. I said to her, I said,

'Annie, the fire was a terrible thing but it happened a long time ago. Get it out of your mind.' I said, 'Doesn't the Bible say let the dead stay dead? . . . ' "

"Let the dead bury their dead."

"Right." She paused for a healthy swallow of Scotch. "Just what I said. You can't stay in the past. Anne lives in a haunted house, all kinds of ghosts drifting around spooking her."

Even a clock that doesn't work is right twice a day. Joan Powers had hit the nail on the head.

"Father Kenny was a big help to her, wasn't he?"

"That creep? She couldn't stand him. Really couldn't. Whenever she had trouble, he'd show up allegedly to console her with that dying-sheep look in his eyes. She'd have to dry his tears."

"She was explicit about this?"

"She sure was, as explicit as she was about ever disliking anyone. I wish Father Kenny would leave me alone. And I said, 'Brush him off,' I said, 'he's a creep.' And she says, 'I couldn't do that, the poor confused priest.' Now's she exhibiting his pictures. I said to her, I said, 'Annie, you're asking for trouble if you do that.' "

Her second accurate comment of the day. It was time to go.

"He was, ah, romantically involved with her, do you think?" he said, standing up and thanking God for a celibate commitment that had delivered him from the remotest possibility of choosing someone like Joan as a mate.

"Romantically involved? I said to her, I said, 'Honey, he can't wait to get your pants off,' not that he would be able to do anything if he did."

"Interesting."

Joan Powers lived in the past, nursing grudges from long ago because her present life was so unhappy. Posters of the Big Bands, of Betty Grable and Harry James, and of the Irving Berlin film *Stage Door Canteen* hung at cockeyed angles from the walls. Old records, movie magazines, and pictures of Clark Gable and Vivien Leigh littered her overfurnished parlor. The world has stopped for her about 1947.

When he was two years old, Blackie reflected as he

drove back to the Cathedral on North Avenue, evading rush-hour traffic. He considered the possibility that Des Kenny's restless soul might have come back to haunt Anne. While he was an agnostic on all but a few matters (a good Catholic doesn't believe very much, but what he does hold to, he holds to passionately), he couldn't in principle exclude the possibility of certain phenomena involving the dead that were beyond one's current capabilities to explain.

The Des Kenny who died at Marian was a harmless little old man who puttered around the garden and said Mass for the nuns, who prevented him from leaving out the essentials. How could he want to come back to haunt anyone?

However, the Des Kenny who painted "Divine Justice" was an angry and vindictive man.

He must have actually got Anne's pants off—to use Joan Powers's infelicitous phrase—at least once. He did paint her as the naked girl trying unsuccessfully to escape from hell, a vision of Anne's present spiritual predicament that was remarkably accurate. He also sculpted the lovely, respectful figurine that revealed the essence of her selfhood.

Could his restless spirit be hanging around the Reilly Gallery, demanding attention the way he had in the past?

Blackie doubted it. And, furthermore, if he was there in Blackie's parish what the hell was he going to do about it?

Get rid of the son of a bitch, that was what. As Anne should have got rid of him forty years ago. And as she should have dumped that prealcoholic idiot from whom Blackie just escaped.

If she dismissed the pests, she wouldn't be herself. He had to admit he liked her the way she was, pests and all. So long as she didn't dismiss the nonpests.

Most notably Mike Casey the Cop, with whom she should bed down in permanent union as quickly as was decent and even more quickly than that if possible.

And also she should surely not dismiss Blackie Ryan the Priest. Where would she find a better purveyor of the Sacred Oils at odd hours of the day and night?

Where indeed?

Was Blackie half in love with her himself?

Of course he was. He gave the impression, quite deliberately, that he was immune to the gentler human emotions. He realized that it didn't fool anyone, but it was a useful ploy. He was, however, quite capable of being smitten by appealing and helpless women.

So, sure he was captivated by Anne O'Brien Reilly. More than somewhat. The more he learned about her from his investigation, the more captivated.

That was a serious mistake. Love sometimes blinds one to the obvious.

41

"I'm all right, Mickey. I'm fine. I came over here to see to some of the arrangements for the next showing. Maria Donlon stopped by to help, Peggy's daughter-in-law. I'll go home in a few minutes.... There's nothing to apologize about. It'll be all finished in a day or two and I may go down to the beach for a weekend. Maria offered me their house for some R and R. . . . Don't be silly. I haven't time to go to Paris."

Her hand was unsteady as she hung up the phone. *A couple of weeks in Paris with you is what you mean. It would be so wonderful, even if we never left the bedroom.*

I didn't think that. Yes, you did. And you enjoyed it.

She was caught between two powerful opposing energies. On the one hand there was her love for Mickey Casey, a love that was passionate, preoccupying, and more overtly physical than any love she had ever known before. It promised her many years of joy and emotional comfort. It would be a fulfillment of something begun long ago and never finished.

On the other hand there was her fear of what she might do to him. Her other loves had been destroyed, one way or another. In the core of her self Anne was trapped in the unshakable conviction that she was fated to be an unintentional instrument of destruction: a landslide tumbling down a mountain and obliterating a ski resort, a truck whose brakes had failed careening into a school bus, a winter blizzard snuffing out the lives of motorists marooned on an expressway, a locomotive smashing a car stalled at an unguarded railroad crossing. She could bear losing Mickey if she had to lose him. She could not bear destroying him. Her physical hunger might overcome her fear of such destruction. So she had to resist that hunger and even dismiss it as the result of the other force that was tugging at her.

She could have met Maria and her cuddly little daughter Margaret Mary for lunch at L'Escargot, Maria's favorite restaurant, down the street in the Allerton. She suggested the gallery because she no longer had it within her power to stay away from the gallery. She would promise herself that she would not enter the building until Mickey came back or without Father Ryan. Yet she would find her footsteps moving irresistibly north on Michigan Avenue and west on Oak Street. There was always something to do, phone calls to make, invoices to check, shipments to monitor, buyers to placate, an occasional agent who wanted to describe the wonders of his new discovery. She could keep busy in the gallery, but she knew that she ought not be there.

Anne continued to think about flying to Ireland, but it was only a possibility that existed in a world of make-believe. How could she worry about keeping her Irish-Gypsy painter, when there were so many other things to worry about?

What was that red-haired woman's name anyway?

Half the time she would doze off, to be awakened by the telephone or the door chime, as she was when the bumptious, breezy, and uncannily brilliant Maria appeared. She was not sleeping well at night. All four of the fire dreams were now coming in the same night, five if you counted . . . the last one.

She woke up screaming several times. Had the neighbors heard? Although the walls of the old building were thick, she had a pretty powerful voice when she was of a mind to scream.

Her weariness, however, was more than merely the result of lack of sleep. She was infinitely tired, as if she had carried heavy luggage for miles and had to continue to carry it for many more miles.

All the burdens of her life, probably. Warring with her desire for Mickey was a world-weary despair, a deep and powerful current of death desire.

Thanatos, Freud called it. She should phone Dr. Murphy and make arrangements to see her next week. She could no more make that phone call than she could escape the gallery.

Her salvation, she knew, was to be found in getting rid of every trace of Desmond Kenny's work. Sending it over to the Cathedral, or to Quigley, which was even closer. She should call the seminary at Mundelein and demand they take it back. Ask the Cardinal or Blackie to remove it. Particularly "Divine Justice." She did not look at it anymore. Father Ryan had been wise to move it into the basement. She knew, nonetheless, what terrible tortures the demons were visiting on the poor girl.

The poor girl is you.

She no longer had the willpower to order Father Kenny out of her life. He was dead, yet he was still in her life, as troublesome and as perversely appealing as he had always been.

When Mickey came back and Sandy was out of the hospital, they would do it for her. She could hang on till then.

Sandy was much better and would be released from the hospital in a day or two. As always, she was pathetically grateful for attention and love. She had, however, no recollection of what had happened to her.

"I prepare to go home, Missus. Open purse. Then all is black. Is very hot, then is very cold. Then is nothing."

"Hurry back, Sandy, I need you."

"Yes, Missus. Real quick."

Anne had her lawyer wire word of his wife's illness and money for a plane flight to Colonel Kokoshka. Of course they wouldn't let him out. The bastard did not even reply.

Next week Mickey would be home from Washington and Sandy would be back in the gallery. They would make her expel Father Kenny.

It was really a battle between him and Mickey, wasn't it? All over again. She would have to decide. She made a mistake the first time. She must not do it again.

She wanted Mickey. Did she have the strength to choose either way? Or would she merely drift between one energy and the other, giving herself finally to whichever was stronger?

She prayed silently to her first love, as she did when she was in deepest need.

Dick, long ago you said you wanted me to be happy. You promised to help me, even if you didn't come back. Please ask God to help me to do what is right. Please.

In that prayer she found some peace. And some restful sleep.

Later she was awakened by a knocking on the front door. Struggling out of her chair, she stumbled into the gallery. A strangely dressed man was knocking politely but persistently in the twilight.

She waved him away. "Closed. Come back later."

The man, wearing an overcoat that was much too warm for the pleasant late-September day, continued to knock insistently but cautiously, apparently afraid of angering her.

Probably some salesman. Not doing very well or he would not be out this late. Poor man.

Nice looking man, too, she thought as she opened the door. "Yes?"

He bowed ceremoniously and kissed her hand. "Kokoshka. Just now I come from aerodrome. To see Pani Kokoshka. My wife."

"Of course. You poor man. Pani is well. You understand. Hokay?"

"Hokay," he said, probably not understanding at all.

"Come in, come," she dragged him inside. He followed her docilely.

I need someone who can take care of him after he sees

her. Where should I look? Why not the Church? What else is it for?

She punched out Father Ryan's number.

"Cronin."

"I'm sorry, Your Eminence. I was calling for Father Ryan."

"I like to sit in his room. It makes me feel important. He's not here now, I'm afraid."

She hesitated and then plunged on. "I need a Polish-speaking priest."

"I know one in Rome, lives in the Vatican palace. Has a job now, but might like working in an art gallery. Speaks pretty good English. A few other languages too."

"No, no." She explained her problem.

"Of course, Anne. I'll have someone stop over at the hospital this evening. Thanks for giving us a chance to help."

"That's what the Church is for," she said, astonished at her impertinence.

"We forget it now and then," he replied with a laugh.

She collected her purse, the light sweater she had worn, and the Colonel, who had been waiting patiently for her. The poor man had to be dead tired.

She pointed out the sights as they strode rapidly toward the Passavant Pavilion of Northwestern Hospital—"Hancock, Water Tower, Magnificent Mile, Northwestern University."

He nodded dutifully, glancing at the buildings, but never breaking his military stride.

You are an idiot for letting her get away, yet you obviously still love her. Maybe you've suffered enough.

She explained to the women at the nursing station. They nodded approval. "She's fine now, Mrs. Reilly, sleeping but doing real well," one of them said.

Anne paused at the door of the private room she had insisted on, hoping Sandy was wearing the lacy blue nightgown she had bought her.

"Pani Kokoshka." She pointed at the door.

The tall man nodded gravely. Tears were pouring down his strong square face. He kissed her hand again, took a deep breath, and opened the door. He smiled at Anne and went in. She closed the door after him and strolled down the corridor to the visitors' lounge, wiping away her own tears.

Fifteen minutes later a broadly grinning Cardinal Cronin got off the elevator.

"Couldn't find an authentic Polack," he said. "Where is this Communist?"

She led the Cardinal to Sandy's room, and knocked lightly on the door. The Colonel opened it, his face illuminated by a broad smile.

Thank God you used your head Sandy.

"Thank you, Missus," Sandy called from the bed. She was beaming happily too.

"I'm going to find him a place to sleep. He's dead tired."

"Thank you, Missus."

"Cronin," the Cardinal said, shaking the Colonel's hand.

"Kokoshka." He bowed formally.

There followed a conversation in Polish in which Cronin explained that he would find the Colonel a place to stay and Polish-speaking people to help. The Colonel was deeply if formally grateful.

"Can he see his kids? I mean like immediately? Five minutes ago? He's dying to see them, but these people are so formal and polite . . . "

"I'll drive him up. Right now."

"I will. You don't speak the language. Remember?"

When Sean Cronin turned on his reckless Irish charm, he was one of the world's most attractive men. What kind of tragedy lurked in those sad brown eyes?

"Has he figured out who and what you are?" Anne asked.

"Not yet. He'll about die. By the way, I think he's come to America to stay. His boss probably knew that when he let him go."

"Just like our ancestors," Anne said fiercely.

"Right . . . Did you send him the money to come?"

"Of course. It was the least I could do."

Cronin hesitated for a minute. "Look, Anne, this really isn't any of my business, but you've done a wonderful thing for this man and his wife, the sort of thing about which Jesus preached."

"Thank you, Your Eminence," she said, aware that, drat it, she was blushing.

"I know you have some kind of troubles and that you are in excellent hands with Blackie. . . . "

"Father Ryan is a wonderful priest, Your Eminence."

"That too . . . This comes with ill grace from a bishop. We are often in the business of hiding or obscuring the truth. Still . . . well, what I want to say, Anne, is that a woman like you has nothing to fear from the truth."

"Thank you, Your Eminence."

She watched the broad backs of the two men disappear into the elevator.

The truth! She shuddered. *Dear God, I've spent my whole life trying to escape from the truth.*

Did Dick send him as a messenger? I ask for divine assistance and the Cardinal Archbishop of Chicago shows up.

That's ridiculous superstition.

What would happen if I told the truth?

I would lose everything I have, family, friends, career, all of it. I'd lose Mickey too.

I might be free at last, free of Father Kenny and the other demons who have pursued me through the years. Yes, I would certainly be free. I've almost told the truth before. Tried to a couple of times and couldn't quite make people listen.

Father Kenny listened. Maybe that's what he's trying to do. Maybe before he is free to leave the earth and find peace he must make me tell the truth.

What is the truth?

I don't know anymore. Maybe I never did. Sometimes I wonder how much of it is a story, like the story of my magic princesses.

She walked slowly down Superior Street toward Michigan Avenue. A light breeze was blowing in off the lake. Streeterville, named after the tugboat captain around whose grounded craft the beach that now stretches from Michigan Avenue to the lake accumulated, was bustling with elegant early-autumn nightlife, gorgeous women and handsome men climbing out of cabs and limos—Mercedes, Rolls, BMWs parked and double-parked all along the street.

I'm part of that world of beautiful people now, a mature and marginal member maybe. It's the world of the living. If I tell the truth, I'll be an outcast for the rest of my life. I'll be in the world of the dead, where I belong.

Or perhaps I would be, however much a pariah, in the world of the living for the first time.

It's easy enough for you to say, Sean Cardinal Cronin. Her thoughts were furious. *You'd be the first to turn your back on me.*

42

The face that stared at Michael from the dilapidated mirror looked like that of an aging, weary gunfighter in an old Western, a cowpoke who knew his last shoot-out was at hand.

"Do not forsake me, oh, my darling," he hummed ruefully, imagining himself as Gary Cooper.

Sternly he told himself to be serious. When he thought of Annie, he acted like a love-struck teenager.

And you don't look much like Gary Cooper either.

As an afterthought he said a prayer for Grace Kelly, poor woman.

To distract himself from both love and melancholy nostalgia, he permitted himself to be angry at the foolishness of this trip to Washington. The three-day meeting was a waste of time, the food at Justice was rotten, and the hotel for which his travel expenses provided was rundown, noisy, and uncomfortable. He could afford to use his own money and stay in the Ritz-Carlton or the Madison. Cops from other parts of the country would raise an eyebrow. The Chicago papers might find out and make a big thing out of it. "Casey Junkets to Washington Again, First Class All the Way!"

After he retired next year, he would junket all around the world, and deluxe all the way too. Alone?

Not if I can help it!

The press was right about these Washington meetings. They were a waste of time. They were also essential. The Feds needed consensus from the police departments all around the country to change the crime-reporting procedures. That meant bringing in the local cops and going through the motions of consulting them—even though the Feds had already made up their mind what they were going to do.

So cops from small cities had a chance to blow off steam and drink and whore in Washington. Given to none of these pleasures, Mike had to listen and make an occasional polite remark.

It went with the job.

Why did it have to come when Anne was in trouble?

He finished shaving, dressed for breakfast and phoned Anne.

She was wide awake, as she had promised she would be, and watching the *Today* show. "Jane Pauley looks so lovely pregnant" was her first comment.

"You sound much better." Her joy crackled on the line. No, that wasn't it. He could feel her joy across seven hundred miles of countryside.

She poured out a story about Sandy's husband and the Cardinal. Love and goodness had given her a new lease on life.

"I hope you're not going to the gallery today."

"Only for a few minutes. I'm having supper with Mark and Tessie tonight."

"Fine. And you've cleared out the Kenny pieces?"

"Most of them. Sandy will be back Monday and she'll help me with the rest. You too if you want."

"I'll be delighted. I'm afraid I can't escape from this madhouse till tomorrow night. I have to eat an early supper with the Director and his wife. Big-deal Chicago cop. I'll see you Saturday morning."

"Don't worry about me. Everything is fine. The worst is over."

"I'll stay in touch today anyway. Now do what you're told."

"Yes, sir, Commissar, sir."

She did sound happy. Maybe the worst was over.

Annie Reilly was no longer an option or a possibility for him. He had to have her.

Even if I have to take her by force, he thought as he put on his jacket and walked down the steps for breakfast, disdaining the slow and dubious elevator.

Force sex on a woman, he told himself, *I could never do that.*

Make her protest strongly if she wants to refuse?

Might that not be exploitation of a lonely and troubled woman?

Hell, I'm a lonely and troubled man and she's exploiting me.

We'll see what happens on Saturday. Balance respect and strength. Not easy with an elusive woman like her.

She wants me too. I know it. I've always known it.

She can still say no if she wants to. I'll leave her alone if she does.

Deep down inside I know that she will say no.

Why? Des Kenny again. Alive or dead, the man is the enemy.

I wonder if she has moved any of that crap out of the gallery.

43

ANNE'S STORY

I triggered the eventual breakup of our marriage, not deliberately, not even unconsciously scoring points. What I did was the result of fear. I was looking for a little insurance against the end and my search for security caused what I most feared.

I went back to school in 1964 to earn my master's degree. Mark, our youngest, was in grammar school and the two oldest were already in high school. I had literally nothing to do in the morning.

I was not a frustrated suburban woman trying to renew a career to give meaning to her life.

I was a worried suburban woman, trying to make certain I could earn a living if something happened to my marriage or my husband. It was money, not self-fulfillment, that sent me to Hyde Park two mornings a week.

I had a little money from my parents, money that in my mind was set aside for the college education of the kids. I could always borrow from Aunt Aggie. The Reillys would of course take care of the children if worst came to worst. That left me with no source of regular income and no skills to earn a regular income. I couldn't live off Aunt Aggie forever.

Divorce was so far from my mind that I didn't realize Jim would have to support me even if the marriage ended.

I knew nothing about our family finances. Jim paid the bills, mine as well as his, and gave me an allowance every week. His male image required that his wife be completely dependent on him financially. He would complain frequently and loudly about how irresponsible with money I was, but he would not permit me the decisions and the information that would let me become responsible.

That's what I say now with hindsight and after some feminist reading. Then I accepted the situation as a matter of course. Daddy had paid the bills and complained about Momma's extravagances too.

We had stumbled through the fifties, somehow. Bethie ridicules that time. She says we were materialistic, complacent, racist, wasteful. I'm afraid I didn't enjoy those simple days as much as others. I did have a house, a car, fur coats, as Joan Powers was so fond of telling me. I didn't know much about racial injustice—Jim was furious about Eisenhower's use of troops at Little Rock. I had no idea where Vietnam was or that it was. I drove a car that went ten miles on a gallon of gas. I had a comfortable house on a lake and a motorboat to go with it. We spent a few days in Florida every winter.

I had all these luxuries, not necessarily because I wanted them but because my husband insisted I have them. Not to have them was a reflection on his success. Whenever I asked if we could afford something, he became angry and shouted, "Let me worry about that."

We could afford the luxuries, as I later learned, because his mother gave him a check every month, a subsidy that she took to be authorization to complain at family gatherings—they were always with his family because I had no family left—about my expensive tastes.

"It's not fair," I protested on the way home one Christmas. "You make me buy these kinds of clothes and your mother criticizes me for wearing them."

"You'd do well to imitate my mother more often," he replied. "And you know I won't tolerate a word against her."

"You tolerate her words against me," I said bitterly.

"That's a different matter," he said. "She's right."

So I worried about money and played chauffeur and den mother for the children and was active in the parish and fretted about how time was slipping away and often drank too much.

The beatings came in cycles. A couple of years would go by without any. Then, without any reason I could see, he would hit me several times in one week. Usually they were not too severe. Sometimes they were terrible. For two days after I conceived Mark, I was not able to move out of bed. I should have gone to the hospital, but I was afraid to embarrass him.

I talked to priests about it, in confession, of course, and was advised to pray for my husband and to try to be a better wife to him. One priest even said, "If a husband beats his wife, nine times out of ten she deserves it."

Many times he beat me because he claimed I was flirting with other men at dinners or parties. He wanted me to be attractive and friendly, particularly with his business partners. It was impossible for me to tell what would offend him. Some nights he would be furious because "You sat on your ass all evening and didn't say a word."

Other times he would rage and slap me because "You were acting like a goddamn whore again."

Other men did make passes at me, which I briskly rejected. I knew he slept with other women, usually, I learned later, very expensive ones. Again I was told by confessors that it was probably my fault.

The night Mark was conceived I might well have been flirting. My dress was too low-cut, I suppose, and I was drunk. There was so little sex in my life, I needed an occasional approving glance from a man to know that I was still worth looking at.

"You were offering your tits to every man at that party," he shouted as he started to beat me.

"You're not interested in them anymore," I shouted back. Those were the last words I said, other than to plead that he stop. I thought he was going to kill me. He might have. It wasn't his fault that he didn't.

The next morning, seeing my blackened face and bruised body, he muttered, "You had it coming, Annie. I hope you learned a lesson."

Looking back on the late fifties and the early sixties, I can't believe I tolerated it—he wouldn't even let me campaign for Jack Kennedy and I had to swear to him that I'd voted for Nixon. I wasn't the only upper-middle-class Catholic woman who struggled to survive husbands like Jimbo. Some had it worse than I did.

I endured because after a while our marriage seemed almost normal; it was the only one I knew, because I didn't see any alternatives, because I was afraid to risk life alone, and because I was convinced that the Church and hence God wanted me to stand by my husband, for the children's sake if for no other reason.

I'm not trying to excuse myself or to blame anyone else. I'm trying, rather, to explain what happened, and to acknowledge that much of what I suffered I brought on myself.

Shortly after the Cuban missile crisis the government investigators showed up at Jim's office. Mrs. Reilly's subsidies had not been enough for his expensive gambling habits and his expensive women. He'd been using customers' money and in the process making a mess of the customers' accounts, thus causing them to miss tax payments for which the IRS was penalizing them.

For a couple of months it looked like jail was inevitable. The company was insured against loss, of course, but my Jimbo had offended many of his partners, who wanted to see him suffer. He sobered up and was scared and earnest, even kind to me.

I was terrified because I imagined that I might have to support myself and the kids alone.

Now I think that maybe if he had gone to jail for a year or so he would have changed and we could have stayed together. I still feel we failed the children, Beth and Davie, anyway.

The troubles were smoothed over. His mother picked up the tab, as she always had. She even found another company to hire him. He celebrated his "beating the rap" with a weekend binge, during which I was frantic with worry because I couldn't find him. I didn't know then what were his favorite whorehouses.

So I went back to school, taking two classes a quarter while I worked on my paper on the early Flemish masters. I had no thought of pursuing a doctorate then—I didn't think I was nearly good enough for that. I simply enjoyed the challenge of the classroom to my dormant intelligence.

I asked Jim's permission, of course. He gave it grudgingly. "You don't seem to care what the guys will say about me. Do what you fucking want to do." The guys were his high school classmates, most of whom now avoided him.

He did not ask about my progress at school. In fact, he pretended that I wasn't going there, except when he complained about the tuition bills. His mother asked sticky-sweet questions about whether I'd become a Communist yet.

"Like Milton Friedman and George Stigler," I said, foolishly, because it made Jim angry and neither he nor his mother had any idea who those two very conservative economists were.

It was during that time that he was particularly hard on poor David and Mark and flirted incessantly with Beth. He was afraid of Jim, who was already bigger. I worried greatly about the children. It was all right to beat me, even kill me. I had enough sins to do penance for anyway. But he could easily kill the children. I pleaded with him not to hurt them. His only answer was, "You've spoiled them rotten. Someone has to teach them the meaning of life."

I graduated with my M.A. in March of 1965. My professors were very pleased with my work and recommended me for the doctoral program, even spoke of scholarship help, despite the mink coat I foolishly wore to class during the first winter.

Jim would not come to my graduation and forbade the children to do so. Jimmy wanted to come, but I persuaded him to stay home for the peace of the family.

I came home not to peace but to a bloody donnybrook. David was unconscious, bleeding from a broken nose. Mark, with one arm already broken, was huddling in the corner, while Jim beat him with a strap. Beth was locked in her room, crying. Jimmy had disappeared. The Beatles were singing "Eight Days a Week" on Davie's phonograph, the cause of the outburst, I later learned. Jimbo was too busy beating up the kids to smash the phonograph.

So when I came into the room, he pulled out the plug and threw the machine at me. The speaker cords halted the turntable in mid-flight and sent it crashing to the floor.

"How many of those Communists did you fuck today, you fucking cunt?" he screamed and tore off my blouse. I tried to run away, but he knocked me down and started in on me with the strap he'd been using on Mark. Next would come sex and then more brutality. I think he might have beaten me to death if Jimmy had not arrived with the police.

I told the officer that, yes, I would press charges and that I wanted him in jail, where he could no longer hurt my children. I took all of us to the hospital, then drove to Aunt Aggie's. I called Mrs. Reilly and told her where she could find her precious little boy.

The quiet, meek little bald man whom Rita brought to dinner at Beth's last summer hardly seems the same person as the raving maniac who beat my shoulders and back bloody the day I became a master of arts.

His mother made a much better choice the second time around.

My war was over, except for the unpleasant divorce, precisely at the time President Johnson was escalating a war which would cost me, one way or another, three of my four children.

44

Al Bender had been a priest so much longer than Blackie had that he thought Blackie's real name was "Johnny," which is what he called him throughout the last, fruitless interview of Blackie's campaign to solve the case of Anne Marie O'Brien Reilly.

Short, stocky, bronzed from the sun, with an honest and open face, Bender had recently retired after fifty years in the priesthood, and was living most of the year in Arizona. He was an artist, a musician, a craftsman, a man of taste and discretion and wit, as charming and cultivated a person as one could possibly imagine. The Church did its best not to ordain men like that in his time, and for many years after too. Doubtless he survived because he was such a nice man—and because two terms of military service kept him out of the mainstream of clerical culture during critical years in his life.

Blackie visited him in the small rectory room where he stayed when he was in Chicago, a room filled with his own paintings and photos, the latter developed by himself and both in frames he himself had made. He was poring over the score of a composition on which he was working.

"Sure, Johnny, I knew Skip Kenny. We were classmates and we both fooled around with painting, so I got to know him pretty well. I went down to the exhibit the other day. Crazy stuff, some of it not bad. Not the kind of stuff he did at the seminary."

"What did he do there, Father?"

"Hell, call me Al. You're the rector of the Cathedral, aren't you?"

"Boy rector."

He thought that was hilariously funny and offered Blackie another drink, which he declined.

"Pious stuff, fold-out magazine cover, if you know what I mean."

"Jesus with a permanent wave and Mary without breasts."

"Yeah, pretty much. Some wild colors occasionally. Mundelein liked them, though. One gory picture of Saint George and the dragon really pleased the Cardinal. Gave it to him on the Feast of Saint George. Made his career, everyone said. Between you and me, the old man didn't know much about art, despite all the stuff he bought."

The stuff he bought proved he didn't know much about art.

"Skip—that's what we called him—was an intense little guy. Worked hard, too damn hard, if you ask me. Here's one of his paintings from those days, I saved it. Not much, but it'll give you an idea."

It was a decorous Saint Elizabeth embracing a restrained Mary. The only reason to think they were women was that they both had long hair. Neither showed any sign of pregnancy.

"What changed him?"

"Why, the fire, of course. He never quite recovered from that. And Mundelein's death."

"You were with him the day of the fire?" Blackie asked, finally reaching the big question.

"Hell, yes. We were playing handball at the Chicago Athletic Club. Poor Skip tried hard at that, like everything else. He was no good at all. So I was stuck with him as a partner."

Blackie's only theory went down the drain. Skip Kenny had not started the fire.

"He was enraged when he heard the news. Said something like, 'I told that woman to get the varnish out,' and lit out for the State Street trolley. That was Skip for you. Intense and dramatic, but not much common sense. He could have got there a lot sooner in a cab. 'Course, priests didn't think of using cabs in the 1930s. Hell, it was an emergency, wasn't it? Here, let me show you something."

Bender shuffled through some files and found an old piece of paper, a yellowed clipping from a parish bulletin, headed "Divine Justice."

"I don't know why I saved this. I guess it struck me as being typical of Skip. I dug it out the other day after I saw his painting with the same title."

We may think that God does not see us when we commit terrible sins of the flesh. We may think he forgets the hideous illicit pleasures we enjoy with the sacred bodies he has given us. We may deceive ourselves into believing that there will be no day of reckoning on which we will have to pay a thousandfold in pain for every single passing moment of perverted fleshly amusement we experience. But God is just, God remembers, God punishes, God turns pleasure into pain, God uses the very organs of our sin to punish us with unspeakable suffering for all eternity. When you sin with a part of your body, which ought to be the temple of the Holy Ghost, say to yourself that someday that part of your body will become a source of eternal pain to you, so great that you will wish you could cut it off and cast it into the fire. Then it will be too late. You will suffer unbearably forever. And even if you almost escape from hell, even if you have slipped away from its raging inferno, even if you begin climbing the high hill to heaven, you will not escape. God will send the laughing demons to pursue you and to drag you back, screaming with despair to the hell in which you belong.

"He wrote that after the school fire, of course?" Blackie said.

"Hell, no. He wrote it for the parish bulletin a couple of years after he was ordained, right after he came back from Rome. The pastor was away in Florida. He was fit to be tied when he saw it."

Lovely man, Skip Kenny, Blackie thought. *Wonder what happened to him in Rome to bring that out? A crazy little guy, but harmless. Al kind of liked him.*

Could such a man come back from the dead and haunt the living? Surely we are entitled to a more impressive ghost than that.

Blackie took his leave of Al, not knowing much more than he had a couple days earlier. Except that Father Desmond "Skip" Kenny had not started the Mother of Mercy school fire.

45

Indian summer had come to Chicago, with warm windless days, crisp nights, golden light, serene and lazy sky, crystal-blue lake waters. It was Anne's favorite time of the year. Always sensitive to the weather, she was lulled by Indian summer into its own mood of lethargic and peaceful surrender.

It would be more difficult to resist Mickey if such love-inducing weather continued on Saturday. Fortunately, a cold autumn storm was forecast to roar down from Canada on Friday night.

To resist Mickey was a decision she had made as firmly as she could. She would seek his help and Sandy's to clear out the gallery on Monday morning and that would be the end of it. She'd had enough of love and enough of marriage. Her life was happy and untroubled without men in it.

Yet she was caught up in the overflow of Sandy's happiness. Jerzy, the Colonel, was not much, perhaps. Or maybe he was. Maybe Sandy had risked everything and won, something that Anne never tried. In any event Sandy had her man back and they both seemed ecstatic.

It was nice, just not for her.

The mixture of lethargy, desire, and physical exhaustion that had her stumbling around like a drunken woman befuddled her thoughts. She had lost her willpower on the subject of the Kenny exhibit and she was in the process of losing her mind about Mickey.

No, Mick. Thanks, but no thanks. Help me on Monday and then worry about the World Series.

She had lost Shelaigh O'Cathasaigh, as she knew she would. Peter Ruben had staged a press conference, with the Irish Consul General and a monsignor from the south suburbs present, to announce an expanded O'Cathasaigh exhibition in February.

"He's welcome to her," she'd told Renee bluntly. "I'm surprised she sold out that cheaply. But then, maybe she figures it's not a large enough advance so that he'll try to get it back when she doesn't deliver."

"You don't think she has any paintings?" Renee said, her voice hushed with artificial horror.

Anne knew she would be quoted and didn't care. "I have to ride herd on her every week for two months before shipment, every day the last couple of weeks. Peter won't do that. He'll have an empty gallery in February and an empty wallet."

She had not thought of that scenario before. In foretelling it to Renee, however, she realized that it was very probable. The O'Cathasaigh needed a keeper. Next year she would be back, without apologies, taking for granted that Anne was still her keeper.

Only next year Anne would be out of the gallery business, an old woman living in a coach house in River Forest, passing the day at her knitting needles, and gleefully checking off the names of her friends who had beaten her to the finish line of the grave.

Now the problem is not Shelaigh, but closing down the Kenny show. I'll need help to do that. Will I be able to ask for help? Will "Divine Justice" seal my lips? Anne wondered.

It doesn't matter. He and Father Ryan will remove the picture no matter what I say or don't say.

Automatically she answered the ringing phone. "Reilly . . ."

"Old Buttermilk Sky" again.

She slammed down the receiver.

The phone rang again. She hesitated. Perhaps it was a client. She picked it up. "Good Night Irene."

Someone was trying to drive her mad. Or was she imagining the calls? There had not been any for several days. Who could possibly know? Had she told anyone during that summer?

I must not stay here and brood, she thought. *I must get out of here, go home and have myself a good night's sleep.*

Wearily she shuffled away from her desk. The last checks had been signed. Sandy would be pleased. "Missus kept the books straight; is that not wonderful, Jerzy?"

Except that Missus forgot to put stamps on the envelopes with the checks in them.

She returned to the desk, affixed stamps with trembling fingers, and gathered up her purse. And then she spread her arms on the desk and lowered her head.

I'm not drunk, she told herself, *only tired. Maybe tonight—the weather is so nice—I'll be able to sleep. No dreams tonight.*

The door was locked. Strange, she had not locked it. No, the doorknob had turned easily in response to the pressure of her hand. The door was held shut by a powerful force. She had pushed against it with all her might.

Dear God, now I'm doing it to myself. No one will find me until I'm frozen to death. I have no children to notice that I am not home.

She resolved not to panic. Unsteadily, fighting for control despite the terror clawing at her throat, she raced through the maze of showrooms back to the comparative safety of her office. She reached for the phone, punched in Father Ryan's number, and held the phone to her ear.

It was dead, as she knew it would be. She was alone with "Divine Justice" and with her own oncoming madness.

God in heaven, Dick, someone, help me!

She heard laughter, sick, demented laughter. She spun around, looking for the source. It was behind her, in front of her, all around her.

I'm doing this to myself, she insisted firmly; this is all in my imagination. I've locked myself in.

Slowly the laughter died out.

See, I can stop it. I have stopped it.

Then the laughter returned and with it demented moans, cries of the damned from the bottom of hell. *No, no, I must stop it. I will stop it.*

How can I fight all night long? It, he, whatever, will get me eventually.

She leaned on her desk with both hands, breathing heavily. *I won't give up easily.*

There was a noise behind her. She wheeled around and screamed with lunatic terror.

Whirling around in the air was a pillar of fire, perhaps two feet long and several inches thick. It was dancing in front of her face, moving slowly in her direction.

Wailing hysterically, she fled from her office and dashed around corners and through showrooms toward the door of the gallery. The familiar lights of Oak Street had disappeared. A thick black curtain seemed to have fallen in front of the gallery. She pounded on the window, begging for help.

The pillar of fire moved inexorably toward her.

She picked up a pedestal and threw it. The pedestal paused in midair, bounced against the fire, and recoiled toward her at great speed.

She ducked. The stand flew over her head, hit the blackened window, and fell harmlessly at her feet. The pillar moved again, slowly, leisurely, closing in on her.

She was screaming now automatically, trapped in despair and fear. She was going to be burned to death. Divine justice had come out of the painting to pursue her.

Instinctively, like a deer trapped by hunters, Anne fled from the front of the gallery, dodging around the hovering flame. Hysterically she plunged down the stairs, into the workroom, and slammed the door shut.

She sank to the floor, greedily gasping for breath. The room was as black as an Egyptian tomb. *It can't come in here, I'll be all right. Mickey will phone tonight sometime. He'll call Father Ryan and I'll be saved.*

The door flew open. Easily and confidently the pillar of fire slithered into the dark room.

She waited, helpless and passive, as it drew close to her and its heat warmed her face.

She took a deep breath and then leaped under the fire and out of the door of the workroom, just as she had escaped from the blazing classroom long ago.

She locked the door, leaned against it for a moment to catch her breath, and then raced to the basement door from which the smoke had erupted a few nights before.

Behind her she heard the noise of the workroom door breaking open. She looked over her shoulder. The door was swaying violently as the pillar of fire spun into the exhibition hall and followed her.

The basement door was as immovable as the one on the first floor. She pounded furiously against it, pleading for help and mercy. The heat of the fire breathed on the back of her neck. She tried to dodge it again. It moved with her, closed in against her body, and singed the buttons on her blouse. She slipped away, leaving most of the blouse on the floor behind her, and rushed crazily up the steps and into her office. The pillar of fire followed her implacably.

She dodged into the bathroom, grabbed for the French shower nozzle, turned on the water, and aimed the jet of water at the fire. Momentarily the fire sizzled and diminished. With trembling hands she advanced on it with the shower cord.

Then the cord exploded in her hand, the water flew

around the tiny room, and the nozzle jumped out of her grasp. The fire closed in again, forcing her back toward the dressing room and closet in which Sandy had almost frozen to death.

She dodged again, refusing to be pushed into that frozen trap.

The fire moved quickly this time, closing in on her again and singeing the front of her bra. The garment disintegrated.

It's stripping me, she thought, as she ran down the stairs again, *playing with me the way a cat plays with a grasshopper.*

She slipped on the landing and tumbled down the stairs. A sharp pain stabbed through her knee and another through her shoulder. Blood streamed from her nose. Dazed and as terrified as the girl in the painting, she lay on the floor, trying desperately to think of an escape. She wanted to pray, but there were no words left in her hoarse, aching throat.

Again the heat on her back, snatching away the remnants of her blouse.

She knew what was going to happen. Until now it had all been an act. She was playing her own part, amusing her implacable foe until the time came for the conclusion of the drama.

Knowing that it was foolish, she tried to run again, stumbled a few paces, turned a corner into another alcove, and fell to the floor, hurting her other knee.

Resolutely she tried once more. She stumbled through the exhibition rooms toward the basement door, and discovered that she was lost in her own maze. Confused and uncertain, she wondered where she was and how she could find her way either to the stairs or the door. She rushed madly from room to room, becoming more hopelessly lost as she dashed through each beckoning doorway. She thought she heard footsteps following her. She wheeled and threw a Kenny painting at the fire and then fell over backward.

Anne looked up. She was directly under "Divine Justice," pushed into the small alcove where it hung—a helpless prisoner of God's wrath. She struggled into a standing position, back against the canvas.

"Please, Father, don't!" she screamed in a voice from her past.

The fire toyed with her, darting at her belly, her face, her throat. Then when she was about to faint from fright and exhaustion, the pillar of fire jabbed at her breast, lingered, danced away, and then jabbed again. She screamed with brute animal anguish as excruciating pain swept through her body.

The pillar of fire unfurled into a massive curtain that enveloped her and pushed her, shrieking for mercy, into the fire on the painting, where the other demons were waiting for her.

BOOK
FOUR

46

She wandered listlessly through the dark, silent corridor of the school. When she walked close to the drab beige walls, she heard the buzz of classroom activities. Then she would drift to the center of the corridor so that she would be isolated from the children in the classroom and feel completely alone.

She liked to feel completely alone. Then she could pretend that she and God were the only persons in the world. She would have God all to herself, like she would have her mommy and daddy all to herself when the older kids went away to college.

She sighed. There was always so much noise in the house. The boys fighting with each other, the girls fighting with each other. Boys and girls fighting. Her mommy and daddy fighting with all the kids and sometimes not being nice to each other. Some days everyone was angry at her. They called her "little brat" more often than they called her by her own name.

Well, maybe she was a little brat. When she grew up to be a great woman, they'd all be sorry. Just like Joseph in Egypt, a story she really loved. Still, she was not sure that she wanted to be sold into slavery just so she could get even with the rest of the family.

She was always the outsider—the boys, the girls, and the baby. Or the big kids, the little kids, and the baby. The baby never got to do the things that even the little kids could, like going to the movies or staying up late on vacation.

She was an outsider in her classroom too. Sister was nice to her sometimes. But not today. She had ordered her out of the classroom because she was fighting. Told her to "march right up to Sister Superior's office."

Sister Superior was the scariest person in the world, probably a very wicked demon disguised as Sister Superior. She was terrified at facing that frightening lady with her story.

"I fought with the other kids and disturbed the class because they made fun of me."

"Why did they make fun of you, young lady?"

Sister Superior always called you "young lady," although you were not nearly old enough to be a lady.

"Because my parents are rich and because Daddy's chauffeur drives us to school when the weather is cold."

"Do the classmates of your brothers and sisters make fun of them?"

"I don't think so."

"Then why do your classmates?"

"Maybe because I know the answers to all of Sister's questions. And because I ask too many questions. They think I'm a show-off."

"Are you?"

"No. "

"No what?"

"No, Sister Superior."

"Do you always put up your hand when you know an answer?"

"Yes, Sister Superior."

"And do you ask questions in school every day?"

"Yes, Sister Superior."

"Then you are a show-off and a very wicked little girl."

"Yes, Sister Superior."

"Sit down there at that desk outside my office and write 'I will not be a show-off in class' two hundred times."

As she did so, the kids and even the teachers who came into Sister Superior's office made fun of her. "The little O'Brien brat is in trouble again," one sister said.

"I don't want her in my classroom next year," said another. "She's too smart for her own good."

It was always that way. Her mommy often said, "Annie, you ask too many questions for your own good."

Especially when she asked the fascinating question of where babies come from.

Her daddy said, sometimes with a smile, "You have too much spunk for your own good, Annie."

Spunk was apparently a good thing to have, if you didn't have too much of it. She wasn't quite sure what it was.

Her classroom teacher, who liked her most of the time, said once, "Anne Marie, you know too many answers for your own good."

Kathleen had said to Connie only a few days ago, "That little brat is too pretty for her own good."

She sighed again. It would be nice if people let her worry about what was her own good.

She had been especially embarrassed the last time in Sister Superior's office because her face became warm and red very easily.

"Look at the little brat blush," said a big girl, maybe from fifth grade. "I'd blush if I had all that money while other kid's fathers aren't able to find jobs."

That made her blush all the more.

Anne definitely was not returning to Sister Superior's office, no matter what happened.

She wished she could disappear forever in the basement of the school, never to be seen again. Then they all would be sorry.

She walked into the hallway that led to church, through the place where the altar boys and the priests prepared for Mass—she couldn't remember its name—and on to the altar.

What did God think of her situation? He was probably a lot like her daddy, eager for her to receive her First Holy Communion this spring the way her daddy was usually happy when she came in from play, but also upset about all her "escapades."

Whatever an escapade was, and she wasn't quite sure; not going to Sister Superior's office, when you'd been ordered to do so, was certainly an escapade.

She talked it over with God and didn't receive a satisfactory answer. Like all grown-ups, He expected her to do what she was told, even when it wasn't fair.

I'm only in trouble when they make fun of me; and

they make fun of me because of Daddy, she thought.

That didn't seem to make any difference to God.

She sighed again, made the sign of the cross, genuflected on her left knee—she never could remember which knee to use—and left the altar.

There were a lot of matches lying around the altar boys' place. Silly careless boys. Her mommy said *never* to play with matches.

She returned to the school corridor disconsolately. Maybe the bell would ring and she could sneak out with the others. That wouldn't work. Her fight with the other girls started right after they came in from the playground. Anyway, Sister would talk to Sister Superior and find out that she had been disobedient.

It was a mortal sin to be disobedient to Sister. She would have to tell it in her first confession. What would the priest say? Would he tell her she was too wicked and too stubborn for her own good? Then her face would really become hot, even if the priest could not see it.

He'd know who she was, of course. Everyone would know that there was only one little girl in the whole parish who did not go to Sister Superior's office when she was told to do so.

The wicked little O'Brien brat who was too pretty for her own good and too smart.

She hated the girls who called her a spoiled brat. They did it all the time. She had a headache today and a stuffy nose and that made her angry. She supposed she shouldn't have pulled Betty Jane McCarthy's hair.

She hated everyone in the class for laughing at her when Sister said she was a "bold stump."

She hated everyone in the whole world. They all laughed at her and made fun of her and made her cry.

Even God. Well, sometimes.

She wished she could get even. Maybe by dying. Then they'd be sorry.

Some men were carrying ladders and cans of varnish and the cloths they used to cover desks when they painted the school. They put them underneath the staircase.

She loved the smell of varnish. It was so sweet and clean.

"The old crow won't let us take this stuff away until she inspects every floor," one of them said.

"Personally," said the other, imitating Sister Superior.

"Kind of a fire hazard to leave it all here, isn't it?"

"Her orders. Did you ever win a fight with a nun? Anyway, there isn't going to be a fire."

They walked away, not even noticing her.

Why might there be a fire?

Her daddy was very cross with her mommy once when she let the boys leave some rags soaked in turpentine in the basement. "They could burn down the whole apartment building."

Could rags soaked with paint or varnish start a fire? There was a lot of old paper and boxes beneath the stairs too. Paper burned very brightly in their fireplace at the lake.

She considered the problem. If there was a little fire underneath the stairs, the school fire alarm would go off, the kids would have to rush out in a fire drill, she could slip back into her class, and Sister would be so upset by the fire, she'd forget about her disobedience.

She went to the church, took some of the matches from the altar boys' place, and returned to the stairs. She looked carefully in either direction. There was no one in the corridor or on the stairs. Gingerly she lit a match.

"Damn," she said, a bad word her father used when a match with which he was lighting a cigar went out.

She tried again. The match went out again.

She stamped the floor in frustration. It was such a splendid idea. She couldn't do it because a silly old match wouldn't light.

She struck another match very carefully and tried to hold it steady. It flickered as if it were going to die out like the others.

She cupped her hand around it the way her daddy did. The flame steadied. *Now*, she thought.

She forgot that the matches were not very long.

"Ouch," she yelled as the fire burned the tips of her finger and thumb.

She quickly decided that maybe the fire was not such a good idea after all. She flicked the match away from her hand so it would not burn her again and threw the box on the pile of cloth covers.

The match missed the covers and landed in the papers behind them.

I shouldn't have done that. It was a very wicked thing. Now everyone will be mad.

The papers burned quickly. In a few moments there was a big blaze, like the fire in the coal furnace in their basement.

She began to run, screaming that there was a fire.

But her feet would not move. She was trapped forever in the burning building.

47

From a long distance, far away in the night, she heard a phone ring. *I don't want to answer it,* she thought. *I want to lie here and die peacefully.*

She was a mass of pain—arms, legs, chest, stomach, head. *Has Jim been beating me again?*

The phone continued to ring. *The hour is later, the day is at hand. Saint Paul. Advent liturgy. Wake up before it is too late.*

She forced her reluctant eyes open. They were heavy, as if burned by a conjunctivitis infection. They blinked closed. Once again she forced them open. She was in the basement exhibition room. All the lights were on.

She staggered toward the phone in the corner of the room. It stopped ringing as she picked it up.

She slumped back to the floor, phone in hand. What

time was it? Why had she fallen asleep on the basement floor?

The phone rang again. She looked around the room, searching for it, then discovered it in her hand. She answered it on the fourth ring.

"Reilly Gallery."

"Mother?"

"Yes, of course, Mark." She tried to sound like the brisk, competent business woman, her favorite public persona.

"We've been so worried. Tessie and I have been frantic."

"No need of that, darling," she said. "The old woman can take care of herself."

"Do you know what time it is?"

"Not exactly . . . "

"It's midnight."

"I guess I've been working so hard that I didn't notice how late I'd stayed. I'll go home now."

I don't even have enough strength to walk upstairs, much less home.

"You were supposed to have supper with us tonight, did you forget?"

Oh, dear God. Mark is the only one who loves me and I've hurt him.

Silence.

Tell the truth, Cardinal Cronin had said.

"I won't fib, Mark. I've been under a lot of strain from the Father Kenny exhibition. I fell asleep this afternoon and didn't wake up till just now when I heard the phone ring. I'm terribly sorry."

Her voice caught. Darn it, she was crying. *Why? I do have children who worry about me. I said last night I didn't. How could I have been so wrong?*

"Don't cry, Mom. I'm just relieved to know nothing has happened to you. We'll give you a rain check."

"Silly fool old woman."

"Only 'woman' applies." He laughed. "Can you come tomorrow?"

"If Teresa will let me make the salad and the dessert."

"I'll negotiate it with her. An early supper because we're going to the Notre Dame game Saturday. I'll pick you up after the market closes."

"Don't trust the absentminded old lady in a car, huh?" She tried to make a joke out of the truth.

"Not at all. I want to show off my new diesel Mercedes. See you about two at your apartment."

"Fine, darling. I'm really sorry."

As she hung up she remembered what had happened. She looked around the room. No trace of the pillar of fire. She glanced at herself. She was fully clothed, her blouse untorn. It had all been a stupid, foolish dream.

She rubbed her eyes and her head. *It's my imagination. I'm doing these terrible things to myself. I've got to get rid of the Kenny show and call Dr. Murphy for an appointment.*

Not now. I need more sleep before I try to go home.

She shoved herself off the floor and climbed weakly up the stairs to her office. She shed her slacks and blouse, wrapped herself in a blanket she kept in the closet, turned off the light, and cuddled up on the couch. *I'm so tired I don't care if I'm surrounded by demons.*

She felt a sharp pain in her right breast. Uncurling herself, she reached for the light switch. She was certain what she would see: a brand mark above her nipple, from a devil's claw.

Nothing.

48

ANNE'S STORY

I was in my middle thirties, intelligent, very well educated, attractive, and utterly lacking in any sense of how to take care of myself or my children.

I had no thought of divorce when I walked out on Jim. I knew only that I did not want ever to stay in the same house with him again, or sleep in the same bed with him. I had left impulsively, not as the result of long and careful reasoning. But I was never returning, never. As far as Aunt Aggie was concerned, the kids and I could stay with her forever. The boys did not want to return, either. Beth informed me that I was being ridiculous, but showed no inclination to run home to her father.

There followed a period of pressure for reconciliation— from his mother, his brothers and sister, Joan Powers, and then the parish priest, his mother's parish priest, of course.

"You must forgive Jim and give him another chance," Monsignor Crowley, a slick, handsome pastor of the wealthy, said smoothly. "Just as Jesus forgives you your sins. Forgive as you wish to continue to be forgiven."

"So he can have another chance to kill me or the children, Monsignor?"

I could not believe I was standing up to the Church. Maybe that was the day I began to grow up.

"Jim is sorry. He promises it will never happen again."

"I know that. He tells me every day on the phone. I don't believe him."

"Under no circumstances would you consider returning to your wifely obligations?"

"If he signs himself into an alcoholic treatment program and agrees to see a psychiatrist for a year when he is released from the program."

I knew he'd refuse or I would not have made the offer. Jimbo was terrified of anyone probing his psyche.

"It would be only fair for you to agree to therapy too," the priest said dourly.

"If I want therapy, I'll do it on my own. I'm not an alcoholic and I don't beat my children."

"Very well," he agreed. "I'll relay your offer. I wish you could be more forthcoming. You know, of course, that you require the Church's permission to live apart from your husband."

I'd had no idea of that. "I need the Church's permission

to stop him from beating me? Do you want to see what he did to my shoulders, Monsignor?"

"No, no, of course not. I mean for a long-term separation."

"Then I'll get the permission."

"For the sake of the children, I beg you to reconsider." He paused dramatically at the door of Aunt Aggie's apartment.

"For the sake of the children, I won't reconsider."

So I drove the kiddies back and forth to school every day, fretted about what I was going to do with the rest of my life, and began the process of obtaining the Church's permission to live apart—which included the right to seek a legal separation ("But not, of course, a divorce, my dear").

The first phase was "counseling" by the parish priest, our own parish priest in River Forest. The man we saw was young and looked like Father Placid. He listened carefully to both sides of the story, nodding but offering little comment of his own. He seemed unmoved by Jim's tearful pleas for one more chance.

"If you go into therapy," I insisted.

"There's nothing wrong with me," he said, remorse turning to anger. "I can pull myself together if I can only get a little bit of help and encouragement from you. You're quite a cold woman, you know, Anne."

"Mrs. Reilly's request does not seem unreasonable," the priest said guardedly.

"Are you on her side, Father?" Jimbo exploded. "What's this, a setup? My mother's priest, Monsignor Crowley, says she should come back and be a good wife to me for a change."

"I'm not Monsignor Crowley, Mr. Reilly," the young priest replied calmly. "And I'm on no one's side. I'm simply saying that under the circumstances her request does not seem unreasonable."

"No one is going to shrink my head!" Jimbo exclaimed.

Later the young priest was interviewing me alone. "Do you intend to remarry, Mrs. Reilly?"

"Of course not, Father," I said, startled. "The Church does not permit remarriage after divorce."

"You're a young and attractive woman. Your children will be raised in a few years. There will be men who will want to marry you."

"Once is enough."

"You must not judge the whole male half of the human race by your husband."

"I won't break the Church's law, Father. The sacraments are too important to me."

"If you are firm in that resolve, your life might be very lonely."

"Are you suggesting I go back to Jim so I won't be lonely, Father? Believe me, I'd much rather be lonely."

"No, Mrs. Reilly, I'm not suggesting that at all. In fact, I think you're quite right in insisting on long-term therapy for your husband. Of course, you know as well as I do that he won't accept that condition. I'm merely worrying about your future. There is, as you know, not a chance of an annulment under the present legislation. . . ."

"I don't want an annulment, Father. Jim and I were married."

The proceedings at the chancery office separation court tribunal were more legalistic and unsympathetic. The priests who take care of such matters, Father Ryan told me later, must hide their emotions behind the mask of formalism, lest they lose their minds. It did not take them long to recognize that ours was a case in which there was no hope of reconciliation.

Then one afternoon, when I had driven the kids home from school, there was a process server waiting for me at the entrance to Aunt Aggie's apartment.

Jim was suing me for divorce, charging desertion and adultery, and demanding custody of the children. He and his mother had not waited till the Church gave us permission to separate.

"He's a damn fool," Aunt Aggie raged. "And she's worse. They'll never get away with it."

"What can I do, Aunt Aggie? I'm all alone."

"The first thing you can do is get yourself a lawyer. If you weren't a damn fool too, you would have done that the day you moved out of the house."

So I met Ned Ryan, a kind quiet little man with silver hair and a crystal blue smile to match his eyes.

"I don't even have to ask you whether the adultery charge is untrue," he said after I had told my story. "I know it is."

"Not that I didn't have the opportunities . . . " I said, feeling the need to defend my theoretical possibilities.

He smiled, a shrewd, kindly smile that I came to admire and respect. "Hardly . . . they will, of course, make a good deal out of the fact that you left the day you received your master's degree."

"I'll pay him back for the tuition."

"No, you won't. The testimony of the doctors who treated you and your children will be quite sufficient to wipe out that nonsense. We will win enough support for you to complete your children's education and to provide a comfortable life for yourself."

"And the children themselves?"

"Mrs. Reilly has overreached. They don't have a chance to win custody."

"I don't want support for myself. I'm going back to finish my doctorate—I can take care of myself. . . . " I faltered because I was not at all sure that I could.

"Nevertheless, we'll get you something until you finish your degree or until you remarry."

"I'll never remarry, Mr. Ryan. I'm a Catholic."

"Of course. . . . May I say I'm sorry, Mrs. Reilly?"

"Sorry?"

"For all the pain you've had and all you will have."

So I began to grow up, to learn how to take care of myself, to make my own budgets, to pay my own bills, to plan my own life. It was hellish. I was on my own, alone and scared stiff. There was no family to help me, except Aunt Aggie, and while she's wonderful, she did not understand. To the Church, I was a divorced woman and hence constantly under suspicion. To my children, I was a hopelessly inadequate mother, unable to cope with their need for a man in their life.

I learned, slowly and painfully, that the world is not designed for women who are alone and that women are not designed by our culture and society to be alone. Still, I made it. I became an adult, more or less. I'm a feminist model of what a woman can do by herself—at the price of enormous personal suffering, much of it imposed by other women—if she wants to.

I'm not sure I buy all the feminism. Maybe I'm too old. I often think that I'd love to have a husband who had so much money that I didn't have to work. Then I could travel around the world in idle luxury the way I have always dreamed.

I'm fair about it. I think it would be wonderful if men didn't have to work, either.

Then it occurs to me that Mark has made enough money in my accounts so that I could retire tomorrow. What, I ask myself, would I do without my gallery?

In 1967 I moved to Washington to escape from the attempts of my husband and mother-in-law to win my children away from me, attempts sweetened by huge cash gifts. Beth was already enrolled at Bryn Mawr, where she majored in social protests, I guess, and from which she never graduated (degrees were not "relevant"). Jimmy attended Georgetown Prep before he left for Colorado Springs and the Air Force Academy. Dave and Mark went to a parochial school in D.C. I chose Washington because one of my professors at Chicago had obtained for me a scholarship and teaching job at American University. He was reluctant to see me leave. A degree from American was not nearly as prestigious as a degree from the University of Chicago. But he sympathized with my problem and assured me that the program at American was presentable and that all my Chicago work would be accepted.

I moved into an inexpensive and comfortable apartment in a redbrick building on the edge of Georgetown and settled down to being a serious academic, promising myself that I'd finish in two years because school was as unreal a world as suburban housewifery.

There was an abundance of pot in the graduate student community. I was curious but didn't experiment. I didn't trust myself enough to lose control of my emotions.

I was entranced by the soft lights of Jan Vermeer's

"Delft," the blues and yellows, the shy yet confident women, the quiet domesticity with faint hints of passion, the rich tablecloths, and the jugs, baskets, plates, and pitchers with which his women seemed so competent. I kept a print of "A Lady Writing" on my desk, lusting for her yellow jacket with the fur trim.

"Only a woman would think those things important," sneered the young punk who was my adviser.

"Vermeer thought they were important enough to paint," I shot back at him, silencing him more or less permanently.

Poor Vermeer. The top of the Dutch wave, he died at forty-three, insolvent and in debt to his mother-in-law, leaving eight children. Poor Mrs. Vermeer too, with so many children to raise. What right did I have to feel sorry for myself?

I was still an innocent, and often lonely, naive. I paid little attention to the news. I barely read about the Tet offensive. I was delighted when Lyndon Johnson withdrew from his campaign for reelection because I thought that would mean the end of the war and I was terribly worried about my handsome young Air Force cadet. The murders of King and Kennedy sickened me, as did the riots in Chicago—which then seemed so far away. Only later did I learn that Beth and Ted, with whom she was then living, were in the thick of the riots.

I attended my classes, did my work, corrected my papers, luxuriated in the lights of Jan Vermeer, and ignored the rest of the world. I felt guilty about my noninvolvement. I didn't need Beth to tell me that I was part of the problem. But before I could do anything else, I had to put my own life in order.

Then, without expectation or warning, I fell in love.

49

Michael eased open the manila folder so that the Texas sheriff who was dozing next to him in the Justice Department auditorium would not see the article in the unlikely event he woke up before supper. There were three questions that merited an answer. As he had insisted in *Principles of Detection*, the most important skill of a good investigator was "to ask the right questions as clearly as possible."

And as early as possible.

The air conditioner in the auditorium hummed monotonously, counterpoint for the equally monotonous babbling of the two bureaucrats who were trying to explain the obscurity of "uniform crime reports" to an audience of snoozing cops, who probably were mentally complaining that DOJ had not provided more comfortable seats for their afternoon naps. The air-conditioning system was as useless as the lecture. It did not so much circulate the dense, heavy air as slowly rearrange it. Thank heaven the ideologues didn't let anyone smoke.

His eyes returned to the article in the folder.

Although Reilly is a successful entrepreneur in a highly competitive business and a member of the contemporary Chicago establishment, she insists that she is "spiritually" part of the 1930s and the 1940s.

"I guess I'm a feminist in many ways," she says. "But often I think I'm from another planet. The Depression and the Second World War are more real to me than Vietnam and Watergate."

What the hell does that mean? She lost a son in Vietnam and she was in Washington at the time of Watergate. Two of her other children are permanently alienated because of that era.

Two of his three questions were easy to answer:

1)Did he want Anne Marie O'Brien Reilly after all these years?

2)Did she want him?

The answers to both questions were a qualified yes, an affirmative hedged in with reservations, hesitations, and doubts, especially on her side. The more time he spent with her or even thinking about her, the weaker grew his will to sustain his own qualifications.

3)What was wrong with her?

That was the hard one.

Why not ask her?

That was a new thought.

Cautiously he turned to the first page of the article from *Sunday*, the magazine section of the *Chicago Tribune*. The brief feature on Annie was the third in the story about "Chicago's Mature Beauties." Nonetheless, the *Trib* editors had had the good sense to put her picture on the cover.

Wow, as he'd said with reprehensible lack of restraint when Patrol Officer Lopez placed the back issue of the magazine on his desk, commenting with a glint of even white teeth that it might contain material useful for his investigation.

"What's this business about mature beauties?" he had asked with forced disdain, to cover up his initial reaction.

All the women's magazines were running such articles, she'd assured him. Older women bought the magazines too and, anyway, she'd added with passionate conviction, they had as much right as anyone else to feel attractive and sexy.

"Sounds like an excuse for fantasizing," he had replied.

"Men and women both. Different fantasies, however."

"Nothing wrong with that," she'd informed him. Moreover, Don Miguel (a faintly disrespectful title that replaced "Jefe" when she was impatient with him and that hinted at "Don Quixote"), she personally felt that it was a good thing that Joan Collins would be a *Playboy* centerfold in December. It would prove that erotic appeal did not end at thirty.

"Who's she?"

Didn't he ever watch television? Didn't he know about *Dynasty*?

He didn't, but since it was Wednesday, he turned off

Brahms's Fourth on the FM that night and tuned in Channel 7, and decided he was rather sorry his scruples forbade him to buy *Playboy*. Besides, Annie was both prettier and more durable than Joan Collins.

Patrol Officer Lopez had not only secured the back issue of the *Trib* magazine; she had made a number of editorial comments in the margin. One paragraph was marked "absurd!" in Spanish.

> Although twice divorced, Reilly says she is free in the eyes of the Roman Catholic Church to marry again. However, she does not think that she will do so.
>
> "I'm carrying around too many memories to burden a husband with," she says with a vivacious smile.

Absurd, yes, Patrol Officer, but a clue. Memories from the Depression and the War! Dick Murray!

Ask her. Why not!

Annie, darling, what is the strangeness I perceive in you! In those occasional moments over the last four decades when our souls have been linked like a key and a lock, why have I found you so appealing and so disturbing! What is the pain that you shared with me long ago and for which I have no name!

He shifted uneasily in his chair. A stupid question. She wouldn't have the faintest notion what he meant.

Yet he knew she would understand his question. He also knew she would not answer it. Could not? Would not? He wasn't sure.

"What do you think of the article?" he'd asked Deirdre guardedly.

It was a wonderful article about a wonderful woman, Don Miguel. No, she didn't seem strange at all. No—with some hesitation—why should it seem odd to remember the Depression and the War if you've lived through them?

They were so long ago.

Despite his disdain for fantasies, he couldn't take his eyes off the cover picture, more erotic in its own way than a centerfold. So understated and dignified was the eroticism of the portrait that no one could possibly object to her tasteful silver and gray and ivory sex appeal—silver and gray hair, silver and gray strapless dress, ivory throat and shoulders as appealing as they had been on the raft, a simple crosslike silver pendant emphasizing the firm line of ivory cleavage. *Ah, Annie, you look like at least an archduchess and maybe an empress. Serious, intelligent, capable, and yet with a hint of laughter in your crackling gray eyes.*

A hint of something else too. What is it? It's the reason I have always been attracted to you and yet afraid of you, why I didn't pursue you after our romp in the snow, why I didn't hold you in my arms on the raft, why I didn't make love to you before I went to Korea, why I didn't write to you when I was in the foxholes there, why I've avoided you since 1952, and why I let you get away the other night when I almost had you.

He considered the picture carefully.

How many men of all ages wanted you when they saw this picture? Yet you are so aloof that no one can call you a tease.

Reilly laughs quickly and her conversation is easy and amusing. Yet one catches occasionally in her quick gray eyes a touch of profound wisdom purchased at the price of great pain.

"You try to laugh as often as you can," she says lightly. "Otherwise you would cry too much."

An insight that went beyond the style of the article, a bland mixture of up-to-date feminist vocabulary and women's page fluff, as though you became politically relevant by using women's last names instead of their first names.

Modest Irish Catholic that she was, Annie was surely wearing some kind of ingenious bra under her low-cut evening gown. Its presence and operation, however, were quite undetectable.

Mike swallowed to ease the tightness in his throat, remembering the feel of her warm flesh against his fingers. He shook his head slightly, as if to clear his mind of sweet and paralyzing images.

He glanced uneasily at the Texan. Still asleep. And the

bureaucrats on the stage were droning on. He closed the folder to put temptation out of his mind. *Fine knight you are, Don Miguel.*

He opened the folder for one last look, one final ambivalent fantasy.

Dear God, Annie, I want you so much. I want to talk to you, about the War and the Depression if need be, for every hour that remains in our lives. I want to take off your clothes and make love to you and then continue the talking until we both want to make love again. We have so much to talk about. I want to be with you, loving and talking, talking and loving, from now till eternity.

Yet you terrify me, as you did in the snowdrift outside St. Ursula's. The mystery in you absorbs me and at the same time scares the hell out of me. I really am Don Miguel, a broken-down romantic idealist. I want to help. I want to save you if I can. But from what!

I have finally discovered after forty years that you are my destiny. If I'm to make anything of my life from here on, I'll have to do it with you. Still, at this moment I want to tear up the Trib article and never look at this damn sexy portrait and never see you again.

What is it, Annie, my beloved! Why am I so afraid of you! I want you so powerfully that my fists clench when I look at this picture. Yet I stare into your eyes and I'm frightened. What's happened to you! What will happen to you— and to me if I am close to you! Are you haunted!

The bureaucratic tones were changing. Meeting winding down. He read the final paragraph of the profile again before he put the manila folder in his briefcase. The reporter had used the same word.

"What next for Reilly?" She shrugs and dismisses the question.

"The gallery until I retire, I suppose. It's my last challenge."

Perhaps. But you note the flicker of pain in her eyes and come away from the interview wondering what hidden challenges may still haunt this striking and gifted woman who knows so much and yet reveals so little of herself.

Why, Mike Casey wondered, *did the reporter choose the word* haunt?

Must I fight the dead for her?

Perhaps the question to ask her is, Who are the dead that I must fight?

50

Mary Kate and her Pirate were lying in bed side by side, shoulders touching, covered with sweat, and breathing heavily and happily. They had had a fight, provoked by her, and a reconciliation, equally of her making.

"I want to consult," she said incongruously.

Joe laughed weakly. "Of course. What else?"

"I wasn't thinking about it while we were screwing," she protested in her own defense.

"You can think about anything you want, woman," he said, "as long as you make love like that."

"Pig," she said complacently. "What makes me think of the case now is that the patient is a lot like me."

"Lucky man," Joe said, now overflowing with compliments.

"Not necessarily." She told him the story.

"Wow," he said when she was finished. "No wonder you're worried." They were now nestled in each other's arms like a pair of teenagers. "My gut instinct says there's a strong possibility of a wrenching, perhaps unhinging, psychotic episode."

"Precisely. All that strength has been built up through the years at the price of repressing huge amounts of guilt and pain and anger. Now she's at a turning point and she must either deal constructively with these energies or her personality will disintegrate."

"The real issue," Joe said, "is that she has been worked over—*fucked over* would doubtless be your term—all her life by her family and by the Church. She's been a good little Catholic girl, pulled herself together, and pushed on. Now she wants someone to love her and make the pain go away. So she chooses a therapist and a priest who are children of a lawyer who was one of the few men who were unselfishly kind to her. The Ryans are to be her family. You're not her therapist but a mother who, unlike her own mother, wants her."

"And she has always been in love, in a peculiarly intense and spooky way, with another member of the clan."

"Poor woman. Maybe it would have been better if she'd fallen apart a long time ago. Think of the guilt, M.K., the tremendous guilt. All those deaths in her family—we are guilty when our loved ones die because of our ambivalences about them. Failed marriages and disastrous love affairs. Add breaking the role models of her childhood and you have a tremendous burden of sins to expiate."

"Role models?" she asked, stroking the back of his neck.

"Look," he said patiently, "you come from a proto-feminist family. It would have been a disgrace for you not to have a career. Yet look at all the confusions and guilts that harass you. Think of the soul-rending an older woman with no family support would experience."

"She's a terribly passionate woman, Joe, and she's had to repress her passions most of her life."

"So you said," he agreed, kissing her gently. "They don't die when you turn fifty."

"Thank God . . . and she's also psychically sensitive."

"That's all we need."

"I agree with you. If she doesn't come to terms with all that's bottled up in her and find someone to love her, she'll probably experience a psychotic episode, one that might institutionalize her for a long time"—she hesitated, reluctant to say the horrible—"or even permanently."

"You can do just so much, M.K.," he said, his caresses becoming challenges.

"I have to take care of her. She's made herself family."

"Too much role overlap," he murmured, insidiously preparing her for another romp.

"And she's not telling me everything, not by a long shot."

"That's her funeral."

"The hell it is."

Much later as Mary Kate was drifting into pleasant dreams, Joe said sleepily, "I never heard about the fire before."

"You're from Boston."

"Did they ever find out who started it?"

"I think I read somewhere"—she yawned—"that it was a pyromaniac, a teenager who spent the rest of his life in a mental institution."

51

Anne woke up at five in the morning, still groggy and sore, and forced herself to dress and drag herself home.

She indulged in a long warm shower and a sip of sherry. She noticed as she slipped on her nightgown that although she still hurt, there was no trace of a burn mark on her breast.

"Imagination," she said sleepily.

She woke up at ten, called the Jarecki Warehouse, which stored her excess paintings, and asked in her most charming voice if they could make a pickup after lunch.

"For you, Missus Reilly, anytime."

Dressing in slacks and a sweatshirt, she hurried over to the gallery, propped the door open to capture the Indian summer warmth, and began packing the Father Kenny pieces. She worked furiously for two and a half hours, like a horrified Polish-American homemaker confronted with a house that had not been dusted in three months, shoving the paintings and sculptures into boxes and cartons in slapdash style and sealing them with packing tape. The last painting was "Divine Justice."

She glanced at it before she dumped it in an oversize box. The girl in the swamp was still running.

"All imagination," she muttered.

She sealed the box and placed it against the pile of packages just as the truck from the warehouse arrived.

As the driver and his helper loaded the truck, Anne found herself drifting into a trance. The world faded away from her, time stood still, her movements were automatic, she was a zombie with no mind or will of her own.

Prisoner of a superior power, she pushed the "Divine Justice" box across the floor and into one of the storerooms. She locked the door and, still in a daze, returned to the workers.

"Just a few more," she said, breaking out of her hypnotic stupor. In the back of her mind there was a vague memory that something strange had happened, yet she couldn't quite remember what.

She gave each of the men a twenty-five-dollar tip, overcoming their routine protests without too much difficulty, and rushed back to the apartment for a quick shower before Mark appeared.

"It's finished now," she told herself, "and I didn't need Mickey Casey or anyone else to help me."

As she set to work on her face in front of the mirror, a vague, nameless trouble stirred in the back of her head.

Something was still wrong. What was it? As though there were a sin she'd forgotten to confess.

Nonsense, you're just a compulsive old woman. Settle down and work at that darn face. You have to be radiant for your son and his family tonight. Look and act like you're the most beautiful mature woman in Chicago.

Which was exactly what Mark said she was when he

lifted her off the ground, kissed her soundly, and spun her into his 300SL diesel.

52

Michael's sexual longings had wilted, like a stiffly starched shirt on a humid day when the air conditioner is not working. Government meetings were spectacularly effective as a libido depressant.

He'd managed to stay awake during the final afternoon sessions, which were the finest cure for insomnia since sheep. Most of his colleagues had succumbed, victims of the peripatetic evenings and nights that seemed to be typical in the nation's capital. All that Mike had accomplished was to fill several doodle books with drawings of Ronald Reagan as a cowboy and mildly irreverent distortions of Washington's most solemn buildings

How could anyone have sexual appetites in that city? Most of what they did was boring and boredom dulled desire more than a cold shower, Mike thought.

Dinner at the director's house has been pleasant but hardly exciting. The director and his wife clearly were exhausted, merely going through the motions. The director had asked about the World Series in Chicago.

"The Mayor might say we haven't enough money to put extra details on for the traffic," Mike said, making a face. "Stay home."

Now, waiting at the nearly empty Baltimore International for his plane, delayed of course, he shook his head in amused dismay at his passion of a day ago for Annie O'Brien. *We were a couple of old geezers,* he thought, *acting like horny kids. She has more common sense than I have. I'll travel around the world alone.*

Monday morning I'll make sure she's thrown all that crap out of her gallery and then forget about her. I'm too

old and too set in my ways to become involved with a woman.

That's kid stuff.

53

What a wonderful evening, Anne thought as she snuggled into her couch and rewarded herself with a sip of very expensive port, which brushed her tongue with the delicate sweetness of the first south wind of spring and the electric pleasure of the first tentative touch of foreplay.

Almost as good as sex, she thought, considering the dark liquid carefully, *and not nearly so much trouble.*

Not that I know that much about sex or port. In my old woman's apartment in my old woman's building. Which, I wonder, will collapse first, me or the building?

My youngest son and his pretty little wife are maturing into very interesting human beings, as well read as the academic crowd and with more common sense. As Dr. Murphy predicted, I'm beginning to realize that I loved him all along. Silly guilt feelings were in the way.

Virtuously she had put a CD of the Brandenburg Concertos on her phonograph. No teenage music tonight. She tilted her glass in a humorous toast to Vermeer's "Girl with a Red Hat," who watched her from the wall at the other end of the couch—even though her hat hardly fitted the color scheme of the room.

Mark and his wife must have vast amounts of money to live like they do, and it's all spent tastefully too. They give a lot of it to charity, I think, from the few hints she gives me, kind of reassuring Grams that they are not materialists.

Hell, kid, I was a much more empty-headed material-ist at your age.

How long ago that was. Yet it seems like only yesterday.

Their children were lovely too, well-behaved little elves with the glint of mischief in their eyes. And charming guests, a hasty dinner party arranged in her honor—"my mother the celebrity!" Mark had toasted her.

I hope I didn't drink too much champagne and make a fool of myself.

Nonsense. You were perfectly charming, the witty, sophisticated mature woman.

The phone rang. "Mother? Beth. I was humiliated at a dinner party tonight. Everyone seemed to know about the crazy things at the gallery but me."

Beth clearly had drunk too much at her party.

"It was all in the papers, hon. Some problem with the gas mains, I guess. Everything's all right now."

"What can I do, Mother, to make you understand how embarrassing these things are to us? Every time you do something screwy, it means trouble for Ted and me and the children. Can't you ever think about us?"

Beth was not concerned about her mother's safety, only about her own image. *I will not let her ruin this evening. I will not.*

"I don't have much control over the gas mains, hon."

"You can stop trying to play the role of the smart Near North Side art dealer. It really doesn't fit you at all," Beth ranted. "I'm afraid of the impact of all of this on Ted's business. Do you want to take money out of our pockets?"

Tears gathered in her eyes. *Dear God, Bethie, why do you hate me so much?*

"We'll see about it next week, Beth. I'm tired and going to bed now."

"Well! I hope you have a good night's sleep because I know I won't!" Beth hung up, her goal of hurting her mother successfully accomplished.

Anne considered her port glass and virtuously replaced it on the glass coffee table.

You can't expect to be successful with all your children, she told herself.

Thus partially reassured and still savoring the success of the evening, she went up to her bedroom, changed into a grape-colored nightgown that seemed perfect for Indian summer, and opened the small window of her bedroom. The light, caressing night air floated in, surrounding her.

To hell with it, she thought. *I'm entitled to another glass of port after all I've accomplished today.*

Anne donned the matching robe and went down for the port. But instead of bringing up the whole bottle, she compromised. She half-filled a brandy snifter with port and, giggling, returned to her bedroom.

She sipped the wine, savoring the night air and the sights and sounds of Michigan Avenue and Lake Shore Drive.

In a mildly pleasant daze she drew the curtain closed, went to the bathroom to rinse the snifter, and removed her contact lenses. She hung up her robe behind the door of her bedroom, then thanked God on her knees for the blessings of the day and went to bed, floating away into the land of sleep, serenely confident that on this magic night there could not possibly be any bad dreams.

Yet there was still something strange; something had not been quite right about this soothing day of renewal.

54

Michael napped intermittently on the ride from Baltimore to Chicago, falling asleep over Detroit. The grating voice of the cabin attendant, warning him to fasten his seat belt (which, as a man who believed in keeping the rules, he had already done), awakened him abruptly and caused him to mutter some words of mild protest of the sort he would not be reluctant to pronounce in the presence of the virtuous Patrol Officer Deirdre Lopez.

I'll probably sleep in the cab and then stay awake all night when I finally get to my apartment. That thought merited a few more expletives.

He did not sleep in the cab, however. The serene night air and the splendid panorama of the Chicago skyline glowing against the stars held his attention and made him feel intolerably sad, a bittersweet weariness with the quickness of life and the wonder and brevity of its pleasures.

"Get off at Ontario," he told the driver, "and take me to Nine Hundred North Michigan."

"Yes, sir."

The driver probably wondered if there was a whorehouse there about which he didn't know.

Mike stood in front of the old building, suitcase on the sidewalk next to him, hands shoved in his pockets. When he had been a kid going to Quigley Seminary, 900 North Michigan, the stately Drake Hotel across the street, and the Palmolive Building (the maiden name of the Playboy Building) were all that existed at this end of the Magnificent Mile, as it wasn't called then.

What would my spiritual director at the Q think if he knew I was going to attack a woman inside this building forty years later? He was one of those who didn't leave the priesthood, as I remember.

He thought of Janet. Her body had been in the ground for a little more than a year. Now he was chasing another woman with more passion than he had ever felt for his wife. Janet had insisted that he should marry again. "You won't survive alone," she'd said bluntly.

But why the ungodly rush?

It was ludicrous. A grandfather lusting for a grandmother. No respect for the dead and no taste in behavior toward the living.

Disgusted with himself, he picked up the suitcase and walked to the curb to flag down a cab. Don Miguel, indeed.

Two of them drove by, both with passengers. Then the supply of cabs seemed to dry up. He could walk over to the cab stand in front of the Drake. There were always cabs there.

He could feel himself being drawn back toward the

door of the building, as if caught by an invisible rubber band.

She wants me to be with her.

Let the dead bury the dead—he heard the phrase run through his head. A cruel, cynical statement. Who had said it?

Slowly he walked the few yards to the stoplight. He told himself that he could not betray the sanctity of the past for the fleeting pleasures of the moment. Life was too short to make a fool of himself at his age over a woman.

Who was the cynic who'd said let the dead bury the dead?

It was in the Bible, wasn't it? Jesus?

No doubt about it. And Jesus was hardly a cynic. Maybe he knew something the rest of us don't.

Mike walked back to the door of the apartment building. *I really am a Don Quixote*, he told himself ruefully. *Thank God Patrol Officer Lopez can't see me now.*

You do want me, don't you, Annie.

He walked into the lobby, wondering in the last seconds whether it really was a dictum of Jesus.

It didn't matter anymore. He was going up to her apartment, of that there was no longer any question. He would play it by ear once he got there. He wouldn't quite refuse to take no for an answer, but it would have to be a pretty strong no.

The elevator man nodded politely. Security was excellent, unless you were the Deputy Superintendent of Police.

Or maybe unless you were a presentable-looking male who'd been seen going to her apartment before.

He paused at the door of her apartment, not altogether sure he would knock. He was on a damn fool enterprise that violated both principle and common sense. He was losing his mind. His intelligence and convictions were being destroyed by passion.

Desire was stronger than reason, as it usually was. He knocked on the door, almost without realizing that he was doing it.

I'll say hello and see how she's doing, nothing more than that.

Thus reassured, he knocked again. And again. *Damn it, woman, wake up.* He turned to leave, a mixture of Hamlet, Miles Standish, and Caspar Milquetoast. *Put on the running shoes and scramble.*

"Yes?" A muffled voice from inside.

"May a weary traveler say hello?"

"Mickey?"

Hesitation while a peephole was opened. "All right, just a minute. I have to open all the locks."

A powerful surge of emotion tore through him, affection, tenderness, want. His heart pounded against his ribs. *It's too late now to turn back. Forward, Don Miguel.*

The door opened. She was hesitant, blocking the way in but still smiling, attractively frazzled in a purple robe and gown, the robe held closed at her waist. "You didn't have to stop on the way from the airport. I'm fine. I've cleaned out the Kenny exhibit . . ."

Her voice trailed off as she saw what must have seemed a hard light in his eyes. She reacted like a frightened bride, curious and pleasantly flattered by the man at her door. She drew the robe more protectively around her.

"May I come in?" he asked cautiously, half-hoping she would tell him that at this hour of the night he certainly could not.

"I suppose so," she said slowly and then, dismissing her fears, "yes, of course. Was it as bad in Washington as you look?"

He placed his suitcase on the floor inside the door, at a precise right angle to the wall. He glanced around the room—polished and tasteful, pin-neat, blue and white and crystal, restrained yet inviting. He turned off the instructions from *Principles of Detection.* All the love and the lust of decades exploded within him. Good-bye, Don Miguel. Hello, super Jefe.

"The worst part was that you weren't with me."

"I don't think I would have been much use. . . ."

Carefully, so as not to hurt her, but firmly, so she could not stop him, he removed her fingers from the robe and pushed it from her shoulders.

Gently but with a determination not to be denied, he

began to kiss her. Lips, eyes, chin, nose, ears, lips again, throat, shoulders, and then back to the lips, lightly and then with a surge of passion. Then as her body stiffened in surprise, he slipped his fingers under the lace of her gown and began to explore and lay claim to her breasts. One, then the other, nipple rose in response.

She backed away from him, shoulders pressed against the wall, superbly defenseless. "Please," she murmured uncertainly. "We're both too old."

"The hell we are!" he laughed. "I'm enjoying this immensely, and so, woman, are you! Come back here!"

One of his arms captured her so that she couldn't slip away. Delicately he eased the straps of the gown away from her shoulders and in one quick movement pushed it to the floor.

I have her naked at last, he thought. *Forty years of fantasy are over.* He renewed his campaign to arouse her, encountering feeble and uncertain resistance. She was tense, embarrassed by her nakedness, afraid of his embrace and explorations, shamed by her own warring emotions. But not ready to fight back.

Now is the time to say your loud no if you want, he thought. He pressed his lips against hers to silence any pleas and held her tightly to overcome any resistance.

For a few seconds she held herself back, reserved and aloof, protesting by nonresponse. Then her body began resonating with his. Her lips returned his kisses and her arms encircled him, moderating the fierceness of his assault and imprisoning him so that he could not change his mind.

Mike lifted Anne off the floor, carried her to a leather couch that seemed to be designed for lovemaking, and, underneath a Vermeer print, consummated the love that had begun forty-one years before in a snowdrift under a streetlight at the corner of Mayfield and Potomac while American marines were fighting not in Lebanon but on a forgotten island called Guadalcanal.

55

I can't believe this is happening, she thought as her body eagerly gave itself to him on the leather couch. *It's a dream, another crazy dream. I'm being raped and loving it.*

The girl with the red hat did not seem particularly impressed.

No, it's not rape, not when a woman wants it with a man she loves. It's the opposite. Too bad it's all a dream.

No, it's not a dream; it's really happening. I'm too old for this sort of thing. I should stop him. I don't want it to stop. I love it.

His body was lean, hard, and disciplined, like that of a paratroop general who prided himself on his ability to jump with his men. And she was a prisoner of the paratrooper, willing to be ravished, indeed more than willing, but not given all that much choice in the matter.

Their first union was not very satisfactory. They were both too awkward, too hungry, too nervous. It didn't matter. The barrier had been broken, the beginning had been made. Pleasure was less important than that they were together, healing, soothing, comforting. The mystery that had bound them did not, as she had feared, demand revelation of terrible secrets. It did not require explanation of the reasons for pain. It did not pry into the dark origins of guilt. Rather it sought out suffering, and exorcised it.

Anne held his head against her breasts and stroked his back. "You really are quite direct, aren't you, Michael Casey the Cop?"

"At the last minute I almost lost my nerve and ran."

"Once you were inside my house," she said, astonished at her own words, "there was no way you were going to escape."

Mike leaned on his elbow, inspecting her closely. "You're incredibly beautiful, Annie. I don't know how you do it."

"The same way I do everything else. Sheer, raw, shanty-Irish willpower. And hang the costs."

"That must hurt after a while." His fingers were tracing the outlines of the beauty he admired.

I know there are terrible problems I should be worrying about, she thought in a quick distraction. *But I'm not going to let them, or anything, ruin the joys of this Indian summer evening.*

"Hurts like hell. Then you stop noticing it. It's a way to survive and it's not all bad."

"It's all good, so long as other things are not left out."

"Like?"

"Like me, for instance." He kissed her tenderly, setting off chain reactions of affection and need within her.

"There haven't been opportunities for other things—family, Church, and God all in the way."

"They shouldn't have been."

"I don't know, Mickey. All I know is I love you. And I don't ever want to lose you, as I lost all the others I loved."

"I'm not about to be lost," he insisted.

She prayed briefly that he would not be.

56

ANNE'S STORY

I fell from grace the day Richard Nixon was inaugurated, as easily as a leaf falls from a tree in a light October breeze. For two wonderful years I lived in sin, paying no attention to God or Church. They were the happiest years of my life since Dick Murray went off to die as cannon fodder in the Hürtgen Forest. I matured into a self-possessed adult woman, capable of taking care of herself, of giving and receiving love, of participating in society with intelligence and wit.

These two years came to an end suddenly, as I knew they would. Many of the possibilities they had opened for me as abruptly closed. I returned to Chicago with a classic broken heart and a renewed sense of worthlessness and failure. I'm still paying the price today for those years of sinful pleasure. Yet, while I deeply regret the sins and the self-deception, I also regret the loss of the love and my failure to stand by the lover.

To make my regrets worse, the outcome could have been different. The Catholic Church changed the rules and didn't tell me.

At first my life in Washington was not glamorous. I made breakfast for the two boys, drove them to school, went to Mass, taught my classes, worked on my dissertation, picked up the children, made supper for them, helped them with homework, corrected tests or prepared classes, did some reading, watched the first part of the TV news, said my night prayers, and went to bed.

I voted for Hubert Humphrey without much hope and was surprised that he almost won. I rejoiced at the end of 1968, convinced that the following year could not be worse. I dreaded the Nixon inauguration and resolved I'd stop watching the TV news. I was fascinated by the changes in the Church, all of which I liked, and astonished that most Catholics seemed prepared to ignore Pope Paul's decision on birth control. So much had changed so quickly. It was for me, of course, only an academic issue.

I had done my best for my children. Much of the time I had no idea where Beth was or what she was doing. She called only when she needed money. Jimmy, now the apple of his mother's eye, a slim, handsome, good-humored young man who reminded me so much of Dick Murray that it made my heart ache, called me every Saturday morning. Dave was a quiet, inoffensive little teenager, already drifting into the world of rock music. Mark cared only for football and basketball. I knew that they needed a man in their life, but certainly not a man who would kill them in a drunken rage.

I had had enough money to get by on, more than enough in comparison with others, I suppose, and had persuaded myself that, all things considered, I was reasonably happy. Although it was not the kind of life I would have chosen when Joan Powers and I had prayed at Mass every morning that someone would invite us to the Fenwick sophomore hop, it could have been much worse. I had learned, I thought, to live with the pains and the loneliness. I was a woman turning forty who was able to survive because she had learned to have very modest expectations.

I suppose that the one factor I hadn't taken into account was my own physical appeal—its impact on others, and my own resonance to their reaction.

I did not date. There was no point nibbling at the appetizers when I couldn't savor the main course. I went to an occasional departmental party, fended off the creeps, and went home to my virtuous bed, feeling that perhaps celibacy was not all that bad an idea.

I had begun to put on weight and had lost interest in makeup and clothes. What did it matter whether I was attractive or not? Then Jimmy protested at Thanksgiving, "Mom, you're getting fat. Shape up."

Of course I did, making a resolution that I've kept since, though I'm not able to explain why. Vanity, I suppose. Maybe I'm afraid that the propositions will stop. If you've been attractive as a girl, you dread the day when men no longer notice you. (I don't understand how Beth can possibly want to look ugly. No good my asking her, however.)

Anyway, I went on a crash diet—fasted through Advent—and swam every morning after class in the university pool. My genes blessed me with a body that responds quickly to good treatment. By the time I met Senator John Duncan at a departmental holiday party (you can't call it Christmas lest you offend those who don't like Christmas), I was again a presentable woman, if I do say so myself.

The other side of the coin of being good to your body is that your body responds by activating hormones you thought you didn't have anymore.

Senator Duncan stopped at the party because he and the chairman had become friends when they'd served on a National Endowment of the Arts panel that the Senator had organized. As soon as he came into the room, my head started to spin and my heart to pump wildly. I had been living as a nun for several years, which is all right so long as you don't drink too much eggnog and stay away from dazzlingly handsome men whose eyes light up when they see you.

John was a liberal Democrat from a western state (he's called a neoliberal these days), a tall sandy-haired Gary Cooper type with penetrating brown, plainsman's eyes, a lean, handsome face, and a slow-magic smile that made me glow inside.

I was introduced as a specialist on Vermeer, one of his favorites.

"I'm happy to meet you, Dr. Reilly," he said, melting me completely.

"A semester away from the Doctor, I'm afraid, Senator," I stumbled incoherently.

"A doctor-elect, then." He grinned and bowed with courtly respect, the white hat cowboy talking to the girl he had helped off the stage after chasing away five hundred Indians. "What aspect of Vermeer is the subject of your dissertation?"

"Domestic utensils, tools—that sort of thing," I stammered, wanting to spill out all the details about who made the plates and bowls that Vermeer's women used in their kitchens.

"Fascinating," he said, his voice a smooth rich brown to match his eyes and his carefully tailored suit. "We must talk more about it. It sounds like a delightful topic."

He moved on, the skilled politician working the crowd, any crowd, because it was there.

He likes me, I thought helplessly, *he likes me as much as I like him.*

One of the other women graduate students, a bra-burning, man-hating, scrawny feminist who disliked me from the day we met, was infuriated by the attention I had received, and probably by my restored sexiness. She also had had much more eggnog than I had.

"How does it feel to be the centerfold of the freshmen boys," she demanded, "the premier sex object of undergraduate instructors? Don't you realize that you're part of the problem?"

"I'm not aware of having posed for a centerfold," I said shakily.

"Don't tell me you are unaware of how they ogle you in the swimming pool," she ranted.

"I can't help it if they look," I replied miserably. My swimsuit was a very chaste tank model.

"Irish Catholic whore," another radical feminist snarled. "A frigid prick teaser who promises everything and delivers nothing."

In the distance I saw Senator Duncan bidding good-bye to the chairman while he watched and listened to what was being said to me. I felt doubly assaulted and humiliated.

"I'm sure you never teased anyone," I replied weakly, a clever answer perhaps, but one designed to bring the cry of "false consciousness" from every feminist in the room. In those days the Movement was new and I did not know the rhetoric with which to diffuse an attack.

No one else rushed to my defense. The rules of the game in the academy at that time were that a radical woman or black could say anything and not be challenged and attack anyone with no fear that defenders would stand up to fight back. Others would whisper in your ear the next day how horrid the radical was. In open and public confrontation, however, the more horrid the radical's diatribes the more totally the victim was abandoned.

I'd seen it happen to others. I knew that no one, not even my close friends or the moderators of my dissertation, would speak up for me. I grabbed my coat and, with tears streaming down my cheeks, tears that humiliated me all the more, dashed out of the house.

Senator Duncan was waiting outside.

"I couldn't help but notice that, Mrs. Reilly. These are terrible times. They'll pass. In the meantime, do you have a ride home?"

I didn't. My dissertation director and his wife had picked me up. I protested through my tears that I could catch a cab, hoping that he wouldn't listen.

He didn't. "Not in this area at this time of night, ma'am."

So he drove me home in a beat-up old Chevy. I told him about Vermeer's dishes and he told me about his wife, whom he married thirty years before when he was a junior and she a freshman at the state university. She'd been in a mental institution for five years, suffering from depression.

"A sweet and gentle girl, ma'am, and the light of my life. I visit her every weekend and not a single time without hoping I'll bring her home. I blame myself because I feel the political life may have been too much for her."

"Do the doctors think the demands of your life are responsible?" I asked, prying more than I had any right to.

"No, ma'am," he said sadly. "They think it would have happened anyway. I can't console myself with that thought. I keep asking the Good Lord what I did wrong."

A reaction I understood perfectly.

I should explain that it took me several months to learn that even though he often sounded corny when he did the pious cowboy act, it did not follow he was insincere. He could sound like a phony, though never to the people back home, and be absolutely authentic. He did love his wife and missed her enormously. He did not play around much either, not until I came along.

"Will she recover soon?" I asked, still uncertain whether to believe his concern.

"The doctors tell me that short of a miracle, she'll never be herself again. So"—he shrugged his marvelous broad shoulders—"I pray for a miracle."

Then he kissed me good night lightly on the forehead.

I was quite overwhelmed by Senator John Duncan. No man had absorbed me with his eyes that way for a long, long time. I told myself that it was an absurd reaction, that I would never see him again, that I was acting like a silly schoolgirl. I pretended that I'd dismissed him from my mind. I paid no attention to the evidence that my body and soul were longing for companionship. I did not even recall the warning of the young priest in River Forest that it would be hard to live the rest of my life alone.

When he called me after New Year's to invite me to a

Democratic party on inauguration night—"kind of a wake, I'm afraid"—I quickly and gratefully accepted.

The next week I rediscovered another aspect of womanly life that I had forgotten during my years as the less-than-gay divorcée, fashion. (I haven't let that slip away, either. What will Bethie say when she sees me in the *Sun-Times* as one of the best-dressed women in Chicago?) I found a cream-colored formal, strapless (of course, with my build), with a narrow waist and wide, flowing skirt and a white mantle to be worn ad lib. At least they noticed me at the Democratic wake. Vanity returned with a vengeance.

Intoxicated by their notice and my own obsession with John Duncan, I babbled throughout the evening and found to my astonishment that I was considered to be intelligent and charming as well as gorgeous. Such unexpected success made me all the more intoxicated. I didn't need any wine or bourbon to be deliriously giddy.

And happy. Happier than I had been in twenty years.

To show you what a naïf I was, I had no thought about going to bed with John. I dismissed my desire for him as a teenage crush. I paid no attention to the way his eyes drank me in, like I was a goblet of sparkling champagne.

I was a virtuous Catholic woman for whom the idea of adulterous sex was unthinkable. I did not yet know myself well enough to realize that the hormones and the emotions pay little attention to what is thinkable and what is unthinkable.

John put his arm around me in the car and drove not to Georgetown but to the Watergate complex, where he lived.

He stopped in front of the wedding cake building, put a hand respectfully, almost reverentially, on my breast, and said, "I'm head over heels in love with you, Anne. I want you."

The only word I could say was *yes.*

57

Dressed in her robe—he was told it was grape, not purple—but not her gown, Anne went down to the kitchen to make breakfast for Mike. Her face and body glowed with complacence, a self-satisfaction of which she seemed both acutely embarrassed and inordinately pleased, a bride astonished at the forbidden acts in which she had engaged and proud of her excellence on the first try.

He shaved with the portable shaver in his suitcase and put on the one clean shirt left in the case. There was no ambivalence in his feelings. He had made her his woman and made her like it. He felt like a fullback who had gained two hundred yards against the best defensive line in the league, a detective who had solved a crime that had baffled the police for twenty years, a pol who had won a landslide victory. His sense of irony reminded him what a timid late-night invader he had been and he laughed at his masculine arrogance.

The laughter didn't prevent him from yelling to the kitchen as he buttoned his shirt, "Make me some coffee."

"If I have any," she replied dutifully.

He smiled at the cowpoke in the mirror with yet more arrogance. "You'd better have some," he shouted, as though he owned the place.

She found enough coffee to make him a pot. "Buy some when we go out," she said.

He was not, then, to be summarily ejected, great big successful sexual conqueror who was still ready to leave if he was told to.

"Do you realize, woman," he said, looking up from the *Tribune* which was delivered to her door, "that when you were seducing me last night, history was being made. For the first time since 1959 the Chicago White Sox are one victory away from a pennant."

"Me seducing you?" She grimaced. "That's not quite the way I remember it. You didn't even ask."

"I did too, kind of," he said, with a tinge of guilt.

"More than kind of." She touched his face approvingly. "You cut it close, but the message was clear."

"I can't quite believe I had the nerve," he admitted.

Her hand stayed on his cheek, fingers gently playing with his face. "You're really quite a good lover, Michael Casey the Cop."

"Better than the others?" he asked.

She pulled her hand away in mock disapproval. "Jealous male egotist?"

"Only kidding," he pleaded.

Her hand came back. "The answer, if you must know, is that you are much better. Strong, direct, determined, and yet very sweet. You know me too well already. Now eat your pancakes."

She was exaggerating. They were still learning the needs of each other's bodies and emotions, learning very rapidly, however. Anne was in bed what she was in life, a superb sexual partner, open, generous, stylish, elegant.

Where had she learned to be so responsive? Mike wondered. Probably from John Duncan, God bless him. Not aggressive exactly, maybe that would come later, but certainly ready for a man's initiatives.

"When it comes to compliments"—he put the paper aside—"I want to pay a few too. . . . Hey, what's the matter, did I say something wrong?"

Her face was frozen in a frown. She rubbed her forehead, blinked her eyes. "What, Mickey . . . ? Oh, no, nothing wrong. I thought I forgot something. Can't remember what it was. No big deal. What were you saying?"

"Are you sure you got rid of all that cr—material from the Kenny exhibition?"

"It's all in the warehouse. That's finished, thank God. I never should have attempted the exhibition anyway. Call it crap if you want. In a way it is."

She was wearing no makeup. The network of lines at her eyes and mouth and on her throat was clearly visible. To him, they made her all the more appealing—vulnerable, human, subject to the aging process like everyone else, and utterly delightful.

He considered not praising her, as he had planned. It would serve her right for not listening to him. Then he decided that he would never, repeat never, do that to her. Time was too short.

"I was paying you a compliment," he said.

"Oh, Mickey," she said, filled with remorse. "I'm so sorry I wasn't listening." Her hand found his.

"No problem. I'm always willing to repeat them. Now I better find a way to make it good."

"Yes?" She squeezed his hand and smiled expectantly.

No wonderful poetry came to his lips. "You are a woman worth waiting for, Annie," he said lamely.

She burst into tears. "Oh, Mickey," she sobbed. "How wonderful!"

She threw herself into his arms, upsetting the passage of a syrup-soaked chunk of pancake to his lips. He retrieved the piece of pancake, swallowed it, and dried her tears, wondering at the look of abstracted bafflement that once again crossed her face.

58
ANNE'S STORY

I would have been very happy as John Duncan's wife. If you sleep with a man two or three or even four nights a week for two years, you come to know his weaknesses as well as his strengths pretty well. Sometimes John was shallow, his political ideas were borrowed and not always from heavyweight thinkers. He was vain about his physical appearance, even more vain than I am, and so obsessed needlessly about his public image that sometimes it seemed there was no substance to him at all.

I was stern with him on the subject, telling him to cut it out if he wanted to be anything more than a senator, which he obviously did.

"Substance without image is no damn good," he insisted.

"If you keep on worrying about your image, you'll have the image of a man obsessed with image," I shot back. "You're defeating your own purposes. It's sick."

This conversation, like most of our serious dialogues, was pillow talk. Only lovemaking slowed the Senator down. He was so content with me as a lover that I could say almost anything to him while he basked in afterglow and he would listen.

"Maybe you're right, ma'am," he said dubiously.

Just the same, he followed my advice and occasioned two national columns on the "New John Duncan," thoughtful, mature, substantive.

By then, as you may have guessed from the fact that I dared to challenge him, he was listening carefully to my counsel. He listened more carefully after the two columns. Unlike many men, he had no problems about giving me full credit for my suggestions.

He was on occasion inconsiderate to the point of boorishness, not merely forgetting a promise, but dismissing it as unimportant. He could be as peevish as a little boy from whom you'd taken an ice-cream cone and as spoiled and selfish as a little girl with a hundred dolls who refuses to share even one with a friend. I took none of it from him.

"You sure are a real terror," he said ruefully one night, slapping my butt. "No one's ever gonna tame you."

"Don't even try," I snapped back, squirming away from him.

"I never will, ma'am," he said apologetically.

I let him recapture me.

He liked my fighting spirit, as he called it, and did a lot of cleaning up his act in response to my feisty demands. His staff on the Hill made common cause with me whenever he was doing something especially dumb. Soon all of them were on my side.

"You're going to make one hell of a First Lady," said a well-meaning Mexican-American aide one day.

"Don't you ever say that again, José," I said, boiling mad. José apologized instantly, not understanding why I was angry, but fearing my wrath. A couple of days later I apologized back.

In retrospect, I think I might have made a good First Lady. It was not to be, of course. Time is running out for John now. He's in his early sixties and the woman he finally did marry is too much like his first wife, sweet but ineffectual. One more man I failed.

He doesn't hold it against me, God knows. Whenever he's in Chicago, there is always a brief but very cordial phone call. Oddly enough the calls don't stir up many memories for me—I suspect they do for him. I can't quite believe that this corny-sounding political cowpoke is the same man with whom I enjoyed so many nights of delirious pleasure.

On the positive side, John was kind, generous, funny— a dedicated idealist beneath the cant and the image mongering and an excellent lover, except when he'd had too much to drink, when his problem was impotence (for which he was deeply apologetic), not brutality, like my good old Jimbo.

He was also deeply religious, maybe more sincerely and less selfishly than I am. I assumed that I was committing adultery and would go to hell if I died suddenly. I learned to live with the fear, especially since I took damnation for granted because of earlier sins. I was defying God because he had already rejected me. I had the courage of one for whom the final outcome was already written.

John simply refused to believe that what we were doing was sinful. "I know it's kind of like adultery, ma'am," he said. "Your priests and my ministers don't approve at all. I sort of feel that the Man Upstairs understands and doesn't mind too much. I think He'll say, 'Well, maybe you shouldn't have done it, but you sure were a good influence on one another.' And that'll be that."

His Man Upstairs was a frequent contributor to John's talks, especially when constituents were in his office. It did not follow that he didn't profoundly believe in that God. When he found out that I said my night and morning prayers every day, often whispering them after we made love, he insisted that we pray together.

"I was kind of ashamed to let a little Catholic girl know I was praying," he said.

Praying with someone else is for me even more embarrassing than taking my clothes off, and that is still terribly embarrassing even when I love the person for whom I'm doing it. I'd never be able to join one of your modern Catholic prayer groups.

John insisted, so we prayed together. The joint prayer added enormous strength to bonds that were tying us together—and improved the sex too.

Certain that I was damned (I went to Church every Sunday, of course, not wanting to increase the number of my mortal sins), I set out to enjoy the time I had left before the demons came to collect me. I discovered that I had a body that was perfectly designed to provide pleasure to a man and to myself. I learned that I had a mind that was quite capable of making a contribution to national policy. I found that I had the wit and the charm to be a welcome guest not only at the big parties and dinners on Embassy row, but at the small and discreet evenings at which the upper echelons of Washington's power elite made what they thought were the big decisions, which sometimes really were. Even at those parties, I was listened to with respect because I was beautiful, smart, and outspoken.

I loved every minute of it.

I'll never forget the night I lost my temper at the most discreet of discreet small parties in Georgetown (I was quite sober, as I had been watching my propensity to drink) because the liberal Democrats present were lavishly approving Nixon's accomplishments.

"He's crazy! Look at the way his hand movements and words are disconnected; it's the aesthetics of dissociation!"

"A wonderful phrase, Professor," said the charming host. "What we would expect from an art historian!"

"Don't patronize me," I shouted. "He'll be reelected, he'll overreach like such men always do, and you'll have to impeach him."

Everyone laughed but me.

"All right! I'll bet each one of you a hundred dollars

that an impeachment resolution will be reported out by the fall of 1974."

There were twelve people at the party. The eleven others took my bet. A couple of them paid up on the day the Judiciary Committee voted, including John. Most of the others sent their check when I sent a polite reminder. The host and hostess never did pay what they owed.

I obtained a Ph.D. with honors, published an article in an obscure journal, and was hired by the Catholic University of America, where no one seemed to care (probably because they are so out of it at that place) about my relationship with the handsome Senator.

The lovemaking was at his apartment. For my kids, he was merely a date. Jimmy, the oldest, already bent on a career in the military, guessed first that there was more to it and, manly, generous young man that he was, was cordial to John. Beth knew too and was very rude to me ("Mother, how can you go to bed with that redneck lackey?") and as seductive as she could be to John. Dave, already drifting into the world of drugs and meditation, didn't notice John or much of anything else. And Mark loved to shoot baskets with him.

I don't know what kind of a mother I was in those days. I was a happy woman. Maybe that made me a better mother. Mark says it did—and I didn't even ask him (I was afraid to). I spent as much time as I could with the kids, tried to be a mother and a father to them, lavished attention and money on them, and gave them as much love as I had.

Realistically I know that it was already too late, that my life with Jimbo had its terrible impact on all of them, and that even my best as mother and father could not wipe that out.

I still felt guilty. It was not right that I should be enjoying so much physical and emotional pleasure while their lives were taking shape beyond my power to influence them.

But guilty or not I was not going to give John up.

Now I look back at the kids and wonder whether I might have been a better mother, with them and for them, if I had been able to control my damn guilt.

His daughters, both of whom were married, were extremely friendly, apparently sharing his view of the relationship as being good for both of us.

In a way, Father Ryan did too. I asked him once how
grave was my sin with John.

"Are you willing, Anne, to live with a Church that lays
down principles and then says that in practice it's impossible for us to make judgments about individual cases?"

"That's not the Church in which I was raised."

"It's the Church now. . . . Look, I don't approve of adultery, for the very good reason that innocent parties are often
hurt. Who is being hurt in your love with the Senator? Not
your husband, God knows. And not his wife, either.
Doesn't that diminish the sin somewhat, even in your moral system?"

"Are you saying that it was not wrong?"

"Leave aside the rules you learned from Healy's *Moral
Guidance* at Mundelein College. Look at it from the outside. Would you say it was terribly, terribly sinful if you
saw someone else in such a relationship?"

"Probably not, but I'm not supposed to judge others,
only myself."

He sighed, as he often did with me. "Even the old mo-
rality taught that circumstances diminish full moral responsibility. Surely you and the Senator were in terribly
difficult circumstances."

"That doesn't make any difference, Father. I thought it
was wrong. So God might send me to hell. He has the right
to do it, doesn't he? I broke his laws."

"Do you know any man who doesn't fall a quarter in
love with you, Anne, once he gets to know you?"

"No . . . " I replied, a little shocked, and also flattered,
at the implication that Father Ryan could fall a quarter in
love with me.

"Do you think God is any different?"

"Probably not," I admitted.

"What kind of a God would it be who sends a lover to
hell?"

I wish I could believe that. If God does love me as much

as John Duncan did—and maybe still does—then I will not go to hell.

Do I miss D.C., now that it's deep in my past? I miss John, sometimes terribly. I miss the excitement of Washington too. My own little art dealer's world is much smaller and less important. Yet I learned toward the end of my relationship with John that there is tremendous phoniness in D.C. and a lot of hollowness. Many of the conversations that made me shiver because they seemed so fraught with importance and significance were merely puffed up pretense.

I would never have given it up on my own. And I would have cleaved to John with all my heart.

The Catholic Church wouldn't let me.

59

"I have made reservations at Le Perroquet for supper," Anne said. "And don't think it was easy. My treat, I absolutely insist. It's another lovely Indian summer day. We can walk along the lake and then . . ."

"Fine," Michael said, putting his stack of dirty dishes in the kitchen sink and opening her dishwasher.

"And then . . ."

"Be quiet." He removed the detergent box from her hand and held her wrist in a grip of steel.

"No," she said weakly, scared and embarrassed all over again.

"Yes," he replied, "definitely yes."

She wriggled ineffectually, halfheartedly trying to escape. *With Matt, sex was routine,* she thought; *with John it had been episodic but passionate; with this man it will be all-pervasive. He's so powerful and so intense that I won't escape from him easily. Not that at this moment I want to.*

He untied the belt on her robe, pushing away her feebly resisting fingers.

"Please," she said weakly. "Not in the kitchen."

Very clever man, she thought to herself. *Proper balance of force and arousal. Skillful seduction of dubiously reluctant woman.*

"Very erotic place," he argued, removing the robe.

"Oh, God," she exclaimed, part plea, part prayer, part celebration. Total contentment with her own womanliness oozed through her body as he pressed her against the kitchen counter. A sweet apathy submerged her reason, making her reckless, sensual, perverse. *Do anything to me. Do everything.*

Delicately his hands explored her while his eyes admired every inch. Memories of another such experience flooded into her consciousness, making her want to scream and run away with terror. She clenched her teeth. She could not hurt Mickey by confusing this time with that time.

"I'm going to take you around the world and in every place find the beach where there's nude swimming," he said, "so I can see you come out of the water, dripping wet and glowing."

"That's a fiendishly erotic thought," she said, sighing with a pleasure that forced back into her memory most of the humiliation of the past.

This is different, she told herself, *completely different.*

"Furthermore, I will insist that you pose for my cousin Cathy. I'll buy the portrait."

"That's even more erotic," she said, feeling the last bit of her self-control slipping away. She squirmed against the sink, not to escape but to respond.

"And I'll undress you in the kitchen every morning."

"Mickey," she sobbed, dazed now by love and desire as her body, without any explicit instruction, busily prepared itself for lovemaking. A moment of terror teased her brain. What was it which she was still so afraid of?

Then there was so much pleasure that terror was impossible. He knew her fantasies and her delights without her telling him. Sex outside the bedroom, especially in the kitchen. Fingers that found the secrets inside her body teased her to the edge of pleasure and paused to prolong the agony of her rapture.

His lips replaced his fingers as the agents of his adulation.

A stream of unconnected thoughts/pictures raced through her head. *He is better than John. Oh, God, yes. Don't do that. Do. Please, do it again. I must do the same thing to you sometime. Do you know that I find you beautiful too? I can't stand it much longer. Even in the snowdrift I knew he would be doing something like this to me someday and I would be terrified and delighted. I will never be able to give him up. The Church won't take this lover from me. Dick, is he the one you sent? It took a long time, but he's worth waiting for. That's what he said to me earlier. Stop, stop, I can't go on. Don't you know, you damn fool, that women have limits? Never, never stop.*

"I do have a comfortable bed upstairs"—she was barely able to breathe the words—"unless you have a fetish for kitchen floors."

"Wonderful."

"You're going to have to carry me."

As he lowered her, as if she were one of the precious statues on loan from the Vatican to the Art Institute, onto the soft rose-colored comforter of her bed, the feeling of terror returned, now more persistent and demented.

I don't care what it is, she told herself. *I will live for today and worry about tomorrow when it comes.*

60

Holding hands, they walked along the lake shore to North Avenue and then through part of Lincoln Park, chatting happily like two lovesick adolescents. Mike found that he was proud of the second and third glances the smartly handsome woman next to him attracted.

He marveled to himself about his new skills as a lover. With Janet, he had been at best ordinary in bed; nothing more was required or expected or possible. With Anne, after the awkwardness of their first union last night, he had been become effortlessly spectacular. No great credit to him; he heard no voices in his brain, but he knew what Annie wanted and rejoiced in giving it to her.

They ate at an ice-cream bar in the park and then returned to her apartment via North State Parkway and Astor Street, enjoying the courtly charm of the Gold Coast's most expensive homes, whose trees were tentatively turning red under the sweet and soft Indian summer sky. It was the sort of setting in which, if it were not for the large imported cars parked bumper to bumper, one might expect to encounter Henry James or some of his characters. Then they walked down Michigan Avenue, gawking at the tall buildings gleaming silver in the sunlight.

They stopped at his apartment so he could pick up a suit that was appropriate for Chicago's most expensive restaurant. Their arms around each other, they watched from his balcony the boats sailing beyond the breakwater, strips of cloth pinned to the blue board of the lake.

"Do you sail?" she asked languidly, leaning against him.

"No," he replied. So much to learn about each other. "Do you?"

"A little. A couple of times in boats out of the harbor here. And in a beach boat across the lake at Mark's in the summer. He wants to buy a twenty-eight-footer. Tessie and I both drew the line. First thing we know, he'll be in Perth trying to bring the America's Cup back to Chicago."

He drew her closer, his fingers lightly touching the smooth fabric of her blouse. "Have you watched the Bears on TV?"

"And seen the skyline?" She nodded in the direction of the red and white and silver and black line of buildings against the hazy autumn blue. "Doesn't it look wonderful, especially on days like this when they use a haze filter. If I were the mayor I'd pay them to fill the game with background shots of the lake and the skyline. Eventually everyone would know we have the most beautiful city in the world."

"The national media would never admit that."

They both sighed, happy in a shared experience. Anne, blushing furiously, opened the top button of her white blouse, creating a windstorm of sudden and sweet need within him. He unbuttoned the rest of the blouse and unzipped and slipped away her skirt.

"Inside," she gasped as he fumbled with the front hook of her bra.

As a concession to her insincere protests, they made love on cushions inside the door of his balcony. Under the hazy sky and with the wind caressing them, their love was at first leisurely and relaxed. Then it changed as though enormous currents of energy had been unleashed in their bodies. They struggled and rolled and twisted and shouted and yielded completely to the power of their joint energy. Sweaty body pressed furiously against sweaty body, both struggling to give totally and absorb totally. She was even more wanton than she'd been in the morning, a source of mind-shattering, rib-bursting, life-draining pleasure, ecstasy that Mike Casey had never known before and of whose existence he had never dreamed.

For all her Catholic modesty and piety, Anne had somehow learned the secrets of driving a man mad with the promise of pleasure and then even madder with her fulfillment of the promise.

Afterward he lazily traced the puzzle lines of blue veins under the pale, milk-white skin of her breasts. A body of a mature woman indeed, but unbearably appealing. Genetic luck, hard work, and profound self-regard.

"What thinking?" she asked sleepily.

"That a woman has to be your age to have known enough of the bittersweetness of life to make such a generous and totally delicious gift of herself."

She flushed, both flattered and embarrassed. "Too old to be all that delicious."

He kissed her, lingering lightly on her lips. "You'll never be old, Annie. And neither will I as long as I'm with you. I was getting old till a few days ago. You've given me a new start, life betting against death, joy against corruption, light against darkness. . . . I suppose you're wondering what kind of a cop lapses into poetry like that."

She held his face against hers, gray eyes misty with mystery. "A good cop. . . . Did I really give you all of me, Mickey? I guess I did. All of me isn't very much, but for the moment it belongs to you."

Then he slept peacefully for a quarter of an hour or so. He heard her call from a distance. Rolling over on the floor, he reached for her and found that both Anne and her clothes were gone. Only the sweat marks on the cushions from her body remained.

She called again. "Mickey." A cry of soft surprise. He knew what she had found and was both pleased and a little angry.

Half-dressed, the skirt held in symbolic modesty at her breasts, she was in his study, flipping through the stack of paintings that leaned against the wall.

"I'm astonished," she said quietly.

"You shouldn't explore a man's apartment."

"A man should lock up things he doesn't want seen," she replied, not at all perturbed by his mild rebuke. "I was looking for a bathroom. I deserve credit for looking at these after I came out."

"Want to buy them?" he asked lightly, putting his arm around her waist. His passion temporarily spent, he was able to be more objective about her attractiveness.

Absently she snuggled closer to him. "You bet I do. New wave realism is fashionable these days. And with the Art Institute School in this city, we're being deluged with clinical Chicago scapes. But you're a realist of the mind and the heart. You love these Slavic neighborhood homes and stores and churches and police stations."

He was embarrassed and enormously pleased. "I've taken some courses through the years. Turned to it for distraction after Janet died. Are they really good?"

"Very good. I want them. How much?"

"I'll trade them for your body," he said, prying the skirt out of her fingers and kissing her throat and strong, graceful breasts.

She accepted his affection with a sigh of pleasure and then considered him with her serious gray eyes as though she had never seen him before.

"You paint the way you make love," she said. "With single-minded and delicate ferocity."

"Is that good?"

"In this picture . . . Bridgeport? Pilsen . . . ?"

"Cannaryville. St. Gabe's."

"You absorb the church front and the corner grocery with the undertaker's next door the way you absorb me when you're inside me. You capture it all, as you capture me."

"Bad or good?"

"Good and scary. Will you let me exhibit them?"

"If I can have you."

"I can't believe you're saying that."

"I mean it." His tongue lingered on the salty-tasting skin of her breast. "Grow old along with me! The best is yet to be, the last of life for which the first was made."

She turned away from his lips and rested her head against his chest. "A cop who paints and quotes Browning. . . . "

"And devours women with delicate ferocity," he replied, feeling that he wanted to protect her and laugh at her forever.

"Sex is only a small part of intimacy."

"For people like us, it will always be an important part."

She eased out of his arms, picked up her bra from his desk and slipped into it. "I'm hungry."

"Small wonder," he agreed.

They ate a Reuben sandwich in Sherlock's Home, an imitation English pub in her building, and drank a glass of beer. Then she insisted on Häagen-Dazs and a chocolate milk shake, only one this time.

"Lent starts next week," she assured him with a kinky grin.

She picked up the tab, observing that she was keeping him today.

"Let's look in at the gallery," he suggested lightly.

"So you can check to make sure I really got rid of the crap? What's the matter, don't you trust me?"

"Certainly I trust you," he said lamely. "It's just . . ."

"That you don't trust me. Come on, forget about the gallery till Monday. We have time for an hour's nap before supper."

"A nap is it?" he said.

"If after last night and this morning and this afternoon you need anything more, then that's up to you," she sniffed.

Later, with her dozing serenely in his arms, he wondered if she had deliberately seduced him away from the gallery.

No, Anne wouldn't do that. She was not that sort of woman. Still, there was terror in that place, terror that ate at her soul. On the subject of the Desmond Kenny Retrospective Exhibition she was not altogether rational. She might do something strange without realizing it.

Why was Kenny still a hang-up for her? What was the pain and guilt, undefined and looming, that still lurked in her soul? It was there all right—now he knew it beyond any doubt—but it was veiled, hidden, obscure.

She wanted it revealed, of that too he was certain, and was terrified of the cost of revelation.

What the hell could it be?

He would have to talk to Blackie Ryan about it on Monday. This time he would not let her slip away.

61

Every cell in her body seemed to tingle in blissful satiety. Men, she thought, never know this kind of contentment with themselves. She felt like a scholar who had won a prize, an actress clutching an Emmy, an artist who had painted a masterpiece. Her womanliness had been put to the test of intense sexuality and she had performed brilliantly.

You won, darling, she informed herself. *He thinks he's won and that's all right because in a way he has too. But you know he thinks he's won and he doesn't know that you know you've won.*

She giggled softly. *You really were quite splendid.*

At my age many women are finished with sex, and with a sigh of relief at that. I seem to be starting to discover what I am capable of as a woman. I'm going to have to be very good at sex to keep up with this man, and even better to stay slightly ahead of him as I am now. The others were never a challenge. None of them knew me so well or made my pleasure so important.

She let herself fantasize that she was a wealthy empress and he a clever and skillful slave who had been brought from the far reaches of the empire to devote himself entirely to discovering and fulfilling her pleasures, to surprise her each time with new delights, and to drug her into continuous complacent self-satisfaction.

She was two women. One was a passionate sensualist who looked forward to responding to the sexual challenge of Michael Casey. The other was a pious pragmatic who knew that on Monday morning the challenge would have ceased to exist and would be replaced by pain and terror.

She dismissed the pragmatic for a few more hours and buttoned up the black satin sleep shirt she'd put on, as much to attract him as to protect herself. He was sound asleep, poor man. A lot of exercise after a hard time in Washington. She grazed his skin with her fingers, from his belly to his thigh. He sighed happily in his sleep.

A good man. You deserve better than me.

His paintings made the gallery come alive again in her head. Perhaps it wouldn't be necessary to give it up. Mickey was good, better than he realized, much better than that old bitch Shelaigh. His neighborhood oils would be very commercial. Chicagoans would be delighted by the shining colors and the revelations in his highly original perspectives.

The one with the Italian sausage stand on Taylor Street against the foreshortened Skidmore, Owings and Merrill glass-and-steel canyons on Wacker Drive was an absolute winner.

The fact that he was a famous cop who had turned down the top job in New York City would make his work even more popular.

I can talk him into the trade—his paintings for my body.

She stretched her legs luxuriously. It was a pleasantly wicked idea.

Strange that he and Father Kenny were both artists. A cop artist and a priest artist.

Father Kenny was a freak. Mickey was utterly normal. And a lover.

Anne kissed his bare shoulder affectionately. *You only know a little bit about me, but you do very well as a lover. You'll improve. Then I'll really go mad every time you touch me.*

She napped for a few moments. And dreamed. Not about Mickey but about Father Kenny. When she was awakened by Mickey stirring beside her she felt not peace but anxiety.

She ordered it out of her mind. Nothing would spoil the perfection of this day, whatever evil tomorrow might bring.

62

She wore a daring black cocktail dress for supper, one with no back at all, only the most minimal front, and long slits at either thigh.

"I've seen you put that dress on, and I still don't believe it stays up," he marveled. She had laid aside the mantle she wore with the dress when they were seated at their table in the overwhelmingly proper and dignified Le Perroquet by

Jovan, the owner, who bowed over Annie's hand as if she were at least a countess.

"Don't experiment to see if it will fall off easily," she said, looking nervously around at the decorous waiters and sophisticated captains. "Not here, anyway."

Annie had the professional fashion model's knack of revealing most of her body and still seeming tasteful and chaste. She could give the impression that she was fully clad when she was, save for absolute essentials, virtually naked to the waist.

Modesty was a state of mind, he told himself wisely, not a state of dress.

"Staring," she murmured, blushing and lowering her head in the familiar novice gesture.

"Mind?"

"No." She laughed. "Mind if you didn't. Little less obvious. Not *that much* less obvious."

They both laughed at their private joke and she gave the captain orders for both of them, complete with details of sauces and dressings without looking at the menu, and asked to see their new wine list.

Mike tried not to feel out of place in the quiet grandeur of the restaurant—red chairs, oriental rugs on the walls, orange and green theme lines on the tablecloths, waiters who raced to take the spring-water bottle out of your hand before you committed the cardinal gaffe of filling your own glass.

"Hey," he said, as her hand rested on his thigh. "What's that about?"

"A way of saying I love you," she replied simply, her eyes tearing.

"I love you too," he replied, a catch in his voice. "We will have great times together in the years to come."

She put two fingers on his lips. "Hush, Mickey. Don't talk about the future. Let's live for this Indian summer weekend on which the White Sox won the pennant."

He was not sure he wanted to give up the future quite that easily. But neither did he want to break her sense of the magic of the day.

"They haven't quite won it yet," he reminded her. "They have to win tonight."

"Would you like to go home and watch it on TV?" she asked, forsaking his thigh for the wine list.

"Certainly not. I want to go dancing."

"You don't know how to dance," she said accusingly.

"I do. I'm great at disco places. Don't do it much anymore." He couldn't bring himself to say that Janet had hated discotheques.

"With Señorita Lopez, I bet," she said, eyeing him shrewdly.

"Once, I admit, but with a lot of other women cops too."

"Well, we'll see how good you are at it after supper. Don't drink too much." And to the wine steward, "Let's try the white Châteauneuf; that's about the Commissar's speed."

"*Oui*, Madame Reilly," he replied.

"You will let me exhibit your paintings in December?" she said in a conspiratorial whisper. "They're really very good and the show will be a wonderful success."

"I didn't paint them to make money," he said doubtfully. "It's only a hobby."

"You don't want others to admire and enjoy them?" she said, with an unerring instinct for hitting at his weak point.

You're a bit of a huckster, my beloved. That makes me want you even more.

"My offer stands," he said calmly.

She blushed. "That's very wicked." She turned to her French roll.

"Unpleasantly wicked?"

"No," she said, after some hesitation. "How do you work? Do you sketch?"

"Sometimes. A lot of the scenes are fictional anyway. I mean they're not any special barrio *supermercado*. Sometimes when I see a place I want to try, I drive back at the end of the day with my Polaroid. And I carry a doodle book with me when I go around in the car. Everyone takes it for granted."

"Patrol Officer Lopez doesn't know what you do with the book when you sneak back into your studio at night?"

"If she does, she keeps it to herself. Dee-dee is not afraid to advise me about my love life. She has sense enough to leave my artistic life alone."

"I'm becoming persuaded," she murmured, "that the young woman is an ally and not a rival."

He permitted himself to savor all the loveliness across the table. "No one is a rival to you, Annie."

She turned away, crimson and flustered by his consuming desire for her. "I shouldn't be talking business with you tonight anyway."

"Suit yourself."

There were a few moments of silence. *Of course you can sell my paintings, Annie. You want them. I want you. Simple.*

Her hand returned to his thigh.

Best of all you want me too.

"You keep that up, Madame Reilly, and you won't be doing any dancing tonight."

She smiled and then turned serious. "What is between us, Mickey? What goes on? We're both wondering and we're afraid to be up front about it. Though we both knew that night in the snowdrift that we were bound to each other, it didn't start there."

"When did it, whatever it is, start?"

"It started," she said grimly, "the day you came into the classroom. I knew it and you knew it too. Here, eat this pâté—it's outstanding. Never eaten here before?"

"No, not the kind of a place for a cop."

"Don't be silly."

It was too complicated to explain that Janet would not have been at ease and that other cops would whisper if he hung out there. One night didn't matter. And in a year he could do whatever he wanted.

"As to my question," she continued, sipping her sherry.

He tried his sherry too, not a cop's drink at all. "Maybe it was simply love at first sight. Couldn't that be it?"

"Nope." She shook her head in vigorous disagreement. "I know what that is. I had it with John. Nothing at all wrong with it, mind you. It goes away, however, or it can go away. What's between you and me isn't ever going to go away, not after forty-one years, not after four hundred."

He spilled a drop of pâté on his lapel. Absentmindedly he dabbed at it with his napkin. In an instant a waiter was next to him with a napkin soaked in soda water. Annie's eyes were dancing with amusement.

Despite her old-fashioned religious piety, she was an extremely intelligent and very shrewd woman, he thought. She'd be a better deputy superintendent than he was if she set her mind to it.

"It feels to me," he said speculatively, returning to the question of the ties that locked them together, "like a lock, maybe like an emotional handcuff, pleasant most of the time, obnoxious occasionally, ecstatic if we have the courage to permit ecstasy. Could it be that . . . well, that we have the same kind of sympathies, that we live on the same emotional wavelength, maybe? We both are supersensitive, passionately eager to help, and very easily hurt."

He thought she might make fun of his admitting that he was easily hurt. She didn't.

Rather, she waited till the salad had been delivered with the ceremony appropriate for a coronation at Versailles and the Rhône wine had been poured, tasted, and pronounced acceptable.

"My shrink says the same thing. I do have a shrink, you know. Offended?"

"Of course not."

"Maybe she's right. Maybe we both saw someone who needed our help more than anyone else in the world. Maybe we've been trying to help ever since."

"I need you, Annie, for sure," he whispered.

Her hand, which had been preoccupied with the salad, squeezed his thigh tightly. "I know you do, darling."

They savored the moment of love. Then she pursued her catechism. "Have you had a secret, Mike? I mean besides being a closet painter?"

"Not really," he replied with a startled laugh. "When I

first knew you, I was terribly worried about my mom and dad and later very angry at them. It wasn't a secret. And as I told you, I finally worked it out with them."

"Something you never told anyone?" she persisted.

"That I'm a romantic masquerading as a cynical cop?"

"Don't be ridiculous. That's obvious. Even Deirdre knows that."

Does she, now?

"What makes you ask? Do you have one? A secret, I mean."

"Who? Me?" She dismissed the possibility. "Here, you must have more of this sauce on your tournedos. That's the whole point of them."

I'm too good a cop to be fooled this time, he thought. *You do have some kind of secret that worries the hell out of you. I need to find out what it is. But not tonight. The smart detective waits for the opportune moment.* Hadn't he written that in his book *Principles of Detection*? He must give her a copy someday. A best-seller in its field. *I bet she doesn't know I wrote it.*

So he ate the best meal he'd ever had in his life, complete with a raspberry flambé and breathtakingly expensive port.

Then she dragged him to a Rush Street discotheque, where she attracted considerable attention from men young enough to be her grandchildren, and danced him into exhaustion.

"Washington?" he asked.

"Of course not. John had too much Baptist dignity. Matt Sweeney, would you believe?"

They walked slowly, hand in hand, back to her apartment and, cuddling quietly in each other's arms—passion temporarily spent but promising to return—watched the Sox win the pennant. Anne opened a bottle of champagne and they drank a toast to a World Series victory.

"You will require . . . ?" She put the cork back in the bottle.

"Sleep," he said with conviction. "I haven't been so tired in years."

"Old man," she sniffed.

He collapsed almost at once into her bed. A few minutes later she emerged from the bathroom, dressed in a sleek white nightgown that hid more of her than last night's entry, but made her not one bit less attractive.

"Please note," she said as she slipped into bed next to him and turned off the lights, "that this gown is much too expensive to rip."

"Who, me?" he said sleepily.

He was not so sleepy as to be unaware that she made the sign of the cross after she turned out the lights. Night prayers, of course.

"Pray for me," he whispered.

"Hush," she replied. "I always do."

Thus reassured, he was soon asleep, a deep and happy rest.

Later he was awakened by screaming. Someone in bed with him . . . what the hell . . . and screaming. Janet? No, no, Janet was dead.

He groped for the light switch, couldn't find it. *Where am I? My God, she's screaming bloody murder.*

He fumbled for something, anything, knocked over a large solid object, found what seemed to be a lamp, searched for a switch, and turned it on.

Annie . . . oh, yes . . . yes, of course.

She was still asleep, cowering against the headboard, face contorted in terror.

Gently he took her in his arms. "Annie, Annie, it's all right. I'm here. I'll take care of you. Don't worry."

She opened her eyes, saw him, and began to push and shove to escape. When he wouldn't let her go, she punched him in the chest.

"Annie, cut it out." He shook her vigorously. "It was only a nightmare. You're all right. No one's going to hurt you."

She blinked, realized who he was, then collapsed into his arms and wept bitterly.

He soothed her and quieted her, reassured her and calmed her. Then she was filled with apologies about being a silly old woman with drunken nightmares.

He held her in his arms and promised her that he would

make the nightmares go away. Gradually she relaxed. He turned off the lights and drew the covers over them.

"Mickey," she whispered in his ear.

"Yes."

"Are you still awake?"

"Sure am," he said.

"Would you do me a favor if it's not too much of a bother?"

"Name it."

"Make love to me again, very gently and sweetly."

"My privilege," he said.

As he prepared her for more love he wondered what were the names of the demons he was fighting.

63

ANNE'S STORY

Super Bowl Sunday 1971 was a day of gray skies and snow flurries in Washington. I played hostess to a group of John's friends at a party in his apartment. To everyone's surprise, the Baltimore Colts, for whom we were all cheering, beat the fearsome Dallas Cowboys 16–13, paced by a kicker improbably named O'Brien, who, I gather, was never heard from again.

The wives were to come for cocktails after the game, John wisely reasoning that there was no point in forcing them to pretend they were interested, so I was the only woman present.

I was worried about Jimmy, whose flight training was beginning at Colorado Springs. Nixon had ordered the Christmas bombing of Hanoi that winter and it now seemed possible that in another year or two my son would be dropping bombs on other women's children. Bethie had left school without her degree and was living with Ted while he finished his architect's training in Philadelphia, both of them being supported by his family. Her time was divided between rock festivals and marches on Washington. She told me, eyes glowing with a martyr's fervor, that a sex-and-drugs blast in rural New York two summers ago was "the most important religious event since Jesus Christ."

Davie had flunked out of Georgetown Prep, mostly because of indifference. I managed to find a small private boarding academy for him in the Maryland hills that guaranteed college admission, but Davie insisted that he didn't want to go to college. Rather, he wanted to be a farmer, "somewhere out west," and live the simple and natural life for which we were intended. Mark was captain of his class basketball team.

I often wondered if my affair with John made things worse for the kids. I did my best to spend time with the two younger boys, even awkwardly trying to provide sex instruction—information that seemed to interest neither of them. Yet I was obsessed with John; he was my love, my husband, my father, my son, my everything. I suppose I cheated on the kids. To be fair to myself, I also suppose it was too late by then to make any difference.

As the game ended and the first dark clouds of night scudded up the Potomac, the phone rang. I answered it as I usually did when there were parties at the Watergate apartment. I was very much in charge.

"Senator Duncan's residence," I said brightly.

"This is Dr. Clark of the Springwood Home. May I speak to the Senator?"

I knew instantly what had happened. The one weekend John had not visited her. I felt my stomach knot and my throat tighten.

"Of course."

"John," I whispered in his ear, amid the din created by celebrating Colt fans. "Springwood."

His eyes caught mine. He winced with anguish. We both knew.

Sue had died of a sudden attack of viral pneumonia. "Nothing we could do," Dr. Clark had insisted.

John never forgave himself. If he had visited Springwood the day before, he told me often in the next two weeks, he might have noticed that she was "not up to par" and warned the doctors.

The din in the apartment subsided instantly when John, white-faced and stricken, returned from the phone and said grimly, "Sue's dead."

His friends quickly drifted away. I called his children while he sat on the couch, looking out at the gray river, hands on his head, as if to shut out the sounds of his grief. I held him in my arms for a while, sensed that he wanted to be alone, kissed him quietly, and slipped out of the apartment.

I grieved for him, but fool that I was, I didn't suspect that Sue's death would have any effect on our relationship.

I remained in the background at the funeral, despite pleas from John and his daughter that I grieve with the family.

"Why not?" the girl asked. "You're part of the family."

"Irish Catholic hang-ups," I pleaded.

She shook her long blond hair slowly. "I don't understand, Anne, but I respect your religion."

I guess I didn't respect their tastes on the subject. What would people say? The ancient battle cry in the Irish quest for respectability.

Our life continued as it had before. John mourned for a week and took me back into his bed. I wasn't sure that it was proper. But I missed him and we needed each other. His love was, if anything, more intense and more abandoned.

At the end of February I met him for supper, after a late session of the Senate, at the Monocle, a restaurant around the corner from the Capital, frequented by senators, congressmen, highly paid lobbyists, high-priced whores, and occasional congressional mistresses like myself.

John was glum and preoccupied. He had a second bourbon and water, which was most unusual.

"Things have to change between us, ma'am," he said halfway through the second drink.

"Oh," I replied nonchalantly, the mistress coolly prepared to accept her marching papers. My heart was already pounding and the mental voice in my head screamed in pain and protest.

"I want to marry you," he said, reaching for my hand. "Not right away, of course. In the spring, maybe June. My daughter and son are strongly in favor. My constituents will love you as soon as they get to know you. My staff thinks it would be a very wise move. . . . "

Consult the staff and the family before the woman, I thought furiously, even though I understood.

"I'd love to marry you, John," I said slowly, now seeing the whole pattern, which I had blindly missed after his wife's death. "I can't. I already have a husband."

"You're divorced," he said, baffled. "I don't understand."

"Catholics can divorce, but they can't remarry. In God's eyes I'm married to Jim Reilly for the rest of my life."

"But, ma'am, you love me. I know you do."

"More than I love life itself. I still can't do it. I'd be excommunicated."

I'm not sure now whether I would have been. Yet the notion that a remarried Catholic was excommunicated was so strong in the Catholic culture in which I grew up that it was beyond question.

"The Church has changed so much," he argued. "You eat meat on Friday; you hear Mass in English. Haven't they changed on this? Or won't they in the next few years?"

"Absolutely not, John. We view marriage as a sacrament. Even God couldn't dissolve my marriage to Jim Reilly."

"Can't you get an indulgence or something? It doesn't matter what it costs. I have to . . . "

"An annulment? I don't think so. Maybe. I'll try."

I felt a hint of hope. Maybe there was a possibility. Then I knew how much I loved John and how passionately I wanted to be his wife.

He had to remarry, of course. His state would never send back to the Senate a liberal Democrat who was reputed to be a playboy about town.

For the first time that night, our love was not satisfying. The bloom was off. The daydream was over. The demands of the real world were closing in.

Catholic U then was a madhouse (I guess it still is) pretending to be a university. It was a collection of seminaries, a decent liberal arts college, a terrible graduate school, a clerical faculty locked in combat with the bishops who were its trustees, a sycophant administration that fawned on the trustees, and a lay faculty that hunkered down, held its classes, and minded its own business.

I had published two more papers on Vermeer, rather cynically spinning out nonsense about the utensils in other Dutch painters' works. Even though I was a woman and was paid two-thirds the salary of male assistant professors, I was a likely candidate for tenure. Publishing faculty members were so rare that the deans were delighted when they found that by some mischance they had one.

So I didn't consider talking to a member of the canon law faculty there. I'm not even sure I knew we had one.

I asked my chairman a hypothetical question and he suggested I see a priest at the Washington chancery office. I made an appointment with the man for the following week.

The Washington archdiocese was a battlefield at the time and the chancery, behind the old redbrick civil war cathedral (where I half-expected to see Abraham Lincoln kneeling in the back in silent prayer), a fortress under siege. Cardinal O'Boyle, with a stroke of his lordly pen, had dismissed half a hundred of his priests for publicly dissenting from the birth control encyclical. The other bishops had paid lip service to the papal ruling but refrained from trying to impose it on their priests and people. They had ducked a fight and O'Boyle seemed to want one. On the other hand, only in Washington did the clergy challenge their archbishop in a public confrontation.

So there was not much time for divorced women who wanted annulments so they could remarry. The priest, a haggard, unhappy man with stringy hair and dirty fingernails, asked me some blunt questions. Was Jim a homosexual? Did he intend never to have children? Might he have been married before without my knowledge? Could he have in the presence of others explicitly repudiated the permanence of our union before we were married?

I listened to the litany of inquiries with a feeling of helplessness. They had nothing to do with the ordinary life of ordinary human beings. They had been put together in a dusty and arid old room in the Vatican by men who had been taken away from their families as small boys and who had never known the sting of desire or the joy of love.

"I don't see much chance for you under the present legislation," the priest said briskly. He did not add what others could have added and transformed my life. There was a strong possibility that the annulment legislation would change.

"It would appear not," I said sadly. "There's not much room in the rules for compassion, is there?"

"The Church is not interested in compassion, Mrs. Reilly," he said superciliously. "Our presumption is in favor of the sacramental bond. We must protect the sanctity of the bond, even if the cost is human suffering. People are not important, sacraments are."

"Yes, Father." The familiar docile assent of the loyal Catholic woman.

"Are you contemplating remarriage, Mrs. Reilly?" he asked bluntly.

"There is a man who wants to marry me," I said, not even shocked by his impertinence.

"I must solemnly remind you that you put his and your immortal souls in grave jeopardy if you attempt such a marriage."

"I know that, Father. I won't marry him."

He didn't believe me. "Should you do so, you will cut yourself off from the Church's sacraments and from God's love for the rest of your life."

"I know that too, Father," I said firmly. "I have no intention of doing so."

I walked all the way down to DuPont Plaza in the biting March wind. Somehow I didn't think Jesus would have been so stern and unsympathetic with me.

The door had slammed shut. I was numb with sorrow. I had always known that my relationship with John couldn't last. I was mentally prepared for its ending some day. But I hadn't thought it would end so soon. Nor had I any idea it would end because John wanted to marry me and was now free to do so.

I ate supper with him that night at the Sans Souci and told him the worst. I thought he wouldn't believe me but he did.

"It seems a cruel kind of Christianity, ma'am," he said sadly, "begging your pardon for saying so."

"Faith isn't supposed to be easy," I replied, filling up with tears.

"You understand that I have to remarry, don't you?" he said, pleading with his eyes for my understanding.

"Of course I do, John. This is my fault, not yours."

We made love that night with the bloom restored. That weekend we flew to Sea Island. John played golf, I swam, and we loved each other with all the affection and desire we had.

"There's no rush about any of this," he said. "I have a couple of years to work it out."

In a couple of years, oddly enough, we could have worked it out.

Perhaps I should have waited. I argued with myself that he was right, that there was no hurry.

I responded to my own arguments by saying that separation would only become more wrenching with each passing month, that I was risking John's career and his happiness, and that I was living in a state of mortal sin.

The last was decisive. I had hidden from my own sinfulness for two years. It was time to return to the Church of my childhood and seek forgiveness. I reread *Brideshead*, my favorite novel from the Catholic fiction course at Mundelein, and was impressed by Julia's sacrifice and the good effects it had on the lives of everyone. Perhaps my sacrifice would win me forgiveness and Beth a return to her faith and Jimmy survival in the war.

I made up my mind the night I finished rereading the book. I would do it as a prayer for myself and Jimmy and Beth. And John too, who would be better off without me.

God seemed to accept my sacrifice all right, but he didn't answer any of my prayers.

I'm sure you'll ask, Dr. Murphy, why I didn't walk out on the Church that was so cruel and insensitive to me. Your background is enough like mine that you know the answer. I had better write it down for the record. I didn't even think seriously about that alternative. My parents were certainly not especially devout—I suspect my mother must have used some kind of birth control after I made my unwelcome appearance. Nor was I a very good Catholic; how could I be when I had such a long, illicit love affair?

To be a Catholic was as natural to me as being American or Irish or a Democrat or breathing air or drinking water. It was unthinkable to be anything else. Two of my children were that way—Jimmy in the few years he had and now Mark. He and Tessie are more explicit about their reasons than I was able to be (or can be even now). Yet it's in their blood. You couldn't drive them out of the Church if you wanted to. Dave and Beth left the Church as quickly as they could, the one in indifference and the other in anger. Maybe that's not a bad performance for those of us whose kids grew up in the late sixties.

Whatever my kids do or did, I've become more stubborn in my Catholicism as I've grown older. The Pope himself could tell me I had to leave the Church now and I wouldn't go.

I knew that I couldn't break up with John and remain in Washington. I would resign my post at Catholic U, return to Chicago with Mark (leaving Davie to board at his academy, where perhaps he would be better off, away from me), and hunt for a job.

John and I dragged on until the end of the academic year, neither of us enjoying the relationship all that much, but both of us too addicted to end it.

He drove me to the airport on Memorial Day and kissed me good-bye, big tears in his brown plainsman's eyes.

64

Of course they went to Mass on Sunday morning, to give thanks for the White Sox victory.

Anne donned a lemon-colored early autumn dress, to match the persisting Indian summer skies and, arm in arm with Mickey, walked up Michigan to Chicago Avenue and over to State Street and Holy Name Cathedral.

"You're not going to receive Communion, are you?" she asked him.

"Why not?" he replied, astonished at her question.

"Aren't we both in the state of sin?"

"Speak for yourself, woman. I'm not."

"Don't you think we've been sinning these last two days?"

"What sin?"

"Fornication."

"That's something kids do."

"Sexual intercourse without marriage is fornication, no matter how old you are."

"I don't believe it," he said flatly. "Do you think God will send us to hell because we finally are brave enough to admit that we love each other? I suspect he's pleased with us."

She hesitated. She was truly not sure. The rules were very clear. Yet maybe God wanted her and Mickey together. Friday night she had not even thought about sin. Yesterday she was so happy that sin didn't seem to matter. Now, with the doors of the Cathedral standing open above them, she wished that there might be a way out.

"I hope not," she said slowly.

She guided him into the church, slipping by the rector's eye without, she thought, being noticed.

Although the priest who said Mass was her favorite preacher, she did not listen to his words.

What am I to think? she asked the Lord repeatedly. *I love him. It seemed good. We're not married. If I turned him away—not that I even thought of that—we would never be married. We're both too fragile to risk rejections. He loves me. I love him. Was it wrong?*

There were no answers.

The terror that had made her wake up screaming the previous night still lurked in the back hallways of her brain, edging through all the little rooms where the secrets and guilts and failures of the past still lurked. Creeping down those dark and dismal passages was another fear, the one to which she could not quite give a name.

Then the question subtly changed. No longer was it whether she should receive Holy Communion. Now it was whether she should continue with Mickey. It was an absurd relationship, was it not? An old man and an old woman pretending they were young again. She had left sexual passion behind when she boarded the 727 at National Airport on Memorial Day 1971. She had also left behind a man she had hurt terribly, and, as it turned out, needlessly. How could she run the risk of that again? Would she not fail Mickey the way she had failed all her other men? Was not the blight on her life permanent? Wouldn't she always be punished and wouldn't that punishment always affect those she loved—her daddy, Dick, Jimbo, Jimmy, David, John, Matt? Could she expose Mickey to the same danger?

Mike stepped out of the pew at Communion time and waited for her to accompany him. Sadly she shook her head. He winced, more hurt than she thought he would be, and went by himself to receive the Body of Christ.

Dear God, am I being a fool?

As they left the church the rector was waiting for them.

"Aha, Mike Casey the Cop! You tried to sneak into my church without greeting me. Doubtless you're attempting to escape your solemn obligation to accept collection envelopes. I herewith present to you your own personal box of envelopes, personally autographed by the rector—me, of course. Alas, the Cardinal is off at some meeting in Rome or we would have his autograph too."

Blushing profusely, Mickey accepted the box from his cousin and automatically gave it to Anne. Just as automatically she put it in her purse.

Father Ryan's nearsighted little eyes danced with amusement.

65

Mike watched Anne's joy dry up, slowly at first, then rapidly as Sunday burned itself out. Her contagious effervescence and vitality withered as rich black earth turns dry and brown under the heat of a long summer drought.

After Mass and breakfast at the Magic Pan, she dragged him into the Esquire to see a double feature of *Star Wars* and *Return of the Jedi*, reprimanding him severely for having missed both masterpieces. They held hands at first and then cuddled in the relatively empty theater.

He took her back to the apartment and made love to her again, insisting that the scantily clad Princess Leia had aroused his passions. She cooperated, but the wantonness had disappeared. They ate supper at the Mexican restaurant called La Margarita, one of the few Near North eateries open on Sunday. She was listless and absentminded throughout the meal.

"What gives, Annie?" he asked as they walked along the lake shore after dinner.

"Emotional letdown, that's all," she said.

"Are you sure?"

"Of course I'm sure," she replied testily.

"Can I help?"

"Am I not entitled to a little privacy?" she almost shouted at him. "Haven't you taken enough of me already?"

"I'm sorry," he said, surprised and hurt.

They continued to walk in silence.

"No, I'm the one who ought to be sorry. Please, forgive me. I have some things I have to work out with my shrink. It's not you. You're wonderful."

Paying no attention to a young couple approaching from the opposite direction, she threw her arms around him and kissed him enthusiastically, pressing her body firmly against his.

"Hey, rapist . . . " he protested.

"I really am sorry . . . nervous letdown, some emotional problems. I'll be all right and I do love you."

About the love he could have no question. But he was not at all sure she'd be all right.

In bed her love was generous again, yet something was missing. He slept with one cop's ear tuned for the sound of a screaming woman. This time, however, she slept peacefully enough.

When he kissed her at 5:30—his rules required that he be the first one at 11th and State every Monday morning—she muttered sleepily, "I still love you."

It was, nonetheless, all wrong. He didn't like the explanation he had come to in the course of the night, by a process that was the very model of the empirical logic he had praised in *Principles of Detection*. As he himself had written, the fact that a detective didn't like a solution and found it highly improbable didn't mean he should fail to pursue it with all the resources at his command when it was the only explanation that fit the available evidence. There was no room in modern detection for the dogmatic exclusion of the highly improbable or almost impossible.

What resources had he at his command?

Not many.

It would require a conversation sometime today with a highly improbable character who would never fit the ideals of *Principles of Detection*.

Blackie Ryan the Priest.

BOOK FIVE

66

Anne woke up about an hour after Mike left, uneasy and ill, feeling like a permanent invalid. Her Indian summer allergies had returned with characteristic punctuality. Her sinuses were blocked and her head hurt as if she were suffering a massive hangover. Moreover, she didn't want to go near the gallery. True, the Father Kenny exhibition had been shipped off. Yet the tricks that her imagination had played on her had changed the gallery from a place she loved to a place she dreaded. There was something distasteful waiting there for her this morning. Probably it was something she had forgotten to do and would have to do. It would be so much easier to swallow some decongestant pills and go back to bed to sleep for several more hours.

It was a tantalizing temptation. By labeling it a temptation, she mastered it. That was what one was supposed to do with temptations. Sandy would be in for the first time since she'd been hospitalized, determined to compensate for her absence, and would have to be sent home early. And the final proofs for the Peggy Donlon catalog would require careful attention. She'd have to negotiate with a number of agents about future exhibitions. No, this was not a day to succumb to temptation.

She sighed, dragged herself out of bed, and took a quick shower. Only as she was dressing did she realize that for the first time in many years she had missed her morning prayers and that she had no intention of going to Mass this morning. Why kneel in the back of church when she couldn't receive Holy Communion?

Did that mean she was not yet ready to confess her sins with Mickey?

She considered carefully as she buttoned the jacket of her light-gray suit. She needed time to think through the

319

problem, to make sure there would not be another tragic mistake. She had been back in Chicago several months before she finally worked up enough nerve to seek forgiveness for her sins of the flesh with John Duncan in the mass production confessional anonymity of St. Peter's in the Loop. The old Franciscan priest chewed the hell out of her, warning her that since she didn't deserve the grace of repentance this time, she had no reason to expect that if she yielded to the sins of the flesh again she would ever receive another opportunity to be forgiven.

"You must spend the rest of your life expiating for these sins!" he had bellowed at her.

She could have told him about expiation, and worse sins than those of the flesh—which would haunt her until the day she died.

I can't go on with Mickey, she thought. *It simply won't work; and I'll hurt him, I know I will.* She realized, nevertheless, that when her sensuality was aroused it wasn't easily put back into mothballs. Only when she'd placed six hundred miles of American countryside between herself and John Duncan had she been confident she wouldn't succumb to the sadness of his eyes and the strength of his arms. It wouldn't be that easy to run away from Mickey Casey. *What a damned fool I was*, she reprimanded herself, *for letting him in on Friday night.*

Fifteen minutes later, after buying the usual croissants, she stood in front of the gallery, key in hand. It seemed perfectly peaceful inside, the first posters for the Donlon exhibition gaily decorating the window. Yet she did not want to go in. What if her imagination continued to play tricks on her, even though the Father Kenny pieces had been safely deposited in the warehouse?

She squared her shoulders in the door and strode briskly in, the competent and mature historian and art dealer.

Nothing unusual happened, and she sighed with relief. It was probably all over, a nasty interlude she brought on herself.

Everything was in order in her office and in the tiny living suite behind it. She shuffled through a large stack of unopened mail on her desk. *I kind of let things slide last week*, she thought. *Sandy will be upset with me.*

She decided to make a quick survey of the basement exhibition rooms to be certain they were in good order for the arrival of the Donlon pictures at the end of the week. "Lunch with Maria," she wrote on her note pad. And then above that notation she wrote, "Call Dr. Murphy." She underlined it three times and then added in large letters, "TODAY!"

She bounced out the door of her office and down the stairs, sighing with relief that the wall space on the landing was empty. She turned on the floodlights at the foot of the stairs, the better to chase down any specks of dirt that might embarrass her, and even more Sandy, at the Donlon show.

She entered the L-shaped room that was the first in her basement network and saw it hanging there on the wall, just where it had been, "Divine Justice" demanding her reparation. "Oh, my God," she exclaimed. "What is it doing here? I know I packed it and shipped it to the warehouse. How did it get back?"

What will Sandy say? And Mickey—he'll call and maybe come over to make sure that all of Father Kenny's pieces are gone. How did it ever get back here?

Hurriedly she took it off the wall and carried it to the storeroom. It seemed much heavier than it had before. She leaned it against the wall, gasping for breath, and only then noticed that the storeroom door, which she always kept locked, was ajar. She flung the door open and, to her horror, saw a torn and broken carton inside. Something had happened in this room over the weekend.

"I didn't leave it here," she said. "I know I didn't. I packed it and shipped it off with the others!"

She tried to recall. There was an odd memory in her head that, no, she hadn't shipped it away with the others. She had locked it in this room. Why in God's name would she have done that?

Hastily she grabbed the carton and stuffed the heavy

canvas into it, then closed the door and locked it. She leaned against the door from the outside, breathing heavily, as though by the weight of her body she might keep the hideous painting inside the storeroom forever.

Then a familiar hypnotic stupor seeped through her veins, numbing her much as a tranquilizer would. *This happened before. I won't even remember what happened when I get back to my office.*

Anne returned to the main floor of the gallery in a zombielike trance and noticed, back in her office, only that her sinus headache seemed worse. She called Maria at the bank and made the appointment for lunch the following week and called Dr. Murphy and was told that her hour tomorrow was still available. "Thank you for keeping it for me," she said humbly.

Dr. Murphy was noncommittal. "See you then."

Sandy arrived at 9:30, breathless and apologetic for being late. "It won't happen again, Missus. Colonel Kokoshka and I go to dinner last night, Polish neighborhood. They dance polkas, old-fashioned Polish peasant dance, all night."

"I know about polkas." Anne laughed. "They beat the Nautilus and jogging for calorie destruction."

Sandy was pale and thinner, but her eyes were sparkling. Anne's cautious questions led to the disclosure that the Colonel had not been as yet permitted into Sandy's apartment to stay. He was, however, being very respectful and was not drinking.

"He's courting you?"

"You bet! Is nice."

"Don't keep him waiting too long, Sandy," she warned.

"Not to worry, Missus!" Sandy replied, using one of Anne's favorite phrases.

All would presumably be well between the two of them, as well as it ever could be between a man and a woman. Then Mickey called, terse and military, very much the Deputy Superintendent of Police again.

"Everything all right?" he snapped.

"Sinus headache," she murmured. "Everything else is fine. Sandy's back and she's fine too. Everything is hokay."

"Good. Excellent. Can I buy you supper tonight?"

"I need time to think, Mickey," she said slowly.

"Think about what?" he barked.

"About us," she replied.

"What's there to think about?"

"I told you I had these personal problems, Mickey; give me a few days to work them out. Please."

"Sure," he said, the police officer's stiffness going out of his voice. "I don't mean to push you too hard. I love you so much that I miss you after I'm away from you for two hours."

"I love you too," she said, sincerely enough. She loved him far more than she ought to.

"Can I call you tomorrow?" he asked.

"Of course. Please do."

She hung up, her hands sweaty and her eyes smarting with tears. What a terrible way to treat a wonderful man. *I'm doing the same thing to him that I did to John, only more quickly. Would it be such a horrible mistake to risk another marriage? I don't know, I just don't know. And I'm not sure where to turn for help. Father Ryan? Dr. Murphy? Who else is there? They won't understand unless I tell them the truth. Has it finally come time to tell the truth? Can I tell the truth and still live?* She brushed such questions aside, pending her next session with Dr. Murphy, and began to work feverishly on her TRS-80 Model IV computer to catch up with last week's mail before Sandy discovered how far behind she was.

"The priest is here, Missus," Sandy announced.

"Cathedral rector?" she asked, once again subconsciously imitating the Polish language's obsession with titles.

"Yes, Missus," Sandy said.

"I think Madame Kokoshka is not altogether convinced that I have either the maturity or the dignity appropriate to be the rector," said Father Ryan, his hurt leprechaun smile just hinting at the total lack of impressive qualities—part of his Father Brown game.

"You can go right back to Holy Name Cathedral," she

said, standing at attention, "and call the Deputy Police Commissioner and tell him that you've inspected the gallery and you can find no trace of the paintings of Father Desmond Kenny."

"Skip," said Father Ryan.

"What?"

"His nickname was Skip. Did you know that?"

"I can't remember," she said nervously.

"Strange nickname," Father Ryan said, glancing around in mystification, searching for the chair that was always in the same place whenever he came into the gallery.

"Then you don't deny you came here on instructions of your cousin, Mickey Casey the Cop?"

"You *are* psychic," he said, totally unimpressed.

"I don't have to be psychic to know that. Of course you searched the gallery from top to bottom before you came round to my office?" There was a jab of fear at her heart, sudden and inexplicable.

"I looked around," he admitted casually. "I would have come even if Mike Casey the Cop hadn't called me. I'm glad to see the Kenny show is gone."

She relaxed and sat down on her side of the desk. "So am I, Father. So am I."

"You and the Superintendent made an attractive couple at Mass Sunday," he observed guilelessly.

"It would never work, Father."

"I didn't say it would." He shrugged his shoulders an inch or two. "As I told you before, the simple parish priest is not a matchmaker."

"The hell you're not!" she said in a rare outburst of profanity.

His eyes twinkled. "Let me know if I can help, Anne. I mean that."

"I will, Father," she said fervently. "I will."

He waited in his chair, inviting her to say more. *He really is more non-directive than his sister the psychiatrist.*

"Well," he said, standing up. "I guess I'd better be going. See you in church next Sunday, if not before."

"You'll see me alone, Father," she said with as much determination as she could muster.

"Maybe," was his only reply.

After he left she returned to her computer, hesitating with her fingers on the switch. *God sent me someone who offered to help, the most helpful priest I've ever known.* She remembered his patience and kindness the first time she'd met him, when she'd exploded at him with more rage than ever was aimed at a priest before. *He offered to help, he wants to help, maybe even he can help, and I sent him away without saying a word.*

Whatever happens to me I richly deserve.

67

"Am I ever likely to forget it?" Tim Guinan's almost-blind hazel eyes burned fiercely.

"I don't suppose so. You were on duty when the alarm came in."

"Was the captain ever around? Weren't those the days when they were all either at the track or in whorehouses every afternoon? Did not they expect the lieutenants to cover for them?"

Tim had been born in County Mayo just before the turn of the century, fought in the Western Brigade of the IRA during the Troubles and the Civil War, and fled to America when the Free Staters won. He must have joined the force a few weeks after he arrived and then, by ability and clout—and probably bribery—rose rapidly enough to be the second in command of the precinct in which Mother of Mercy parish was located. A thin little man with bushy white hair, a deeply lined face, and a quick impish smile, he reminded Mike of an ancient bantamweight prizefighter whose movements began with the cockiness of his past and then faded into the vague confusion of weariness and age.

Tim remembered very few things that had happened since he retired as chief of uniformed police (as they were called in those days) the month John Kennedy was killed.

Had be been a crook? By the standards of the old days he'd "taken" less than most. But his expensive home in Palos, with its tasteful early nineteenth-century antique furniture and its plush light blue parlor carpet, suggested that he hadn't been sternly honest either.

Like all true Sons of Erin, he routinely answered questions by asking others.

"A terrible thing—the fire, I mean," Mike said, following the rules of discourse of an Irish cop of the old days.

"Wasn't it worse, even, than the stockyards fire?"

"The records indicate your lads did a thorough investigation, probably better than we'd do today."

Dead silence. *Never answer a question, even with another question, when you don't have to,* Mike thought.

Mike had driven to the southwest suburbs because of a little background digging he had done. Opening the files he'd ordered from the archives on the Mother of Mercy fire, he'd discovered that Tim Guinan had been on the spot and done the legwork for the Blue Ribbon Commission.

"And they never caught the arsonist after all the work you people did?" he said sympathetically to the old man.

"Whoever said there was an arsonist? Didn't the Commission say it was spontaneous combustion?"

"The word was that there was a pyromaniac from the parish who was already in a mental institution by the time the report came in."

"Was there ever any proof of that, now?" The old man's sightless eyes glinted shrewdly.

"That was supposed to be one of the reasons he was never brought to trial. He was so sick that he would never be released; there was not enough evidence for a conviction, and it would renew the pain of the families."

"Is that what they're saying?"

Mike filled Tim's tumbler with more bourbon. "It seems to me that it wouldn't take much evidence to get a conviction."

"You might think that, might you not, especially with

the Church so eager to escape the blame—and the lawsuits?"

"I might."

"I'll tell you one, Michael Patrick Casey." The old man emptied his glass in one fierce swallow. "I may have done some things as a cop that you wouldn't do today, but has anyone ever said that Tim Guinan would let a mass murderer escape if he had any evidence beyond mere conjecture?"

"Not in my presence," Mike said, knowing what the answer was and also having his own answer.

The young man in the mental institution, who was reputed to have died in the early forties, might have started the fire. Probably he'd started it. But there was not a shred of hard evidence to prove it. Moreover, the rumor that he had was a useful escape for both the police force and the Church.

Dear God, where does that leave us?

68

ANNE'S STORY

"We certainly can't offer you an assistant professorship," Father Matt Sweeney, the president of St. Columbanus University, said. "The best we can do, I'm afraid, is an instructorship, and that only two-thirds time."

Sweet Matthew Sweeney was a handsome, curly-haired black Irishman, with sparkling blue eyes, a quick and kindly smile, a gift for turning phrases, and the glad hand of a ward committeeman. His doctorate was in education. I guessed even then that he'd never looked at a research paper—one of his own, or anyone else's—since the day Fordham University awarded him his degree. He was, however, precisely because of his City Hall style, an extremely effective fund-raiser, greatly admired by the wealthy Catholic women of the Chicago metropolitan area, people like my aunt Aggie, who had set up my interview with him.

"How many class hours is that?" I asked, my heart sinking.

"Well, let me see; that comes, well, let's say twelve hours. It's three courses and our normal load is four, but since you only have two preparations—freshman history— it still adds up to two-thirds." He smiled winningly. "I wish we could do more."

"No courses in art history?" I asked.

His smile expanded into a broad grin. "Ours is a teaching university, Dr. Reilly. We train nurses and accountants, teachers and doctors and lawyers. Business or nursing majors or prelaw or premed aren't much interested in art history."

"I was in tenure-track at C.U.," I said tentatively.

"Your publication record is impressive," he said; "we're happy to have someone with your training and productivity on our staff. It's late in the year, however, and our budget is limited. I wish I could do more. Of course, when we consider you for assistant professor next year, I'm sure your publications will weigh heavily in our decision. I have to remind you, however, that ours is a teaching university."

"I understand," I replied mechanically.

He was far too gracious to say it, but the only reason I was in his office was that Aunt Aggie was a major contributor to St. Columbanus. Hiring me was a favor to her and not a compliment to my academic productivity.

"Come on," he said cheerfully. "I'll buy you lunch. The faculty dining room here isn't very good—like everything else, I'm afraid—but, still, we have a pretty fine spirit and with some breaks we're going to make this the Catholic Northwestern."

In the dining room he greeted every member of the faculty present by first name, inquired about their wives and children, and introduced me, always with the respectful title Dr. Reilly, as someone who was going to be "playing on the team" next year. The men on the faculty looked me over appreciatively, save for a few elderly priests. The two women professors did not approve at all.

So I went to work at St. Columbanus. And, the next year, in fact, I was made an assistant professor, but didn't receive a raise. I was also appointed to four faculty committees and showcased as "one of our most productive scholars." I needed the job so badly that I didn't argue.

It was impossible not to like Matt Sweeney. Ten or fifteen pounds heavier than when he was star basketball player at Columbanus, he was always genial, relaxed, and informal. He agreed with your criticisms and complaints, promised that he'd do what he could, although there wasn't any room in the budget. "The treasurer won't let me do it."

John Leary, the treasurer and academic dean (at St. C.'s they were not thought to be incompatible offices), was a mean little man with pop eyes and a lisp. He was one of the priests who'd turned his back on me in the dining room. The members of the religious order that taught at St. Columbanus praised him as a financial wizard, a man with vast business experience before he entered the order. I found out that that meant he'd worked as a clerk in his father's shoe store.

' Matt was expert in the self-fulfillment psychological jargon that seemed to have replaced the Baltimore Catechism party line for the new post–Vatican Council generation of Catholic priests. "We really have to focus our resources to facilitate the individual developmental processes, to maximize the students' experience and fulfillment, and to orient them for productive and creative and self-satisfying lives." Such was the type of exhortation at faculty meetings over which Matt presided. Either the other faculty members didn't mind the jargon or they had heard it so often as to be immune to it or, most likely, they simply didn't mind because Sweet Matthew was such a likable human being.

"Matt is one man who is never going to go through a mid-life crisis," Joe Harris, a colleague in the history department, told me. He could not have been more wrong.

I took the job at St. Columbanus because I needed the money. I hadn't saved anything in Washington, I was in debt to Aunt Aggie, and my support from Jimbo diminished after I received my doctorate. Though Mark was the only one in the family left at home, I was still afraid to touch the money my parents had left me, feeling that someday the children might need it. I needed a job to pay the bills and to maintain my carefully developed sense of personal independence. "It's not much of a school," Aunt Aggie warned me, "but you had to come back to Chicago, so it's about the best we can do."

Occasionally I reflected that if I had not fled to Washington to escape my husband and mother-in-law, I might have finished up at the University of Chicago, and be teaching at a distinguished university. Now I was doomed to be forever mired in a Catholic backwater.

Perhaps I deserved such punishment. Wasn't I, as one of the religious studies faculty told me, guilty of pride and stubbornness in thinking that a woman, who ought to be a wife and mother, was entitled to success in the university world? (The religious studies department was, by the way, an all-male enclave that had much of the atmosphere of a country club locker room at the end of the day when the golfers were beginning to drink.) I wasn't sure then that he was wrong, even though there were consciousness-raising groups all around me, both in Washington and in Chicago.

I moved into a small apartment in the Jefferson Park district on the Northwest Side, enrolled Mark at Fenwick— which meant driving him to high school every day before I went to the university—and settled down to prepare lectures on freshman history for future nurses and accountants, most of whom were taking history because it was convenient for their schedules. About the content of history they couldn't have cared less.

I cried myself to sleep almost every night that first winter, a bitter, bitter cold Chicago winter, because of my loss, of John Duncan. The pain gradually lessened and life went on, but I was desperately tired at the end of each day, exhausted by the fruitless effort of trying to stir up a modicum of intellectual curiosity in the bland Eastern European faces that stared at me in my classrooms. Still, I worked on two more articles about Vermeer. One expanded my work on household utensils and now included such contemporaries of his as Pieter de Hooch and Nicolaes Maes, both of whom had even more numerous dishes and plates and goblets in their paintings, though they were not nearly as gifted as poor Jan Vermeer. The other compared versions of the "Procuress" as portrayed by Vermeer, Van Baburen, and Van Bronckhorst. I argued that Vermeer's effort—with its splendid glass and tumbler and carafe—was the most domestic, the most chaste, and the most erotic because the girl was smugly enjoying the petting. I even threw in some mumbo jumbo, which I half believed, about the feminism of Vermeer's vision.

Mind you, such academic game-playing is tolerable only when it is viewed as play and not as serious business, especially at a "teaching university." But I did them anyway, for my self-respect. Later I would find that my publication record could be used against me on the grounds that it showed I was not sufficiently interested in the students. In fact, as one colleague pointed out, "You'd make the rest of us look bad, and you a woman at that."

I haven't given up academic pretensions, Dr. Murphy. Despite the demands of the gallery, I still write an article every year. I even have a contract, a tiny advance, and a half-finished manuscript for a "coffee table book" on household utensils in painting from the Middle Ages to the present. I enjoy such work most of the time. And even when I'm dead tired at the end of the day and my eyes hurt, I still plug away. It's important to me to know that the money that went into my Ph.D.—none of which I earned—was not wasted.

I hated St. Columbanus University. It stank of mediocrity. With the exception of a few people like myself, who felt tied to Chicago, and some faculty spouses from Northwestern and the University of Chicago or Chicago Circle, the faculty was fourth-rate, innocent of publication records and teaching skills. They were cynical, disillusioned, bitter. They moped their way through life, realizing they were failures, the dregs of their classes in graduate school who'd been sent to a Catholic university because it was the only institution inept enough to hire them. They bitched about the administration and the religious order that ran the school, made fun of the Catholic Church (most of them were more or less practicing Catholics), pretended to be sophisticated and well-informed about things Catholic because they read the *National Catholic Reporter* and *Commonweal*, and looked down their noses on the ordinary Catholic laity and especially their students.

"Our typical student," Joe Harris once told me, "is a racist, a superpatriot, a crude materialist, and a male chauvinist even if she's a woman. They've come to college to play a game—answers and tests for grades will get them jobs so they can move out of the city, get away from the blacks, and buy a tacky little suburban house they can fill up with children who are no more sophisticated or intelligent than they are."

"That's Chicago Catholicism for you," said another history instructor who'd not yet finished her dissertation at the University of Chicago and never would. "The kind of people who make Mayor Daley a hero."

"Why don't they go to Chicago Circle?" I asked on another occasion.

"Because they want a Catholic education," said Joe derisively. "Matt smiles his genial smile at their parents, promises them a 'solid Catholic formation and an opportunity to enrich their personal growth and development,' and your typical ethnic parent is willing to shell out five thousands dollars a year. It's a living."

"They're exploiters of the poor and the oppressed," a faculty woman agreed. "They deserve to be exploited themselves."

I didn't argue. Later I would learn that they were both wrong. There were some young people in my class with first-rate minds and imaginations who were desperately eager to learn and to whose curiosity and ability our faculty was immune. Columbanus was probably no worse than most of the Catholic institutions in the country that claim to be universities. Its mediocrity and cynicism simply resulted from the fact that the religious orders that run the universities are quite incapable of comprehending what a quality educational institution is. You pack the students in, process them through their courses and credits, collect tuition fees, announce an annual retreat, award them their degrees, and tell yourself you've done the work of the Lord.

Catholic U. had certainly been no better. But when I was there I had had something else to live for; now I was older, drifting toward forty-five, with almost no expectations, barely surviving emotionally. I suppose I enjoyed wallowing in the muck of mediocrity at St. Columbanus. I was disgusted with life and myself. It seemed singularly appropriate that I be on the faculty of a disgusting school. I was filled with self-pity, indeed enjoyed feeling sorry for myself, content although bitter at what I thought was the rock-bottom of my life. At least things couldn't get any worse, I told myself.

And I was dead wrong.

69

Maria folded her towel neatly and placed it on the locker bench, a strict Italian housekeeper even in the locker room of a pool.

"You're compulsively cautious, Anne. It comes from having had something to lose in the Depression. We were too poor to lose anything, so I'm never afraid to take chances—prudent chances." She chuckled. "In case I don't look the part just now, I emphasize that I'm a responsible bank president. Anyway, a gallery in the Oak Park Mall is a prudent chance. New-rich western suburbanites like me can buy art too. Not as much taste as your limousine liberal clientele, but just as much money. Men and money are the same. If you don't take chances, prudent chances"—she waved a hand flippantly—"you don't make anything and you don't get made either."

Maria had a rhetorical style all her own, kind of postexpressionist, Anne thought. Leaping from splash of color to splash of color and yet always making excellent sense if you were willing to leap with her.

After lunch she had dragged Anne unwillingly to the pool, and made her swim for twenty minutes. Then relax in the whirlpool and swim for twenty more minutes—and all the while urging her to open a Reilly Gallery in the Oak Park Mall, in whose survival Maria's bank was deeply interested.

For a few moments in the shower room Anne felt bathed clean spiritually, as if steam rising from the slippery floor, astringent liquid soap, thick suds, and the piercing sting of hot water against her skin could penetrate her soul and wash away its filth. She left the shower temporarily renewed.

Now while they dressed Maria drove home her point, leaning—arms akimbo—against the locker room wall, not so much immodest in her trim nudity as unconscious of it, a graceful retired ballerina, perhaps, with the body language of a svelte female Puck from *A Midsummer-Night's Dream*.

"How can you give me a loan," Anne asked, "when the gallery I already have is in trouble because of that Irish—"

Maria dismissed the faithless Shelaigh with a wave of her hand. "No bitch like her can do you in. Anne Reilly is a magic name. After what the banks have put into Brazil—not mine, I might add—you're a triple-A risk. Your very name is worth a loan. No one goes out of business these days because of one mistake. Just like with a man. When a man and woman love each other and want each other and they're both free, they're crazy not to take a chance. Hey, I don't have any clothes on. See what preaching does to me?"

Maria's homily had shifted back and forth from the Oak Park Gallery to Mike Casey, about whom she'd demanded to know as soon as Anne had joined her at L'Escargot. "Who is he, Anne? I can tell that he's it from the look on your face."

As Maria rummaged in her purse for her glasses ("no time to put in the contacts today") Anne's admiration for her friend's smooth and agile beauty crossed the subtle line that separates curiosity and admiration from the first faint beginnings of erotic desire.

What's wrong with me? Too much sex, I suppose.

"You make sense, Maria," she agreed. "If I were as young as you . . ."

"Age has nothing to do with it." Maria waved her hand again, this time quite unaware she had a bra in it. "Oops, I should never try to talk and dress at the same time. Anyway, when you stop taking chances, you stop living. And you're very much alive."

"I've never taken a chance in my life when I could avoid it," Anne said candidly.

"I think you really believe that," Maria said, fastening the slippery garment into place. And then in a deadly serious tone, quite uncharacteristic of her, she added, "Now's the time to change, kid, now or never."

Anne didn't ask whether her friend meant the new gallery or Mike.

70

Blackie was awakened early Monday morning, even before his usual hour for rising, from the sleep to which the just are entitled, by a phone call. "Blackie? Mike."

"Ah. Mike who?"

"Mike Casey, who else? Do me a favor. Go over to the gallery sometime this morning and make sure she's cleaned all that crap out. She says she has, but there's something fishy going on."

"Ah. The Reilly Gallery, you mean?"

"What other gallery? I'd do it myself, but I don't want it to look like I'm snooping and I've got a hell of a day lined up here."

"You seemed tolerably happy at church yesterday," the priest offered.

There was a pause at the other end of the line. "Happier than I've ever been in my life. Now, will you go over there and make sure she's buried all that crap someplace?"

"I had every intention of doing so, Michael. I'll let you know."

"I'll call you, say, after lunch?"

Blackie hung up and smiled. Mike Casey the Cop was in love, not just in love the way he was the afternoon the Skip Kenny exhibition opened. He was in love the way a man was who'd begun to possess the love of his life. The glow on both their faces before the 10:30 Mass yesterday could only be attributed to highly successful sexual intercourse, a fact which Blackie discreetly refrained from mentioning. He rejoiced, not necessarily over the sexual intercourse, but rather because of the appropriateness of their love. Sometimes it took the One In Charge a long time to work things out.

As far as Blackie could tell from a cursory inspection of the gallery, there was no trace of Skip Kenny. But Anne was a different woman from the one who had bounced cheerfully down the steps of the Cathedral the day before with Mike Casey the Cop on her arm. Her shoulders sagged, her fingers played nervously with a ballpoint pen, her gray eyes were like Lake Michigan on a dreary December day, and her lips were tight, as though she were holding back a cry of pain. Blackie offered his help but was politely sent on his way.

Yet he had had it in his power that morning, in her office, had he only known it, to crack the problem, to lance the abcess and begin the cure, to beat Des Kenny to the ground the way he deserved to be beaten a long time ago.

But he blew it.

"I couldn't find anything," he said cautiously to Mike, who called promptly at 12:30.

"How did she seem?" Mike demanded.

"Not as happy as she did yesterday," Blackie admitted.

"Damnation!" he exploded. "Blackie, can I come to see you this evening? Something has got to be done."

"By all means come," Blackie said. "But, candidly, because something must be done it doesn't follow that there is anything that we can do."

"There has to be," Mike said. "I love her so much."

Which, coming from Mike Casey the Cop, was an incredible statement.

After Mike hung up, Blackie reviewed the events of earlier in the day. The word *haggard* applied to Anne for the first time since he'd known her. She'd held herself together for a long time by feistiness and intelligence. More was required now. And whatever that more might be, she didn't seem to have it.

71

By the end of the day Anne was so tired, she had to read a letter three times before she understood it and then forgot its contents as she tried to type a reply. Her head ached, her back was sore, the contact lenses hurt her eyes, her stomach was tied in knots.

Maria's therapy had relaxed her for an hour or two, but the old anxieties had soon returned, draining her of the physical well-being she'd felt when she'd bid her friend good-bye promising she'd think seriously about her advice.

She'd sent Sandy home early because the Polish woman was still quite weak. Almost the moment she'd done so the phone rang. She knew what it would be.

A different song this time—"White Cliffs of Dover." "There'll be bluebirds over . . . "

She hung up quickly. Was that one of the songs he'd played over and over while he was painting and sculpting the statue of her? She didn't think so. Or maybe someone else remembered better than she.

There was nothing she could do about it, so she went back to her work with dogged determination.

She sealed the letters, stamped them, put them next to her purse and laid her head momentarily on the desk. *I must go to the basement to make sure the lights are off before I leave for the apartment.*

The rooms were already dark. Sandy must have taken care of that before she left, she said to herself. She felt as if she'd entered an eerie cavern swarming with vampire bats or perhaps a sewerlike dungeon on whose walls she'd find the chained skeletons of torture victims.

She turned on the lights and looked around, then half-gasped, half-screamed as she caught sight of "Divine Justice" hanging in the L-shaped room where she'd found it earlier, seeming to stare at her, balefully, implacably.

She felt a hot flame at the back of her head, like an overheated blow-dryer. The pillar of fire was back, moving slowly down the steps toward her. She tried to dodge around it and escape to the main floor, but the pillar was not to be evaded. Inexorably it drove her back against the wall next to "Divine Justice." She ran to the other door of the L-shaped room and collided with a solid wall. The room had been sealed. She was trapped.

Then a fierce winter wind swept through the gallery, overturning pedestals, swaying the floodlights, and chilling her to the bone. The temperature of the room dropped from late September warmth to January cold. The ferocious wind, seemingly of hurricane force, slapped her hard against the wall and held her there so she couldn't move.

"Dear God, no!" she pleaded.

The only answer was fiendish laughter, laughter that seemed to fill the room to a symphonic crescendo, laughter that pounded in her ears, beat against her chest, assaulted her all over.

I'm going to hell, she thought. *I'm being dragged down into the depths of the inferno.*

The wind tore at her clothes, ripping them off slowly and tantalizingly, as if reveling in her shame, savoring every second her humiliation could be prolonged. The more desperately she clutched at her slashed garments, the more insidiously the wind tore them off. She felt herself being stripped before thousands of people in a sports arena—inspected, appraised, laughed at by the contemptuous throng.

Invisible bands clamped themselves around her neck and ankles, nailing her against the wall. *No, no, no, no . . .*

Then foul, unseen hands began to violate her body,

pinching her flesh with savage, cruel twists, then tickling her lasciviously so that she screamed and laughed uncontrollably at the same time.

The hands and fingers continued to squeeze, hurt, degrade. Every imaginable obscene thing that hands can do to a woman's body were done to her time after time, until she was worn out with humiliation and pain and yearned to die. The tormenting, teasing fingers would pause a few seconds while she recaptured her breath and then begin again. Each time she would scream for mercy. Each time slimy paws seemed to relish her debasement all the more because of her pathetic pleas.

Yet she couldn't suffer in silence. The demons wouldn't permit her the luxury of pride or nobility. It was essential she be totally abject in her desire to escape.

Nor was she permitted the luxury of losing consciousness. On the contrary, every sense, every nerve ending, every feeling, was pushed to a fine point of sensitivity. She prayed that she would lose her mind, that her selfhood would be destroyed so that she might not realize what was being done to her. But her awareness became even keener and her body raced desperately toward grotesque pleasure and release. The obscene hands, however, would not permit her that, either. They forced her body to the brink of satisfaction, then retreated, only to return again and make her suffer more. *This is what hell is like for women*, she thought—*sexual degradation that never ends, always exciting you and never satisfying.*

The exhibition room gradually disappeared. She was outside now, in a dark, dismal forest, surrounded now by a wall of flames. Within the seething inferno were men and women who were watching her in macabre fascination, fiendishly amused as she squirmed and twisted in a hopeless effort to escape the foul hands of her tormentors.

Then the hands were removed and she fell to the ground. She supported herself on her knees and her hands, gasping for breath and searching for the energy and courage to attempt to break through the wall of flames.

She was thrown suddenly on her back, her hands pinned to the ground, unseen weights cruelly pressed against her arms, her legs painfully pulled apart. The demons prepared to rape her.

Her cries and pleas caused more sniggering laughter from the observers within the flames. One by one, unseen demons entered her and debased her, harshly and brutally using her for their pleasure. Hell for a woman was endless rape.

Hazy faces floated in front of her eyes, faces belonging to the demons amusing themselves with her body, but not the faces of demons. Rather they were the faces of the men in her life—her father, her brothers, Dick, Jimbo, John Duncan, Matt Sweeney, her priests, her teachers, her clients, her colleagues. Only Mickey, Blackie, and Father Kenny did not make sport of her. Sometimes the faces were so vivid she actually believed she was being raped by her father or by her long-dead lover. Other times she guessed that the demons were putting on masks of the men that she loved. What did it matter, finally, whether her tormentors were real or illusory? She had become a vile and used thing, a crumpled tissue paper, a torn, dirty paper napkin.

They did not let her hold her spirit or her mind aloof from their pleasure. She was forced to cooperate mentally and spiritually as well as physically, to enjoy the coarse and sordid degradation, to experience at the same time the heights of physical pleasure and the depths of emotional degradation.

Then they left her. The lascivious hands no longer pawed at her, the flames faded away, the laughter was silenced. She was left to lie on the floor of her gallery, totally exhausted and utterly disgusted by her own corrupt worthlessness.

Why didn't the priests tell us that for women hell is eternal sexual degradation and rape? Probably because it never occurred to them how terrible such suffering could be.

72

"You require another Jameson's," Blackie said to Mike Casey the Cop, pouring a generous amount of the twelve-(now eighteen) year-old special reserve into his glass. No ordinary visitors to his rooms at the Cathedral, only very distinguished visitors, such as cardinals, deputy superintendents of police and perhaps popes, were permitted the luxury of the twelve-year reserve, and Cardinals only sparingly.

"Thanks," Mike said grimly. "I need booze a lot these days."

"Ah," Blackie said. "Love."

"I certainly do love her," Mike conceded unnecessarily. "She drives me out of my mind."

"A not-unfamiliar lament of those in love."

"There's something terribly wrong over there, Blackie," Mike said, his Basil Rathbone face clean shaven, gaunt, and handsome, and his twisted frown revealing deep concern. "I don't know whether it's the gallery or her, but something has to be done."

"Saturday and Sunday she loves you. Today she doesn't want to see you. That's not particularly unusual behavior for lovers."

"She said she has serious personal problems; they've been bothering her intermittently through the whole weekend. She said she would have to work them out with her shrink before she decides about me. Is her shrink Mary Kate, do you know?"

"Probably. Good ethical therapist that she is, Mary Kate has never mentioned her. Good ethical priest that I am, I have never asked."

"We've got to help her, Blackie!" he exclaimed.

"What can we do? She won't tell any of us what's bothering her. How can we help?"

"Goddamn it! I love her!"

"How do you think I feel!" Blackie shouted back, deciding that it was now appropriate for him to reveal some emotion. "How could anyone know her and not love her? You can only help those you love when they're ready to let you help them. Trying to force help on her will just make the problem worse, whatever it is."

"We're taking an enormous chance if we leave her alone," Mike pleaded, disposing of most of his Jameson's in a single, wasteful gulp.

"A price we have to pay for respecting other people's integrity, I'm afraid, is that we let them take their own risks. The only consolation is that they're going to take them anyhow."

"It's that slimy little son of a bitch Des Kenny, that's what it is," Mike insisted.

"Father Kenny is dead. He's been dead for over a year; his mind was around the bend for more than thirty years. How could he be hurting Anne?"

"What do you know about obsession?"

"That might be a better question for Mary Kate than me. Obsession, I guess, is when you wash your hands all the time, polish doorknobs repeatedly, or rush back into the house to make sure you haven't left the faucet on. Candidly I don't think that's Anne's problem."

"I didn't mean that kind of obsession."

"What other kind is there? The kind that's like diabolic possession? Maybe. Only, the demons attack you from the outside instead of taking possession of your soul." Blackie leaned forward. "Mike," he said, "the new Church really doesn't take that sort of thing seriously, despite exploitation films like *The Exorcist* and novels by Mr. Blatty."

"I don't give a goddamn what the new Church takes seriously. I think she's being obsessed by the ghost of Desmond Kenny."

"Should I find us an exorcist? I have a hunch it wouldn't work. I don't think I'd try it unless Anne takes us into her confidence and asks for our help. In the meantime all we can do is keep a careful watch over her and be available when she needs us."

"Damn it," Mike said, still angry. "Then what can we do?"

"Perhaps Mary Kate will recommend a brief stay in the hospital. You might suggest it to Mark. There will be someone to watch her, maybe some strong tranquilizers to calm her down. . . ."

Mike erupted from his chair. "Fuck the tranquilizers! Are you so goddamn dumb you don't understand that it's only her mind that has kept her sane all these years?"

"Huh?"

"She's been surrounded by idiots all her life, men and women who blame her for their problems and demand that she take care of them." His face was purple with rage and he was screaming at the top of his lungs. He paced about my room like a man trapped in a sealed cave.

"Her family was wiped out when she was a kid and she feels responsible for that and for every fucking disaster and tragedy that has happened to anyone close to her since. If you were run over by a car this afternoon, it would be her fault."

"I think I know that," Blackie said cautiously.

"Then why would you sedate the mind and will out of her and take her away from the world from which she draws her strength? Institutionalize Annie for a couple of weeks and you'll have a vegetable on your hands."

"You're right, of course." Never argue with the insights of those who see with the eyes of love. Father Blackie's lesson for the day.

"How can she fight the demons alone?" Mike continued, calming down.

Blackie eased him back into his chair and refilled his glass. "First of all," he said, "she's not necessarily fighting demons. Remember, she did refer to personal problems. They might be quite serious, but I think we had better leave them to her and Mary Kate. Secondly, she's not fighting demons alone. She has at least three guardian angels. I'm going to see her every day, you're going to talk to her every day, and she's probably spilling her guts to Mary Kate several times a week. If there's a war in heaven going on, and I'm not altogether convinced of that, she's not without some allies."

"A worn-out cop, a sawed-off priest, and an Irish woman shrink!"

Blackie found that hilariously funny.

"Did Des Kenny start that goddamn fire?" Mike continued.

"No way. I talked with the priest who was with him when he heard the news."

Mike raised an eyebrow. "So you've been poking around?"

"And banging into dead ends wherever I turn."

"And I'm supposed to be content to be a guardian angel to her?"

"Or an archangel," Blackie insisted. "Indeed, Saint Michael, the Archangel, your patron, whose feast comes around this Saturday, I believe, together with Raphael and Gabriel and the rest of that crowd."

"My feelings for her are not archangelic."

"How do we know how archangels feel about a lover?" Blackie asked.

"I think I'll have Deirdre Lopez take a ride over to the Jarecki Warehouse and make sure Des Kenny's hell is safely locked up."

"A haunted painting in a haunted gallery, Mike?"

"There could be worse things going on."

73

The fires had come back to burn her for her sins, only now they tortured not one part of her body, but many. They darted, teased, tickled, and then jabbed, lingering lovingly. She screamed in hysterical anguish, begging incoherently for mercy. The fires of hell, she'd been taught in school, were all the more terrible because the pain does not eventually consume the suffering organism. The fire does not destroy the body, but rather heightens its sensitivity. The pain does not last for a few seconds or for a few moments, but forever.

The walls of flame had closed in around her. The sniggering demons watched her intently, delighting in her suffering with glittering hard-eyed fascination. Somehow they looked familiar, friends from long ago who had a score to settle with her.

There was scarcely an inch of her flesh that was not seething from pain and shock. The nauseating smell of her own burned flesh revolted her stomach. She vomited till her gut was dry. Then she continued retching while the damned howled with laughter at her agonized writhings. Yet in the back of her brain a small voice repeated, *This is not real, this is your imagination, you're making it all up. You're doing it to yourself as punishment for your sins. Stop it, it will end when you make it end.*

She no longer believed that voice. The demons had come for her to take her off to hell for all eternity, to degrade, debase, and torture her forever.

A wave of liquid swept across her face, thick, rancid goo. Someone was throwing buckets of filth at her. She tried to twist away and was cruelly pinned to the floor as bucket after bucket was dumped on her. Then she knew what it was—her own vomit, multiplied a hundredfold and swirling around her like water in a shallow pool. For a few seconds the smell and the slime were too much; she lost consciousness, fading away in a sea of stench.

Then she was slapped viciously back into full wakefulness. The assault of vomit had stopped. Already the goo was caking on her body. *What will they do next. Will they ever run out of dirty tricks!*

She shivered violently. The temperature again changed dramatically. She was outdoors once more, naked and dripping wet, in a fierce winter blizzard. Snow quickly piled up, covering her feet, her ankles and climbing up her legs to her waist. She shook with teeth-grinding, bone-shattering shivers. Even though her body was becoming a pillar of ice, it couldn't stop its fearsome quaking. *If this keeps up, I'll shake myself apart.* "Dear God, help me to shake myself apart; please let me die. If you give me another chance, I won't do it again," she said aloud.

Her prayers produced only convulsive laughter from the damned souls now only a few feet away from her, smacking their lips, it seemed, over the suffering the combination of fire and ice had caused. And her hell was only beginning.

Gradually the blizzard died away and she found herself lying again on the floor of the office in her gallery. Maybe they were finished with her this time. Maybe she could crawl off somewhere and find a gutter and die. Slowly, painfully, her body racked with fever, she shuffled toward the door.

74

Anne was naked and shivering in Aunt Aggie's coach house at the lake, even though that August of 1942 the temperature outside was in the nineties. She thought she would die of shame and humiliation. Father Kenny's phonograph, which ran all day long though he never seemed to listen to it, was playing "Good Night Irene."

She had never been naked in the presence of a man before the previous weekend. It was proper punishment, he'd told her then, for her terrible sins. She hadn't believed him; he had no right to impose his own punishment. Then he'd threatened to tell the truth. She'd refused again, wanting to run, but unable to move off the old throw rug on the floor of the guesthouse porch. He'd picked up the phone and dialed the police.

She'd given in then and began unbuttoning her blouse. Trembling with fear and humiliation, she stood in front of him while with a frenzied paintbrush he slashed across the canvas. "You're an evil whore," he screamed at her. "You killed your brothers and your mother and father, and you killed all those innocent children. That wonderful little body of yours, of which you're so proud, will suffer in hell for eternity!"

"I'm not proud of my body, Father," she said, through clattering teeth. "It's just an ordinary woman's body."

"It's a stinking swamp of evil, a vile trap for men, like every other woman's body, all shiny and beautiful on the outside and filled with corruption and the stench of dead men's flesh inside."

"That's the Scribes and Pharisees, Father," she said, remembering what she'd learned in her religion class.

"A woman's body is worse than the worst of all Pharisees," he ranted at her, all the time brushing paint rapidly on the canvas. "A vile stinking swamp, a cesspool of filth and corruption and death."

She felt soiled, as filthy as a worn-out dishrag. She had been deprived not only of her clothes but of her human value, humiliated, degraded, corrupted. She knew she'd carry the marks of her shame with her for the rest of her life.

This is a nightmare, she told herself. *It isn't happening. It isn't happening. Father couldn't be doing this to me.*

He'd made her come back every day, take off her clothes, then pose for demented paintings of women suffering in hell. She'd never got over her embarrassment, never become accustomed to the painful humiliation, never adjusted to his ranting and raving. Each day had been a new experience of hell on earth.

"When I'm through, your stinking, filthy body will never be able to tempt men again. You'll be useless to them. You'll have to go into a convent and do penance for the rest of your life. All the bodies of women should be locked up in convents forever!"

At first he hadn't touched her. He'd avoided coming close to her, even looking at her. Then, when he looked at her, it wasn't with an expression of enjoyment or desire, but of disgust and revulsion, as though she made him want to vomit.

But then, when he molded the pretty figurine, he'd drawn very close to her, his breath and perspiration filling her nostrils with stench.

He's going to rape me, she'd thought. *Father's going to rape me, and there's no one I can turn to for help. Aunt Aggie wouldn't believe me and Mickey Casey would hate me if he knew what I had done. Dear God, please don't let him rape me.*

The next day he'd hugged and kissed and caressed her as soon as she had removed her clothing, shouting that she was a fire demon from hell coming to destroy him. She'd begged him to release her, not to hurt her, to let her go. He'd slapped her and knocked her to the floor, then stood over her triumphantly: "You'll have a miserable and unhappy life, you'll die a terrible death and suffer in hell for all eternity. You're no longer human; you have no rights as a person. Anything I do to you is part of God's punishment."

Then, again purged of his rage, he had slumped into the canvas chair next to his easel and sobbed bitterly. Her fear and hatred yielded to a helpless compassion. Trembling, she had held his poor, sick, shaking head against her breasts. She had soothed him and made him go into his bedroom to get some sleep.

She did not return to the coach house again. But she never forgot that at the last moment she felt not disgust for him, but a strange, perverse emotion, something like love.

75

The patient was tired, beaten, and—the first time I would have used the word to describe her—old. Moreover, she had proven me a false prophet: jeans, a T-shirt (admittedly with Monet water lilies), sandals, and a dirty raincoat. For the first time, too, she wore no makeup. If Caitlin the Clown had seen me go out of the house that way, I would have heard about it for the next five months.

"I haven't been feeling very well," she said, collapsing

on my couch with none of the mixture of feminine modesty and sophisticated elegance that formerly marked that entrance.

"I'm sorry to hear it."

"I have a confession to make."

"Oh?"

"You've heard enough of my autobiography to know that your father was my lawyer when I was divorced."

"Yes."

"He's still well, I hope?"

Strict theory said my response ought to have been something like "You're wondering about my father's health—I wonder why?"

It was men that put that theory together, however, so I said, "Extremely well for a man of his age."

"I hired another lawyer when Matt Sweeney left me. I guess I didn't want your father to know that I was a two-time loser."

"I'm sure he wouldn't have reacted that way."

"I knew you were his daughter when I called for my first appointment."

"Oh?"

"And that you were the sister of Father Ryan, my pastor."

"Indeed."

"You say that just the way he does."

"Now do you want to explain why you didn't tell me these things before?"

"Your father and your brother are wonderful men. I trust them both. I knew I could trust you. I was afraid if I told you, you wouldn't see me."

"That was a pretty powerful assumption, wasn't it?"

"You wouldn't have, would you?"

"Why was it so important for you to have some kind of family guarantee about me beforehand?"

"Because I was so afraid."

"I see."

"Are you going to stop seeing me now?"

"Do you think I ought to?"

"I wouldn't blame you."

"It was necessary that my trustworthiness be guaranteed, but you still didn't trust me enough to tell me the truth."

"It's very dangerous to tell the truth."

"It's even more dangerous, when in treatment, not to tell the truth."

"Yes, I know. I really need help terribly now. Please don't throw me out."

"Let's talk about it."

"And there's another thing too."

"Oh?"

"I've been lying to you all along."

"Have you?"

"Yes, there's something terrible in my life that I've been hiding from you. I suppose you've guessed that already."

"Do you expect me to make you reveal what it is?"

"No . . . I know I can't solve my problems unless I tell the truth. The Cardinal told me the other day that I had nothing to fear from the truth. I think he's wrong."

"Cardinals are often wrong. This particular time, though, he's right. Truth may be frightening but untruth is even more frightening."

"Yes, I know. But if I tell you, I will have to tell others and everyone will hate me. I'll die."

"Is the truth that terrible?"

"Oh, yes, it is."

A long silence. The patient was weeping. I was groping for a way to break out of our short-sentenced dialogue.

"Does the truth have to do with the police person?"

"Oh, I forgot about that. He's your cousin."

"Yes, I know. He was not, however, part of your initial deception. Has he brought on this crisis in your life?"

Another long pause.

"No, I don't think so. Maybe he's made it worse. I love him so much and I don't want to hurt him."

"And you're sure that if you and he continue your relationship, you will hurt him?"

"What I've done hurts everyone I become close to."

"Are you going to tell me what it is?"

"Yes, if you give me a little more time. I'm not quite ready."

"How soon will you be ready?"

"Very soon, Dr. Murphy, or I'll lose my mind."

Mary Kate pressed the pause button, composed her closing remarks, then released it and began to record again.

The patient's fears are totally justified. She is very close to being prepsychotic. The absence of concern about her physical appearance, given the fact it has been a very important part of her life, is quite troubling.

This is no ordinary case; the demons with which we are wrestling are strange and powerful. What has been tormenting this rather wonderful woman for all her life?

Dear God, what can we do?

76

ANNE'S STORY

The aftermath of my affair with Senator Duncan ended with a singularly abrupt communication from the Archdiocese of Chicago.

"What the hell is this?" I shouted at the young priest I'd cornered at the rectory, flinging the letters and the questionnaire in his face.

He was a cute little man with short curly brown hair, sweet blue eyes lurking behind thick glasses, and a kindly elfin smile.

He picked up the papers from the floor, glanced at them, and said, "A letter and a questionnaire about an annulment."

"I know that, you asshole," I screamed at him. "I want to know how dare the Catholic Church send me something this offensive."

"The Catholic Church," he sighed, "has an incredible

facility for doing offensive things, especially to those who love it."

I never use that language with anyone, and especially not a priest, but I was hurt, angry, felt terribly cheated.

Despite Nixon's resignation—and I'm afraid poor John waffled too long on that one—1974 was a terrible year for me. It began happily enough, with the news that Jimmy was to be married. I was surprised when he called and told me that he and Jennifer, a girlfriend about whom he'd talked several times but whom I'd never met, had decided to get married before he went overseas. I couldn't blame them, not with my memories of Dick Murray. She was Irish, she was Catholic, and from the pictures he'd shown me, she was pretty. So I flew to Denver for the wedding with a light heart. I feared then that Beth would never marry Ted, and never have children. "Marriage and children are ridiculously out of date," she told me. So it was nice to contemplate the prospect of an ordinary marriage in the family and ordinary children to be born in the marriage. Jennifer was very pretty, indeed, and also, I thought, very intelligent. Unfortunately, she took an instant dislike to me. I suppose she was too young and too insecure to be at ease with her groom's obvious devotion to his mother. I think that at the rehearsal dinner she had already defined me as a lifelong rival and would never change her mind.

It hurt a lot. Mothers lose their sons to wives. That's the way the human race seems to operate. I was willing to lose Jimmy to her. She would henceforth have prior claim on him, but I did not think that that claim needed to make us enemies. She didn't see it that way.

We were civilized but distant with each other during the wedding celebration, and Jimmy was so hopelessly in love that he didn't notice the strain between the two of us. There was resentment in her eyes, however, when he kissed me good-bye.

So I returned to St. Columbanus after the wedding, feeling more lonely than ever and also feeling that I probably deserved it. I prayed for the two of them, and especially prayed for Jennifer that she would be a better mother to her sons than I had been to Jimmy.

Jimmy was assigned to a squadron in Thailand, much too close to the Vietnamese war for me not to worry. The war was winding down, however; we were doing virtually no bombing in Vietnam or Cambodia and it was rare for an American plane to be shot down.

Jimmy died the same way Dick Murray died. He was a perfect officer and gentleman, the ideal service academy product—brave, loyal, respectful. He would have been chief of staff someday, his commanding officer's letter said.

I wondered if I deliberately raised him to be a substitute for Dick, a man as unlike Jimmy's father as anyone could be.

Or maybe Jimmy chose that for himself.

His plane simply didn't come back from his first reconnaissance mission over the Parrot's Beak area of South Vietnam. He didn't survive a single day of war. The pilot in the plane nearest him said that he looked around and Jimmy's plane simply was no longer there. Probably engine failure. He was never found, nor was his plane, and now all these years later he is still missing in action.

Jennifer was pregnant, before the marriage obviously, and bore a son who was called James Reilly. She remarried a few years later and is living in San Diego now. I visited her and her new husband a couple of years ago for a few hours. Young Jim Reilly looks like his father and his great grandfather (my father) and seems to be a happy and well-adjusted young man. His mother and stepfather have several other children, and the marriage, as far as I can tell, is relaxed and happy. Jennifer was not pleased to see me and she made no effort to hide that fact. Her husband was astonished by her rudeness, unfamiliar, it seemed, with that dimension of her personality.

She blames me for Jimmy's death, I think. She hates me so much she has to blame me.

They never come to Chicago and I doubt I'll ever be invited to visit them in San Diego again. I'm sure she won't ask me to any of young Jim's graduations. The little kid kind of liked me too.

I always send them Christmas cards with a cash present for Jim. I wonder if he gets it. Sometimes she sends me a Christmas card and sometimes she doesn't.

I pulled some strings and managed to enroll Davie in a Catholic college in Iowa. He failed all his courses the first semester of his freshman year and all but one the second semester. The president of the college, after a personal plea by Father Matt Sweeney, agreed to give him a second chance. After the Thanksgiving vacation, during which Davie did nothing but listen to rock music all day, he left to return to the college but never arrived. We searched frantically for him, without success. After New Year's, I received a postcard telling me that he had joined a commune in northern California, dedicated to living a "natural life." The only times I hear from him are when he needs money, and then it's always in a soft and vague voice that sounds mildly offended, as though a regular check I was supposed to be sending him hadn't come.

I tell myself it was a bad time to raise children. I remind myself that an MIA, a permanent dropout, and a life-style radical are not at all untypical for American families who grew up during the late sixties and early seventies. My children could well have become what they are if their father and I were still happily married. (Jimbo and his mother pretty much lost interest in them after we moved to Washington, writing them off, I guess, along with me.) I tell myself that women much less responsible than I for family tragedy have been forced to suffer the same alienation of their children.

All that doesn't help very much. They were mine, I loved Beth and Jimmy with all my power. I did my best to love Davie. They're all gone now, one way or another, and how can I help but feel that in some way, deep down, it's my fault?

Mark was then all-city tackle in his second year at Fenwick, the only child for whom I never had much concern, perhaps because I didn't have much concern left.

My contract meanwhile was renewed at Columbanus, but only for one more year. I felt that my teaching (I won the best teacher of the year award) and my publications (one or two every year) entitled me to a three-year contract with tenure review at the end. Matt Sweeney promised me, "I'll do everything I can, Anne, absolutely everything I can. Your credentials are excellent. You would be promoted to tenure now if the budget would allow it."

The budget didn't even allow a three-year contract.

"Gosh, I'm sorry," Matt said sadly. "I did everything I could. Pulled out all the stops. The budget committee can't see its way clear to giving a woman a three-year appointment when we have male faculty members with families who've been here a lot longer, and we can only afford to renew them one more year. It's this damned inflation, you know."

I ended up consoling him. I assured him I knew how hard he'd tried and that I could wait till next year if I had to.

"Damned sure we'll get it then," he said. "I'll resign if we don't."

"Sweet Matthew let you down, huh?" said Jim McQuade, a priest in the theology department, later.

"I don't think so!" I protested. "He did his best. He said he'd resign next year if he couldn't get me a three-year appointment."

"That's Sweet Matthew for you," McQuade said. He shook his head as though disapproving of a playful but slightly wayward boy. "John Leary might never smile and he might be a mean old son of a bitch and he might be one of the worst academic deans in the country, but at least he gives you a straight answer."

"You don't think that Matt meant his promise about next year?"

"Oh, sure, he meant it. And the only reason he made it is that he's damned certain there won't be any problem next year. Between you and me, I'm convinced he could have gotten you a three-year contract with a hefty raise this year. He traded you off for someone else."

"That's a rotten lie," I snapped at him, turned on my heel, and stormed away. Now I'm not so sure.

I was feeling the inflationary pinch like everyone else, though I was now being paid a full-time assistant professor's salary—at the lower end of the range. My annual increments were trivial. Some of the active feminists on campus said I should sue, but while I knew I was the victim of sexist discrimination, I didn't want to get into any more trouble than I already had.

Matt Sweeney, moreover, was very kind to me when we received word that Jimmy was missing in action. I realized I had no one to turn to, no family, no parish, very few friends. Joanie Powers blamed me for letting him go to the Air Force Academy in the first place. Bethie said that he'd died before he'd become a war criminal. Aunt Aggie was off in Paris. While I went to church on Sunday and received communion, I avoided any other contact with my own Northwest Side parish. Jimbo and his mother seemed quite uninterested. So when Matt offered to say a Mass in the university chapel, I was delighted. And when more than five hundred faculty and students attended the Mass—pressured into it by Matt, I was sure—I broke down and wept with gratitude.

"Gosh," he said, "we ought to be grateful to you. You gave us the chance for personal fulfillment that a liturgical exercise like this provides."

I certainly was not falling in love with Matt Sweeney. I was in no emotional condition to fall in love with anyone. I was grateful, though, for his kindness and his sincerity and his friendship and profoundly offended by what seemed to me to be the envious cynicism of the other members of his religious order.

I was in no condition, then, for the official letter from the Matrimonial Tribunal of the Archdiocese of Chicago explaining to me that my husband, James Reilly, had presented a petition for the annulment of our marriage.

There were six pages of detailed questions: "Describe the circumstances under which you met your spouse ... Were there any characteristics that struck you as unusual or problematic that you disregarded? ... Give a brief description of your married life together ... Did you engage in extramarital relations? ... What means of birth control did you use? ... Was this marriage ever a good marriage ... What were the circumstances that led to the breakdown of the marriage? ... What is your opinion of the present stability and maturity of yourself and your former spouse? . . . Have you ever been physically aggressive or violent toward anyone? . . . Are there any recurring fears that bother you? . . . Have you ever seriously contemplated suicide? . . . Please describe your own sexual tendencies and activities . . . Have you often repeated the same mistakes? . . . Are there circumstances in which you might lie or cheat? . . . Do you spend money on things you cannot really afford . . . Have you ever been treated for a nervous breakdown? Please elaborate. . . . "

There were detailed questions about my psychiatric history—then nonexistent—and forms that authorized the release to the tribunal of my medical and psychiatric letters.

Jimbo and Harriet were trying to prove that I was insane.

I became hysterical, stomping around my apartment, throwing pillows, even smashing dishes—the first time in my life I'd ever done that.

I was only slightly less crazed when I cornered the young priest at the rectory.

"In 1967 and in 1971, Father," I yelled at him, "I was told that there was not the slightest possibility of an annulment. Now I find that my husband is applying for one. Will he get it?"

"Probably, Mrs. Reilly. Of course, the annulment will apply to you too. Most such petitions are granted these days."

"How could it have been that I was permanently bound to him three years ago and now he's not permanently bound to me?" I shouted.

"Where did you try three years ago, Mrs. Reilly? Surely not in Chicago."

"In Washington," I shouted. "You mean I could have a valid marriage in one archdiocese and not in another?"

"I'll try to explain, Mrs. Reilly, if you'll give me a chance," he said. "You have every reason to be furious. If I were in your position, I would be furious too. I warn you beforehand my explanation won't be at all satisfying. It does have the merit, however, of being the truth. Now, if you'd be so good as to sit down. . . . "

I sat down and listened.

"We're in the process of an enormous change in the Church's thinking about the nature of the sacrament of marriage. We are beginning to see clearly once again that marriage is not permanent because it is a sacrament; rather it is a sacrament because it is permanent."

"What the hell does that mean?" I demanded. "I was taught that a valid marriage contract is a sacrament and never can be broken. Jim and I were married, Father, not very well, I admit, but we were still married. Now the Church comes along and tells me that we were not married?"

"You were married," he said gently. "But if an annulment is granted, it will mean that the Church has decided that the marriage was not sufficiently mature to be a sacrament."

"We had four children, Father. Isn't that enough for us to be married? Are you trying to tell me our children are illegitimate?"

"Even when an annulment is granted," he said cautiously, "the Church specifically states that the children of such a union are to be considered legitimate."

"Then we were married after all," I said triumphantly, wondering why I cared that much about a marriage that had always been a burden.

"A decree of nullity, Dr. Reilly—and you must excuse me for sounding legalistic—does not deny the reality of the relationship or say that it was entered into with ill will or moral fault. . . . "

"Then what the hell does it say?" I demanded furiously. "What kind of sick games are you playing with human lives?"

"It says that the relationship fell short of at least one of the elements which are essential for a sacramental, that is to say binding, union and hence is not viewed by the Church as a source of continuing marital rights and obligations."

"Gobbledygook. What does it cost? How much money does the Church make on this shell game?"

"Not nearly as much as you'd think," he replied with a

hint of a grin. "In fact, we lose money. The costs are over five hundred dollars a case and the offering is two hundred, which we waive if the petitioner cannot afford it. Since you're not the petitioner . . . "

"How can you justify this nonsense?" I demanded, refusing to be mollified by his patience. Then I calmed down. He was, after all, a nice young priest. None of it was his fault. "I'm sorry, Father. I'm not the kind of person who shouts at priests. Forgive me."

"Shout all you want." He grinned impishly. "Maybe we need to be shouted at more. Anyway, a sacrament, Mrs. Reilly, or should I say, Dr. Reilly"—the young priest tried again—"is a revelation of the power of God's love in the world. Marriage is a sacrament because the permanence of the union between a man and a woman reveals the permanence of God's commitment to us. Would you say the relationship between you and your husband was of that sort?"

"No," I said sadly.

"Precisely. The Church now understands that a man and a woman have to be sufficiently mature to contract that kind of a union before their marriage becomes sacramental. Short of that, it is possible for them to separate and to remarry. In this view of things, Dr. Reilly, sacramental marriages are much harder to come by than we used to think. It is not nearly enough for a man and woman to exchange consent. Rather, it is required that their consent be sufficiently mature and sufficiently deep as to reveal the maturity and depth of God's love for us. I don't expect you to approve of what we've done to you, but I hope you at least understand the reasoning behind the new policy."

"How many marriages are that way when they begin?" I demanded, impressed by the reasoning but ready to be furious again.

"I wouldn't want to say, Mrs. Reilly," the young priest said, and smiled, a most beguiling smile. "The idea, of course, is that a sacrament evolves very slowly, beginning the first time a man and a woman catch each other's eye and culminating in true sacramental permanence, maybe only after they've survived their first major crisis together."

"It sounds like pop psychology to me."

"I don't like cheap psychology either." He fussed with a paper on his desk, reluctant to look into my angry eyes. "Yet the Vatican Council said with great wisdom that sacramental marriage is not merely the handing over of rights to one's body but a gift of the total person. If there is no interpersonal communication possible, if man and woman do not achieve a certain bare minimum of sharing of their personhoods with each other, then there is no communication and no sacrament."

"Jimbo and I never did that. He would never have been able to share his personhood with a woman. Perhaps not with anyone," I said wearily, and then my anger returned. "Do you realize, Father, that I was very much in love a few years ago with a wonderful man who wanted to marry me and who was free to do so? I turned him down because I believed in the Church's teaching. Are you telling me that if I had waited a few years, or if I had come to Chicago, I might now be able to marry him?"

"I'm afraid so, Dr. Reilly," he said sadly.

"So I've sacrificed a life of happiness because the Church didn't change its laws quite soon enough?"

"I hope you still find happiness in your life, Dr. Reilly," he said.

"What if I had married him? What if I had left the Church and been excommunicated? What if we were married now and I came seeking annulment? Could I have received it?"

He sighed and said, "Yes, indeed, Dr. Reilly. I will say it for you. Because you were a good Catholic laywoman and did what the Church told you to do, you've been abused, cheated, treated unjustly, unfairly. I wouldn't blame you if you walked out of this office and out of the Catholic Church and never had anything to do with us again."

"That's precisely what I intend to do!" I screamed, grabbed the questionnaire, and rushed out of the rectory, sobbing with grief and frustration.

I had a long conversation the next day with Matt Sweeney—"talking the whole thing through," as he put it—and decided I was being very foolish.

I returned to the rectory the following week, apologized

profusely to the young priest, and asked him to notarize my responses to the questionnaire, which was, on reflection, as sensitive as the poor priests who were responsible could have made it under the circumstances.

"Fifty pages," he said, impressed by the heft of my story—which had helped me to understand what went wrong in our marriage. "Only half of those who apply ever complete the document."

"I'm an academic, Father. I like to talk about myself. I suppose that the poor people who don't fill out a report are not very articulate."

"I'm sure you're right," he said mildly, making me feel guilty all over again.

"I really don't use that language ever, Father. I'm very sorry for having shouted at you. I know it's not your fault. And to tell you the truth, Father, I'm sorry, but I never did learn your name."

"Ryan," he said. "My Christian name is John. Most people call me Blackie, which is short for my middle name, Blackwood, and I won't bore you with the story of how I came to be called that."

That was where the kindly eyes came from. "I knew your father long time ago," I said softly. "I'm even more sorry for shouting and cursing."

"Be my guest," he said with a smile. "Incidentally, why did you come back?"

"It may not be much of a church, Father, and I'm furious at what it's done to me, but it's still the only church I have."

77

Mike Casey dragged Blackie away from his lunch table for the second time in a week. "Blackie? Mike," he said over the phone.

"Of course. Who else?" Blackie thought Mike sounded as if he'd been in forty-eight hours of marathon negotiating with a band of mad terrorists who were threatening to massacre scores of innocent hostages.

"Deirdre searched all through the warehouse and couldn't find that damned painting."

Blackie didn't like that one bit.

"You mean she's been lying to us?"

"How well did you search the gallery?" Mike demanded impatiently.

"I didn't have a search warrant, Superintendent," Blackie answered. "I wasn't able to explore the workrooms or the closets or the storerooms. Do you think she's keeping the picture there? Or might it be in her apartment? And why is she lying to us?"

"Have you been over there today?" Mike asked, ignoring Blackie's questions.

"I was there this morning and spoke with the lovely Alexandra, who assured me that Missus was not present. I'm not altogether convinced that was the case. I think that just now Anne doesn't want to have anything to do with her simple parish priest."

"What are you going to do about that?" Mike challenged.

"What I'm going to do, Superintendent, is suggest that you, who in your role as lover are far more qualified to be physical than the aforementioned simple parish priest, go over there this afternoon and raise blue bloody hell."

"Might that not be kind of risky?" Mike asked nervously.

"It might be risky not to. If you have one ace left, you might as well play it."

"Then what do we do?" he demanded.

"Then we pray, Michael; we pray very hard."

78

Most of Anne's time now was spent in a trance. She could not sharply distinguish between waking and dreams. She stumbled through the waking hours in a stupor, her world shrouded in a haze in which she had to squint to recognize the objects of everyday life, almost as if she were losing her sight and couldn't explain this to others because she was also being deprived of her power of speech.

Terrible things had been done to her, or seemed to have been done to her. But there were no marks on her body of burns or frostbite. She recognized the images in her memory as fantasies, half-dreams created in her imagination because of the stress and strain of the Desmond Kenny exhibit, but at the same time, they seemed to have acquired a life of their own. She had stopped going to church in the morning and managed to be unavailable when Father Ryan came to see her. She dreaded phone calls from Mickey, knowing that she would have to put him off for another day or two, pleading that her "personal problems" were still unresolved. Whatever compass she had in her life was no longer functioning. The only goal she had was to survive until her next conference with Dr. Murphy, at which, she promised herself, she would spill everything and at last be free, no matter how high a price she would have to pay for her freedom. At least the confusion would be over and the dreams would come to an end.

But despite the seemingly drugged trance through which she moved, she was still able to function as director of the Reilly Gallery, respond brightly to Mark's phone calls, make a date with Maria Donlon the following week, sign contracts for the two exhibitions in mid-January, and listen sympathetically to the nervous Sandy praising her husband.

"You're going to take him back, Sandy, let's face it," she said on one occasion while in the gallery. "You're going to run the risk that his intelligence and kindness will return now that he's out of that terrible police state."

"It's so difficult, Missus," Sandy replied sadly.

Probably even more difficult for the poor man, especially now that you look so lovely.

In these moments of lucidity she was firmly convinced that the problem with the Desmond Kenny exhibition was behind her. It had been a mistake, but the mistake was finished and now she must get on with life. A few seconds later she was back in her stupor, uncertain about everything and especially uncertain about the three people who were available to help her—Mickey, Father Ryan, and Dr. Murphy.

In her semitrances she was haunted by obsessive lust, her fantasies filled with wildly obscene, frenzied, and vivid images. It was, she supposed vaguely, the result of her intense sexual episode with Mickey Casey. Yet with Mickey, sex, however powerful, had also been graceful and healing. The images, the pictures, the desires, that flooded her brain now were cruel and destructive. "This can't be me," she told herself. "I don't have such a dirty mind."

Since her brief erotic attraction to Maria in the locker room, everyone had become a sex object to her. Man and woman, young and old, stranger and friend. Her frantic eyes disrobed not only the men on Michigan Avenue, but also the women. Consumed with reckless, violent curiosity, she found herself following two thinly clad late-teenagers, probably coeds at Loyola, down the street for a half-block, fantasizing that she was an Empress who had the power to seize them and use and abuse them for her own pleasure.

"Dear God, help me," she prayed as she turned and virtually ran in the opposite direction back to the gallery.

The most powerful of her obscene desires, because they were not violent but sweet, were aimed at Sandy. She loved the Polish immigrant woman, of course. She was happy that she had been able to offer Sandy a new life, dependent on her help, grateful for her wide-eyed admiration and impressed by her physical attractiveness.

But Sandy was only transiently a sex object, an occasional flicker of interest in the depths of her fantasy life, the kind of appealing but ridiculous notion that humans had, she was convinced, about their friends of both sexes.

Now she wanted Sandy so badly she had to clench her fists to keep her hands off the woman.

She was helping Sandy to apply makeup before a Friday evening date with Jerzy, as Colonel Kokoshka was now called almost all the time. Sandy had not bothered to acquire the skills of the typical American woman, with her almost unlimited supply of makeup, until Jerzy reappeared. Now she was on a crash course to learn those skills.

Sandy was sitting on an unsteady wooden chair in front of the minute vanity mirror in the gallery's living suite, dressed in her underwear and smelling of shampoo and soap.

"Is not much of a face, Missus," she said sadly. "Has no character, like yours does."

"Nonsense," Anne insisted. "It just has a different kind of character."

She had always found women with Sandy's kind of beauty—full-blown and classic—more aesthetically appealing than women of her own lithe and modern construction, probably the result of the grass seeming greener in someone else's front yard. Now she was dizzy with admiration and longing for Sandy's generously curving hips and large, exquisitely shaped breasts. *Dear God*, she pleaded silently, *please don't let me do it.*

Finally she got Sandy zipped up in a sleek maroon cotton-knit dress that spoke of autumn warmth and promised spring sunshine.

"You'll knock 'em over, Sandy. Are you going to take him back tonight?"

"Not tonight, Missus," Sandy said with an attempt to sound firm and determined.

"I bet you do." Anne laughed and, without seeming to be awkward, evaded Sandy's grateful kiss, lest something terrible happen as a result of their embrace.

Jerzy entered the gallery just then and stood patiently at the door. He was wearing a nicely fitting three-piece gray suit and looked very much the successful Polish-American businessman. He shook hands with his wife and bowed respectfully over Anne's hand, which he kissed.

"Have a good evening," she said solemnly.

"Is hard to begin, Missus," he said in painfully chosen English. "Is harder to begin again. Yet must do. Is not so, Sandy?"

Ah, now she was Sandy even to him.

"Is so," Sandy said cautiously.

"Is so, Missus?"

"Is so, Jerzy."

The three of them laughed and then Jerzy and Sandy left, walking as close to each other as they could without touching.

I hear messages from strange sources, Anne thought as she watched them walk down the street. *The Cardinal says I should tell the truth. Maria argues I should take chances before it's too late, and Kokoshka advises me that I should begin again.*

None of them knows what they're suggesting I do. What if they are really messengers, guardian angels sent from God? . . .

> Angel of God
> My guardian dear
> To whom God's love
> Commits me here
> Ever this day
> Be at my side
> To light and guard
> To rule and guide . . .

That's silly. Why should God send angels to me.

Wearily she walked back into her office and sat at the desk, her imagination sparkling with fantasies of a night of sweet caresses in Sandy's bed—sometimes with the Colonel present and sometimes without.

"Hi," said Mickey Casey, standing in her doorway with a half-apologetic and lopsided grin.

"Oh!" She jumped up, startled. "I didn't hear you come in."

"So I noticed," Mickey said. "The chime did ring, and I did knock kind of lightly. Hard day?"

Mickey was being careful, no longer asking how she felt or inquiring, like a Prussian field marshal, whether she had shipped off Father Kenny's "crap."

You are really trying to be sweet, aren't you, darling! What a shame it is that I'm such a terrible mess. "A real hard day," she said wearily. "I'm beginning to think I need a long vacation."

"I might be able to find someone to come with you," he said tentatively.

"Mickey, that would be wonderful," she said without thinking.

Instantly she regretted her words. *I have to tell him to go away, to give me a few more days, to let me work things out with Dr. Murphy. After I've told one person the truth, it will be easier to tell others. I can't afford any more titillation with Mickey.*

"I have some furlough coming," he said, "I suspect I could clear the decks and get away by Monday. And to beat you to the punch, Patrol Officer Lopez probably can run the police force without me."

"Oh, Mickey," she said sadly, "it would be so wonderful, but we can't do it, not yet."

"Father Ryan tells me that Saturday is my feast day. It might be a nice time to go to Bermuda."

Quickly, his arms were around her and his lips were pressed against hers, throwing gasoline on the fires of desire that were already burning inside her.

"No, Mickey, no. Not now. I can't do it now. Please," she begged.

He started to undress her, pulling her T-shirt up over her breasts. She squirmed and twisted and fought and finally punched him.

"Let me go," she screamed.

"Sorry," he said apologetically. "I guess I misread the signs."

Something tore apart inside her, a barrier that had been holding back both lust and love. She glared at him furiously, opened her mouth to order him permanently out of her office, and said, "Not here. Come into the dressing room."

She pulled the T-shirt the rest of the way over her head

as she led him into the private suite and locked the door. Imperiously she pointed at the tiny couch. "Over there."

And then as he watched open-mouthed, she undressed tauntingly, tantalizingly, as though she were an erotic dancer. Then she threw herself upon him, attacked him, and made reckless love to him. It was now a man's turn to be the one who was used.

79

Mike was both shocked and frightened by the ferocity of Anne's attack. He was being used by a woman who was desperately hungry for sex, something which had never happened to him before, and he wasn't sure he liked it. He also resented being used as a sex object.

Her hungry rage, however, was quickly appeased by her affection for him. And then he knew the tranquil bliss of a man who has surrendered himself to the ministrations of a determined and skillful woman who cares deeply for him, the exquisite oblivion of having his mind wiped clean of all thought, and the sweet narcotic of losing his identity to her sweaty body for a few rapturous moments.

In those moments he knew her worry and knew how to heal it. When his ecstasy was over, he had forgotten what he had learned. Only a vague trace of it remained.

"Wow!" he said weakly.

"I'm sorry if I was too rough," she said contritely.

"You are one hell of a woman when you turn aggressive."

"Only when I turn aggressive?"

"Especially," he said. "I'll be all right in a couple of days when I start breathing regularly again."

"Silly." She laughed. "I don't know what got into me."

"I should explain that to you?"

She pushed him away lightly. "Now you really are being silly. I was like some kind of she-animal in heat."

"Nonsense, it's just that you find me irresistible," he insisted.

"Let's take a shower and then go have supper someplace and get thoroughly drunk," she suggested.

"It's a pretty small shower, as I remember it," he said dubiously.

"All the more fun, then." She laughed at his hesitation.

"I'm not sure I'm strong enough for another one of your she-animal romps."

As it turned out, he was strong enough.

As they finished dressing she said, "You're going to have to take me someplace like Hamburger Limited, where they don't mind women who are not among the ten best dressed in Chicago."

"I'll pretend I don't know you . . . Oh, hey, I'm hesitant to mention this, and please don't be mad, but they tell me that 'Divine Justice' isn't in the warehouse."

"Checking up on me, were you, you goddamn son of a bitch?" she shouted. "Who gave you the authority to check up on me?"

"I was only trying to be helpful," he stammered.

"This is my business. I've run it my way successfully for a good many years; I don't need a cop snooping around. Do you understand?"

"I'm sorry," he said contritely. "I really am. Please don't be angry."

"Now you go and search every single corner of this gallery and see if you can find that painting," she ordered. "Go ahead, do it. Look in every room, every closet, every empty place you can find, and see if the painting is there. Then come back here and tell me you didn't find it."

"That's not necessary, Annie," he said meekly.

"Don't give me that bullshit," she yelled. "Go ahead, search!"

So he searched as carefully, as systematically, as thoroughly, as *Principles of Detection* demanded. He opened every carton in the storerooms and the workrooms. He flipped through every stack of paintings, looked under every table, explored every closet. There was no trace of "Divine Justice."

"Well?" she said, for an instant seeming almost to hope he had found something.

"Nothing."

"Then get the hell out of here and leave me alone!"

"Please, Annie, isn't there some way we can talk this out?"

"I've had it in life with men who want to talk things out," she exploded. "Now get out of here and never send your stupid cops to check up on me again."

He left, bowled over by the savagery of her anger and her language.

Savage sex, savage rage, savage words. *She's in deep trouble and I've cut myself off from her. I'm a bumbling ninny.*

80

Blackie was sitting in Mark and Tessie's parlor, drinking Diet Pepsi and entertaining their daughter, Anna, on his lap. Small children of both sexes had, unaccountably, a predilection for leaping on his lap as soon as he sat down, much as they flocked to his cousin Catherine when she appeared anywhere, but especially on a beach.

"Living up to all her own rules has always been a problem for my mother," Mark said thoughtfully. "Now it seems to have become an obsession. She's more ready than she used to be to excuse others from the rules and less ready to be tolerant of herself. Even when we were growing up she was easy on us and hard on herself. Now the demands are implacable—and harsher than ever."

"Indeed."

"Mom never permits herself a bad day. When I was

playing on teams in grammar school and high school—poor woman, she always came to the games—and fouled up, she would tell me not to worry about it: everyone had bad days; it was part of being human. My failures were the result of the frailty of human nature, hers the evidence of moral weakness."

"She loves us so much," Teresa agreed, "and she's afraid to become too close to us for fear she'll fail us."

"She probably thinks she's responsible for the alienation of your brother and sister," Blackie suggested.

"Beth and Dave are both children." Mark dismissed his siblings with a wave of his hand. "Beth is into anger and Dave into self-pity. Those emotions are okay when you're a teenager. Adults grow out of them. If my brother and sister don't want to grow out of them, that's their problem, not Mom's."

"Indeed." The young man was a trader, not a psychologist. However, he understood human nature, as traders must, Blackie thought. He and Anna exchanged funny faces.

"Look," Mark went on. "I can take a dumb position in the morning, hang on to it stubbornly all day long, and by the time the bell rings have wiped out a month's profits because I've been stupid. I can say to myself, 'Reilly, you were a damn fool,' and come back the next day to start winning it back. When Mom does the same thing—that Czech fellow . . ."

"Sobanek? . . ."

"Yeah. She says to herself, 'You're morally worthless and you're being punished.' Mistakes for her are sins. I don't like to use the word *old* because she's not old . . ."

"Heavens, no," his wife agreed, replenishing Blackie's drink.

"But as the years go on, she sees more mistakes and more sins. She has some problems at the gallery just now and won't ask me for help. It would be wrong to use my money to commit more sins."

"Ah."

He was dead right.

"Do you believe in diabolism?" Mark asked.

"Diabolism?" Blackie repeated. He recalled discussing precisely this question with Steve Riordan, the theological tower, at the seminary the week before.

"Junk like *The Exorcist* frosts me because it trivializes evil," Riordan had said. "Would that our only problem was demons that sneak out of pits in Iraq occasionally and force little girls to use dirty words. Our ancestors postulated demons because the explanation fit the data. Hitler and Stalin were bland, sick little men. They killed fifty million people. The disproportion between the cause and the effect makes you wonder. Or a crazy little nut like Lee Harvey Oswald changes American history. We used to say they were possessed. Now we say they're sick. Maybe there's a truth somewhere in between.

"Maybe they're not Dante's or William Blatty's devils," Steve had continued, "and certainly they're not little tricksters with horns and pitchforks. Rather, they could be irrational and malicious powers that are barely held at bay and that periodically break through the restraints and do incalculable harm. Only the most naive Lockean optimists deny the power of superhuman evil. We're wrestling with principalities and powers, Blackwood, principalities and powers."

Blackie slowly shook his head. "That's a question I haven't resolved yet," he said, surprised.

"Is there anything that can be done to make her change her rules?" Mark asked in a tone that showed he was deeply worried about his mother. "Anything that would cause her to lose this obsession?"

"That man she's involved with," Teresa continued, "would he put up with it?"

"For about thirty seconds," Blackie replied.

When he finally returned to the Cathedral that night, Blackie sensed he had in his possession not merely the raw materials of a solution, but many of the details.

In his fantasy life he enjoyed the harmless illusion that he was a medieval swordsman who went about whacking with his broad sword those who persecuted his family and his friends and his people.

Fine. But how does one whack an angry ghost who may

have made a deal with the principalities and powers of darkness?

81

ANNE'S STORY

Why did I marry Matt Sweeney?

The only answer I can think of now is that he asked me to and when I said thanks but no thanks he said he needed me. Jimbo's annulment petition had been granted; I was free to get married, and no one else applied.

Moreover, Matt's application was made with a heart-rending plea for support and help in a "terribly difficult and painful transition in my life." I've always been a sucker for such pleas. I can't say I loved him, but I didn't love my first husband, either, not the way I came to understand love in my relationship with John Duncan. The union with Matt Sweeney offered me a kind and sympathetic companion. I needed kindness and sympathy. So, too, apparently, did Sweet Matthew.

Not that I hadn't been warned. Before the annulment was granted, I was summoned to the Chancery Office for an interview with the judge in our case, a hulking blond linebacker with a gentle voice named Father Stefan Varga.

"Your biography is remarkably complete, Dr. Reilly," he began carefully, fingering my lengthy self-description.

As usual, I felt my face turn warm. "We academics live by our language skills, Father."

"Quite," he said, averting his eyes from mine. "That's not what I mean, however. You're remarkably mature in this document about admitting your immaturity. Such paradoxical self-awareness is rare."

"Yes, Father."

"As you know," he said hesitantly, "we sometimes request psychological interviews to complete our file of evidence. On other occasions we impose therapy as a condition for remarriage. . . . "

"Are you telling me that I must see a psychiatrist?" I demanded.

"Oh, no." He blushed too. "Hardly. I am perhaps being too much the priest and too little the judge. If you permit me . . . "

"Of course, Father." How could I be angry at this gentle Slavic giant?

"You are aware that you will shortly be free to remarry?"

"I hadn't thought about it," I replied. "Perhaps I've learned my lesson."

"I wonder . . . "

"What do you mean, Father?"

"By your own admission, Dr. Reilly, you entered your union with Mr. James Reilly in great part motivated by a sense of compassion and a desire to help; as you say in your biography, you take care of birds with broken wings."

"Are you saying that you're afraid I might repeat the same mistake unless I see a therapist?"

He blushed again. "I hope you won't be angry at the suggestion, Dr. Reilly."

"Not at all, Father," I replied crisply. "I appreciate it very much."

As you know, Dr. Murphy, I didn't follow his advice. I told myself while walking to the parking lot that I had had it with broken-winged birds and would never make the same mistake again.

And promptly made exactly the same mistake.

Matt and I had gradually become friends from my years at St. Columbanus University. We went out to dinner together and occasionally to films—nothing too heavy, Academy Award–winners like *One Flew Over the Cuckoo's Nest* and *The Godfather, Part Two*. I took him to the opera one night; I lent him my record of *A Chorus Line* (or rather, Mark's record of *A Chorus Line*). He didn't wear the Roman collar when we went on these occasional "dates"—if one

could call them that—but few of the priests at St. Columbanus wore collars, anyway.

At the end of the date there was a routine handshake
and a peck on the cheek, not a hint of anything sexual.

Then one day Sweet Matthew invited me to come to
his office, thick carpet, solid mahogany, heavy drapes—the
gift of some wealthy patrons, according to the party line—
and said to me, "I have come to a very painful decision,
Anne. I haven't told anyone except a few close friends and
my religious superiors. I wanted to keep everything secret
till the matter was concluded."

He played nervously with his gold Mark Cross pen and
continued unsteadily, "I came to the conclusion two years
ago that I had given all of myself I could to university administration. I saw that I was becoming a burned-out case,
shallow, superficial, and without any depth of sincerity or
authenticity. I realized that my creativity was gone and
that I was receiving no more self-fulfillment from my work.
I talked it over with a very solid and wise counselor and
decided it was time for me to make a mid-life change, to
seek a new area in which I could find more genuine authenticity, so I applied to the Pope for a dispensation. My petition has been acted upon. I'm resigning next week as president of the university and leaving the priesthood."

He was not a passionately committed priest (like Father Ryan, whom I could not imagine leaving the priesthood), yet beneath his casual and laid-back style I could not
have imagined there was any frustration or unhappiness.

"What are you going to do?" I asked.

"Oh, I'm going to stay here at the university. I'm a
tenured professor in the education department. I want to
get back into the classroom, catch up on the research literature, and begin to do some scholarship work of my own
again."

It didn't seem to me to be necessary to leave the priesthood to do any of those things. "I'm sure you know what's
best for you, Matt," I said carefully. "They'll have a hard
time replacing you."

He dismissed that with a light wave of his hand. "Oh,
come, anyone could be a college president. . . . Now, there's

another question, Anne. And this applies to you personally. I'm convinced that the kind of fulfillment and personal growth I need requires that I marry. Not immediately, of course, but perhaps next summer. I realize this is a very poor way of putting it, but in my circumstances, I don't have much choice. Would you consider being my wife?"

I was flustered and dismayed. "No," I told him, "it's not you, Matt. You're a wonderful man. It's just that I'm not ready to marry again yet. Probably never."

He seemed surprised and a little hurt. "I really need you, Anne. Promise me you'll think about it for twenty-four hours."

I promised.

When I came back, determined to say no, I found him weeping in his office. So, of course, I changed my mind.

To be fair to him, it was easy to change my mind. I was so lonely then, and so worried about the way inflation was consuming my income, and so terrified about what life would be like when Mark went off to college, that I hardly noticed. I thought about it for a week, asked myself why not, and accepted his proposal.

The following summer, the weekend that the United States celebrated its two hundredth anniversary, Sweet Matthew Sweeney, sometime president of St. Columbanus, and I were joined in the bonds of holy matrimony in a private ceremony in the university chapel.

It was never an unpleasant relationship. I had few illusions about Sweet Matthew. He was more a son than a husband, though, unlike Mark and Davie, hardly a troublesome son. He had had no prior sexual experience and required careful guidance lest he be humiliated during our honeymoon in Cape Cod. At first he was very interested in sex, "as a fulfilling experience I'd never had before," though he scarcely wore me out. After a while it became a relatively minor routine in our lives, like buying and reading *The New York Times* on Sunday morning.

We moved into an expensive apartment on Lake Shore Drive—Mark was going away to college in September—and settled down to what was, if not exactly exciting marital happiness, as least tranquil domesticity. It seemed to me that it was the best I could possibly expect and more than anything I had a right to.

I was genuinely sorry when it ended, and only then realized what a fool I'd been.

BOOK
SIX

BOOK

SIX

82

"Did you know that you met Mike Casey the Cop for the first time as a very little girl at the Century of Progress World's Fair?" Father Ryan asked in a tone of voice that suggested the wide-eyed wonder of a museum guide.

His phone call had awakened Anne at 10:30 in the morning. "I beg pardon, Father," she said somewhat stiffly.

"You and Mike Casey the Cop encountered each other on an open-air bus on the way to the Enchanted Island, and that's not in the South Pacific, but was the children's section of the World's Fair at the Century of Progress in 1934."

"I can't see what difference it makes."

"I'm sorry, Anne," he said. "I fear I have awakened you."

"Not to worry, Father," she said, calling on her last reserves of courtesy and respect. "I've really been under the weather the last couple of days. Sandy and Jerzy and their two children have gone off for a couple of days of watching the leaves at the Wisconsin Dells and I've been trying to shake off a bout of the flu."

"I'm sorry to hear that you haven't been feeling well," he said, a solicitous tone in his voice. "And I'm even more sorry to have disturbed you."

"Not at all, Father." She wished everyone would leave her alone, especially this clerical busybody.

"I thought you would be interested in my World's Fair discovery, courtesy of my niece Caitlin, who presides over our family archives. Marge Ryan Casey, Mike Casey the Cop's mother, kept fairly extensive records—a diary, and then, later on, copies of letters to her husband when he was a war correspondent in Ethiopia and other strange places."

"How interesting."

"You don't remember the encounter at the World's Fair?" he said gently, pushing her for a response.

"Of course I remember. Mickey doesn't. He claims the first time we met was when he walked into our classroom at St. Ursula's. Women have better memories than men."

"A point I will not dispute."

"I'm sort of a World's Fair buff," she said, reluctantly being drawn into the conversation. "I have a couple of scrapbooks of memorabilia tucked away someplace and I was able a few weeks ago to sneak up to the Chicago Historical Society to see their exhibition of pictures. It was a much more spectacular event in my memory, I guess, than it was in reality, although it was pretty spectacular in reality. To a little girl, it seemed like another planet. That's why I'm so enthusiastic about the World's Fair in 1992. I hope our new mayor doesn't prevent it. I'd kind of like to be involved, if I live that long."

"God willing, I'm sure you will. Did you find Mike Casey the Cop an interesting toddler?"

A nasty word of protest sprung to her lips. She cut it off. After all, Father Ryan meant well. "I thought he was a marvelous little boy." She laughed, despite herself. "He really hasn't changed all that much, Father. As a little kid, he was sweet and quiet and gentle. The hard-nosed cop mask came later. It doesn't fool those of us who really know him."

"We all wear masks, don't we, Anne?" the priest said pointedly.

"What's that supposed to mean?" she demanded.

"Oh, nothing. I merely thought you'd be interested to know that your acquaintance with the Deputy Superintendent long antedates the Mother of Mercy fire."

"And what is that supposed to mean?" she demanded.

"I'm not quite sure what it means, Anne," he said softly. "You're going to have to tell me what it means."

"Father, I don't want to hear another word from you ever about Mickey and me. It's over; it's a dead issue."

"Don't call me, I'll call you. Is that it, Anne?"

"That's it precisely, Father Ryan. Leave me alone for a few days until I get over this flu and am not in such a snotty mood. Please, please, leave me alone and don't ever talk about Mickey again. Is that clear?" It seemed impossible to offend him or even to annoy him.

"Oh, yes, it's quite clear, Anne. You want me to slip out of your life for a while. I may do that, and then again, I may not. Good priests sometimes don't vanish, even when they're told to. Get better."

The son of a bitch didn't even give me a chance to have the last word, she thought furiously.

Anne was no longer sure what the day of the week was, or even the time of the day. She shuffled around her apartment in her robe, drinking port and herbal tea and munching on crackers. She was uncertain when she'd eaten last. She slept most of the time and talked to no one. She begged Mark not to call her for a few more days, "until I get over this nasty case of the flu."

She felt indescribably tired. The spunk her father had once said she had too much of had disappeared. There was no reason left to cling to life—the two men she had loved, and she couldn't quite remember their names—were gone. Her children hated her. The art gallery was a waste of time. All the efforts she'd put into her physical appearance were vanity. It was time to let go, give up, flow back into the natural processes from which she'd emerged during the Great Depression. She'd struggled for long enough. Now was the time to let happen what would happen.

As she lay in her bed after Father Ryan's call, suspended between consciousness and unconsciousness, trying to remember what day it was, her bed tilted, slanting toward the window of her bedroom, almost perpendicular to the floor. She clung desperately to the headboard so she wouldn't slip off onto the floor. Then the bed tilted in the opposite direction, toward her bathroom. Slowly at first, then swiftly, it swayed back and forth, each movement becoming more rapid, until the bed was spinning like a roller coaster at Riverview. No, Riverview died a long time ago. It was Great America now, she thought irrelevantly as the bed rose from the floor and spun around like a centrifuge. She held on with all her strength lest she be hurled through the window onto Michigan Avenue.

The centrifuge slowed down gradually, and then her bed clanked into place with a severe jolt that sent her reeling to the floor, dizzy and terribly sick. She pulled herself to her feet, leaning against her dresser, and staggered into the bathroom, where she vomited again. Again? All this had happened before. Many times. Many, many times.

When her stomach was too weak to retch anymore, she stumbled back into her bedroom and collapsed on the bed. For a few moments there was blessed peace, and then the bed began to shake, bouncing up and down like a pile driver, jarring her bones, grinding her teeth, banging her head.

Dear God, please make it stop, she begged. Her prayers were no longer heard, if they ever had been, and the bed continued to pound against the floor as if it were trying to smash through several layers of concrete.

When the pile-driver ride finally stopped, she felt as if she were just barely alive. She crawled off the bed and descended the stairs to the first floor of her apartment, clinging to the railing all the way down.

On the first floor, still disoriented, she swayed toward the door of the corridor outside, remembered that that was not the right way, and then, leaning on the wall, eased her way into the kitchen. There were two empty port bottles on the sink and one half full. She poured the port into a water tumbler, filling it almost to the top, swallowed a large gulp, and, with a last, final effort, dialed Dr. Murphy's office on her kitchen phone.

"This is Dr. Murphy speaking. I do not have office hours on Wednesday. If you wish to leave a message, please tell me your name and phone number and I will return your call. If you wish to cancel or change an appointment, please indicate that too. Wait for the sound of the beep and then give me your message."

Wednesday already? What time Wednesday?

"Anne Reilly, Doctor. I'm afraid I won't be able to keep any more of my appointments for this week or next week. I'll be in touch with you later."

Why did I say that? she asked herself. *Why did I cancel my appointments? I called her for help. I thought she might be able to prescribe some medicine for my flu.*

Painfully she hobbled into her dining room and opened the curtains. It was dark outside. The clock across the street on the Playboy Building said the temperature was 49 degrees and the time was 2:30 A.M. A powerful rain was beating against her window and the northeast wind off the lake was howling down a virtually deserted Michigan Avenue.

Thursday morning already. She must have slept through a whole day, perhaps two. The sleep hadn't helped much. Perhaps she had a fever. Delirious. All of it in her imagination.

She reached for the tumbler of port and remembered she'd left it in the kitchen.

Confused again, she couldn't remember where the kitchen was, and then, picking her way around the dining room table, she finally discovered it. Yes, sure enough, on the sink was the tumbler of port. With one hand on the table, she reached with the other for the kitchen door and dragged herself from the dining room into the kitchen. She leaned on her dishwasher and reached for the glass. The dishwasher began to bounce and jump and shake, just as her bed had. She clutched the port tumbler in her hand and raised it to her lips. The floor of the kitchen was vibrating, jumping about like a high-speed elevator plunging out of control. The glass of port flew from her hand and shattered on the floor. She reached for the half-empty bottle on the sink and it, too, was wrenched out of her hands and shattered against the icebox. Hanging on to the sink with the little strength she had left, she felt the kitchen being wrenched out of the apartment building and hurled into space. Then it hung for a moment at the top of its climb and plunged sickeningly back toward the ground, like a burned-out Fourth of July rocket.

All was blackness. For a long time. And then she awoke, lying on the floor of the parlor, her face on the first step, her robe partially pulled off. For a moment everything was clear to her. It, they, whatever, had come from the gallery to her apartment. She had cut herself off from all help—Father Ryan, Mickey, Dr. Murphy. She felt as if she were marooned on a planet at the far end of the solar system, to which no human had come before or would ever come again.

She would have to face her end as she had lived her life, isolated and lonely.

83
ANNE'S STORY

I lost my job at St. Columbanus because I married Sweet Matthew. After our honeymoon, I came back to teach the second summer-school session because John Leary, the acting president, pleaded with me to do so. "Your classes are popular," he said, his eyes twitching nervously. "You're an easy marker, I guess."

I wasn't a particularly easy marker, though I didn't believe in failing kids simply because they were at the lower end of a curve. My classes were well attended because, unlike most of my colleagues, I still prepared my lectures and, to tell the truth, the kids also seemed to like me. The young women identified with me, telling me they hoped they could be as attractive when they were forty (an enormous compliment, if an inaccurate estimate of my age). The young men delighted in the opportunity to stare at a well-proportioned woman for fifty-five minutes three mornings a week. That flattered me too.

Well, I never denied I was vain. I like to be stared at. No, I am not beautiful. But you should have seen the handful of other women who were permitted on the faculty in those days.

I had come to like my students. Many of them were intelligent and curious young people who were open to learning and who had assumed the pose of dull indifference to protect themselves from the sarcasm of the self-proclaimed Catholic intellectuals on the St. Columbanus faculty.

I was assured verbally in June that the Tenure and Promotion Committee had approved a three-year renewal of my contract and that there was a line in the budget for the following academic year to provide my salary. However, I would not receive the contract until the end of the summer because the budget would not receive its final approval before August 30. It all seemed reasonable, or at least reasonable enough, given the way St. Columbanus was administered. Then, on the last day of the summer session, I was summoned to John Leary's office and given the bad news.

"I'm sorry about this, Dr. Reilly; however, I have no choice. We are forced to terminate your appointment at St. Columbanus College effective today."

"Why? What have I done?" I gasped in dismay.

"You know very well what you've done, Dr. Reilly," he said primly. "You married the former president of this college, who is a priest. It would be a grave scandal to the students and their parents if you were to continue on the faculty."

"Matt is remaining on the faculty, isn't he?" I said, clutching his desk so my dizzy head wouldn't betray me.

"Of course," he replied, as though I were a fool for asking the question. "Professor Sweeney has tenure. You don't."

"If I had a three-year contract, you wouldn't void the contract, would you?"

"We never break our word, Dr. Reilly. But you don't have a three-year contract."

"I was promised one, in the spring," I said uncertainly.

"That was in the spring," he said. "You've changed your situation since then."

"Matt had a dispensation from Rome," I continued to argue. "Our marriage is valid."

"That's not the point, Dr. Reilly. There are certain standards here that must be preserved."

"This is a violation of academic freedom, Father Leary. You know that as well as I do."

"I would hope you don't bring the matter to litigation," he replied. Now speaking in the stiff and formal tones of a judge: "If you do, the matter will linger in the courts for many years and will be an enormous embarrassment for Professor Sweeney."

I stumbled out of his office, blinded with tears and furious. My husband was at home (he wasn't teaching second summer semester) and I phoned him from a public booth down the corridor from the President's office.

"That's a terrible thing, dear. I'm very sorry to hear it," he said soothingly. "I can see John's point, of course, but I think it's terribly unjust. We shouldn't be surprised. Don't worry; my income can take care of us for a while, even if we do have to tighten our belts a bit."

It would be more, I knew, than just tightening our belts. One income would not be enough to pay the rent on the apartment, which Matt had chosen. I would have to find another job, and find it soon.

I applied the next day at the Chicago city colleges and discovered that they would be very pleased to have someone with my credentials on their faculty. "Very pleased indeed, Dr. Reilly," the dean said. Moreover, although the city college was merely a collection of junior colleges scattered all over the city, the faculty union was very tough and someone with my credentials and experience would earn fifty percent more than I had earned at St. Columbanus.

However, there was a catch. Their budget, too, was committed for the coming academic year. They might be able to find room for me in the spring. Perhaps there would even be a single evening course sometime after the first of the year.

I stormed up and down the streets of downtown and the Near North Side of Chicago, my sundress wilting in the summer heat. I was angry, disgusted, repelled. It was typical of the Catholic Church. As I had told Father Ryan several years before, it was a pretty terrible church. Yet, it was still the only one I had. The thought of my conversation with Father Ryan reminded me that I had not seen him in over a year. Somehow I did not want to tell him about my marriage to a priest, however valid that marriage might be. Now, however, I needed not the support of a priest-husband who sympathized with me and held me in his arms while at the same time saying he could understand the university's position. I needed a priest who would be as angry as I was.

So I turned off Michigan Avenue and went over to Wabash to Holy Name Cathedral Rectory, where I'd heard Father Ryan was now stationed. He obliged me with anger, even more than I had expected.

"Those miserable, filthy, hypocritical sons of bitches!" he exploded.

"Your language is as bad as mine, Father," I said, not even trying to hide my satisfaction.

"If I wasn't in the presence of an elegant and charming woman," he said, his eyes glinting with fury, "I'd use much stronger language. I'll get them for you, Anne; don't worry, I'll get them."

"Vengeance is mine, saith the Lord."

"Don't quote scripture when I'm angry, woman!" he shouted. "Those people are a disgrace to the Catholic Church and they must not be permitted to continue their hypocrisy."

"I don't want the job back, Father. The place smells of mediocrity anyway. I'm well rid of them."

Father Ryan cooled off after a bit.

"I shall still have a word with my Lord Cronin, who likes those people not," he said. "He has a marvelous nose for phonies. However, that is another matter. What do you want to do, Anne?"

I told him about the Chicago city colleges.

"Has it occurred to you that perhaps there is another area of endeavor at which you might be happier?"

"My training is in art history, Father. I know quite a bit about art criticism. I'm not much of an artist, however. What else can I do besides teach?"

"There is," he said thoughtfully, "a slightly dotty but rather benign elderly woman named Cornelia Graham. . . ."

"Of course, the Graham Gallery over on Oak Street."

"Indeed. She has been variously described as a tough old bitch, a sweet old lady, and a shrewd old bandit, all of which titles are appropriate. She is a loyal and faithful member of the parish, though I must confess, none too enthusiastic about the English liturgy. She's slowed down a bit in recent months and I believe is looking for an assistant. In fact, she seems, unaccountably, rather fond of me. Thinks of me as a 'cute little priest,' a sentiment I believe you also entertain, despite my occasional uncanonical language. In any case, Mrs. Graham has asked me to keep an eye open for an assistant. She's contentious and difficult, at best, which I suppose would make her an excellent match for you. Are you interested?"

I'd never thought of working in an art gallery. The idea, nonetheless, struck me as very interesting.

"At least till a job opens up for me in the Chicago city system," I said tentatively.

"Excellent. I'll call her now and see if you can walk over and make an arrangement with her."

Corny, as I came to call her, was certainly no more than four feet eleven inches tall and really thin, but even in her upper seventies, she had sweet eyes and a pretty face. I was escorted through the gallery and asked to comment on the pictures hanging on the walls and waiting in the storerooms.

"That's nice," I said of one, "and I suspect it will sell, but it's not likely to grow in value."

"Humph."

"And that one is terrible. It doesn't deserve to hang in your gallery." I pointed at another. "This one is skillful, and is worth probably more than the price tag you have on it."

"Humph."

"And this one"—I paused over a marvelous blue-and-white watercolor, "this one is the work of a brilliant young painter."

"Humph."

At the end of the tour Cornelia considered me thoughtfully. "You only made one mistake, Dr. Reilly."

"What was that?"

"Peggy Donlon, who did the watercolor, is considerably older than you and considerably younger than me."

"Youth and talent don't necessarily correlate with chronological age," I replied promptly.

Cornelia's face, which had been frozen in mild disapproval until then, lit up in a bright smile. "I really must call you Anne, and you really must call me Corny, young woman. And if you want it, you have a job."

It was a job I loved instantly. Somehow it seemed designed for me and it challenged my strange combination of skills and energies better than anything I'd done in my life. I did take the one night a week course at Loop Junior College because I wanted the opportunity to teach art history, which the city college system offered, even though St. Columbanus didn't (it attracted not late-teenagers, but adult students, many of whom were substantially older than I was, and a couple I suspect even older than Corny).

Moreover, though Corny, classic skinflint with money, didn't pay very much, she still payed more than St. Columbanus.

Matt was delighted with my job and pleased that I was happy. He made one or two mild complaints about hasty dinners but then laughed the complaints away and said, "When feminism cuts close to home, it doesn't look nearly as appealing as it does in principle. I guess I'll have to learn to cook."

He tried, poor dear, but he never was very good at it. He didn't even know how to use the disposal in our kitchen sink. Our marriage was easy, relaxed, friendly. I'd learned enough about human nature, particularly male human nature, not to make too many demands on my new husband. By temperament, Matt was incapable of making too many demands on anyone. As a cure for my loneliness, being Mrs. Matthew Sweeney was a useful role. As an occasion of intermittent sexual release, which was better than no sexual release at all, our marriage bed was mildly satisfying. To tell the truth, however, it was more important then to have someone in the same apartment with me than in the same bed. After a reasonably long life, I told myself, one learned to live with one's investments and thereby limit one's losses.

The gallery was more fun and more challenge than my marriage. Corny increasingly relied on my taste, my business judgment, my common sense, and my tenacity (I had become her Sandy, I guess). I sometimes wonder in retrospect whether my grandfather, who reputedly was one of the worst pirates in the First Ward in the old days of the Everleigh Sisters, Bathhouse John Coghlin, and Hinky Dink Kenna, had bequeathed some special gombeen genes to me and perhaps, through me, to Mark. Indeed, I've even wondered whether I might not have done very well in one of the pits on the Board of Trade, a suspicion Mark confirms by rolling his eyes.

My husband increasingly became involved in the Catholic Charismatic Renewal. I accompanied him once or twice to Catholic Pentecostal meetings in a parish near the campus of St. Columbanus. They were not my cup of tea.

"I don't mind the speaking in tongues," I told him. "I suppose it's just a form of enthusiastic prayer. But I can't buy the simple-minded theology. The world is a lot more complex, and so is human life. You can't solve your problems by flipping open the Scriptures, choosing a page, and assuming that that's God's personal message to you."

"The Charismatic Renewal in the United States began in the theology department of the University of Notre Dame," Matt said, disagreeing mildly. (All his disagreements were mild.)

"Which merely proves what a rotten theology department they have," I responded.

"It's the most important movement in the new Church," he said. "The Charismatics and the Liberation Theologians *are* the new Catholicism."

"We've abdicated our own heritage, Matt. The Charismatics are Protestants and the Liberationists are Marxists. What the hell happened to the Catholic tradition?"

"It's finished," he said mildly. "We have to look elsewhere for a vision of the Catholicism of the future."

I didn't argue because one of the implicit rules of our union was that I did not overwhelm my husband with superior knowledge and intelligence. Nonetheless, I couldn't see that a tradition that had produced Augustine, Aquinas, Dante, Notre-Dame, Rubens, San Pietro, Michelangelo, Newman, Chesterton, and contemporary writers like David Tracy and Karl Rahner—neither of whom I understood—was exactly bereft of vision or importance. I let it go.

Matthew, however, attended Charismatic Renewal meetings twice a week, one of them on the night I was teaching at Loop College. Indeed, the Charismatic Renewal occupied so much of his time that his own research, which he'd promised to do when he stepped down as president, was never begun.

So we lived for two years. I can't be certain whether I would have been satisfied in our marriage if it hadn't been for the Graham Gallery. For the first time since my graduation from high school my life was occupied with activities that weren't unpleasant. My responsibilities and my guilts and my sadnesses all remained, but I was so deeply involved in my work that I paid little attention to them, save for worrying about Mark when he married Tessie at such a young age.

We'd been married for two and a half years when Matt went on a week-long Charismatic retreat, the first time we'd been separated for more than a day since our marriage. I was curious about what my reaction would be, half-fearing, half-hoping that I would not miss him. The first few days were fine. The apartment without Matt wasn't very much different from the apartment with Matt. The gallery kept me busier than usual because Corny was in the hospital for a checkup, a checkup that worried me because she seemed to be tiring more easily than she had even a few months earlier. But by the fourth day of the week, I confess, I really did miss Matt and decided that an apartment with a man in it was substantially better than one without. For the first time in our marriage I concluded that he was not merely a pleasant companion but someone I had begun to love.

On Friday afternoon—Matt was due back Saturday afternoon—I closed the gallery early and went over to Passavant Hospital to visit Corny.

"I have a business proposition," she began briskly. "Would you be interested in buying the gallery? Not all of it, maybe only fifty-five percent? I'm going to have to put it up for sale, you know."

"Oh, no!" I cried. "You can't sell!"

"I'm afraid I have to. The doctors tell me it's time to retire and relax. My daughter and son-in-law have been begging me to join them in San Diego and help in a little gallery they run on the side. I figure if I don't do it gracefully, I'll be carried out of the gallery in a pine box. I don't want to rush the Lord's plans. I'd like you to turn the Graham Gallery into the Reilly Gallery.''

I wept because of affection and concern and gratitude. I would much rather have had it the Graham Gallery and had Corny around than take over on my own.

When I got back to the apartment that night, I dug out my financial records, considered the money my parents had left me, notably enhanced by the prosperity of the forties and fifties, and then sadly deflated by the inflation of the late sixties and the seventies. I realized I was fifty thousand dollars short of what Corny needed for her "grub stake" when she went to San Diego. Perhaps I could get a bank loan, I thought, yet I was reluctant to sink all my money into a new enterprise and go into debt too. I'd learned enough in two years with Corny to know that many business people embark on much riskier ventures on the strength of their credit line in the bank. The memory of the Great Depression and what the Crash did to my father still terrified me. I called Mark and asked his opinion. He told me that he would look into it but that, on the face of it, it sounded like a much less risky venture than those he participated in every day.

I was filled with possibilities and fears that I wanted to share with my husband as soon as he came home, especially now, as I had determined that, after a fashion anyway, I loved him.

Matt was exhausted when he finally arrived late Saturday evening. It had been an emotionally exhilarating retreat, but there hadn't been much time for sleep.

"The Holy Spirit really spoke to me this week, dear," he exclaimed. "For the first time in my life I see things clearly. What a blind fool I've been through the years, but I'm now filled with God's grace and I *know* what I should do."

I wanted to tell him about the gallery, but he seemed to need the opportunity to talk more than I did.

"Might it not be a good idea," I asked, "to sleep on it before you decide anything drastic?"

"There's no sleep necessary, dear," he replied. "The Holy Spirit has shown me the way. He has provided me with his guidance. I must do what I must do."

I was becoming a bit uneasy. "What do you have to do, Matt?"

"My relationship with you, Anne," he explained slowly, "has been the most meaningful relationship in my life. I have grown and enriched my personality, I have fulfilled myself. I've become a much better human being because I have lived with you and loved you and shared life with you these years. Now I feel I must go on to the next phase in my life, that I must respond to the call of the Holy Spirit and become an even richer, deeper, more authentic, and freer human being."

"What does that mean?" I asked, hardly able to believe my ears.

"I'm going to have to go back to the priesthood, Anne," he said solemnly. "The voice of God has spoken to me through the Holy Spirit this week, and I realize that I must go back to the priesthood."

"You're married to me!" I insisted. "How can you go back to the priesthood when you're validly married to me?"

"You won't release me?" he said sadly.

"How can I release you, Matt? We were validly married in St. Columbanus's chapel. We're husband and wife till death do us part."

"No we're not, Anne." He shook his head as though I did not fully understand. "In God's eyes, of course, we've been married, but not in the eyes of the Church. From the point of view of the official Church, I was not free to marry. I am not validly married now, and if you will release me, I can go back to the priesthood. I suppose I will have to go to a monastery for a year or two to reestablish my relationship with the Church, but I'm sure they will permit me that if I end my relationship with you."

"You told me that you'd applied for a dispensation and that the Pope had granted it," I exploded.

"I didn't tell you that, Anne," he said in the tone of a full professor lecturing a freshman girl on the first day of the term. "I told you I had applied for a dispensation and the Holy Father had acted on it. Fortunately, his action was to deny it. They're pretty reluctant over in Rome now to give dispensations to people who have positions of responsibility—bishops, religious superiors, college presidents."

"You lied to me," I shouted.

"No, I didn't lie to you, Anne," he insisted, hurt by my lack of sympathy with his problem. "I told you I was free to marry. In my heart I was free. I believed that God wanted me to marry so that I could enrich and grow and develop and become a more authentic human being. This week I've learned that I misunderstood the voice of the Spirit. I'm terribly sorry if I have hurt you. Can't we talk this through, work it out, understand one another, and part friends? If you care about me, and I believe you do, Anne, don't you want me to be authentic? Don't you want me to respond to the voice of the Spirit?"

I was dazed, incredulous. This couldn't possibly be happening. Two husbands, two marriages, both of them from the Church's point invalid, the first because long after the fact the Church had decided Jimbo Reilly and I were not emotionally and psychologically capable of contracting a marriage, the second because the Church had never given my husband permission to marry. Thanks a hell of a lot, Church!

"Get out of here," I told him. "I don't want you in this apartment for another hour. Pack whatever clothes you need and go someplace else. Go back to the dorm at Columbanus, where you belong. Get out and stay out."

"I paid the rent on the apartment," he protested with an air of offended innocence.

"I don't give a goddamn what you paid. You're a fraud and a faker and a phony."

"You won't release me so I can follow the call of the Spirit?" he asked anxiously.

"I'll release you with an enormous feeling of relief, Sweet Matthew Sweeney," I bellowed, "just so long as I never have to look at your pious, phony, hypocritical face again. Now get out!"

"You'll regret this," he said, his voice trembling with what from anyone else besides Sweet Matthew would have been called rage. "God will punish you for your cruelty."

"Out!" I screamed, grabbing an iron from our fireplace. He left.

I was too angry and too disgusted to even bother to cry. I told myself that in a few weeks I'd hardly know he was gone. It wasn't that easy, however. Living in the same apartment, sharing the same bed, occasionally coupling your body with someone else's—all of these things create ties that have demands of their own, even if you're unaware of them.

The divorce was not messy, just depressing. I had no idea how I would survive financially, although I did realize I would have to move out of my luxury apartment and find something cheaper. I also knew I would have to find a new job unless whoever bought the gallery from Corny wanted to keep me on.

The fears, the guilts, the responsibilities, the anguished memories of the past must have been lurking in the closet because on the night Sweet Matthew left, my dreams began again. In the morning, I woke up screaming, something I hadn't done since before I went to bed with John Duncan.

Then my Mark, unbelievably, miraculously came to the rescue. He appeared one afternoon in the gallery— Corny was in California, arranging things with her daughter and son-in-law—and dropped into my hands two sets of keys. "The first is for an apartment over at Nine Hundred North Michigan, which is smaller and doesn't cost quite as much as the one you're in but is closer to the gallery," he said. "I've paid the rent for the first six months. And the other is a new set of keys for the Reilly Gallery. I know you've got your own set, but I wanted you to have this set as a memento. Corny and I closed the deal on the phone today and she's as pleased as punch. Now, you'd better make a lot of money so that if I ever get tossed off the Board of Trade, you can hire me as a messenger boy!"

He was grinning like a cat who had swallowed a railroad car full of canaries.

"Can you afford it, Mark?" I asked in disbelief. How could this boy, this child, this former delinquent, have that sort of money? He laughed enthusiastically, not even mentioning that it was a question I often asked his father and then hugged me even more enthusiastically. "Don't worry, Mom! I can afford it, all right. I won't even have to trade in my Mercedes or Tessie's Jaguar."

So it came to be that I lost a husband and acquired a gallery. On the whole, an excellent trade. No, I must say more than that, drat it. I lost a husband and acquired a son.

No, that won't do either. I found I always had a son. A good son.

I fell in love with my new apartment and was only mildly frightened by being now completely alone for the first time in my life. Mostly it worked out. After a while I stopped missing Matthew, though to tell you the truth, Dr. Murphy, I still wish I had a man. In fact, I wish I had not John Duncan necessarily, but a man who is as passionate as John is. Does that sound strange, a woman of my age really yearning for a passionate lover? I suppose it does, but I can't help it.

The gallery flourished and I became very much a part of the Chicago establishment and society scene. I did not lack for suitors and there were more than enough passes made. Having been burned a couple of times, I was going to be very wary before I embarked on the matrimonial seas again. This time the man would have to be passionate, gentle, sympathetic, intelligent, and, above all else, I guess, totally unattached. No one like that has come along. The tentacles of depression continued to poke at my personality—indeed, more insistently now than they did after Matthew walked out on me, or perhaps I should say, after I ordered him out.

I suppose the depression is all mixed up with things deep in my past and may even stand in the way of my making an intelligent decision about a man to spend the rest of my life with. So that's the reason why, Dr. Murphy, I began to see you.

Father Ryan asked me again why I'd stayed in the Catholic Church.

"How can you possibly remain with us," he said, his pale blue eyes consoling me, "and stay in a church that's done such terrible things to you?"

"Same answer as before," I replied. "It's the only church I have, and I don't know what I'd do without Midnight Mass at Christmas."

"Huh?" he said, a rare confession of surprise from my cute little priest with the hurt leprechaun smile.

"I'm not sure what Easter is about," I replied. "Sure, Jesus rose from the dead and that's wonderful. I'm not sure, though, what it means for my life. But I do know what Christmas means. God somehow joins himself to a little baby and we celebrate with old carols at midnight of a cold, dark Christmas day. We know that life is stronger than death, love is stronger than hate, good's stronger than bad. If anyone takes Midnight Mass away from me, I have nothing left to live for. Don't you let those crazy people over in Rome abolish Midnight Mass."

"No way," Father Ryan said.

Now you know the whole story, Dr. Murphy. I've read over all of these chapters and I guess I understand myself a little better. Since I'm kind of an academic and since academics are into summaries, I'll offer a summary of my problem: I am a very lonely woman. I guess I always have been. Since Dick was killed anyway and I probably have romanticized that romance too. I've been lonely as long as I can remember. I was too busy with Jimbo and the kids for many years to notice. John Duncan was a temporary cure. Matt Sweeney was a pretense that loneliness didn't matter. Now that it's too late for me to be anything but lonely, I wonder what I might have done differently.

Someone said that men want sex and accept intimacy as a necessary condition and that women want intimacy and offer sex as a necessary preliminary. I hope I'm not a freak, Dr. Murphy, but I've discovered that I want both very badly. When Mike Casey consumed me with his gorgeous baby blue eyes at my gallery the other day, I realized how terrible it is to live alone, no man in your apartment, no man in your bed, no man's body in your body, filling you with happiness. I've lived that way all my life, even when there were men around.

It's my own fault, of course. I'm being punished for my sins and there's no way to escape. Sartre was wrong when he said hell was "the others." In fact, hell is the absence of "the others." I've been in my own self-created hell for a long time. Now that I recognize it and know that I can never escape, it becomes an even more lonely hell.

Yet, I kind of feel sorry for me, if that doesn't sound too self-indulgent and too self-pitying. Somehow I ought to be better than I am. I can't say that I don't know where I've failed because it's pretty clear to me where I failed. And I think I also know why I failed. Sometimes I wonder, however, whether maybe God may not have made demands on me that were much too big for a very little girl.

84

Dizzy, sick, unbearably weary and beaten, Anne slumped head down on her kitchen table. Light was coming through the window, so it must have been morning. She didn't know what day of the week, or even month of the year, it was. The end was coming, however, of that she was certain. Those who wished to destroy her would do so today. The evil spirits in the gallery had now taken possession of her apartment. She was cut off, alone, without any help or protection. They were toying with her, playing with her, amusing themselves with her before the final destruction, which would plunge her into the anguish of hell forever and ever.

There were no prayers left, no God on whom to call, nothing but the certainty of doom. The last plea had been rejected, the last stay granted, the last appeal turned down.

Now there remained only the short walk on shaky limbs and stumbling feet to the gas chamber.

With sore, swollen lips she tried again for perhaps the hundredth time to murmur the words of the act of contrition, a last desperate, pathetic plea that God might forgive. The gates of heaven were closed against her. There was no one listening. God wouldn't even deign to give her the grace to say the final prayer, which she had murmured so many times in the confessional for almost half a century.

The frigid arctic wind was suddenly there in her house, sweeping through the parlor, knocking over lamps and tables, pulling prints and paintings from the wall. It invaded the dining room, smashing furniture, overturning the table, and then found her in the kitchen, lifted her from the table, and deluged her with snow and cold.

She abandoned her resistance. They would play with her as long as they wished and then they would do whatever they had come to do. The foul hands were back, pulling off her robe, starting again their vile and obscene amusements with her body. Now she was passed from unseen demon to unseen demon, tossed around her apartment as though she were a beach ball, to be even more completely degraded and debased than in the gallery. The flames were everywhere, forming a tight little circle of fire around her and the demon whose turn it was to take his gross amusement in humiliating her. There seemed crowds of human beings now in the flames, scores, perhaps hundreds, their obscene laughter at her predicament echoing and reechoing as they roamed her apartment, smashing more dishes and overturning the few pieces of furniture that were still standing.

She peered at them in the flames, somehow recognizing them, yet not knowing who they really were. Her attempts to identify them seemed to heighten their amusement. Their laughter grew ever louder. Then came the rapists, now with very clear faces, gleefully and fiendishly triumphing over her as they plunged again and again into her body, forcing her to enjoy her own suffering and degradation. Her father, her brothers, Dick, all the men she'd ever known, floated above her as her body jerked in spasm after spasm after spasm. She told herself this was all imagination, a trick of the demons, an illusion of the hell she would suffer forever. These were not really the men who'd loved her. Yet, even as she tried to reassure herself, she wondered how many days into eternity she would be able to remember. Eventually she would forget, and then she would truly believe that the men she'd loved were reveling in their power over her and in the pleasure that came from debasing her.

Ice, fire, humiliation, pain, and torment invaded her now in ever faster cycles so that finally they all seemed to become one. She was being burned, frozen, and raped all in the same instant. This was the essence of an eternity of hell—all possible pains and humiliations, degradations going on at the same time. She prayed for madness, longed for it, begged for it, implored God to take away her sanity so at least she would not be aware of who it was who was suffering.

Then the shadowy figures and the vaguely familiar faces began to emerge from the fire. She recognized them. She had known all along who they were, even if she had not been consciously aware of it. Torn, crippled, disfigured, maimed, they came from the flames pointing their fingers at her in accusation and triumph. Oh, yes, she knew who they were.

They were the children she had killed in the fire.

85

Blackie had not slept well at night since the explosion at the Reilly Gallery. He was sufficiently Celtic to be terrified of the supernatural, even though he pretended to be a more or less total rationalist. Anything that touched the person and the art of Desmond "Skip" Kenny struck him as being a little uncanny. Moreover, he loved Anne Reilly greatly, and was profoundly concerned about her anguish and, even worse, had no idea what to do about it.

So he fretted and stewed and tossed and turned in his bed and thought and figured and calculated and came up with a total, absolute zero. He pretended to his Lord Cronin, and to his diligent if not always adequately appreciative parish staff, that he was sleeping as well as he ever had—after all, was he not the just man who was entitled to his sleep?

Whether or not he succeeded in fooling the Cardinal, Blackie didn't fool himself. In his head he was convinced Anne Reilly was going through a severe crisis brought on by the long series of cruel things the Church had done to her, aggravated by the reappearance of her lifelong, if mostly invisible, lover, Mike Casey the Cop, and brought to a head by the evil art of Skip Kenny in her gallery.

That's what he thought in his head. From the depths of his mordant, melancholy Celtic soul, however, he was fully prepared for Mike Casey's explanation that they were dealing with something monstrous and possibly diabolic. He kept the ritual, the stole, and the holy water on the bedstand so that any hour of the day or night he might rush forth and pronounce the preliminary words of exorcism.

Yet, he didn't quite believe that was the difficulty either.

Moreover, he knew there would be no point in doing much of anything until Anne opened herself to someone and asked for help. Presently she was showing no signs at all of that.

In short, he didn't know what to do.

He called her several times on Thursday, violating her instructions, and she didn't answer the phone. Nor was there a response at the gallery. He assumed she'd pulled the phone plug out. He considered going to her apartment and pounding on the door. That day, however, was a very busy one at the Cathedral: funerals, wedding rehearsals, instructions, committee meetings, irate staff members, recalcitrant teenagers, knife-carrying and drug-peddling grammar school students—these were the kinds of troubles that affected the modern, postconciliar pastor as he purported to teach the good news that God loved the world.

So he didn't go over to her apartment, wasting precious,

precious time when they had none to waste. Worse still, he didn't yet see the explanation, a failure he later regarded as almost criminally negligent on his part. All the pieces in the puzzle were there, but somehow—old age, perhaps, or the confusion that comes with minor ecclesiastical power—he didn't have sense enough to put the pieces together.

About eight o'clock that night he had supper at L'Escargot, Mary Kate's favorite restaurant, in the Allerton Hotel, and refreshed his weary body with some of their marvelous cream of watercress soup. It was Joe's one night a month at the Suicide Center at Northwestern University Hospital. (Joe didn't actually answer the phone calls, but rather monitored the efforts of the psychiatric residents who did answer them.) So all three—Blackie, Joe, and Mary Kate—had an early dinner together.

"This will be a good night," Joe observed, "or a bad one, depending on your perspective. Summer's over, leaves are falling off the trees, and it's been raining for a couple of days. It's enough to make anybody think about their bottle of sleeping pills." Some nights at the center, he added, there was no activity at all and other nights he and his residents talked all night long.

"What are your percentages, Joe?" Blackie asked curiously. "Do you win more than you lose?"

"Oh"—Joe laughed—"we win most all of them. But it still hurts whenever you lose."

"Understandably," Blackie said, reflecting that Joe's patients in many cases were doomed to have suicidal potential.

"I wouldn't last ten minutes in that kind of role," Mary Kate commiserated. "I'd want to get in the car, drive over to their houses, and grab the bottle of sleeping tablets out of their hands."

"Doubtless bringing along The Weapon to smash open their doors if they wouldn't let you in," Blackie remarked.

The Weapon, a family heirloom that leaned against the wall in the Murphys' study on Longwood Drive, was a late-medieval Irish pike, useful for fighting off Norman and English invaders but not necessarily for staving in the front doors of modern, upper-middle-class homes.

After dinner Mary Kate, something less than her usual effervescent self, dropped Joe at the hospital and Blackie at the Cathedral. "You'd think I could do without him one night a month, wouldn't you?" she asked Blackie as he got out of her Datsun 200 SX.

"No, beloved sister," Blackie replied. "I wouldn't think that at all."

In his rooms, Blackie fortified himself with an extra-large helping of Jameson's and went to bed, feeling sure he would have another sleepless night.

The Jameson's worked, however, and he slept deeply, if not peacefully. Then he awakened with a start, sat up in bed, and saw it all—not all the details, to be sure, but the broad outline of the story and the solution.

"But that's absurd," he shouted. "That's goddamn fool nonsense! What's more, I can prove it!"

He dashed into his office and began rummaging through the files that Caitlin had brought from Grand Beach. Blackie searched for several minutes and then stopped, frozen by another insight. "Good Lord," he said to himself, "so that's why she didn't answer the phone all day. Damn, damn, damn, damn!"

He phoned Northwestern Hospital, asked first for the Suicide Center, and then for Dr. Murphy.

"Joe, do you have the Psychiatric Unit's admissions list there?"

"Yeah, it's around here someplace. I can dig it up. Why?"

"Look through it. If you find the name Reilly on the list, call your wife and tell her to get down there just as fast as her Datsun can make it and use whatever clout you have so that there're temporary staff privileges waiting for her when she arrives."

"Got it," Joe said. "I think I know what this is all about."

A few minutes later, Blackie's personal phone rang. "You're right, Blackie. She's here. It looks bad, very bad."

"Have Mary Kate call me as soon as she has some idea what will happen."

Blackie hung up and looked at the pile of old letters and

diaries. The answer was in there someplace, he knew, but now it might be too late to hunt for it. So he went back to bed, suspecting, quite correctly, as it turned out, that Friday might be a very busy day.

86

The phone rang, Mary Kate nudged where Joe normally lay, and said, "Answer it, Joe."

There was no Joe there to nudge, so, dismayed and distraught by his absence, she answered it herself. It was Joe, unaccountably on the phone instead of in bed with her where he belonged.

"Her name is Anne Reilly, isn't it? The patient we talked about the other night?"

"Yes, of course," still trying to figure out why her husband was on the phone.

"She's here in the Psychiatric Unit, under heavy sedation and restraints. She was admitted early this afternoon. Her neighbors heard her screaming in her apartment. The building superintendent finally opened the door and found the apartment in a shambles and Mrs. Reilly hiding in the bathtub, stark naked, in an extremely acute psychotic episode. Blackie thought you ought to know and suggested I get you temporary staff privileges."

"Right. I'll be there as soon as I can." Mary Kate was now fully awake and extremely worried.

"Drive carefully," she cautioned herself as she set out. "You won't be any good to her if you make half the trip in an ambulance."

When Mary Kate walked into Anne's room, she thought for a moment that there was a mistake. This wasn't her patient, Anne Marie O'Brien Reilly, one of the ten best-dressed women in Chicago and easily the most beautiful mature woman in the city. This was a worn-out, battered old woman who had gone quite out of her mind. Mary Kate had to look a second time and even a third to realize that indeed it was Anne and that the psychotic interlude was tearing her apart.

"Treatment, Doctor?" she snapped at the first-year resident in charge.

"That's obvious, Doctor," he shifted his feet uneasily. "Very strong sedation. She's quite manic, you see."

Poor kid is scared stiff of the great Doctor Murphy, she thought. I'll have to help him too.

A nurse stuck her head in the door. "The rector of Holy Name Cathedral on the phone for you, Dr. Murphy."

Mary Kate told her she'd take the call at the nurses' station.

"Sister? Brother."

"Any other rector?"

"For what it's worth, Mike Casey told me a few days ago that if we take Anne's mind away from her with strong tranquilizers, she'll go under. He thinks it's only the strength of her intelligence that's kept off the demons—his word—so far in her life."

"He may be right," Mary Kate said slowly. "She's heavily sedated now. Yet, judging from her movements and facial expressions, she's going through hell."

"The eyes of love often see things we don't," he said tentatively, careful not to influence his sister's professional judgment.

"She was apparently quite violent when they brought her in," Mary Kate said. "Intelligence or no."

"She was alone then," Blackie replied. "She's been alone too long."

"And when she comes out, assuming I take the hypo away from the resident who wants to shoot her up again?"

"She won't be alone. You'll be there."

"Mary Kate the Archangel," she said ironically.

"At least an archangel—more like a throne or domination."

Mary Kate wasn't sure what that meant, but she went back to Anne's room thinking furiously. Her brother had confirmed her own vague instincts.

"Your treatment doesn't seem to be working, Doctor," she remarked gently to the resident. "She's twisting and turning and her rapid eye movements indicate terrible nightmares."

"Nightmares with the kind of sedation we've given her are quite impossible, Doctor," he said, trying to sound like a senior consultant.

"How do you know, Doctor?" she asked. "Have you ever been there?"

"It's standard treatment, Doctor," he replied, a bit shaken.

"No more, Doctor," she ordered. "Not another pill, not another shot, nothing."

"When she revives, Doctor," he said, scarcely hiding his contempt, "won't she do herself serious physical harm despite the restraints? We had a terrible time controlling her when she first came in and getting her into the bed."

"I imagine you did."

"Her family will be upset if she's injured, Doctor," he insisted.

"Then they can sue for malpractice," Mary Kate responded sharply. "Where is the family? Are they here?"

"They're waiting in the lounge," he said.

"Okay. I'll be down there to see them in a minute."

"What treatment?"

"When she comes out of it, it should be sometime in the morning, she'll see my face. And you just watch, Doctor," she grinned like a Halloween prankster, "the calming influence my face has on her."

"It's a very attractive face, Doctor," the kid grinned back despite himself.

"You may have swallowed the blarney stone in Ireland, young man," she jabbed her finger at him. "Want to bet against my treatment?"

"No way."

Mary Kate slipped out of the room, assured the patient's son and daughter-in-law that she had been treating her for some time, and that she had great confidence in the patient's emotional strength. But when she returned to Anne's hospital bed, she was shocked again at how terrible she looked.

"You better be at least as strong as I think you are," she muttered, "or there isn't going to be much we can do for you."

She sat at the side of the bed and watched Anne carefully for the slightest sign of returning consciousness.

"When your eyes open I want you to see a Ryan face, a Ryan smile, and Ryan blue eyes so that you'll know that we are, all of us, pulling for you—including my father, my brother Blackie the priest, and—I will drag him in when necessary—Mike Casey the Cop."

"You see, Doctor," she said to the resident as he drifted in at 7 A.M., "no more struggling, no more rapid eye movement—an exhausted but restful patient."

"I'm impressed, Doctor," he said with a mixture of admiration and dread. Joe Murphy had often remarked to his wife apropos of resident crushes on her that she was too young to be their mother, too old to be their girlfriend, too Irish to enjoy their worship, and too sexy not to attract it.

"Nothing to it, Doctor." She smiled her most winning smile for him. "Now go get me a cup of coffee."

At 8:45 Anne's eyelids flickered and then peacefully quieted down.

As Mary Kate later recalled, she summoned all her resources of love. This woman was her mother, her daughter, her sister, her cousin, her friend, her lover, her patient. She would save her. She would make her well. She would give life back to her.

"Annie," she said softly, touching Anne's hand. "Annie, it's Mary Kate. It's all right. They can't hurt you now. I'm here. It's all right. Everything is all right."

Cautiously Anne opened her eyes, tried to focus on M.K., then sort of skeptically closed them again.

"Open your eyes, woman," Mary Kate ordered pleasantly. "I have a young resident here who, though he doubtless regards me as old enough to be his mother, is convinced I'm a genius. You have to confirm it for me."

Anne opened her eyes again. "Dr. Murphy," she said in surprise.

"Who else?" She breathed a huge sigh of relief, appropriate for a woman who has just given birth, which in a way she had.

Maybe I am a genius!

"I'm so sorry to have disturbed you. I don't remember what happened. . . . I'm not in hell?"

"No, you're merely in Northwestern Memorial Hospital, which, as far as I've noticed, while not an appealing place, is scarcely hell."

She untied the restraints, soothed Anne's hair into place, took her hand, and said, "Everything's going to be all right. We'll have you out of here in a day or two and then off to Bermuda or Sea Island or Tahiti for a long vacation."

Anne sighed peacefully. "I guess I need one. Will you tell Father Ryan I'm all right?"

"You bet . . . Oh, Dr. Reilly, this is Dr. Hoffman, the resident who's been helping me. He's kind of cute. Will you please tell him I'm a genius."

She smiled, her best Anne Marie O'Brien Reilly smile, and shed about twenty of the years she'd put on in the last day. "Dr. Hoffman"—she giggled—"My, there're a lot of doctors around here, aren't there? Dr. Hoffman, Dr. Murphy is a genius."

Mary Kate called her assistant and told her to cancel her appointments for the day. Then she talked to Mark Reilly—whom she assured his mother was fine—the Pirate, and finally, Blackie Ryan the Priest.

"She made it," she told him. "She's going to be all right."

"The battle's over?" he asked.

"For the present. At least we've got her out of the psychotic episode and rational again. There may be a lot of work left to do, but now it's our inning."

Then she went back to Anne's room and listened to her description of the fantasies that had been assaulting her for the last several weeks and that had reached a crescendo at the beginning of her psychotic episode. They had continued while she lay in the hospital bed, strapped to the rails and so deeply sedated she shouldn't have been able to dream.

"Pretty foul-minded images of hell, aren't they?" she asked, grinning weakly.

"Pretty scary, if you ask me. And not all that untypical, either. If women who believe in hell are honest with themselves, they'll admit that the worst possible eternal punishment would be endless sexual exploitation. Those fears are built into our bodies, I think."

"I don't want that to happen to me," Anne said sadly.

"I'm sure it won't," Mary Kate replied briskly. "We have to find out what is causing these fantasies to disturb you so much." And then, with some hesitation she added, "And block out your fantasies with images of a God who says that He—or She—is Love."

"I know what the cause is, Dr. Murphy," she whispered softly.

"Oh?"

"I'm going to tell you the truth today," she said as Mary Kate helped her to sip a cup of tea. "That's the only way to escape from the demons—is to tell the truth."

"I'm all for truth, " M.K. agreed. "When do we start?"

"Would you call your brother and Mickey and ask them to come. I want them to hear the truth too."

"Sure," Mary Kate said, "why not? Why not have a little Ryan family party right here in your hospital room?"

"It may be more like a wake."

87

Mike Casey felt a certain savage satisfaction. He and Patrol Officer Lopez had found a cop harassing a confused motorist from out of town in the middle of 57th Street, just off Lake Shore Drive. The motorist was black and his car bore a Pennsylvania license plate. Clearly he was confused about where he was and even about what law he might have broken. But the cop had backed up traffic for half a mile on the Drive because he hadn't ordered the motorist to the curb or off 57th Street to Cornell.

Michael and Deirdre were in the unmarked car, she in sweater and slacks, appropriate for the cool autumn weather.

"Stop just for a second," he ordered her. Then, leaning out the right-hand window, he yelled at the offending cop, "Get that car off Fifty-seventh Street and onto Cornell. You've backed up traffic for half a mile on the Drive, you stupid idiot."

The cop wheeled on him and bellowed back, "You pull over right there, fuckhead, and I'll settle with you."

"Turn off on Cornell," Mike ordered Deirdre.

"*Sí*, Jefe," she said obediently, cop that she was, doubtless sympathizing with the hapless patrol officer.

A few minutes later the blue-and-white squad pulled up behind them. The cop got out with a drawn gun and waddled arrogantly toward them, as though he were imitating a sheriff in some inane vintage southern movie. "Out, both of you, and up against the car, hands on the top. I'm going to frisk you. You first, muchacha." He leered at Patrol Officer Lopez. "This ought to be fun."

"Put the gun away, Officer," Mike said firmly.

"Don't give me orders, fuckhead. Who the hell do you think you are?"

"Deputy Superintendent Michael Patrick Vincent Casey is my name, and your name, copper, is mud. M-U-D, mud."

"Makes you feel good, huh,' Jefe," Deirdre commented as they drove north on the Drive, having quite demolished the unfortunate policeman.

"If he drew a gun on us, Deirdre, he'd draw a gun on anybody. We don't need psychopaths like that on the force."

"*Sí*, Jefe."

Before he could challenge the reproach in her voice, the reproach that suggested that anyone who was a cop was bound to have a bad day now and then, there was a radio call, a personal emergency for the Deputy Superintendent.

"It's Blackie, Mike. Anne is in Northwestern Hospital. Apparently it's nothing serious—a minor nervous collapse, according to Mary Kate. She's been with her since midnight. Anne wants to see all three of us. Perhaps you could pick me up at the Cathedral. Now."

"I'm on my way," Mike replied briskly. "And, Patrol Officer Lopez, we *will* observe the traffic laws."

A stiff wind was blowing in off the lake. Thick white clouds with dark gray bottoms were racing in from the northeast, alternately hiding and revealing the sun. The lake was gray when the sun was hidden and green when the sun glanced out through the clouds. The whitecaps glistened like scurrying mermaids, strong and defiant no matter what the wind or weather.

"She will be all right, Jefe," Deirdre said reassuringly. "She is a strong, strong woman."

"She's had to be a strong woman all her life, Dee-dee. Even strong women get pushed beyond their strengths."

Blackie was waiting outside the door of the Cathedral rectory and hopped quickly in the back of the unmarked police car.

"She . . . she was admitted yesterday. A severe psychotic episode in her apartment. Screams upset the neighbors. Mary Kate found out last night and apparently brought her out of it pretty quickly. That's all I know."

Patrol Officer Lopez stopped the car at the entrance to the hospital, a grimly modern concrete silo that looked a little like a Cape Canaveral launch pad in the midst of the older Gothic and art deco complex of buildings that was Northwestern University Hospital. On the sidewalk white-coated men and women hurried by, their heads ducked against the wind, with the confident stride of those whose medical skills had given them quasi-divine powers.

"Take the car back to Eleventh and State, Patrol Officer Lopez," Mike instructed. "Tell them on the radio where I'll be. I'll take a cab back later."

The young woman hesitated. "I could wait for you, Jefe."

"You'll do what you're told, Patrol Officer Lopez."

"*Sí*, Jefe. May I stop at the Cathedral to say a prayer for Doña Anna Maria?"

Before Mike could reply Blackie cut him off. "You'd better, Patrol Officer Lopez. And pray for the two of us too."

"Never argue with a priest," Mike said.

"*Sí*, Jefe—no, I mean, no, Jefe."

"They're all in love with you, aren't they, Mike," Blackie said as they rode up in the elevator.

"The female police dogs aren't," Mike replied philosophically.

Mary Kate was waiting for them outside Anne's room. "Where the hell have you been?" she demanded, glancing angrily at her watch, a big and shapely woman with gold and silver hair, a lovely agile face, and the Ryan blue eyes.

"You need sleep, sister," Blackie observed.

"Damn right I need sleep. However, I'm surviving on the adulation of the residents here, who think I'm a genius and keep repeating that assertion at five-minute intervals. Look, let me warn you, she's tired and has been through a rough time. She looks like hell but is a couple thousand percent better than she was last night. She's going to be all right. I want to get her out of here in a hurry. Maybe tomorrow. There's still work to be done and the 'secret' she has to tell us is important. Got it?"

"Yes, ma'am," Blackie said meekly.

"Got it," Mike agreed.

Anne was wearing an unattractive hospital dress and no makeup. She did indeed look like she'd been through hell. But to Mike Casey she was more beautiful and desirable than ever, with the appeal that a woman has for a man who realizes that he has the healing power to revive her energies and restore her life. He vowed that if Mary Kate did release her tomorrow, he would be there to take charge and never let her out of his sight. He leaned over and brushed his lips against hers. "If you were a cop, I'd fire you for insubordination."

She laughed weakly. "Patrol Officer Lopez wouldn't let you."

And to Blackie she added, "You must excuse me for looking so terrible, Father. I've apparently been doing some odd things the last few days."

"I hardly noticed," Blackie said, winking.

"Bastard," Mary Kate said, rising to the defense of all outraged womankind.

"I don't understand," Anne said, now serious and businesslike, "everything that's happened to me. I do know, though, that most of it in some strange way is the result of the secret I've been keeping for more than forty-five years. I've been terrified to reveal the secret because I knew people would hate me. I even thought I'd prefer madness to the public humiliation." She shook her head. "I've had my experience with madness, and I guess that was a mistake."

"No one will hate you, Anne," Mary Kate said reassuringly.

"Yes, you will," she contended. "All I can hope is that you might be able to forgive me."

"I'm sure we will," Blackie insisted.

Mike Casey said nothing, contenting himself with taking possession of her hand, a terribly cold little hand.

"I started the fire," she said calmly. "I was the arsonist who was responsible for the Mother of Mercy fire. I killed my two sisters and ninety other children and nuns. I killed them because they laughed at me and made fun of me and said I was a spoiled brat and that my father had too much money and that it was ridiculous I should be brought to school in a limousine on cold winter days."

The room was as silent as an empty church. Outside, the hospital call bell pinged against the blurred murmur of men's and women's voices.

"Are you sure?" Blackie said suspiciously.

"I'm sure, Father," she said. "I still see it in my dreams, sometimes almost every night. I fight with some of the other girls at the beginning of the afternoon class—you remember how I was for getting into fights in the classroom, Mickey?" She smiled oh-so briefly at him. "Sister ordered me to go to Sister Superior's office. That happened earlier in the year and I was so embarrassed and humiliated I couldn't do it again. So I wandered around the corridors and saw the men put the varnish and the cloth covers under the staircase where the newspapers for the collection drive were already stored. I heard one of them say something to the other about the possibility of fire. I thought that was the solution to my problem. If I started just a little fire and the alarm bell went off, I could sneak back into the class ranks out in the cold and return back to the classroom unnoticed. I thought about it, toddled back to the sacristy, borrowed some matches, and tried to start the fire. The first match blew out; the second match also blew out. The third one burned my fingers and I threw it away and it landed in the paper and that was how the Mother of Mercy fire started."

There was total silence in the room, the silence of frozen antarctic wastes where there was no love, no life, no happiness, no hope.

"You didn't intend to kill anyone," Mary Kate said softly. "You were just an angry little girl, angry like all little girls are sometimes angry."

"All little girls don't kill their sisters and ninety other people," Anne replied. Her voice was calm and controlled, her eyes dry. All the emotion and tragedy had been drained away. Now there seemed to remain in her only infinite sadness.

"Are you going to arrest me, Mickey?"

"Arrest you? Why?"

"I murdered ninety-two people."

"Anne, it was almost fifty years ago."

"There's no statute of limitation on murder. I looked it up once."

Fifty years of worrying about a little girl's innocently intended prank.

"Your mother always warned you about playing with matches," Blackie inquired, "didn't she? In fact, she caught you many times doing it." His eyes were vague and abstract, as though he were contemplating a moon rise on a distant planet.

"That's right, Father. I knew I was doing wrong, even taking the matches from the sacristy."

"There's nothing to charge her with, is there, Mike?" Mary Kate asked.

"If an adult did it," he said firmly, "it would have meant nothing worse than involuntary manslaughter and most likely a psychiatric commitment, but a child . . . Even then, and even with the emotions that must have been fierce at the time, nothing would have been done to a seven-year-old child."

"But I'm an adult now, Mickey. Don't I have adult responsibility?"

"In the United States of America"—he couldn't help but laugh—"we don't punish adults with adult punishments for what they did as children. There's no legal case against you, Anne. There never has been. The hurt and angry little girl who was frightened of Mother Superior has discharged whatever responsibility was hers long ago."

She thought that if he knew she would lose his love. How would he be able to explain that, on the contrary, he now loved her more than ever? Now he knew, finally, what the pain inside her was that he had tried to heal in the snowdrift under the streetlight at Mayfield and Potomac.

"At least I have to tell people," she protested weakly.

"The children have been dead for almost fifty years," Mary Kate rejoined thoughtfully. "The firemen probably are all dead; so are the parents of the children. So, too, are the men who left the varnish and the cloths under the stairs, and the nun who stored the papers there. . . . "

"She died in the fire," Anne interrupted.

"There's no one who needs an explanation anymore, Anne," Mary Kate said. "It's all over. All the prices have been paid. Why impose any more suffering on your children, your grandchildren, your friends, and yourself? Your terrible secret is out in the open. It doesn't mean anything anymore to anyone, not even to you, now that you've revealed it. My brother the priest here is about to say 'let the dead bury the dead,' so I'll say it for him."

"It seems too easy," Anne said dubiously. "Why don't you hate me?"

Mike Casey figured it was his initiative, so he put his arms around her and drew her close, his fingers touching the bare skin at the back of her neck. "Because we love you, that's why, goofy!" he said.

And then there were lots of tears as everyone hugged everyone else—save for Blackie Ryan, who stared out of the dirty hospital room window at a little patch of the gray-green lake in the distance and said nothing at all.

"There's more," Anne said, dabbing at her eyes with a tissue that Mary Kate had magically produced. "I guess it isn't as bad as the fire but I still have to tell you. I confessed the fire to Father Kenny one summer at the lake. He was furious, ranted and raved and denounced me as a terrible harlot, an evil sinner who would be damned to hell for all eternity. . . . He made me take off my clothes and pose for his paintings." She shivered. "It was a terrible, terrible experience. I suppose that having one of those paintings in the gallery, and the little figure he made at the end of the summer, brought all of this on—pushed my imagination over the brink. Don't you think so, Dr. Murphy?"

"Probably," Mary Kate said. "Did he try to rape you?"

"No, not till the end of the summer. Then he felt me and pawed me and I think would have tried to force sex on me if he could. He ended up sobbing in my arms, poor, pathetic little priest. . . . "

"He broke the seal of confession?" Blackie demanded, returning from his far planet.

"He didn't tell anybody else, Father," Anne said. "That doesn't break the seal, does it?"

"Even talking to you about it outside the confessional was a violation of the seal. That miserable son of a bitch. He deserved everything he got," Blackie snorted angrily.

"Now, now, brother," Mary Kate objected. "Forgive and forget. Isn't that what you preach?"

"I don't have to practice what I preach," Blackie said, his face, normally so bland and pleasant, twisted with rage. "That man was a disgrace to the priesthood. He never should have been ordained."

"Oh, don't say that, Father," Anne said, defending a poor, pathetic broken wing once again. "He tried hard."

"Tell us a little more about your dreams," Mary Kate asked.

"There are four others besides starting the fire. In one, I'm outside watching the fire, seeing the children fall from the windows, even seeing Kathy and Connie die. Then I'm inside, in the classroom, while the fire's going on, and manage to escape by dashing through a gap in the smoke. Then I'm at the wakes and the funerals with Mom and Dad. And then finally, I'm at the lake and Father Kenny is painting my picture."

"We can discuss those later," Mary Kate said, resuming a brisk, professional manner—the tears now banished. "I think I'm going to be able to let you out of here tomorrow. And then I'll want to talk to you next week and then send you off for some rest. Presumably your assistant will be back to take charge of the gallery."

"Whatever you say, Dr. Murphy," Anne agreed meekly.

"And you won't be traveling alone, either," Mike said authoritatively.

She merely smiled at him, an enigmatic smile that didn't quite say yes but certainly didn't say no, either.

"Was that the order of your dreams?" Blackie asked, once again examining through the window the slice of lake through the tall buildings in the distance.

"Yes, it was, Father. No, wait a minute—the dream about the men and the varnish was the fourth dream and then about Father Kenny, the fifth."

"They always come in that order?" Blackie demanded.

"I think so; usually, anyway."

"Dreams often follow such sequential patterns," Mary Kate interposed. "Sometimes it's significant; sometimes it's not."

"All my life," Anne said suddenly, "I've wanted to hate God for what He let happen to me. I've tried my best to hate Him. It doesn't work. How can you hate someone who refuses to hate you back? And sends you angels. . . . "

Her voice trailed off. She was crying softly again. Anne held her hand. Mike put his arms around her shoulders.

"The angels of September," said Blackie thoughtfully, "the whole dumb crowd of them. Not nearly as swift as they ought to be."

Tears turned to laughter. Mike kissed her good-bye as affectionately as he could with a priest and a psychiatrist watching, and then he and Blackie left the hospital room.

While riding down in the elevator he said to Blackie, "I suppose you figured most of that out?"

"I woke up in bed last night and realized, much too late, that she assumed responsibility for the fire and that Kenny was mixed up in that responsibility. I called the hospital on instinct and, sure enough, there she was. Maybe some kind of breakdown was imperative before she could tell the truth."

"She seems almost disappointed that we don't hate her."

"What would you do if you'd felt guilty for fifty years and then discovered that it really doesn't make all that much difference?"

"Then it's all over?"

They emerged onto Huron Street. The sun was momentarily so bright, they both squinted to protect their eyes.

"There're still some strange things going on," Blackie said thoughtfully. "I'm not sure it's over yet, by any means."

"At least she's got an enormous burden off her mind," Mike said. "Hasn't she?"

"I don't believe any of it."

"You don't believe she started the fire?"

"Oh, I believe she thinks she started the fire. That may come to the same thing. I've got to do a little more research before I'm sure."

88

Back at the Cathedral rectory, Blackie renewed his search through the correspondence and diaries of Marge Ryan Casey. Somewhere in those diaries, he knew, was the conclusive answer to their problems. Most of what had happened was already clear in his mind. He could make a persuasive case for his own explanation without the documentation. Mary Kate could sort the rest out, perhaps with hypnotism.

He paused in his frantic rush through his aunt's passionate and difficult life. He was convinced he knew the answer to the fire, at least insofar as the fire mattered to them, and he also understood, as did everybody else by then, why the Kenny Exhibition had pushed Anne to the brink of madness and temporarily over the brink.

Yet, there was more that remained to be explained. Granted Anne was a sympathetic and sensitive woman with periodic psychic powers, the explosion and the smoke and later the appearance of a fire seemed to him to be extraordinary telekinetic manifestations, the kind of thing that apparently had not happened before in her life. Now that Mary Kate and he could talk about the case, he would ask her what she thought of that aspect of it. There didn't seem to be, however, any reason for undue concern. Anne's secrets were out in the open and had proved themselves relatively harmless. How relatively remained to be seen. The Desmond Kenny works of art had been removed from the gallery. As soon as he found the documentation he was looking for, the case would be closed. Unfortunate, he would tell himself later, Mike had not told him that Patrol Officer Lopez couldn't find "Divine Justice" in the warehouse out on Halsted. He hadn't told him for the obvious reason that he had searched the gallery himself and had not found it there, and there had not been time to send Deirdre Lopez back to the warehouse to search again.

If Blackie had had the slightest awareness that "Divine Justice" might still be in the gallery, he would not have been nearly so confident or relaxed as he was. They were still struggling with principalities and powers.

89

Mike and Blackie had done their best on Friday night to clear away the worst of the rubble and restore some order to Anne's apartment. They both agreed emphatically that they were not cut out for housework. Anne would be dismayed by the condition of the apartment when she came home the next day, but her shock would not be nearly as great as it would have been if they had not done the preliminary work.

Mary Kate called them while they were in Anne's apartment and said she was going home to her husband and children, and that Anne would be out sometime during the course of the next day. She instructed Mike to pack a bag of clothes and makeup for Anne and bring it to the hospital— also a nightgown so she wouldn't have to spend another night in that terrible hospital thing.

Feeling a bit like a voyeur, Mike collected slacks, a sweater, underwear, shoes, the most obvious pieces of makeup, and a discreet blue nightgown.

She certainly has a taste for lace and frills, he thought. *So much the better for me, I suppose.*

And she keeps things compulsively neat. So much the worse for me.

At the hospital he waited while she went to the bathroom to change from hospital gown to her own nightdress. Then he locked the door to the hospital room from the inside and took her firmly in his arms when she stepped out of the bathroom and kissed her until his lips were sore.

"And that's just a preview, woman. The coming attractions are going to be better!"

She smiled happily. "I don't know what I'm doing yet, Mickey. But I know I like that."

"I noticed," he said.

The pleasant memories of the embrace lingered with him as he fussed over his paperwork the next morning. She was to come back to the apartment in the afternoon and have supper with him, and then he would drive her to River

Forest, where she would stay with her son and daughter-in-law for a few days. After that the program was open-ended, depending on Mary Kate Murphy's clinical judgments and . . . well, on what he and Annie were able to work out.

One thing was certain. He would not permit her to spend another night in that apartment alone, not for a long, long time.

The partly sunny attempt at renewing Indian summer the day before had failed. Thunder and lightning storms were rushing into Chicago one after another, lighting up the sky over the Loop with jagged gashes of flame. It was, he remembered, the Feast of St. Michael the Archangel. "Putting on quite a show for us, aren't you, old boy," he remarked to his worthy seraphic namesake.

At 11:30, Annie phoned him. "What a terrible mess in my apartment. I can't believe I was *that* crazy!"

He decided not to claim credit for the housework he and Blackie had done. "Forget about it until you come home from Mark's. No point in working yourself into a fuss about it now."

"Not to worry. There's no way I could even begin today."

"How do you feel?"

"Fine, a little tired. I think I'll take a nap now. Mark and Teresa want you to join us for dinner, if it won't be too much of an imposition on you?"

"No imposition at all. Call me when you wake up from the nap," he instructed her.

"Yes, master," she said, and laughed.

Then there was a long silence, as though she were tempted to say something else but didn't quite have the courage.

"Something on your mind, Annie? Like maybe that you love me?"

"Silly. Of course I love you." She hesitated. "There is something else. After my nap, I want to go over to the gallery for a few minutes. With you. I want to destroy the painting of 'Divine Justice.' "

"It's not in the gallery, Annie. Don't you remember that I searched for it?"

"Vaguely. You told me that Patrol Officer Lopez wasn't able to find it at the warehouse, didn't you?"

"It was your idea that Deirdre was the one who searched for it. But I looked everywhere in the gallery and it wasn't there."

"It is there, Mickey. I'm convinced it's there. I know it has to be destroyed for me to be free of the past. Will you at least come with me this afternoon to make sure?"

"Of course. Why not? I'll pick you up about four o'clock. Just call me when you're ready."

"Would you bring some fire extinguishers too? I know that sounds crazy. Everything that's happened, I'm sure has been in my own imagination. Yet, I'd feel a lot better if I knew there was a fire extinguisher around."

Was she having a relapse into her psychosis? Mike wondered. She sounded calm, self-possessed, confident—not exactly the "Madwoman of Chaillot." There had been a real explosion and a real fire in the gallery. Why not come prepared?

"I'll take care of it. I'll have a whole battery, and we'll destroy that thing permanently."

He called the communications department, learned that Patrol Officer Lopez was on duty, and spoke to her. "Officer Lopez, would you go over to the fire department and collect a case of CO_2. Not just one extinguisher, a dozen of them, and you and Patrol Officer Mulherne bring them to the Reilly Gallery and leave them inside the door. Stop by my office for the keys on your way. Don't ask me any questions, though I'll answer at least one of those you would ask. She's out of the hospital and she's fine."

"Wonderful, Jefe!" Deirdre said happily. "You better take her out for a real nice supper tonight."

"I believe I'm invited to her son's house," he said tersely. "And if you make any comment on that at all, young woman, you'll be pounding a beat in South Chicago for the rest of your life."

Annie phoned again at 4:30, yawning contentedly. "Wonderful nap. I'm afraid I overslept. Can you come by in half an hour? We'll go to the gallery and then come back to the apartment so I can don my best bib and tucker for Mark and Teresa.''

"I'll be there," he promised, wondering if there would be some free time for love between their work at the gallery and the drive to River Forest. He'd make time.

Patrol Officer Lopez had told him, when he called her in the meantime, that the fire extinguishers had been delivered. "Hey, Jefe, that gallery is some scary place, so bare and empty. Both Lenny and I were kind of spooked by it."

"Spooked by an empty gallery? What kind of patrol officers are you?"

"A superstitious Mexican-American and a superstitious Irish-American. Neither one of us liked it a bit. What are you going to do there, Jefe?"

"We're going to extinguish the fires of hell," he said jokingly. "Don't worry about it, Deirdre, it's no problem."

"*Sí*, Jefe." But she didn't sound convinced.

Why did I say that? I'm not going to fight any hell fire. The only reason the fire extinguishers are there is to reassure Anne. We'll go in, search the gallery for that painting, shred it and that will be that.

A burst of lightning exploded, seemingly right outside his window, and a deafening roll of thunder followed it almost at once. He hoped that Michael the Archangel was not, for some reason, unduly offended.

90

Deirdre paid scant attention to the struggles of the University of Illinois football team on the television in their family home in Logan Park. Her father, a skilled electronics technician, had rigged up his own big-screen television, which, as he assured Deirdre, was better than that in any of the bars in the neighborhood. Moreover, he'd also constructed a fantastically high antenna that drew in Channel 16 from South Bend and Channel 21 from Rockford, the former to see Notre Dame home games on Saturday afternoons and the latter to see Chicago Bear games on Sunday afternoons when Soldiers' Field was not sold out.

Deirdre's father, Patricio Lopez, was as dedicated a member of the Notre Dame subway alumni as ever walked the face of the earth.

"Can I borrow the Volvo for an hour or so, Papa?" she asked Patricio.

"Sure," he replied. "Where are you going?"

"To see a priest," Deirdre said thoughtfully.

"You're not in trouble, are you, muchacha?" Patricio asked anxiously.

"Don't be silly, Papa; of course not. But I think someone I know might be."

She went up to her room, checked her service revolver, and donned the shoulder holster underneath the jacket of her brown suit. *You don't fight demons, necessarily, with revolvers,* Deirdre thought ironically. *But it won't do any harm to be prepared for anything.*

She removed a rosary from her purse, opened the top button of her shirt, and dropped the pendant around her neck. As she rebuttoned her shirt she wondered whether the nuns at St. Scholastica would think her a superstitious spic. She shrugged her shoulders and, for good measure, kissed her fingers and touched them to the feet of the statue of Our Lady of Guadalupe that El Jefe had given her on her birthday.

As she turned on the ignition in the two-year-old Volvo, another thunderstorm roared down the Kennedy Expressway and a terrible flash of lightning cut across the lakefront sky, from the Hancock Building all the way to Sears Tower, from one end of the mountains to the other, seeming to rip the heavens over Chicago apart.

Deirdre made a quick sign of the cross and began to pray to every saint in heaven and the souls in purgatory too.

BOOK
SEVEN

91

Annie paused a moment for breath. "I haven't been necked and petted so much since I was seventeen years old."

It was not, Mike reminded himself sternly, the way you acted toward a woman who had just been released from a hospital after a psychotic episode. But affection had led to tenderness and tenderness to passion. Anne's reaction was first catlike languor and then ravenous passion. She became a tightly wound dynamo of sexual energies; her breasts were so inured to his caresses that she moaned if his hands slowed. Her flesh craved unremitting foreplay the way an actress craved resounding critical praise. Her lips demanded limitless attention from his, as a politician sought media attention. The last broken barriers of her pietistic Catholic prudery were being swept away by a firestorm of physical need.

"Let's forget the damned painting," he insisted.

"No, Mickey. We have to destroy it first. Then I'll be free. Don't ask me how I know that. I know."

Because he himself half-believed there was something supernatural in the gallery, he was prepared to agree with her. "All right," he said reluctantly, releasing her. "We'll go over and do in 'Divine Justice' and then we'll come back here and finish what we've started before we go off to your son's house for supper."

"I'm still confused, Mickey. I'm not sure yet what my future is," she protested, shaken by the flames of passion that had been ignited in both of them. She rearranged the beige sweater that matched her beige corduroy designer slacks. Makeup and expensive clothes—Annie was now vigorously on the mend. Her character was quite incapable of a leisurely rebound. If you were Anne Marie O'Brien, you coped—even with the devil.

"I've made up my mind," he said vigorously. "And that's that."

"You've kind of taken possession, haven't you?" she said, not irritably, but simply as someone making an observation.

"That's right." He helped her on with her raincoat and kissed the back of her neck lightly for both reassurance and challenge. "Come on, let's get this exorcism out of the way. Hey, what have you got there?"

"A knife," she said, waving a large kitchen knife, "to slash the canvas and"—she opened a small traveling case—"a bottle of turpentine to smear the paint." She put the knife in the case, closed it, and fastened the clasps.

"When you destroy a work of art you really do destroy it, don't you, Annie?"

"I think I could become a very violent woman without much trouble," she said meditatively.

"I've noticed."

"You have the fire extinguishers?"

"Twelve of them, delivered by the loyal and faithful Patrol Officer Lopez to the gallery earlier in the day."

So they rode down in the elevator and walked into the driving rain of Michigan Avenue, huddling together under his umbrella. The thunderstorms had driven most people and traffic off the Magnificent Mile. Though the sun had theoretically not yet set, the deserted streets and the low clouds obscuring even the top of the John Hancock Center made it seem like midnight instead of six in the evening.

"The lightning and thunder," he said, as a thunderbolt exploded seemingly right behind the Playboy Building, "is courtesy of my good patron, Saint Michael the Archangel, whose feast it is today, in case you'd forgotten."

"Of course," she said, squeezing his arm. "Happy Feast Day, Michael the Archangel."

"Me or the saint?" he asked.

"Both," she said fervently. "Do you remember the prayer, Mickey? Let's say it."

So at Michigan Avenue and Oak Street, as lightning

continued to split the early evening sky, they prayed as they had thousands of times in their youth, at the end of the old Low Mass: "St. Michael the Archangel, defend us in battle. Be our protection against the malice and snares of the Devil. Restrain him, O God, we humbly beseech thee. And do thou, prince of the heavenly hosts, by the power of God, thrust into hell Satan and other evil spirits who roam through the world seeking the ruin of souls."

The door of the gallery opened easily enough and, just as Deirdre had said, the empty rooms with their off-white walls were spooky, even after Annie had turned on the floodlights.

"Here are the extinguishers, an even dozen of them, just as Patrol Officer Lopez said."

He took one of the yellow canisters out of the box, checked the seal to make sure it was charged, and advanced after her through the network of exhibition rooms toward the back of the gallery.

"My God, Mickey," she cried. "Look—there it is."

She was pointing at the landing on the staircase to the basement exhibition rooms. There, exactly where he'd seen it for the first time, was "Divine Justice," hideously glaring at them.

A fierce wind blew through the gallery and slammed the door behind him. He tried to open it. It wouldn't budge. They were sealed in the gallery with a diabolically possessed painting.

92

"*Padrecito*," the young woman in the brown suit said as Blackie emerged from the confessional, the only priest-hearing on a Saturday afternoon in Holy Name Cathedral in the postconciliar Catholic Church.

"Ah, Patrol Officer Lopez, something amiss?"

"El Jefe had me bring twelve fire extinguishers to the Reilly Gallery earlier in the day. I'm sure that he and Donna Anna Maria are there fighting with the devil. *Padrecito*, we must help them."

"I think, if it's the two of them, the devil's outnumbered. Nevertheless, I'll phone my sister."

Blackie raced back to the rectory and up to his room, leaving the near-frantic patrol officer waiting for him inside the door of the rectory. He grabbed his ritual, stuffed it in his pocket, stuck a stole in another pocket, threw on a raincoat, and put a large spray container of holy water in the raincoat pocket. Then he called Mary Kate.

"Brother speaking. It would appear that our friends Anne and Mike have invaded the gallery, intending to exorcise demons, having equipped themselves, as far as I can see, with nothing more than a brace of fire extinguishers and perhaps invocations to the honored saint of the day— Michael the Archangel!"

"Does he want to put her back into a psychosis?" Mary Kate screamed. "We have to stop them."

"I thought that was the way you'd react. In the company of the stalwart Patrol Officer Lopez, I'm on my way over there, with stole and ritual and holy water, I might add."

"I'll be there right after you," she replied. "I'll bring The Weapon!"

She hung up before he could ask her what possible use a medieval Irish pike would be against demons.

93

"I don't mean to be doing this to you, Mickey!" she cried. "I don't want my imagination to hurt you."

"Divine Justice" was now audibly shaking, pounding against the wall, like a fierce, wounded beast.

"You're not doing this to me, Annie," he said grimly. "There's someone else here in this gallery with us."

"Well, let's get rid of him," she shouted over the roar of the wind. "It's my gallery, not his."

They stumbled toward the painting, eyes smarting from the dust raised from the storm.

"Good God," Mickey screamed. "Look at the painting; it's *alive!*"

The damned souls in Father Kenny's picture were writhing and squirming before his eyes. He blinked furiously, trying to clear his vision.

"It's not very bright," Anne shouted over the roar of the wind. "It doesn't know what I'm going to do."

She opened her travel case and with a quick violent movement smashed the bottle of turpentine against the top of the frame, shattering the container as though she were christening a ship with a bottle of champagne.

"Hold it, Mickey!" she screamed.

Mickey grabbed the sides of the frame and hurled the painting onto the landing, then kicked it into the corner. Anne fell to her knees and slashed at it with her kitchen knife, cutting diagonally from top to bottom in two savage thrusts of the knife. The picture clattered past them and went crashing down the steps.

"After it, Mickey!" she shouted. "Use the fire extinguisher!"

Mickey activated the extinguisher and covered the canvas with its foam. Momentarily the picture, torn and blurred by the turpentine, seemed to acquire a life of its own; then it disappeared under the gray pudding of chemicals.

"We've got it, Mickey," she exclaimed, brandishing the cover of the Monet water-lily-emblazoned trash can.

"We're going to win, Anne!" he exulted. "We've beaten this demon!" He gasped as the wall divider quavered in the wind and started to fall. "Watch out!"

Anne slashed desperately at the painting, ripping it into tiny pieces and throwing the pieces on the floor of the gallery. The painting would not die, however. Like living beings the bits of canvas spun and jumped about the floor and began to merge again. A column of fire rose from the struggling mass, detached itself and moved implacably across the gallery towards Mike and Anne.

The fire extinguisher in his hand fizzed out. He grabbed for another yellow container. It too had lost its charge. He threw it away and yanked another one out of the carton. It would not function. The pilaf of fire bore down upon him, an irresistible power surging up from the depths of hell.

"Anne!" he screamed.

She did not reply. She had disappeared, lost in the fire.

94

All the lightning and thunder in the world seemed to have been concentrated on Oak Street Beach. Then, just as Deirdre and Blackie arrived at the Reilly Gallery, it exploded across Michigan Avenue and down the street after them. The rain falling in huge thick sheets, the lightning crackling just above their heads, the wind whirling and rushing, the thunder booming like the artillery at Stalingrad. Blackie briefly remembered the pictures of Houston during the hurricane that August and fervently prayed that Saint Michael was responsible for the outburst, and that he was on their side.

"I can't get the door open, *Padrecito!*" Deirdre yelled above the furor. "It's slammed shut. They're trapped in there with the demons!"

Blackie turned up the collar of his raincoat, pulled out the ritual, and thumbed through the pages to the rite of exorcism from baptism. It seemed pointless to reach for the holy water. He had more than enough water as it was.

"Stand back, *Padrecito!* I'll try to shoot off the lock!"

Blackie grabbed the young woman's wrist. "Don't shoot, Deirdre. Remember who's in there."

Then, like Grace O'Malley storming aboard a British ship in Lough Carrib, his sister was there beside them, brandishing The Weapon. The door resisted. Inside, the gallery was shrouded in blackness, but they heard screaming and demonic laughter as well as deep, earthquakelike rumbling.

"They're trapped! With the demons. We can't get the door open!"

With obvious relish Mary Kate smashed her pike against the display window of the gallery. The window didn't budge, and the pike seemed to bend, as if it had crashed against armored plate. Not in the least daunted, Mary Kate continued to pound while the rumbling noise inside grew louder and louder.

Then the inside of the gallery began to pulse with light and energy, like the source of a vast laser beam. Great bursts of crackling, blue electrical current seemed to break out of the building and race down Oak Street, across Michigan Avenue, and up into the sky over the lake. Up and down the street electrical charges exploded as though hundreds of live electrical wires were dancing frantically. The marquee of the Esquire theatre collapsed with a loud roar. Across the street the high second story glass windows of a bridal shop dissolved and mannequins fell to the ground, momentarily joining the wild dance. Lightning leapt across the sky, bouncing off the tall buildings of Michigan Avenue and plunging to the ground.

The darkened beacon on top of the Playboy building tore loose from its base, rose into the sky like a vast rocket, faltered, then tumbled down on Oak Street Beach, bounced once like a giant rubber ball and then hurtled out into the lake into which it disappeared with a fearsome sizzle. One of the great TV antennae on top of the John Hancock Tower swayed drunkenly in a sudden burst of wind and then bent to one side, cracked, and hung like a broken toothpick. Stereo sets and VCRs flew out of the windows of shops further up the street and hurled themselves towards the little group in front of the gallery. Mary Kate beat them off with her furiously flailing pike.

Then, as suddenly as it had begun, the sound and fury stopped. Oak Street was as silent and motionless as a graveyard.

95

Mike could barely see, not because the gallery was plunged in darkness but because there was so much blinding light. "Where are you, Annie?" he shouted as he groped toward the white flame that seemed to have taken root over the remains of "Divine Justice."

"Mickey! I'm here, with the lilies!" She slapped the side of the trash can. "Help me put it over the fire!"

He stumbled into her. She'd only been a few feet away. "We can't go into that fire," he said.

"It can't hurt us," she insisted, "unless we're afraid of it. Maybe it's not my imagination but his imagination. It's harmless."

Mike didn't believe her but he figured that if Annie was going to die, he wanted to die with her, so together the two of them thrust the trash can toward the fire consuming "Divine Justice."

They held it in place for a few moments, panting from their exertion, until the light altogether died out. And then, with a great sigh, they sank to the floor, merely a man and a woman in a madly disordered art gallery, holding firmly in place a battered trash can painted with the lovely water lilies of spring.

"You hold it for a few moments, Mickey," she said. "I'm going to fix this painting permanently."

She slashed into tatters the partially reassembled "Divine Justice," threw the pieces of canvas into a wastebasket she had seized from behind Sandy's desk, and then turned the basket upside down on the floor. Both the pillar of fire and the remnants of the painting were now deprived of the oxygen they might need to flame anew.

"We beat him, Mickey," she said as the floodlights returned. "We beat him!"

"We sure did!"

It was over.

"There are people outside," Mike said. "I better let

them in and I better think of a good story for Jeremiah Mullens to explain what happened here this evening."

"Freak thunderstorm," Anne said, with a half-laugh, half-sob.

The door opened easily. Outside in the driving rain on an Oak Street littered with rubble were Mary Kate Murphy swinging a great battle axe, Blackie Ryan, his glasses covered with rain, holding a ritual and a holy water spray, and Deirdre Lopez with a drawn service revolver.

The Angels of September, he thought.

"Come on in," he said, bowing courteously. "I think we need all of you."

96

Mike, Blackie, and Joe and Mary Kate Murphy were all on their second drink in Sherlock's Home, a publike bar in Anne's building. Mike and Blackie were drinking Irish whiskey, and the Pirate and Mary Kate, very dry vodka martinis.

Mary Kate had put her patient to bed with aspirin for her headache—no tranquilizers; they were not going to play that game again. The resourceful Patrol Officer Lopez had been dispatched to facilitate an explanation satisfactory to District Commander Mullens as to what had happened in the freak storm, an explanation that was apparently reinforced by the fact that the United States Weather Service reported extraordinarily rare "meteorological phenomena" along the Chicago lakefront. They were still mopping up the mess behind the bar in Sherlock's Home, where a considerable amount of precious refreshment had been smashed in the tempest that had rocked the Magnificent Mile. The pub, normally far too chic to be compared with its brash, noisy counterparts in England, smelled of spilled ale. The excited voices telling tales about what had happened sounded like a jovial Friday night crowd in Chelsea during the Blitz. All that was needed was sawdust on the floor and cucumber sandwiches.

Damage to the Magnificent Mile and its environs, according to the police, would run into the millions, but miraculously no one had been seriously hurt. Saint Michael the Archangel and most of the rest of the angelic chorus must have been working overtime, said Mike Casey the Cop.

"Was it a tormented soul finally being released from its prison on earth and soaring into purgatory?" asked the Pirate with his typically Jungian perspective.

"It might have been," his wife agreed. "Perhaps it was Skip Kenny coming back to force Anne to tell the truth. Having achieved that, he could go to his eternal reward, such as it may be."

"Oh, nonsense, not to use more scatological language," said Blackie. "She told the truth two days ago. Why try to drive her insane again in there tonight?"

"Was that the goal?" Mike asked uncertainly. "Was it all about robbing Anne of her sanity? Did Des Kenny want vengeance against her and against everyone who he thought might have caused him to lose his mind?"

"Or, might it really have been the devil?" Mary Kate wondered.

Blackie sighed heavily, usually a sign that he was about to pontificate. "Let us consider these hypotheses in order," he said. He arranged a number of pretzels on the table. "One. Diabolic possession. But I ask you, what kind of demon would it be that could be put out of business simply because it lacked oxygen? Hellfire, should there be such, certainly doesn't require oxygen to perform." He flicked away one pretzel.

"Secondly, Desmond "Skip" Kenny comes back for vengeance. Why? Annie never did anything to him except let him intimidate her and then, at the end, simply be kind to him when he turned up impotent. Moreover, he'd been a gentle dottering lunatic for thirty years, hardly the kind of being who, when released from the constraints of his body, would want to come back to settle old scores." He flicked away a second pretzel.

"The third possibility: The young Desmond Kenny, somehow reborn after he died, discovers that he cannot find release on this earth unless he constrains Anne to tell the truth about the Mother of Mercy fire. However, why then try to put her back in the psychiatric ward at Northwestern once she's told the truth, at least the truth as best she knows it?"

"What does that mean?" Mary Kate interrupted. "Do you mean that Anne didn't tell the truth about the fire?"

"As I said"—Blackie allowed himself to look exasperated at the interruption—"she told the truth as she knew it. So we must exclude the likelihood that Des Kenny returned to clear up the mystery of the fire, a mystery about which nobody except the four of us and Annie are all that worried." He flicked away the third pretzel. "By the way, did someone call her son?"

"I did," Mike said. "Told him that Michigan Avenue was a shambles, that the storm did some damage to the gallery, and that we'd come for supper tomorrow night. He laughed and said his mother was a great one for coming a day late. The poor kid sounded like he was worried to death about her—not without some reason!"

"There is also," Blackie went on inexorably, "the possibility that Anne entertains herself, namely that the phenomena we have witnessed are the result of her vivid imagination and extraordinary telekinetic powers. That she has a vivid imagination we concede, but there is no record that anyone knows of that she has telekinetic powers. Moreover, telekinetic types, as far as I've been able to ascertain from a few phone calls, do not want to invoke physical harm to themselves." He flicked away the fourth pretzel.

"So, learned Punk," Mary Kate demanded, "what do we have?"

Her brother shrugged, as though the answer were a matter of little moment. "The important point is we know what we don't have," he said, reassembling the pretzels and beginning to munch on them. "Do you want a hypothesis that covers the data? This may be as close as we'll ever come:

"When Desmond 'Skip' Kenny painted 'Divine Justice,' he was a man beside himself with anger and rage: his frustrated career as a church artist; the terrible fire in his first assignment; the conflict with Mundelein, which arguably may have led to Mundelein's death; guilt for his own temptations and sins of the flesh—might not all of these have invested that painting with enormous psychic energies, irrational forces that we don't understand but certainly know linger in places and things long after the events that produced them have slipped away into the past? For example, visit the shrine at Glendalough in the Wicklow Hills, south of Dublin. There's about one chance in three that you'll become acutely conscious of the presence of persons and energies among all those gray gravestones and ruined rock buildings, persons and energies that are not exactly benign but not exactly evil either, merely scary. Might not such energies be the psychological residues of the terrible things that were done time after time after time at Glendalough when the monastery was sacked and the monks were slain? Who knows? At least there is reason to believe testimony that certain places and things are, if not exactly haunted, at least endowed with uncanny forces that we do not altogether understand. Moreover"—he finished the fourth pretzel and moved the entire bowl in front of him, signaling at the same time to the waitress that he wanted a third glass of Jameson's—"is it not at least arguable that our friend Annie, a sensitive, sympathetic, and guilt-ridden woman with a tragic life behind her and at least some touch of psychic propensities and especially with intense memories of both the fire and of Desmond Kenny and her reaction to the fire, might not, in the presence of such energies and forces, also generate certain energies and forces of her own? Could not those two psychic fields come into proximity with each other, indeed, merge and create transiently a highly destructive reality, a temporary being—if one wishes to call it a being—made up of Anne's guilt and anger and pain, now experienced, and Skip Kenny's anger and guilt and pain poured out with violent and reckless talent into that canvas forty-five years ago?"

"A being, Punk?" Mary Kate asked skeptically.

"A dense, convoluted, and extremely evil if only temporary network of psychic energies," he said thoughtfully. "Does it not fit the data? And does anything else fit the data?"

"It's plausible, Blackie," Joe said, "and I agree with you that it's the only explanation we're ever likely to get. Diabolic possession is a lot more attractive an explanation than a haunting, if only because it's simpler and more historic."

"But might not those cases in the past of alleged diabolic possession, which cannot be explained by mental illness, be of the same kind as I have just described?"

"And the things that happened to her came out of her own unconscious," Mary Kate agreed. "She provided the demon, if we can call it that, with the raw material for her hell."

"Each of us creates his or her own hell," Blackie said mildly. "The dark side of Anne's personality happens to be more spectacularly dark, just as the bright side is more radiantly bright."

"No one was seriously hurt," Mike observed. "The only one who could have been permanently damaged was Annie."

"And the insurance company," Blackie said, "but their pain tends to rub out in the long run of actuarial possibilities."

"What if it comes back?" Mary Kate demanded.

Mike didn't hesitate for a second. "Annie and I will beat it again," he said decisively.

"Doubtless," Blackie agreed. "Whether it was a demon or a lost soul of a madman seeking vengeance, or my temporarily existing energy pattern of evil, or even the imagination of a guilt-ridden and psychic woman, I think we can at least agree on one point: the target was Annie, and whatever tried to get her didn't succeed, thank God and Michael the Archangel."

"Which Michael?" Mickey asked with a crooked grin.

"Both of them, of course," the priest said blandly.

"All because of a fire," Joe lamented, "which she ignited quite unintentionally nearly fifty years ago and which, through an incredible twist of fate, killed her sisters and almost a hundred other teachers and children."

"Oh," Blackie said in the tone of voice of someone dismissing a matter about which he thought there was already universal agreement, "she didn't start the fire."

"What?" they all erupted.

Blackie drew himself up calmly, even complacently. "It should be obvious that Annie didn't start the fire," he said. "In the first place, she's not that kind of person— guilt-ridden, scrupulous perhaps, old-fashioned in her Catholicism in some ways, but not a firebug. No, not even by chance a firebug."

"You'll never persuade her by that argument," Mike said ruefully.

"Fortunately, I won't have to. But consider some of the evidence. In her dream she saw the men put the varnish and cloth covers underneath the staircase next to the paper from the paper-collection drive on the same day the fire started. We know, however—at least we do if we've read the newspapers of that time, as I have—that the papers, part of the Thanksgiving paper drive that used to be the eighth Sacrament in the Catholic schools, like the varnish and covers, were there several days before the fire. Perhaps Annie was in the corridor and did hear the men talk about the possibility of a fire, and perhaps she even considered the idea of setting off the fire alarm to avoid Sister Superior's office, but I tell you this: It is inconceivable that she would actually have gone into the sacristy and stolen matches from the church. For Annie, the Church is far too sacred a reality to take even matches from.

"Furthermore, consider the order of her dreams. First of all, she sees the fire outside the school. Then she is inside the school, suffering with the others. Then, and only then, she is underneath the stairwell, starting the fire. It simply won't wash. Any two of those are a possibility but the three of them, no. Something had to have been made up, or to have happened on another day.

"Third—and I consider this to be decisive—in the newspaper accounts, Anne's mother is quoted as having said that the only reason Anne survived was that she was home the day of the fire. Incidentally, it is altogether possible that Annie could have lied to her mother about her illness and thus enhanced her own guilt about not dying when her sisters did. Does that make psychiatric sense, Sister, and Brother-in-law?"

"Sure it does," Mary Kate said. "But from what she told me about her dreams, her memories of being trapped in the classroom and the flames are very vivid."

"Annie is a woman of very vivid imagination. That's why she's a good art critic. Nonetheless, the records of the fire also show that the primary school children escaped unharmed for the most part because the fire spread to the second floor before the first floor. If Annie has dreams of her own classroom going up in flames, those dreams are clearly fictional."

"I suppose we could get at it with some hypnotism," Joe said. "Play the tapes back for her and find out what her memories of that day really are."

"I would suggest," Blackie continued, "that what you will find is the following: Annie was getting over a case of the flu, which had plagued many children in the parish. Her mother wanted her to go to school, but not particularly liking school in those days, she begged off with a half-fib that she was still sick. Then, when she saw the fire engines and saw the smoke, she bounced out of bed, raced over to the school, and watched the building and her two sisters go up in flames. As a result of the rage and pain her parents felt, she experienced considerable guilt about her own survival, guilt about her fib that kept her out of the fire, guilt about her dislike of her sisters and her classmates, guilt that she'd even considered starting a fire, and guilt because her parents, perhaps quite unconsciously, might have preferred to lose her instead of her two older sisters. She was perhaps too precocious a child for them to understand. In a sensitive and loving little girl like Anne, all of that in the course of a few years becomes transformed into a dream-conviction that she started a fire and then gradually a conscious conviction that she started it. If you read the papers, you'll see that considerable effort was expended by the diocese and by the pastor of the parish to persuade the world that it was not so much negligence on their part, minor negligence, indeed, but still negligence, as the malice of a mad arsonist that was responsible for the deaths. Much better to blame the malice of a madman than the innocent incompetence of good and well-meaning people.

"The more Annie heard her father rant about the guilt of this imaginary arsonist, the more she became persuaded that she herself was the felon. Belonging to a church that at that time emphasized guilt more strongly than anything else, Anne naturally assumed the burden of responsibility for the deaths in the Mother of Mercy fire. And it may be rather difficult for her to give up that responsibility."

"I think we can persuade her," Mary Kate said thoughtfully. "She is—it's trite to say it, isn't it?—a very strong and brave woman."

Blackie agreed. "A very strong and brave woman. And, if you ask me," he said with a wink, "the only diabolism in this whole story is the diabolism of the ecclesiastical institution that was obsessed with sexual sins to the exclusion of all else, which emphasized guilt and punishment to the exclusion of all else, and was staffed by clergy many, if not most, of whom hated and feared women. Blame the Church for Anne Marie O'Brien Reilly's sufferings, not just after the fire, but for all her life."

"Let me go over it again," Mike said, glancing at his watch. "We don't know what caused the first explosion, but we do have a rational explanation: sewer gas. We do know, and I'll explain how later, that someone did sprinkle soot all over the gallery after that. The second explosion was almost certainly a sonic boom . . . dressed up by Annie's imagination. All of this combined with Anne's own pent-up guilt, the memories the exhibition recalled, and whatever was in that painting to unleash what we might loosely call the gates of hell, even if we are not certain how to define them."

"How come 'Divine Justice' kept reappearing?" Blackie asked.

"That's easy," Mary Kate said. "The painting was to be the battleground for the forces in Annie's unconscious. She kept it around, however subconsciously."

"What about the phone calls?"

"Phone calls?" Blackie's audience said in unison, as they were supposed to.

"Anne told me they began the day you and the Cardinal visited the gallery," Mary Kate explained. "Most of the demonic interludes were introduced by a phone call in which someone played a scratchy record that Father Kenny used to repeat endlessly on his old machine in her aunt's guesthouse. She figured it was imagination."

" 'Good Night, Irene'?" asked the priest.

M.K. was astonished. "Yes."

"Don Miguel," Blackie said grimly, "would you find one of your rusty lances and proceed soonest to Western Springs and impale on it a certain Mrs. Anthony Powers? She was the catalyst."

"Would a call to the local police chief do just as well?" Mike said gently.

"No," Blackie replied. And then with a deep Irish sigh he added, "I suppose we'll have to settle for that."

"What about the explosion and Sandy locked in the closet." Mike Casey frowned darkly. "Your theory doesn't explain that."

"I know."

"So?"

Blackie made a small, self-effacing gesture. "No theory fits all the data."

They were all silent, shivering a little from a hint of supernatural cold.

"Principalities and powers." Joe Murphy stirred the ice in his drink. "That's what we struggle with?"

"Sometimes we win," Blackie nodded. "This time we did. Someone with a flair for crooked lines used it to reunite Alexandra with my Lord Cronin's good friend Kokoshka. What can I tell you?"

"How can you be certain she didn't start the fire?" Mary Kate asked.

"Oh, that," Blackie said, casually reaching into the inner pocket of his unpressed black jacket. "Here, Mike, is a letter from your mother to your father—a photoprint actually. Caitlin has the archives on microfilm. It's kind of a present from your family out of the past. Read the passage I've marked in green ink for all of us."

He signaled the waitress, an active member of the Cathedral parish. Apparently she understood the signal, indeed, was waiting for it. As the cop glanced at the letter a bottle of Baileys Irish Cream and four cordial glasses materialized in front of the group. As if he were assisting the Cardinal at a pontifical Mass at the Cathedral, Blackie solemnly filled each glass.

As Mike read the marked passage they all sat around the table in silence, sipping their drinks thoughtfully when he was finished.

"What a magnificent woman she would have been if she could have heard that thirty-five years ago," Joe said when Mike had finished.

"What a magnificent woman she is now, even without that letter," said Blackie.

Mike folded the letter and put it in the breast pocket of his carefully tailored jacket. He opened a brown manila envelope and laid out on the table five pieces of alabaster, the broken statue of a young woman.

"I found this in her office. The one lovely thing that Desmond Kenny made was destroyed too."

"Anne, of course," Blackie murmured. "How beautiful she was."

"More beautiful now," Mike said thoughtfully. "At least to me. I'm going to have this put back together. For the repose of his soul or something like that. You know, Blackie," he added, "it's the same Church that's tormented her that's also helped her become who she is."

"I never said we were consistent, did I?" Blackie replied.

"What time is it?" Mike looked at his watch. "Eleven forty-five—still the feast of Saint Michael the Archangel. Dr. Murphy, you don't mind if I bring this letter up to her apartment, do you?"

"Not in the least," M.K. said enthusiastically.

"Happy Feast Day," Blackie said, wiping his glasses with a paper napkin.

97

Mike banged on the door of Anne's apartment for several minutes. The door finally opened partway, and Anne, a maroon bath sheet clutched in front of her, soaking wet, peeked out.

"I'm sorry if I woke you up," he said awkwardly.

"I was treating myself to a long, leisurely bath," she said, blushing.

"Feeling better?"

"Feeling fine; headache's all gone."

"Can I come in?"

She hesitated, gray eyes uncertain and anxious.

"I have a document I want to read to you. It's important."

"Just a minute." She rearranged the towel so that it became a wrap, stepped back, and opened the door all the way. "I'll go upstairs and get dressed."

"I like you the way you are," he replied.

Her hair was plastered against her head. She smelled of soap and shampoo and bath oils and looked very young and innocent.

"I'm embarrassed," she said, still blushing.

"I enjoy you embarrassed," he replied.

"Sit down. Would you like a drink?"

"Sure," he said.

There was a popping sound in the kitchen and she returned with a bottle of champagne and two champagne glasses.

He glanced around her apartment, a comfortable and stylish cave, a gracefully appointed silk cocoon for two. A few days ago he had come as a dubious conqueror. Now he remained as a willing captive, tranquilized by beauty and intelligence and courage.

"Just happened to have it on ice?" he asked lightly.

"I put it in the refrigerator before we went over to the gallery," she said, filling both their glasses. "I guess I forgot to take it out. Were you drinking downstairs?"

"Only a sip of Jameson's; this won't make me sick."

They silently toasted each other.

"We beat them, Annie," he said again.

"We sure did," she replied, tilting her glass again in his direction.

"There are all kinds of explanations," he began awkwardly.

She shrugged her wonderful shoulders. "Not tonight, Mickey. I believe they're all true, but I can wait for another day or two," she said, sipping from her champagne and watching him coolly over the goblet.

Well, she let me in, she stayed in the towel because I told her I liked her that way, she poured me champagne, which she'd been saving for me. She's still confused and uncertain, but I think Saint Michael and I have routed more than one demon tonight.

Anne bowed her head in her characteristic novice gesture. *Cathy Curran may be right. It may be the most beautiful back in the world.*

"That afternoon in the gallery . . . it was a little bit the demon, but I think it was mostly me."

What a time to apologize for being sexually aggressive.

"Probably," he said, teasing just a little.

"You don't mind?"

"Single-minded and delicate ferocity."

She laughed and looked up at him, this time a sly smile tugging at her lips. "You will let me exhibit your canvases?"

"I suppose."

"In December?"

"I suppose."

"Would you possibly be able to do a few more before

then? I'd like to fill all the rooms on the first floor."

"I could try with proper payment."

Later he would tell her about the two dozen canvases stashed in his daughter Jane's basement in Park Ridge.

She refilled his champagne glass, having accomplished all her assignments. "It's good, isn't it?" she said shyly.

"I have to read you this document." He slowly unfolded it. "That's why I came up at this hour to bother you."

She laughed easily, cheerfully. "Sure."

Another good sign, he thought.

"This is a letter from my mother to my father, written in 1939 when he was in Poland, just before the war started. I'll read you the appropriate paragraph. You can hang on to the whole letter for a while if you want."

She nodded solemnly.

"I bumped into Mary Anne Laverty the other day at Marshall Field's. She had her cute little tyke Annie with her. You remember her, the black-haired, gray-eyed little charmer who played so nicely with our Mickey the day we took them to the World's Fair. Mary Anne was terribly sad, understandably, I guess. She told me the fire was still very much on all their minds and that they'd finally decided that they had to move out of Mother of Mercy and into St. Ursula's. It's outside her husband's ward, but they will maintain an official residence at the apartment house they own in the ward. He's strong enough politically now to be able to get away with that. She thinks the change of scene might help them to forget the fire and at least protect the little girl from the memories she must have every day when she goes to school. The child seems to be as sweet and as feisty as ever, but I can imagine what goes on inside her head. Mary Ann says she is very bright and has an extremely active imagination, always making up stories, and that they're worried about what will happen to her if they continue to live in Mother of Mercy.

"They almost lost the little girl in the fire too. She'd been home sick with the flu and didn't want to go back to school. Mary Anne said she almost forced her to go back but, somehow or other, at the last minute, decided to permit her another day off. Brrr! What a terrible memory for all of them to have to live with!"

He handed her the letter. She read it over carefully and then placed it on her damaged coffee table.

"This makes all the difference in the world," she said slowly. "And yet, in a way, it doesn't make any difference at all. I realized yesterday in the hospital, when I told my secret to the three of you, that I was already forgiven for whatever evil things I might have done in my life, forgiven and loved."

"There's all kinds of other evidence," he said gently: "Blackie dug it up and Mary Kate says she can use hypnotism to confirm it for you."

She shrugged again, sending currents of affection and desire through Mike's nervous system. "That's probably a good idea. I'll listen to what the cute little priest"—she grinned—"has to say. I believe it, though. Of course I believe it."

"It must be wonderful to be free at last," he said awkwardly.

"I'm a permanent flake, Mickey. If I wasn't worried about the fire, it would have been something else. And you just watch—I'll replace it with another guilt in a few days."

"I'll take my chances," he said lightly.

"I'm still not sure, Mickey." She lowered her head in her novice bow again.

"I am," he said bluntly.

"You know"—she folded his mother's letter and returned it to him—"there was always a part of me that warned that I might have made the whole thing up. I was great at making up stories as a little girl. . . ."

"I hope they were filled with handsome princes," he said.

She blushed again, a deep and lovely crimson.

"One or two of them . . . and then yesterday, after I told my silly story to you and Father Ryan and Dr. Murphy, I asked myself if it was really true or whether it was something I'd made up, like all the other stories."

He folded the letter, placed it in his wallet, slid it into

his coat pocket, and breathed a silent prayer to his mother.

They were sitting on the leather sofa, at opposite ends. Anne, head still bowed, was silent and thoughtful. He reached for her neck and very gently drew her face toward his; he placed his lips against her lips tenderly, more a light and sustained contact than a kiss. With his fingers he felt her pulse racing through her throat.

Not bad, for a feast day, Saint Michael. There would be love and champagne and more love and then many sunny private beaches. They could all wait, however. Now he and Annie were together again, the way they were in the snowdrift and the way henceforth they would always be.

He felt lighthearted and light-headed, deliriously content. He moved his lips away from her lips for a moment and murmured, "I guess from now on you're going to be called 'Annie Casey, the Cop's Wife.'"

She threw back her head and laughed, the rich glorious laughter of a young and happy woman. He felt it rumble beneath his fingers in her throat.

"Oh, Mickey, darling, how little you know your crazy relatives. You're the one whose name is going to change. From now on you'll be 'Mike Casey, the Art Peddler's Husband'!"

That seemed a good idea too.

ANOTHER NOTE

Despite the Watsonian Note at the beginning, all the characters, institutions, and situations in this story are products of my imagination. In particular, the Archdiocese of Chicago is never likely to have a cardinal as brave as Sean Cronin, nor is Holy Name Cathedral ever likely to have a rector as ingenious as John Blackwood Ryan, nor does Chicago have a Catholic university of as high quality as St. Columbanus.

It will be clear to those who know anything of Chicago's past that to some extent I have in mind the Our Lady of Angels School fire that occurred on December 1, 1958 (and which is described vividly in the book by Michele McBride, one of the survivors, *The Fire That Will Not Die*); however, the fire in this book occurs twenty-three years earlier, in a different parish, and with details and circumstances and characters that are completely different. Hence, this is not the story of the Our Lady of Angels fire and no one should expect to find in this book explanations for that fire.

I hope, by the way, that it is clear to everyone that the four principal "angels" of September—priest, lover, psychiatrist, and patrol officer—represent the Church at its most effectively caring best.